# FEAST all SOULS

Also by Simon Bestwick

**Novels**

*Tide of Souls*

*The Faceless*

The *Black Road* series

*Hell's Ditch*

*Devil's Highway*

**Novellas**

*Angels of the Silences*

**Collections**

*A Hazy Shade of Winter*

*Pictures of the Dark*

*Let's Drink to the Dead*

*The Condemned*

# The Feast of All Souls

SIMON BESTWICK

First published 2016 by Solaris
an imprint of Rebellion Publishing Ltd,
Riverside House, Osney Mead,
Oxford, OX2 0ES, UK

*www.solarisbooks.com*

ISBN (US): 978-1-78108-462-5
ISBN (UK): 978-1-78108-461-8



10 9 8 7 6 5 4 3 2 1

A CIP catalogue record for this book is available from the
British Library.

Designed & typeset by Rebellion Publishing

Printed in Denmark by Nørhaven

For Cate

# Chapter One

## A Sort of Homecoming

*Higher Crawbeck, Salford, 16th October 2016*

THEY DROVE OUT of Manchester across the River Irwell into Salford, where Collarmill Road began sloping uphill in a long straight line, all the way to Crawbeck.

Dad drove. Mum sat between Alice and him; Alice looked out of the window as tinned-up council houses and bleak low- and high-rise flats swished past.

"Ugh," said Mum. If she hadn't been going grey, the two of them could have been sisters: the same short black hair, pale skin, roundish, small-boned faces and wide blue eyes behind huge spectacles. "What possessed you to move here, Alice?"

"It's nicer further up, Mum."

"Even so."

"I used to live around here when I was a student," Alice said. "You remember. It was nice, too."

"Alice." Mum frowned and sighed. "Sweetheart, I know you've been through a lot, but you can't go back. Living in the past won't do you any good."

"You know you could have stayed with us," said Dad, thankfully before Mum could regurgitate more half-baked psychobabble from one of her lifestyle magazines.

"I need some space, Dad. Some time to myself."

"I would have thought that being on your own's the last thing you'd need, after –"

"Richard," said Mum, and Dad subsided, grumbling.

Alice could have said with equal truth that much as she loved her parents, she could never live with them again; their well-meant fussing would drive her mad. But there was such a thing as too much honesty. She'd learned that the hard way, with Andrew. "It'll keep me busy," she said. "It's a fixer-upper. The last owner rented it out to students. I'll do it up myself, work with my hands. It'll be just what I need to take my mind off things."

Dad grunted, Mum sighed, but they said no more, so Alice looked back out of the window as the dull surroundings gave way at last to Crawbeck's faded grandeur. There were terraced streets here too, of course, but bigger, more ornate buildings – villas and three-storey townhouses – testified to what the district had once been, especially along Collarmill Road itself.

The ground rose higher; to the left Alice saw Manchester's rooftops, through the trees that grew along the roadside. "Well, this isn't too bad," conceded Mum. A Chinese takeaway swept by on the right.

As they neared the top of the road, a line of old, thick trees, their leaves only beginning to rust and fall, rose up ahead like a wave.

"Oh," said Mum. "Well, that *is* nice."

"It's called the Brow," said Alice. "Looks over Browton Vale."

"Never mind the sightseeing," said Dad. "Where is this place?"

"Here, Dad. Just on the right."

They climbed down out of the hired van, stretching tired limbs.

"God," Dad said, peering at the road. "Look at this, Ann! Cobbles."

Collarmill Road carried on another hundred yards or so before ending sharply at the edge of the Brow, but ahead of where they'd stopped, the tarmac surfacing vanished and gave way to cobblestones.

"And look at that, Dad." Alice pointed, knowing it would interest him. "See? The old tram tracks."

"So they are." Dad put his hands on his hips. "Don't see that every day."

"Never mind that now," said Mum. "Oh God, Alice, is this the place?"

She was pointing at the house they'd parked outside. "Yes, Mum."

"What were you *thinking*? Richard, have you seen this?"

The house was semi-detached. On one side lay a builder's yard; on the other, another house of identical build. Three stories high, with black and white eaves above the lone gleaming eye of the attic-room window, it was built of red brick and loomed above a small but wildly overgrown front garden. The garden path's concrete slabs were cracked and sprouting weeds, and the gate's blue paint was peeling from the rotten wood. "Oh God," said Mum again, "and those windows are filthy."

"They'll clean up," said Dad. "Place looks sturdy enough. That's what matters."

"But it's a *big* place, Alice. It's for a family, not –"

"Ann," Dad said. Mum stopped.

"I told you, Mum, I want somewhere with a lot of space. I like to wander about."

"You've got outside for that. What's that place, just up there?"

"Browton Vale." Alice tried not to grit her teeth; even at forty-two, her parents could still make her feel like a sulky teen.

"What's wrong with that for a walk, then?"

"Because – Mum, because sometimes I'm not going to *want* to go outside. Some days I just want to stay indoors."

"You can't do that forever, Alice. What about getting a job?"

"I didn't say I'd be like this forever, Mum. Just for now. Anyway, walking around helps. I'd go mad cooped up in a little flat."

Alone in a house there'd be no people; even in the worst weather, you couldn't guarantee that on Browton Vale. She could rarely settle or rest, not unless she'd tired herself, but she wanted to be left alone. Just her, and her grief. Self-indulgent, maybe, but for now it was what she needed.

"Besides," she said, "it'll keep me busy. I told you – it's a fixer-upper. You won't know the place by the time I'm done."

Light flickered across the upstairs windows. Most likely a bird flying over the tree-tops, but for a moment it was as if two huge eyes had blinked and turned their half-amused gaze on the tiny figure that had dared voice such a challenge.

THE FRONT DOOR pushed a rustling heap of post up against the wall. There was a narrow hallway, with the front room and a ground-floor bedroom off to the left; it dog-legged around the staircase to the kitchen.

"Pongs in here," Mum said. "You want to get the window open, give it all a good airing."

"Yeah, okay, Mum." The air was stale, but it was also October and getting cold.

"Shall we get started, then?" said Dad.

"Okay." Alice handed Mum a carrier bag.

"What's this?"

"Electric kettle, jar of Nescafé, sugar and a pint of milk."

Dad laughed. "Someone planned ahead."

"Didn't get me any mugs, though," said Mum.

"They're in the last crate I loaded into the van. Come on, Dad."

Outside, Dad opened the rear doors. The van was full of translucent plastic crates; here was everything Alice still owned in the world. It seemed excessive, cluttered – and at the same time, ridiculously little to show for a life.

She cleared her throat and pointed. "Kitchen stuff's in that one."

"Right-o." Dad took one end, she the other. He grinned. "And a one-two-three, *heave* –"

It was that phrase that did it, that and the grin; Dad was in his sixties now, grey-haired and balding, growing a paunch, but when she was little and he'd been lean and tanned with a full head of black hair; he'd said the same thing, grinned the same grin, before sweeping her up in the air as if she'd been a toy. Alice lifted when he did, managed to walk backwards down the drive without tripping over the kerb or the uneven path, but in her head he was still holding her aloft, making her soar and swoop through the air while he imitated the growl of aero engines. *The best dad in the world*, she'd put in one of his birthday cards – not *daddy*, because that was babyish, but *dad*.

But then there were the other memories, the ones that surfaced as she stepped back over the threshold into the hall. Dad on the sofa with no tie and his collar undone, flopping like a slack-stringed puppet, lips loose and drooling, while Mum screamed and shouted at him, pointing at the brown envelopes on the coffee table.

Alice hadn't touched alcohol until her mid-twenties because of that, because of the fear and disgust the word *drunk* awakened in her. But there were worse things than drunk. There was the pounding on the front door and the ogreish bellow through the letter box; there were bills in red and Mum crying at the kitchen table, holding her tight and trying to tell her not to worry, but only worrying Alice more.

There had been the time, when Dad wasn't at home, that the front door had been kicked in – the sturdy, reliable old wooden door that had kept the world outside, suddenly smashed inwards, splintered and crumpled and hanging off one hinge. A huge man in a donkey-jacket had stepped through, clutching a pick-axe handle; another, smaller, smoother, in a pin-stripe suit, had followed.

Alice wasn't vain, but she'd been used to strangers smiling at her; everyone said she was a pretty child. But the big man had just glanced at her as if she was nothing, then looked away again, and the Pinstripe Man had looked her up and down with a nasty little smirk. She'd been about eight at the time.

Mum had been shouting; the Pinstripe Man had screamed at her to shut up. He'd screamed some more things as well, but Alice hadn't really heard them. He'd been shouting too fast and she'd scuttled backwards into a corner, hands over her ears to blot out the sound.

The men went at last and Mum had hugged Alice to her breast. They'd both been crying. Mum had a black eye and a split lip. That night, when Dad got home, they'd packed their bags and driven off to stay with Mum's sister on the coast.

"Alice?" She blinked. Dad looked back at her over the crate. "Where are we putting this, love?"

"Sorry, Dad. The kitchen. In the corner so it's not in the way. Should be everything you need in there, Mum."

"Right you are."

Alice followed Dad back outside. That long-ago night hadn't been the first or last time such a thing had happened, but it had been the worst. Soon after, though, Dad had started going to AA meetings, but it had been years before they'd no longer had to struggle financially, before they'd been able to start saving.

"Where does this one go?"

"Put them in the downstairs bedroom for now," she said. "Plenty of space for them, and there's that many rooms I don't know what needs to go where yet."

"Okay, if you're sure. But if it's not done tonight, I don't know when I'll be able to come back out and help you."

"I'll manage, Dad. It'll –"

"Keep you busy?"

She laughed. "Yes. That."

She'd kept herself busy for years; reading, studying, until she was at university, taking a physics degree. That was when she'd met John. She didn't want to think about John now. After that, she'd cared about one thing and one thing only, and that had been hunting down a job that would pay the most, help her save, that would make sure that neither she nor her parents, if she could help it, would ever have to worry about money again.

And then she'd met Andrew, and in due course, Emily had come along. But she didn't want to think about them either.

"MUM. *MUM*. PLEASE. Don't do that. Just don't, please."

Alice shouldered past Mum and snatched the photos from the mantelpiece.

"Well excuse me, Alice, I was only trying to help."

"I know, I know, I just –" Alice hugged the pictures to her chest, felt her voice crack. "I just can't look at them right now."

"You've got to face it at some point, love."

"I know, I know I do. I just can't at the moment. Even seeing a picture..."

Mum spread her hands. "All right. All right. It's up to you. Now are you sure you're going to be all right?"

"I'll be fine. I mean, I'll be okay." She wondered if that was true, or ever would be. She told herself it had to be.

But you didn't expect to outlive your child; of course there were parents who carried on after such a loss, who coped, worked, lived somehow, but there was no knowing for sure what went on behind their eyes. A dead child tore a piece of you away. The wound might heal, but something would always be missing, something hard and dead left in its place.

They hugged her goodbye, muttered "see you soon," and then got back in the van. Mum waved as they drove off into the dusk. Alice waved back, until the red tail-lights were gone, then shut the door, locked it and cried.

She sat curled up against the door for a while, sobbing, till she heard a floorboard creak – that, and felt someone standing over her, leaning down to look. She started, opened her eyes. It was dark, but streetlight spilled in through the glass panes in the front door to show an empty hallway. She got up and fumbled for the light switch. The unshaded bulb clicked; nothing. Imagination, nothing more.

Alice breathed out and went into the kitchen, wiping sore eyes on her sleeve. The cooker wouldn't be here until tomorrow; she had some packets of freeze-dried noodles that she'd only need hot water to prepare, but found herself craving something more substantial.

The Chinese takeaway would only be a short walk, but it would mean going out. She'd have to get a grip, sooner or later. But for now she'd rather stay indoors.

She switched on her laptop, plugged the dongle in, logged onto Just Eat and found a place that delivered: hot and sour soup, salt and pepper ribs, sweet and sour chicken and egg fried rice. She ordered, paid with her debit card, shut down the computer and got up.

Now she paced. She wandered up and down the hallway, in and around the front room, kitchen and the ground-floor bedroom jammed full of crates. The front room was bare except for the armchairs and sofa, the floorboards filmed with dust. She went upstairs. Two bedrooms and a tiled bathroom on the first floor; two more bedrooms at the top.

The top bedroom at the front was the one whose window nestled under the eaves; the attic room, she'd called it. It was like all the other rooms: empty, with bare dusty floorboards and an unshaded bulb hanging from the ceiling. She flicked the switch, but the room stayed dark. She walked to the window, peered out into the night. Streetlights gleamed on tarmac and cobbles, turned trees to silhouettes; below, Collarmill Road sloped down towards the city.

Floorboards creaked; she gasped, then clenched her fists. Just the house settling. She'd have to get used to it, to live here.

As she stepped back, the dead lightbulb flashed into life, turning the window into a mirror. Alice cried out, spinning round.

But, of course, the room was empty. The lightbulb flickered and went out again. Shaking, she crossed to the switch and flicked it a few times, but the bulb showed no further signs of life.

She left the room without looking back, pulling the door shut, and went downstairs, heart still drumming in panic.

A trick of the light, nothing more. At most, the very most, it was her treacherous wounded mind that had made her see – if only for a snatched second – ranks of children standing behind her. Well, in a couple of weeks it would be Halloween. Season of the witch, and of ghosts. But there were no ghosts. There weren't. Even if she sometimes wished there were.

In the front room, she curled up on the armchair, dug a book out of her shoulder bag and leafed through it, not registering a single word on any page, until her meal arrived.

SHE WATCHED AN old film on her laptop – a comedy she hadn't seen in years. Andrew hadn't liked it, and time to watch movies on her own had been hard to find after Emily was born. That thought occurred to her early on in the film and brought with it a sudden surge of pain, but she forced herself not to think about Emily, or Andrew. Instead she focused on the film, wondering as she did what other long-denied past pleasures might await rediscovery, and how far, if at all, they'd compensate her for her loss.

After the film, she dragged her folding camp-bed upstairs, followed by her sleeping-bag, pillows, some folding metal steps and a spare light bulb – she'd made a point of packing several of those.

In the attic room, she replaced the broken bulb. The previous owners had left a pair of curtains; she pulled them shut, then undressed. This was her home now; she couldn't allow herself to fear this or any other room. She hesitated before turning off the bedroom light, but the landing light was on, as was every other light in the house. She'd have to get used to the dark here soon, but for tonight, this first night, she'd allow herself that one small indulgence. She climbed into her sleeping bag and zipped it up.

ALICE DREAMT SHE stood on a bare hillside, under a grim sky. It was daylight, but the clouds were thick and heavy, black with rain. Below her, something moved. She couldn't see it clearly, but it was big, with a pelt of black, bristling fur. She was already turning away when it roared; after that, she was running.

It was behind her. As she neared the summit she knew there was no outrunning this, that her only salvation would be – what?

There was something she had to see. She didn't know what, only that it was here at the top of the hill, and that if she could see it she'd be safe.

But she couldn't. And then there was a roar, and a terrible shadow fell upon her.

ALICE WOKE, BUT only briefly; she was asleep again in seconds, barely even opening her eyes.

In any case she lay facing the wall, and didn't turn around. So she didn't see the small figures that stood beside her bed, watching her until dawn's first light came to drive them away.

# Chapter Two

## The Confession of Mary Carson

*Liverpool, February 1888*

EVERY WORD I utter is to be recorded, verbatim. I know I have made this clear to Mr Muddock here; has he, in turn, made it clear to you, Mrs... Rhodes? Ah, I can see from your scribblings that he has. Very good.

Every word is to be recorded, and the transcript typed. The subsequent fate of the document will be decided at a later date. My chief concern for now is that a record is made.

You're both ready to proceed? Very well, then.

Although I was a clergyman's daughter, I have never been inclined to dabble in theology; nonetheless it has occurred to me on many occasions in life that, perhaps, just as we are rewarded for our good works in Heaven, so we are punished for them here on Earth.

I verge on blasphemy, perhaps. Those who know me would be shocked – to them I am a Godly and charitable woman – but in truth they know me not. None of them do, or have: neither my dear departed husband nor even my beloved children. If they but did they would turn from me, appalled. I have devoted the latter part of my life – that part following the events I wish you to record – to good works, much as I devoted my life prior to it. But how many good deeds are required to outweigh sins such as mine? In that year – Mr Muddock, Mrs Rhodes – I sinned most grievously; blasphemy is a mild offence to those for which I must answer.

Life has, ultimately, treated me well. I am six and eighty years of age, with three children now full-grown and grandchildren almost beyond counting. I may even live to see my first great-grandchild, and I have been well-provided for in my dotage. Perhaps, if we *are* punished for good works, we are rewarded for wicked ones. After all, the way to God's Kingdom is rocky and steep; nothing of value is obtained without hardship, so why should the way of virtue not be harsh and that of iniquity full of ease?

This will be, for want of a better term, a confession of my sins. You are young, Mrs Rhodes, and appear reasonably innocent, while Mr Muddock, I know, is a man of the world, but I suspect both of you will have cause to be unsettled – or alarmed – by this account of mine.

Among other things, you'll both have cause to question my sanity; that cannot be helped. I can only imagine my own disbelief at such a tale, had I not experienced it myself. I do not ask you to believe. Only that you complete this transcription and preserve it safely until my decease, at which time you will follow whatever instructions I have made for its disposal.

So, let us proceed. I shall begin with facts. My father was a country parson; of my mother, I have no memory. She never fully recovered from my birth, dying about a year later. My father always showed me great affection – tempered with a good father's strictness – but my mother's death had left a void in his life which fatherhood alone could not fill.

Had he but married again, both our stories might have been different, but there could never be any other woman for my father. Instead, he devoted himself to a cause. Always sympathetic to the Abolitionists, now he gave freely of his time and wealth to them, which they found a great asset. Not only was he an eloquent writer and orator, but, tall and grey-haired as he was, looked as though he might have come down from Mount Sinai to utter God's word. From childhood I was his helper; I grew to be his secretary and chiefest aide.

Both within the Church and his congregation, his unwavering denunciation of slavery earned him enemies, and in time he lost his living. He found a post at a seaman's mission in Liverpool for a time, before fellow Abolitionists supported him with donations to enable him to fully assist the cause.

Or rather, *us*, for I was his fervent ally. Do not mistake me: I still take pride in all I helped my father achieve, whatever the cost to myself may have been. And there *was* a cost. I turned down two offers of marriage as I grew older. My father, and the cause, needed me.

In 1833, Great Britain abolished the foul institution of slavery. For my father it was an hour of triumph. Yet he had expended the fullest measure of his vital force in the cause of Abolition; overwork, and the harsh conditions in which we had lived, had taken their toll upon his health. Robbed of his purpose, he sank into melancholy and sickness, and three years after his triumph, he died, leaving me, at thirty-three, a penniless spinster.

My father's only assets were his prized books: tomes on theology, philosophy and rhetoric. I sold them and searched in growing desperation for work as a secretary or governess, without success. What work I found was a fitful, hand-to-mouth affair. I had to leave my father's former lodgings for a squalid little room near the Docks, and cursed myself for not having accepted the marriage proposals offered to me; surely I could still have aided my father even while married.

Matters began to look increasingly desperate, and it seemed only a matter of time before I must either starve or lower myself to the most shameful extremity any woman can. But then an old friend of my father's, a Mr Unwin, came to my aid. Moved by my plight, he had made enquiries and learned of a position that had arisen in nearby Manchester, as secretary to a wealthy mill-owner. The post was well-salaried, and included board and lodging. Here, I hoped, was a position that might offer some measure of security, where I could hope to set aside a portion of my earnings to provide for the future.

Mr Unwin wrote to the mill-owner, a Mr Thorne, and after a brief time the post was offered me. And so with some relief I packed my few remaining possessions into a small trunk and boarded the Manchester train the following day.

I arrived in the city one cold morning in the March of 1837 and was met by a coach and four driven by a pock-marked, brutal-looking individual whose name I never learned. The city itself was a foul place – noisy and crowded, stinking and dark. The narrow streets ran with filth and clouds of smoke from home and factory chimneys fouled the air, sooted the walls black and murked the sky above it. And as the factories grew, so the city swelled and spread.

Soon enough, we had cleared the packed, stinking streets of Manchester, and the carriage was travelling up Collarmill Road towards Crawbeck.

My memories are half a century out of date and dimmed by time. I returned to Crawbeck only once after the events to which this Confession relates, and was sufficiently preoccupied that I failed to study my surroundings in great detail. Doubtless the march of so-called 'progress' had effaced much of its beauty and will have done even more so by now.

At the time, though, as I recall, it was still mostly unspoilt. Crawbeck is built upon a hill about a mile to the nor' nor' west of Manchester, up which the sprawl of squalor and filth was only just beginning to spread. A few narrow, terraced streets stood on the lower reaches of the hillside, but these soon gave way to open heath, broken only by a handful of small villas.

Beyond these there lay a further stretch of untouched land, and then at last a high wall which proved to girdle round the entire upper third of the hill. In this was set a pair of black wrought-iron gates; stencilled in gold lettering on each gatepost were the words SPRINGCROSS HOUSE.

Beyond these lay a gravel drive, on either side of which extended well-maintained lawns; beyond these were thick, almost jungle-like gardens.

The coach rounded a bend in the drive, and I saw Springcross House for the first time. I suppose I ought to say that I had some premonition of ill-fortune – were I the narrator of some Gothic romance I certainly might, but I was, and am, nothing of the sort. I shall be honest – what point to a Confession if it is not? – and admit, though it pains me, that I experienced no such presentiment. If any emotion coloured my thoughts, it was a blend of excitement and hope: for here, at last, if I was fortunate, industrious and wise, was the security I had so long desired.

Springcross House was a great grey edifice of ashlar stone, done in some imitation of the Greek or Roman style. Doric columns supported a marquee above the wooden double doors of the main entrance. Flanking these doors, mounted on fluted pedestals, were statues of lions rampant. Elaborate scrollwork surrounded the doorframe and windows.

All the same, there was a strange air of restraint about the building. Men like Mr Thorne, I knew, were *nouveaux riches* – parvenus who'd but lately dragged themselves up from the gutters of their birth – and often proved to be of low and vulgar taste, made all the more unpleasing by the scope to indulge it afforded by their newfound wealth. Mr Thorne, it seemed, was not of their ilk: the building spoke of wealth, indeed declared it, but without vulgar ostentation. There was something almost austere, even ascetic, about it.

A footman helped me down from the carriage. The double doors opened and servants emerged to carry my few cases into the house. The coach clattered away as I was helped up the steps. Beyond the doors, the entrance hall was a bright, circular space, lit by day by a skylight above and by night by a huge crystal chandelier. Staircases rose to the left and right, to a landing that ringed the hall and looked down on it.

A tall man in his forties stepped forward to greet me. "Miss Carson? I am Kellett, Mr Thorne's butler."

Mr Kellett was not unhandsome; he was also well-built, presentable and well-spoken, but something about the man immediately inspired my dislike. And nor, I could tell, did he like me; he eyed me rather as my father's cat would have another tom appearing in the old vicarage garden. Perhaps he feared a new secretary might become privy to secrets he was not, and pose some threat to his territory. I curtseyed. "A pleasure, Mr Kellett."

His lips formed a faint smirk: perhaps he recognised what an innocent he had in me. "Mr Thorne is presently away," he said. "We expect his return this afternoon. In the mean time, your room has been prepared."

I was ushered up the winding staircase to a large bedroom at the back of the house, decorated in white and green, with an adjoining bathroom and water closet. Bay windows and a balcony overlooked the gardens I had observed earlier. Peering out, I saw that lush vegetation grew thick around the back of the house. A large ornamental pond, complete with a fountain, lay almost immediately below.

"Pray make yourself at ease, mistress." Kellett gave me a smile and a low bow. "Mr Thorne will see you on his return."

It must be admitted that I did not – could not – 'make myself at ease' at Springcross – not then, at least. I was used to small, familiar places – the old vicarage near Burscough, the missions and lodging-houses that had been our home thereafter. This place was vast, pristine, and unwelcoming, and Kellett had scarcely bothered to veil his dislike of me, while the other servants had remained expressionless and aloof. Wherever I had gone, I felt as though I would have drawn some withering or pitying glance. The day, at least, was mild and without rain, so I sat out on the balcony, reading a novel I had brought with me.

As afternoon wore towards evening I heard a clatter of hooves and rattle of wheels; I quickly roused myself, bringing in my chair, shutting my windows and completing a hasty toilet. As I did, I heard the opening of doors, running footsteps and raised voices, but none called for me. With little better to occupy my time, I took up my novel again, until, at length, came a gentle tapping at the door. "Come in," I said.

A maid entered: a plump, sallow-faced creature with a permanently sullen expression. "The master's home, miss, and would like to see you."

"Of course," I said. My stomach was a pit of tension, try to hide it though I might; I was suddenly conscious that my dress, while clean, was several years out of fashion, that my stance and carriage might be deemed to lack the necessary poise. These and a dozen other reasons why Mr Thorne would dismiss me on sight and cast me back into penury suggested themselves almost at once. I composed myself as best I could and followed the maid down the staircase to the ground floor and my new employer's study.

This was, oddly, the first place in Springcross House where I felt remotely at ease, for it reminded me greatly of my late father's study – albeit much larger. It had the same deep, rich-coloured wood panelling, the same fire roaring in a grate, the same high shelves stacked with leather-bound volumes. However, it also boasted several stuffed animals under glass, which my father had never been able to abide. A fox, a hare, a wolf, a huge owl, all gazed at me with yellow and amber eyes lit by reflected firelight.

Above the fireplace was a portrait of a tall, upright man in evening-dress, with long, reddish-brown side-whiskers and a stern, commanding countenance; he had something of the air of an Old Testament prophet. If that was Arodias Thorne, as I guessed, then he had so much in common with my late father, at least in his own estimation. But my father, I knew, would never have commissioned such a monument to vanity. Even had an admirer gifted him with it, he would have consigned it somewhere out of the way where neither he – nor, could he help it, anyone else – would behold the wretched thing.

In one corner of the room stood a wide mahogany desk on which rested decanters and crystal goblets, pens and blotter and inkwells, journals and ledgers, all neatly arranged and stacked. Again, I could not help but note the contrast between this and my father's study; my father's effects had lain all a-muddle in a sort of genial disarray, but everywhere one looked here was absolute order: a place for everything and everything in its place.

Beside the desk, gazing out of a mullioned window at the afternoon sky, was a man with greying hair. He had not turned around at my entrance or the door's closing, or at my footsteps on the wooden floor; he merely stood, hands clasped behind his back, as I approached the desk.

"Miss Carson, sir," said the maid.

"Very good, Boswell. Dismissed." The man did not turn round. The maid scurried out, glad, I felt, to be gone.

"Mr Thorne?" I said.

"Who else might I be, Miss Carson?" He turned, and I saw I indeed faced the man from the portrait, which I also saw had contained considerably less flattery than I might have supposed. While not particularly tall, Mr Thorne *was* imposing (and once again, despite myself, I was reminded of my father; however much I strove to resist the impulse to contrast my employer with him, I met with little success).

I still see him now, with absolute clarity. He had a strong face, high-cheekboned and Roman-nosed, with a high forehead that denoted a powerful intellect. The eyes were a dark grey in colour, like cold iron or the clouds of a gathering storm. His height aside, the greatest difference between Mr Thorne in the portrait and in the flesh was that wrought by age. His hair was now almost entirely iron-grey, the lines about his eyes and mouth more pronounced and the lips, while still full, were thinner, and firmly set. Even so, there was still an impression of virility and strength.

"You are Miss Mary Carson," he said, in a cultured, sonorous voice, "formerly of the village of Burscough and the city of Liverpool. I am Arodias Thorne, formerly of the village of Browton and now of Springcross House, Crawbeck." He motioned. "Please. Sit."

I did as he instructed. He sat behind his desk and studied me. Firelight gleamed in his eyes, as in those of the stuffed beasts elsewhere in the room.

"You are well spoken of, Miss Carson," he said. As I say, many such captains of industry were men who'd risen to great wealth from the lower stations of society, and were apt to bear the lowly stamp of their origins. Arodias Thorne, however, had gone to great pains to eradicate all hint of such from his speech; it was almost *too* precise, in fact, perhaps because a style acquired late in life never sits as easily upon a man – or woman – as one learned from birth. I remember, too, how still he stayed – at that interview, and subsequently – when speaking. As with the ordered neatness of all around him, all was ordered and controlled, as if in fear of what might, at a moment's laxness, be let slip.

"I am glad, sir," I said. Mr Thorne permitted himself the barest shadow of a smile.

"You would not be here were it otherwise, Miss Carson. I have no doubt of your qualities, as regards the post, but have heard only the barest details of your career." His eyes did not waver from mine, nor blink. "Perhaps you would be kind enough – in your own words, of course."

How much did he know? I was hard put to believe that Mr Thorne would engage someone – especially in so responsible a position as this – without fully acquainting himself with their history. Perhaps it was a test, to see what I might try to hide.

So I told my tale with my head held high – although it occurred to me, as I spoke, that Mr Thorne might hold my father's campaign for Abolition as a black mark, or my impoverished circumstances as a badge of shame.

"So," he said when I had finished, "you have laboured long and hard to bring about Christ's Kingdom on Earth, Miss Carson. A thankless task, as you have learned: it has left you penniless and a spinster."

I was too shocked by such bluntness to speak. Mr Thorne raised a hand.

"I have no wish to denigrate either your or your father's achievements. He was a remarkable man, by all accounts. But you must understand, I am engaged in no philanthropic endeavour. My object is profit, pure and simple. Do you think that a mean and unworthy end, Miss Carson?"

I sought a diplomatic answer. "It's a necessary one, Mr Thorne."

Again that faint vestige of a smile. "I have known poverty, Miss Carson, and lifted myself from it, through no effort but my own. Any man could have done as much; it is merely a matter of will. I confess, therefore, that I have scant sympathy for those unwilling to do likewise – those who wallow in the mire of their degradation, expecting the industrious to pull them out."

What reply, if any, did he expect? I had no idea, and so remained silent. He went on.

"I have, as a result, a somewhat harsh reputation hereabouts – one I have, I'm sure, done much to earn. My late wife was a boon companion to me, from the very beginning, in my endeavour. Among many other duties, she filled the place that I have now engaged you to fill. I tell you this in honesty, Miss Carson. I have no doubt that your intelligence and aptitude are equal to the position, only whether your stomach is."

"I am in need of work, Mr Thorne," I said at last. "You have engaged me as your secretary, and not your conscience."

Again that shadow-smile. "Good. In any case, you have earned yourself a good measure of credit as regards the life to come. It can do you no ill to now address the needs of the present one. Yes, I think you will do, Miss Carson. That will be all for now." He perched a pair of spectacles on his nose, reaching for a book. "We shall begin tomorrow morning, at five o'clock sharp. Good evening to you."

He opened the book and began to read. Realising I was dismissed – purely in a temporary sense, to my relief – I returned to my rooms.

Later, Kellett brought me a cold supper. I was glad to be spared dining with him and the other servants; I had little desire for their company, least of all that of Kellett himself.

For all its magnificence, Springcross House was a cold place, where affection and kindness had no home. Kellett and the rest were of a piece with it; so, it seemed, was my new employer. Or perhaps not; he was not unhandsome, despite his years, and there was that faint, amused smile...

I chided myself for reading too many romances. I might still hope to find a husband at my time of life, but I should get nowhere by setting my cap at a man like Arodias Thorne. I resolved myself, therefore, to make my first object that of my employer: the amassing of wealth in sufficient quantity to ensure I would not want in later years, even if I must spend them alone. Needs must – Mr Muddock, Mrs Rhodes – when the Devil drives.

# Chapter Three

## The Fire on the Hill

*17th – 18th October 2016*

THE ALARM ON Alice's mobile phone began beeping at 5.30 am. Grunting, she stirred, rolled over in the bed and surveyed the empty room.

She picked up the mobile and switched it off. Her handbag and a plastic bottle of water sat beside it; she picked them up and sat on the edge of the bed, bare toes brushing the floor.

She took the packet of Citalopram out of the handbag, popped one of the antidepressant tablets into her hand and washed it down with a gulp of water. Then she got up, pulled on last night's clothes and went downstairs.

The house was cold. She'd have to put the central heating on. In the kitchen she made coffee; she'd have to go out shortly, get some toast or cereal. She could have just gone straight out, but resisted the urge; she was dressed in last night's clothes, unwashed, bed-hair still sticking up all awry. She'd look like a madwoman, and these days she felt like one too much of the time. Or on the edge of becoming one, anyway. It was all too easy, when you lived alone and weren't working, to slip into behaviour others might mistake for mental illness. Easy to forget to wash or change your clothes, or to hold conversations with your now-ex-husband or your dead daughter.

Alice sucked in a sharp breath, then let it out slowly. The thought of Emily, when it came suddenly and unexpectedly, still caused almost physical pain.

She sat in the front room, cupping the mug in her hands for warmth, and sipped her coffee, then went up and ran the shower. It coughed and spat but finally ran hot enough. She'd forgotten to unpack the shower gel and shampoo the night before, but Mum had laid out a bar of thick, creamy white soap in the bathroom sink. That would do. There was a thick towel on the radiator too. The kind of thing she'd forgotten to think about any more, but that Mum would remember. Alice's eyes misted; she stepped into the shower and let the hot water rinse the tears away.

After the shower, scrubbed pink and clean, she donned new layers of protection: clean clothes and make-up. When she was done, she studied herself in the mirror and nodded, deciding the impression of a woman who wasn't unhinged by grief was convincing enough.

SHE BOUGHT BREAD, cereal, bacon, more milk, orange juice. She ate breakfast, drank coffee, then went into the downstairs bedroom and opened the first of the crates.

Crate by crate, as the day wore on, she unpacked; it filled the gaping spaces of time, stopped her thinking about Andrew, about Emily, about what the hell she was meant to do now. She stopped to grill bacon and make a sandwich, drank coffee until her teeth were clenched and she was juddering. She ventured out again to buy some decaff. And the unpacking went on.

Around two o'clock, she Skyped Teddy, out in Spain. He looked different, but in a good way; he was slimmer, his skin bronzed, and if his grey hair was a little whiter, it was a very nice shade of silver that went well with the new tan.

"So, my dear," he said. "Come on, tell old Teddy. How are you doing?"

"I'm okay," she said.

"Yes? Really?" He raised his eyebrows.

"I'm fine," she said. "As you well as you can expect. You know, I'm not singing Hosanna and doing the Happy Dance every morning, if that's what you mean."

"Perish the thought," said Teddy. "The very image is the stuff of nightmares."

"Oh piss off, you old queen," she said. "How are you and Stefan, anyway?"

"Oh, very well." Teddy smiled. "Retirement's suiting me down to the ground. It's a whole new lease of life."

She smiled back. "I suppose sea, sun, sand and sangria will do that for you."

"Not having a fucking day job will do it even more," he assured her. "I feel like a man twenty years younger. Unfortunately, Stefan's threatened to cut off my balls if I get one."

Alice spluttered and put her coffee down. "You bastard, you nearly owed me a new laptop there."

"I've told you before, you shouldn't drink while Skyping."

"I bloody miss you, Teddy."

"I know. I can brighten a room just by leaving it. So remind me again, darling heart, where are you now?"

"Manchester."

"Dear Lord," Teddy shuddered theatrically. "The horror, the horror."

"Have you ever even been north of Watford?" she asked him.

"No," he said. "I've never been to that city near Chernobyl either – the one they evacuated?"

"Pripyat?"

"Quite. I've never been there, but I know more than enough to be quite certain that a) I wouldn't like it, b) I will miss no vital life experiences by not going and c) the natives would probably fucking eat me."

"There aren't any natives in Pripyat. It's abandoned."

"Don't you bloody believe it, darling. It's probably populated by a horde of hideous Soviet-era mutants who aren't aware that the Berlin Wall's come down and that the Red Flag no longer flies in Moscow. Great hairy flesh-eating brutes with the physiques of gorillas."

"I'd have thought that'd be right up your street."

"Shows how little you know of me. I prefer a rather more refined dancing partner. Seriously, though, Manchester sounds good for you. It's near your parents, isn't it?"

"Yeah."

"Well, that can't be bad. I'm sure being near your family –"

"What's left of my family."

"Alice –"

"Okay, okay. You're right. I'm getting gloomy and maudlin."

"Must be something in the water. Look, for goodness sake, take care of yourself, and get in touch with me if you need to talk. I love you very dearly, my girl," he added gruffly. "Lord knows why."

"Love you too," said Alice. Her eyes stung and she blinked hard so as not to start crying in front of him. "Look, I'd better go."

"All right, then. Look after yourself, chick."

"You too."

The dongle linking her laptop to the internet had almost run out; she'd rung Virgin, arranged for them to connect her, but that would take days. The internet was her link to the wider world, to the distraction she so badly needed to stop her thinking. She'd buy a new dongle tomorrow, maybe two. In the meantime, the television and DVD player were unpacked, so she set them up, turned all the lights on and watched films, one after the other, as the afternoon outside grew dim.

*And that was the first day*, she thought.

* * *

AT ABOUT EIGHT o'clock, she paused the film she was watching. There'd been something. Sounds. Voices, she was sure. Next door, maybe. A television. But when she listened, she heard nothing.

Kids, perhaps, outside. There'd been something about the sounds that had made her think of children.

She switched the film on again. Something flickered in her peripheral vision; something small and dark and child-sized, with a pale blur of a face.

No. Alice dug her fingers into the arm of the settee until they threatened to punch through the leather. No; there was no-one there.

But there were those sounds again. She pressed the pause button, and this time the noises didn't go away when the film fell silent. She wished she hadn't done that, because she could hear them now, quite clearly. Not clearly enough to make out every word, but she could tell what they were and where they were coming from. They were whispers – the whispers of children, she was sure of it – and they were coming from outside the front room door, from the hallway of her house.

That couldn't be right. Alice sat paralysed; they must be on the pavement outside, talking. Probably running around in witch and ghost costumes, rehearsing their trick-or-treat routines for Halloween. But the sound wasn't coming from that direction; it was coming from just behind the living room door.

Children had got in, and not sweet, gentle-natured children, like Emily had been. Feral; that was the phrase, wasn't it? Feral children. Coined by the kind of newspapers she most despised, but even so – children weren't born knowing right from wrong, that a world existed beyond their selfish need. And if they weren't taught it, they could be little monsters – cruel, vicious, satanically demanding. They wanted something and so it was theirs by right; breaking into a house would be nothing to such a child. And if someone else had the temerity to be living there, to put themselves, by the bare fact of their existence, between them and their object –

Christ; one noise in the night and she was turning into a rabid fascist, seeing danger everywhere. But that didn't change the fact of the whispers, still coming from the hallway.

What could she use to protect herself with? She almost sobbed in relief when she saw something she'd forgotten about – a wooden chair-leg, lying in a corner. The chair had been there when she'd moved in, broken and falling apart. The leg had fallen off as Dad had picked it up to carry outside and Alice had toed it into a corner, out of the way. And then, thankfully, forgotten about it.

She snatched it up, brushed away the dust that clung to the haft, and advanced on the door, hefting it in both hands. The whispers grew louder.

*Does she know?*

*Will she help?*

*Help who? Him or us?*

She gripped the door handle, so tightly her knuckles whitened; her arm drew back, ready to sweep her make-do cudgel down.

*She'll help him. It's why she's here. Can't have that. So we're going to have to –*

Alice yanked the door wide and lunged through it, a snarl in her throat ready to become a furious shriek. But the hallway was empty. She spun to her left, brandishing the chair-leg at the stairs, but they were empty too.

The house was silent, but for a faint buzz from the television. Alice gripped the chair-leg tighter, then turned on the upstairs lights and went up.

She checked each room, one by one. In her attic bedroom she was momentarily afraid to look at her reflection in the window, remembering what she'd seen – thought she'd seen – the night before, but the glass only showed her herself, standing in an empty room.

Alice breathed out and went back downstairs, but left the lights on. And when she went to bed that night she took the chair-leg with her, keeping it close under the duvet.

THE SECOND DAY began at the same time; Alice drank coffee, ate toast, showered, dressed and completed the last remaining unpacking. The empty crates she stacked in the downstairs bedroom. She might need them again and it wasn't as if she couldn't spare the space.

That job done, she ventured out. The sky was a dull grey, but there was no wind and the air was mild. Locking the door, she walked up the cobbled street to the edge where it dropped away. There'd been a storm back in the nineteen-twenties or thereabouts, she remembered being told, and part of the Brow had collapsed, turning a section of hillside into 'the Fall,' an almost sheer face that dropped straight to Browton Vale. From further up ahead, where the dual carriageway on Radcliffe New Road ran around the edge of the Vale, came the sound of heavy traffic.

The Vale was thick with rowan, oak and beech; over the years, they'd even sprouted in the steep slope of the Fall, so that they flanked the wooden steps that Alice climbed down. The way was thickly carpeted with fallen leaves: brown, red, russet and gold. After that she was on a muddy, well-trodden footpath that wound through the woodlands.

She followed it as it bent around heaps of overgrown rubble, stubs of walls, the gaping holes of what had been foundations. Houses, caught in the landslip. Leaves, twigs, the bristly casings of fallen beech nuts, all crunched underfoot; two grey squirrels chased across the path and shot up a thick oak's trunk, spiralling round it as they climbed. The woods smelled of damp earth, rotten leaves.

Autumn had always been her favourite time of year, and yet its beauty was so bound up with death and decay.

The path forked. One way led down to the river Irwell; the waterway wound and hooked its way over the miles from its source near Bacup in Lancashire, marking out the boundary between the cities of Manchester and Salford before weaving into, and through, the latter. Alice could hear the shallow water chuckling over the stones. The other path rose higher, led deeper into the woods; she followed that.

Soon she was walking through drifts of leaves so thick that it was an effort to kick them skywards in great, billowing showers of colour and rot. The rich smell of leaf-mould, woody and damp, enfolded her. Something about it took her back to her childhood – the good parts, the safe parts. Walking with Mum while Dad was out at work. The air not cold enough to numb or cause pain, but just enough to make the warmth of coming home, of a mug of drinking chocolate or a bowl of oxtail soup, a real thing, a pleasure that counted.

Alice smiled, pushed her hands into her coat pockets and walked on. Her breath was a pale ghost in the damp air, vanishing almost as soon as it left her mouth. A crow cawed; another squirrel skittered through the leaves, stopped nearby and studied her with bright button eyes, paws raised and twitching above its white bib before darting off. Specks of rain fell in her face, but only a few, only intermittent; nowhere near enough to justify turning back. She glimpsed another walker through the trees – not in any detail, just a flash of the red coat they were wearing – and called out a greeting, but there was no answer.

The path sloped down. Tree branches met and meshed above her, making a tunnel of mossy trunks on either side and russet leaves above and below, with green grass and light at the end. Still smiling, Alice went down. Part of her would be sorry to get clear of the woods, but it would be nice to see the river. She peered through the trees, but couldn't see any sign of the red coat, or even the path they might have been taking. Perhaps they hadn't been on a path; perhaps they'd been slipping behind a convenient tree-trunk to answer the call of nature. Alice giggled to herself; that would be just the kind of timing she'd done so well. She'd met John that way, at university.

She let herself think of John, just for a moment. Lazy Saturday mornings in bed together, her small hand spread on his chest while he slept, marvelling how its whiteness stood out against his skin. Cheap pub lunches on a Sunday. Sharing books in the library. The weekend she'd gone home with him to meet his parents. They'd been tall and handsome and dressed immaculately, as if for the Sunday service at the local Baptist church.

His Dad had been called Elijah; he'd had a neat moustache and touches of grey at his temples. His mother was Dorothea, and her laugh had been musical. Both his parents had spoken with a light Jamaican lilt, in stark contrast to John's own Manchester accent. They'd been good people, although she'd never felt they'd been quite sure of her.

It was time to stop thinking of John. Follow a story too far along its length, it always ends in sorrow. Best to stop now. All of a sudden the trees felt cloying, their looming presence oppressive; she strode faster, clear of them, onto the open ground, into light and clear, fresh air with just a hint of the river's yeasty scent.

She walked across open heath towards the river, trying to determine what had changed. Because something had, beyond doubt. Something felt different.

She stared down the river. Yes, something had changed. There'd been a footbridge over the river, and further down, two tower blocks. She'd seen them from the Brow before coming down the steps, but now they were gone. In their place she could see only rolling heath and running water.

Hallucination. It had to be. Some sort of side-effect from the medication. Anti-depressants could do that sometimes. She'd best get home.

Alice turned the other way – back the way she'd come, towards the house – but that view, too, had changed. The ground still rose where the river bent round – the hillside where Higher Crawbeck stood, rising to a summit at her house – but there were no buildings there either. No telegraph poles, no streetlights, just the green-furred shoulder of the hillside, studded here and there with rocks. A big, crooked one stood roughly where her house had been; beside it something was afire, sending a long stream of flames twenty or so feet up into the air.

Alice rubbed her eyes. Not real, it wasn't real – it couldn't be – but when she looked again, the view was still the same.

Over to her left there were noises: the crash and rustle of something heavy trampling its way through undergrowth. Twigs and branches snapped; Alice felt the ground underfoot shiver, and the branches around the entrance to the path she'd just left shook, leaves drifting downward. Beyond them, she had an impression of movement: something big, bigger than a man, was forcing its way through the woods towards her.

And then there was a sound. Afterwards, Alice could never be sure what it was; it was as if she'd forgotten it almost as soon as she'd heard it. Sometimes she thought it had been a shout, a song, a chant; at other times, the blast of a horn or the sounding of a gong. All she knew was that it sounded, and the air grew still; she looked at the trees and they were motionless, only a last few dislodged leaves drifting to the ground. But up ahead, the fire still burnt upon the naked hill.

She looked behind her. The sound, whatever it was, had come from there.

Parts of the Vale were wooded, and others open grassland; others still were wet and marshy, filled with tall bulrushes. The edge of the small marsh was about fifty feet behind her, and a man stood among the rushes, half-hidden. He wore some sort of red anorak or hooded jacket; the hood was pulled up to cover his hair and ears, exposing only the white oval of his face, which seemed almost featureless.

The man in red was looking directly at her, and put a finger to his lips. Sound crashed in; the rush of traffic on Radcliffe

New Road nearby. She looked up at it and saw the cars swishing past, looked up the river and saw the familiar houses of Collarmill Road. When she remembered to look behind her, the bridge and tower blocks had also been restored, but of the man in red there was no sign.

"God," muttered Alice. Her fingers were shaking, and the Vale no longer felt so calm or peaceful. She hurried along the riverbank, taking the quickest route back towards the Fall and the steps to the street above. She almost staggered down the cobbled street, but managed to compose herself; self-control might be her only defence against outright madness just now.

Inside, she locked the door, made coffee, and sat shivering on the sofa for a long time.

LATER, SHE FELT better. Yes, at the time it had been frightening, but ultimately, what had it been? A brief – a very brief hallucination, that was all. She'd been through a lot in the last two years – not just Emily's death but the breakdown of her marriage, the divorce, and now this move, uprooting herself, abandoning her job for an uncertain future once her money ran out.

In that context, a couple of hallucinations didn't sound so bad. Most likely, she just needed to adjust her medication a little. There was no shame in mental illness any more, no stigma. Allegedly, anyway.

There was a surgery nearby, so she went there and registered as a patient. If things got worse, she'd see a doctor; it made her feel a little safer. After that, she took a bus into Manchester, sitting on the top deck near the front. She'd always enjoyed that, getting to look down at the world from a height. Some teenage boys got on en-route, cursing and shouting and blasting out loud, discordant music no-one dared ask them to turn down. Alice huddled deeper in her seat, wishing she'd brought her iPod and hoping not to attract their attention.

Manchester gathered around her with its choked, milling streets, but it wasn't so bad at first, from inside the bus; she was above it all, and it passed in silence, especially when the boys crashed and stomped down the stairs. Getting off the bus was a different matter; the city's noise crashed in on her like a wave, and Alice was jostled constantly as she made her way along the pavement, feeling off-balance and clumsy, out of place.

"Watch out, love," a man snapped as he strode past. Alice stumbled, blinking, flinching as others glanced her way. *The madwoman*, she thought. That's what she'd become. She squared her shoulders and strode towards the Arndale Centre, hoping that didn't make her look mad or ridiculous too.

If the streets had been bad, the Arndale was worse; bodies streamed in all directions, thronging to worship at this or that altar of Mammon, this or the other golden calf. She struggled to an escalator, climbed on for respite. People glared and grumbled as they stepped past her; how dare she hold them up by not climbing the already moving staircase as fast as she could, to grasp for the next glittering prize?

She stumbled around the upper level; from a shop window, plastic orange jack o'lanterns and a row of Halloween masks – witch, mummy, vampire, werewolf – leered at her from beneath a spiderweb of silly string. She flinched away from their empty-eyed gaze and kept going until she finally found a branch of Curry's, where she bought two replacement dongles. She'd order another off the internet if she had to, but these should last her for the next day or two, even in a worst-case scenario. It would do until they came to put a proper connection in.

Her business done, she gratefully boarded a down escalator and wove back through the crowds towards Shudehill station, where she sat shivering and waiting until another double-decker pulled in. There were no yowling teenagers, at least, on the outward journey; the city passed away in silence, giving way to Salford and finally Crawbeck.

Inside the house, she shut the doors and climbed into bed. It was always tempting to stay there in the morning or go back in there during the day, to cocoon herself in blankets and hide from the world. It was also the kind of temptation best not yielded to: staying in bed would become a habit, venturing downstairs a commute, leaving the house a full-scale expedition to a wild and hostile land. Structure; choice; control. She needed them now, to come back from where she'd been and not slip back.

But just this afternoon, she'd make an exception. One hour, she promised herself. No more.

IN THE END it was more like two hours, but she got up again and went downstairs. By then it was beginning to get dark. She pulled the curtains, switched the lights on. As a child she'd always found something deeply comforting about the sight of house-lights aglow in the dull grey autumn evenings.

She watched a DVD. Her phone rang.

"Hi, Mum."

"It's Dad."

She laughed. "Sorry, Dad."

"How you doing, love?"

"I'm okay. Settling in."

"Yeah?"

"Yeah. Just – you know, getting used to it. It'll take time."

"Mm. Everything... all right?"

Apart from her lost marriage, her dead daughter? But she didn't say that. That was the whole point. Everything, now, was no longer everything. It was whatever she had left with those things gone. "I'm okay. Yeah."

"Yeah?"

"Yeah."

A pause. "Ooh, your Mum's here."

She told Mum more or less what she'd told Dad. She didn't mention the hallucinations or the anxiety because there was no point. To their generation, 'mental illness' still evoked images of someone foaming at the mouth in a straitjacket, or screaming in a padded cell. Christ, it wasn't even just their generation. Most people seemed to feel that way – unless, like her, they'd spent some time on the other side of the mirror, at which point you realised it wasn't so very different. *We treat our minds in a way we'd never treat our bodies*, Kat had used to say.

She thought she'd managed to reassure them, at least. When the call was over, the film had lost her interest; instead she switched on her laptop and curled up on the sofa, surfing from site to site.

After a while, she remembered her Facebook page; she hadn't looked at it in nearly a month. She took a deep breath, then opened it.

Notifications, personal messages – most of them were to be ignored. The notifications were for trivial shit that might have seemed funny or vaguely important before Emily's death, but not any longer. The messages? Mostly from people she'd seen or heard from since the death, the funeral or the divorce.

There'd been some friend requests though. She scrolled through them, smiling a little. A lot of them were from people she'd known at university; it was like pressing the rewind button on her life, going back to before Emily and Andrew. Things had been simpler then; it had just been her and the career she dreamt of, that and finding the right boy. You thought you were so grown up at that age, thought you knew everything and had the world at your feet. But really, you were still little more than a child. Christ, could she really be almost twice the age she'd been when she'd graduated?

Alice studied the friend requests. Nicola Smith: she'd fallen pregnant in the final year. God almighty, her child – hadn't it been a boy? – would almost be old enough for university now himself; his biggest worry would be exams. And girls, of course. Or boys. Whichever way he swung. *That* had been a bigger issue back then, too. Although there'd been a lad on her year – God, she couldn't remember his name at all – who'd allegedly been gay but had slept his way through half a dozen of the girls on the course. *He thinks he's gay because it's in fashion*, Emma – one of the few university friends she'd kept in touch with – had said of him.

Bloody hell, it was all coming back. All the emotions of those years swept through her, despite the numbing effect of the anti-depressants. She'd make an appointment to see the doctor tomorrow. She scrolled through a few more friend requests, clicking 'confirm' on them, one after the other, until one name sprang up.

*John Revell.*

He smiled out of the photo at her. Christ, except for the addition of a goatee beard, he hadn't changed remotely. *Black don't crack*, he would have said, putting on a fake American 'ghetto' accent. The same calm, kind eyes; the same gentle smile. It hurt to look at him.

She reached for the mouse. She couldn't accept this request: time hadn't bought her enough distance, not even a decade and a half after the fact. She was about to click 'ignore', but that would have seemed too cruel, like spitting in that face. She looked at his Facebook page instead, what she could see of it. *Works at Paranormal Researcher*, it said. She sighed. He'd kept on with that foolishness? What a waste. It just made her remember why they'd broken up, why the gap between them was too hard to bridge, even now. Especially now.

She logged out of Facebook, switched the computer off, and let the silence return. It was getting late, anyway; a good time to get some sleep.

The whispering began as she stood up.

This time there was no telling herself that the voices came from the street outside; they were coming from right behind the door. She fumbled beside the sofa, picked up the chair-leg and advanced.

When she flung the door open, the hall was empty, but movement flickered at the periphery of her vision – above, and to the left. She looked up towards the top of the stairs before she could stop herself – and, just for a second, she saw the children standing there.

She opened her mouth to cry out, and they were gone. The blinking of an eye; that was, quite literally, how long she'd seen them for, and yet so vividly that, however hard she tried to convince herself they'd been an hallucination, she could never quite believe it. There'd been boys and girls of various ages – as young as seven or eight, she thought, and as old as twelve – in scruffy, rather old-fashioned – Victorian? – clothing. But they'd been there, looking down at her, even if only for a moment. And they'd been so terribly pale.

At last, she found the courage to creep up the stairs, although she was only able to keep her eyes open for fear of what she might otherwise pass close to without seeing it. She climbed into bed and turned her face to the wall in the dark, waiting and waiting for sleep to come.

# Chapter Four

## G.I.G.O.

*19th – 28th October 2016*

ALICE RANG THE surgery at eight the following morning, spoke to a bored-sounding receptionist and made an appointment for half-past nine. By then, much to her own annoyance, she'd already taken her daily anti-depressant – she'd done it on waking, almost on autopilot. If an increased dosage or different drug was the answer, she'd have to wait until tomorrow before beginning the course.

Even if the new prescription – assuming the doctor gave her one right away – took effect at once (which it wouldn't) that would mean a whole day of waiting for any more unwelcome visions to reveal themselves. Correction: a whole day *and night* of it.

Here she was, clamouring for drugs. From experience she knew what counselling could do for some, what it *had* done for her, but right now she had no time to go digging in her psyche, trying to root out the cause of the things she'd seen and heard. What she needed, for now at least, was a chemical off-switch, something to make them go away until she was readier to deal with them.

In a way, she was in luck. The local practice had about a dozen GPs and God alone knew how any of the others might have reacted, but Dr Whiteley, the doctor she saw that morning, just grunted and nodded, half-listening, as she recounted her woes. He'd reached for the computer keyboard to amend her prescription before she'd even finished speaking.

"Okay," he said. He was a thin, sallow-faced man, unshaven and sunken-eyed. He looked ill himself, or hungover. *Physician, heal thyself*, indeed. "So what we'll do to start with is increase your dosage. If that doesn't work, we can look at upping it again – that, or switching you to a different drug. Okay?"

"Okay, but –"

"Any problems, any side-effects, come and see us again. Otherwise, come back in a couple of weeks and we'll see how you're getting on. Any changes to your drug regime will usually take a few days to have an effect."

"Yes, of course. I understand."

The pharmacy was next door; she bought the new prescription and made her way home. Well, after all, this was Salford; it was known to be one of the most deprived areas in the UK. *You knew that*, she almost heard her mother cry, *and you* still *chose to move back there? What's* wrong *with you, Alice?* But Whiteley and the rest were probably used by now to an endless parade of the walking wounded traipsing through their surgeries, psychically maimed by loss of one kind or another – not only bereavement but long-term illness, unemployment, poverty, debt, domestic abuse or casual Saturday night violence. To him, she'd have been just one more face in the crowd.

At home, she looked longingly at the packet of pills with their increased dosage. Here was peace, here were the answers. She shook her head in disgust and thrust them back into her handbag. Here she was, supposedly an intelligent, rational woman, and she was clutching a packet of pills like rosary beads, or some saint's relic that would heal all affliction. What price reason now?

But then again, that was the point, wasn't it? Alice put the kettle on and made a cup of decaff, treating herself to a couple of teaspoons of sugar. It was her mind, her reason, that was under attack here; she couldn't trust her own perceptions any more. Computer techs had a saying: Garbage In, Garbage Out. You couldn't make decisions accurately if you couldn't trust the information you were putting in.

Simple as that. The brain as a computer. Fix the duff connection and you fixed the machine. She padded back into the living room, switched on the laptop. Was this all there really was to her, then – a softer, meatier version of a hard drive? Runs for a while, then develops faults, finally packs up and ends up on a junk-heap?

It occurred to her that the ghost-children – there, she'd thought it, the dreaded G-word – might be something she *wanted* to see. Because if she was just a hard drive on legs, that was all Emily had been. And that meant Emily was gone – completely, forever. But ghosts? Ghosts meant there was more to the equation, some missing factor...

Alice browsed Facebook for a while – looked again at John's friend request and once again could bring herself neither to delete nor accept it – and finally looked up at the room around her. It was empty. Silent, too. No whispers from the hallway. All the same, she played some music – Jan Garbarek, letting his arrangements of Greig's *Arietta* and Jim Pepper's *Witchi-Tai-To* wash over her.

In a way, the worst part was looking up and seeing nothing, listening and hearing only silence. It meant the sight and the sound were still to come.

But they didn't come, not that day. Not even when she went to bed, to the attic room. She was alone there. But still she turned her face to the wall and refused to look at anything, not until morning came.

* * *

SHE TOOK THE first of the new pills as soon as she woke, then set about her normal routine – up early, coffee, breakfast. Surf the net, read, potter around the house intending to make plans for redecorating and stare at the walls instead. Watch DVDs, and try, above all, to skirt the elephant in the room: what now? With marriage, motherhood and work all gone, what was there?

She could find another job easily enough, she supposed. Despite everything, with her qualifications, it would be a cakewalk. If she wanted a career change, she could retrain – she had savings enough, plus her share of the proceeds from selling their old house. Even a new family wasn't impossible; there was still time to find a good man, to have another child –

And to lose them both, as she'd lost Emily and Andrew. She shook her head. But what *did* she want? She found she hadn't the slightest clue.

Yesterday's tension was still there. Not quite as bad – she was on the new dosage now – but it hadn't gone. The silence waited to be broken, the shadows to give birth.

Alice grabbed her coat and went outside. The air was cool and damp, scented with wet earth. She looked up the road towards the line of trees, hesitated, took a breath, then walked up to Browton Vale.

The fear passed quickly in the woods. She followed the winding paths through the trees and drifts of fallen leaves, and the tension ebbed. In the woods themselves, she'd been safe; it was only when she'd walked out onto the open heath that things had gone weird.

She found an old wooden bench on one pathway. The wood was black with damp and green with moss, but she sat there anyway. The path overlooked a long slope that led down to the river; a thin streamlet zigzagged down it, through banks of earth and stone. Crisscrossing tree branches and the wet leaves that hung from them blocked the Irwell from view; a few dull glitters of light, glancing off its surface, gleamed through the vegetation.

She sat there for a while. It felt safe. No place for whispering ghost-children, and no sign of the modern world; if the cars and houses of Collarmill Road wanted to wipe themselves from existence again, she wouldn't notice, nor see the fire on the hill. But in any case, the dual carriageway was above and behind her and the traffic drone from it was almost soothing. Alice relaxed, drifting, until the first cold specks of rain landed on her face.

She stayed put at first, until the rain picked up, going from a light drizzle to a downpour. She pulled the hood of her coat up; the rain drummed lightly on her head. She started when she heard something crashing through the undergrowth, a voice cursing in the distance – then realised it was just another nature-lover, running to get out of the rain. And yet here she sat, because – why? Because she thought her house was haunted?

*Sanity is as sanity does,* Alice told herself. She got up, flipped back her hood to feel the rain on her face, and jogged home.

AFTER THAT THE spell seemed broken. Self-care was the prime concern again, and she slipped back into her normal routine. She didn't even think about the children until quite late in the evening, close to the point where she was ready to go to bed, when she realised how utterly normal a day she'd just passed.

She hesitated at the door to the hallway, then opened it. It was empty; so were the stairs and landing, and the bedroom. She smiled, went to bed, and slept without dreams.

THE NEXT DAY, Alice began the process of redecorating. A trip to B&Q netted a haul of dust-sheets, paint, wallpaper and tools. She stripped the faded wallpaper from the attic room walls, hung fresh woodchip paper and painted over it with warm, mellow colour – a rich burnt-orange that evoked either autumn leaves or a Caribbean sunset.

She bought carpet tiles and used them to cover the bedroom floor – it would do for now, anyway. For the front room and hallway she bought laminate flooring. She repainted the front room, bought lamp-shades for the bare bulbs, knick-knacks for windowsills and mantelpiece.

Now and again, of course, a little worm of fear twitched – children's voices in the street outside, before she placed where they were coming from; the occasional twinge of irrational dread when she stripped paper from rotten plaster, that a chunk of the wall would fall away to reveal some hidden cavity with a tiny skull grinning out of it. But as those days passed, the fears were fewer and further between, and never justified.

She started with her bedroom – new curtains, a double bed – and the front room as they were where she spent most of her time; next came the kitchen, then the bathroom. The bath was a heavy enamel job, old but in good condition; at some point, she'd have to buy a new one, but for now it would do. She settled for a new shower curtain, a new toilet seat, fresh linoleum for the floor.

Little by little, 378 Collarmill Road was changing, from a house into a home.

The engineer from Virgin Media finally came by, put in an internet connection and installed a wireless router. His name was Ron; he was good-looking in a rumpled, companionable sort of way, and a couple of years older than her. He was also married – "since we were twenty-one," he told her – with two grown-up sons. One had graduated university, and the other would next year.

Alice made him a cup of tea, and they chatted a little. All warm and friendly enough, until she mentioned Emily. A divorcée is one thing, but there really is no name for a parent bereft of a child. It put a shadow over things, and Ron left not long after. Alice was briefly and cruelly tempted to shout, *It isn't catching, you know* after him as he walked, a little too quickly, down the drive to his van.

Still, she now had internet access. She passed more time that way, in between the decorating jobs. She kept looking at John's friend request. If they'd married as they'd planned to, she'd have been a bride at twenty-two or three. And yes, there'd have been children, nearly as old as Ron's by now.

Where would she be, if she'd done that? Less well-off, perhaps. But happier? Well, that was hard to tell. If they'd had a child and lost it – but there'd have been plenty of time to heal, and then try again. Alice had had Emily pretty late, and – she might as well face it – there wasn't much time left for her try for another child. Perhaps with IVF and donor sperm – but that sounded clinical, and selfish too.

*The fruit of our love*, Andrew had called Emily; it was pretty much the only thing she could recall him ever saying that had been remotely poetic. But it was *right*, too; it summed up everything motherhood was supposed to be, as far as she was concerned. It was an organic thing, coming naturally out of a couple's love for one another, their devotion made manifest. Artificial insemination from some unknown donor was something different – to her it would have felt cold and bought and fake, like a nip-and-tuck or breast augmentation. Not about love or devotion, but vanity and ego.

That wasn't fair, she knew, but for her, at least, it would be wrong. And that meant no children for her, no family – not unless her life changed radically within the next few years, and she couldn't even imagine that happening. Over time, maybe, but not in time to beat the change.

And despite herself, she found herself studying John Revell's profile picture on Facebook. His page only showed non-friends the most basic information; if she accepted his friend request, what else would it tell her? That he'd married, had the children he should have given her with someone else?

*That he should have given her?* "Jesus," Alice muttered, and shut the laptop down.

It was dark, it was late and she was tired. She turned off the lights and went upstairs.

She flicked on her bedroom light and plodded into the room, peeling her sweater off over her head as she went. She tossed it over the back of her chair, grinned to herself, then turned and found herself facing the window. As usual, the light had turned it into a mirror; in it, behind her reflection, were the children.

This time they didn't vanish after a split second, didn't go away when Alice blinked. They stood there, their eyes enormous and dark in unnaturally white faces, and fixed on her.

It was an hallucination, she told herself; nothing that wouldn't pass in a moment or that a trip to the doctor's wouldn't solve. But when their reflections reached out for hers with hands like pale, tiny claws she couldn't keep still. She twisted away from the window and found herself staring down at them. They looked real; solid enough to touch, had she wanted to, although there was nothing she wanted less.

She'd thought them all fair-haired, but saw now that it was like straw – bleached and faded. Their pale skin was dry and cracked, like badly-applied plaster or droughted earth. When they smiled at her, their teeth were sharp. And then they reached for her, and their fingers, where they gripped her flesh, those were sharp too.

# Chapter Five

## The Music Room

*The Confession of Mary Carson*

HAVING BEEN ENGAGED by Mr Thorne, I soon settled into a steady routine. I rose at four each morning, made my toilet and presented myself at his study. From there, Mr Thorne conducted the majority of his business, venturing forth only when necessary.

In addition to his mill, he owned tenements in Manchester and warehouses at Salford Quays. He was a shrewd businessman; he could hardly have been otherwise to attain his wealth. The world of commerce, he told me, was like unto that of Nature: red in tooth and claw. Softness or pity had no place in it, and could benefit no-one, least of all himself. On the contrary, it could only expose him to risk, that others would exploit. There could be no consideration other than whether an action brought him profit or loss.

Mr Thorne had learnt to delegate, and picked his subordinates with utmost care. In them he sought two qualities above all. The first was a ruthlessness almost equal to his own; the second, even stronger quality, a healthy fear of his displeasure. These employees he handsomely paid, for they would save him the cost many times over.

I had, of course, known something of Mr Thorne's reputation when I came to Springcross House, but as his secretary – well, I need not tell you, Mrs Rhodes, how intimately one becomes acquainted with the workings of a business in such a role. Hardly a week seemed to pass without an appeal from some public-spirited body regarding the conditions at his mill or his properties. Even by the standards of the time, he was a harsh and pitiless taskmaster. The apprentices in his mills were brought from workhouses and orphanages in the South, paid a pittance and worked harshly. Having no family or friends here in the North, they had, therefore, nowhere to go.

The only act of apparent generosity I saw him perform in relation to them was when two 'prentices ran away. He dictated to me a most full description, to be printed and disseminated across the city, of both boys, down to the very clothes they wore – even these, you see, the apprentices owed to him.

The generosity was in the reward offered, which was handsome indeed. My father had, of course, taught me that no-one is beyond hope of redemption. Here was, I thought, some small seed of compassion and grace, one that might, if nurtured, bloom. But when I complimented Mr Thorne on his solicitude for the boys' welfare, he only snorted. "They are mine," he said, "bought and paid for, and I mean to have them, Miss Carson. There is a principle at stake, and in any case, such ingratitude cannot go unanswered – else every apprentice may try to abscond."

Thinking of all my father had striven for in life, I did not wish to think of how he would have viewed a man who believed himself the owner of the children he employed. Had he lived, I thought, he might have found new purpose seeking to ameliorate conditions at mills such as Mr Thorne's.

As it was, I closely examined my conscience on a daily

basis. If truth be told, I hardly liked what I found, but what alternative did I have, Mr Muddock, Mrs Rhodes? I could not afford grand gestures: my savings were, at long last, beginning to grow, but if I left Mr Thorne's employ they would soon be exhausted on the simple costs of board and lodging. And what prospect of employment then? To leave suddenly might mark me as unreliable, flighty, and I would need a reference from Mr Thorne – one he might well refuse to give under such circumstances.

As for the other servants – if they had ever been troubled by their employer's actions, they no longer were; on the contrary, they were most at ease with them. Among them I found not one to call a friend: to a man and a woman they were base, greedy souls – and in Kellett's case, I shuddered to think what else.

And so my life at Springcross House, in its first phase, was a secure but solitary affair – my physical wants were taken care of, my savings steadily grew, but a deep loneliness soon set in.

I spent my days at the house – even the days off. I knew neither Manchester nor Salford well – to the extent that I knew any city, it was Liverpool – and never quite found the courage to explore it alone. Besides, I had no wish to fritter away my salary on trifles. The great, rambling house, and its gardens, were room enough.

Winter became spring, and the gardens of Springcross House bloomed. Winding gravel paths led through ranks of trees and flowers, some native to Britain, some not. There were forcing-houses, where delicate tropical blooms and fruits were cultivated, and little paved clearings with seats and statuary, ornamental ponds and fountains. Around the back of the house, a small stream ran, winding and glittering and foaming, through the grounds, before vanishing under the girdling wall in the direction of Browton Vale below. Yes, it was possible, on the whole, to find beauty, solitude and a substantial measure of peace in the gardens of Springcross House, and so, indeed, I did.

A gardener – as unforthcoming and charmless as the other staff – maintained them, but to this day I think I may have been the only soul at Springcross to appreciate them. Mr Thorne never seemed to spare them a glance; perhaps his late wife had loved them, I thought, and he maintained them for her sake. But that was no more than a guess, for of her I knew nothing. No picture of her hung in the house; her name was never spoken. But for Mr Thorne's single passing reference to her, she might never have lived.

The gardens were particularly charming when it rained lightly, if one took a parasol, but there were days when it rained so heavily it seemed the Flood was about to come again. On those days, I could only remain indoors, where I spent my time reading, either fiction or instructive and improving works with which I might hope to extend my list of accomplishments.

I have, Mrs Rhodes, led a somewhat lonely life – at least until I met my husband and found myself an anchor in this world – and so can attest there are few companions so constant and comforting as a good book. Reading is an addiction I have never outgrown; indeed, the ordering of new books was my one extravagance at Springcross House.

However, one rain-filled day I finished the novel that had occupied me for the past week and found myself restless and dissatisfied; I possessed several unread books but none, just then, attracted me. I found I would rather be up and about – but the weather, of course, prevented it. The house being empty – it was the servants' day off – I began exploring my new abode.

'Rambling', did I call it? A poor choice of words, perhaps; it implies something wandering and random, and Springcross House was never that. Every part of it had an intended function. However – since the death of Mrs Thorne, I suspected – many rooms remained unused. Most of the disused chambers seemed intended for entertaining guests – which Mr Thorne, I knew, had no interest in whatever. There were guest bedrooms, a ballroom, a drawing-room and much besides, including, I discovered, a music room, of which I shall say more presently. Having no need of them now, he had abandoned them to gather dust – out of sight, out of mind. It surprised me a little that he did not lock their doors, to seal away all memory of his loss – but he was but lately widowed, and perhaps not yet ready to put all memory of Mrs Thorne aside.

It was difficult to tell, as Mr Thorne made it a point of pride to show none of the softer emotions; to the outward observer he seemed as unfeeling and pitiless as flint – indeed, so I had thought him at first, but now I wondered, a little. In any case, the doors opened readily into those forgotten rooms. For the most part I did no more than look into them, afraid I would disturb the dust and make it obvious I'd been in there. But then I found the music room.

I opened its door just as the sun broke briefly through the rainclouds and lit the room with a pale golden light, making the dust motes in the air glimmer. It was an arresting sight, so I stood and viewed the room more fully. It was fitted with a pale green carpet, walls punctuated with fluted columns and adorned with floral wall-paper, rows of chairs, and – the feature which caught my attention most – a large pianoforte.

It was this that sealed my fate, in a way. My father had had one at the vicarage in Burscough. He had played passably, and had instructed me. And, in all modesty, I can say that the pupil outstripped the master. It had brought cheer and gladness to our home, admiration from our few visitors, and had been a pastime in which I'd taken both pride and enjoyment. Doubtless some would say that those sins brought about my downfall.

I looked up and down the corridor to ensure that no-one was there, then slipped into the music room, letting the door swing shut behind me.

Thunder rumbled. A wind moaned, dashing rain against the windows. The gap in the clouds closed, and that pale golden light dimmed and faded. But the pianoforte... the pianoforte remained.

I had had no opportunity to play since we had left Burscough, but now I lifted the instrument's lid, perched myself on the stool and ran my fingers lightly over the keys before attempting a few brief chords – low, hesitant, casting nervous glances at the door lest the unaccustomed sounds bring someone running, even though the house was empty. The pianoforte was a little out of tune – only to be expected if it had been left unused so long – but otherwise in reasonable condition.

After a few moments had passed, I ventured to play the first notes of a piece by Beethoven. When no thunderbolt came to smite me, I continued, feeling my confidence grow. I was surprised at how readily my fingers found their way across the keys, how easily skills I had almost forgotten returned.

I played, faster and louder and more fluently, and as I played it seemed the room brightened once again. The piece was the 14th Sonata and it had always seemed, to me, filled with a kind of aching, ungraspable melancholy, for something that once had been and now was lost. Perhaps it was about love. I would not know; other than my father I had never really known it, and if the tune was about any kind of love, it was a different one from that.

But, like all young girls, I had been in love with the *notion* of being in love – indeed, I blushed to recall how in my youth I had conceived *grand passions* for the unlikeliest of men. (Although this, Mr Muddock, Mrs Rhodes, had more to do with the paucity of remotely eligible bachelors in my immediate circle of acquaintances than any perversity of mind on my own part.) While we all collude in the fiction that a good woman has no such thoughts, a fiction it is! And so I could, perhaps, feel something of the melancholy Beethoven's music seemed to hold – not for a lost love, but for the lost possibility of it.

The music was melancholy, was regret, was sorrow, and I fed it with my own. And still that light seemed to fill the chamber. Do you know the 14th Sonata, Mrs Rhodes? The first movement, the *adagio sostenuto*, does not raise its voice;

it is quiet, it is modest, and it gently fades away. I had played it from memory, with my eyes very nearly shut; now, as the last notes sounded, I opened them again.

The room was still bright, and there were shadows on the floor. Of the chairs, I thought at first, but then I saw that the shapes were wrong. The chairs – all of the chairs – were occupied.

I turned and looked. They were silhouetted against the pale light that shone through the French windows. They were silent and unmoving; I could not make out their faces – which is not, I can assure you both, any cause for regret on my part – but knew that they were watching me. This vision lasted but a moment; as the pale glow faded, so did their silhouettes, like shadows on the air, leaving only the empty chairs behind.

The light was gone, and did not come again. The music room was almost dark now, so overcast with rainclouds was the sky. There was a flash of lightning, a roll of thunder, and more rain streamed in torrents down the glass.

I looked away at last, not a little shaken. Yet, I told myself, I could not have seen the spirits of the dead. It was nonsensical – even should I grant that such things could make themselves manifest; Springcross House was a new building, not some old castle with a rich history of bloodletting. The only death I knew of to have taken place here had been that of Mrs Thorne, not of a whole ensemble of children – for the seated figures had been very small.

Whatever it was, it could do me no harm. So I told myself, at least; convincing my rebellious instincts was another matter. Under other circumstances I would have wanted to continued playing, but now I only wanted to leave. I reached to lower the lid, and as I did looked towards the door of the room.

It was open, and Mr Thorne stood watching me in silence, arms folded, face as impassive – and as awful in its impassivity – as that of some dreadful sacrificial idol.

"Mr Thorne," I stammered, but could say no more. You

may perhaps guess at the tumult my thoughts were thrown in. I had no doubt that my employer was angered, and I could hardly play the innocent – the rooms had not only been left undisturbed but had been intended to remain so, and the mere fact they were unlocked was no excuse.

In that moment I was certain that I was to lose my position, and that there would be no letter of recommendation for me, no reference to help me find another situation. Such money as I had saved would sustain me a few short months, and then I would be facing the same grim choice I had before being offered this position, between the workhouse and whatever other unsavoury alternatives there might be. I had known, how could I *not* have known, that this was, for Mr Thorne, a kind of sacred ground? I was ruined, doomed by my own foolishness, by a few minutes of vain idleness. How could I have been so stupid? What would my father have said, could he see me now?

I cannot quite tell how much time passed before he spoke. It might have been seconds, or minutes, where I tried and failed to meet those stern grey eyes. "You play well," he said at last. "Where did you learn?"

Caught quite by surprise, I was at first lost for words, finding them only when Mr Thorne's eyebrows rose in imperious demand for an answer. "My father."

"Of course. He was clearly a good teacher. Or had an apt pupil, perhaps." He nodded at the piano. "The instrument was my wife's."

My face burned. "I am sorry, Mr Thorne. I –"

"I have little use for company, Miss Carson. My wife, on the other hand, greatly enjoyed the society of others. I can take or leave the trappings of wealth and power. She was neither vain nor greedy, but appreciated the regard those things brought her – it is a truth, deny it as we will, that a book is judged by its cover. And so when I had Springcross House built, there were rooms like this, for her to entertain guests. They have been unused since her death."

"Mr Thorne, I'm very sorry – I meant no disrespect –" I knew I sounded abject, but the fate this job preserved me from was still very much on my mind. Pride comes more easily to someone who has no such fear hanging over her. But he went on.

"She played very well," he said. "I'd forgotten... how pleasant it could be."

His face remained as stone, his voice level, but the words – they did not come easily. It was a little like hearing a machine forced to perform in a way it was not used to: cogs and gears creaked and struggled, unfitted to the task, and yet accomplished it. Arodias Thorne, I realised, though appearing made of flint, might be of a more varied composition after all.

He gestured towards the piano. "Please, Miss Carson. Continue."

I rested my fingers on the keys, tried to pick up the sonata's threads. I had finished the first movement, the *adagio sostenuto*; now came the second, the *allegretto*. After the first movement's quiet melancholy, this was bright, joyful, full of sunlight and hope. I let my thoughts turn to the love I'd hoped to know – that, perhaps, only perhaps, I still might. When that ended I plunged, without hesitation or a glance at Mr Thorne, into the final movement – *presto agitato*, full of storm and fury. By now I was playing with a kind of mad, exhilarated defiance, no longer knowing or caring what game was being played, caught only in the heady moment, at last doing something that gave me joy.

At last I finished the final movement and was at rest, spent, leaning over the keys as the last notes echoed away and the room once more was silent. Only then did I look up and turn towards Mr Thorne for a response.

But the door to the music room was closed, and he was not there.

# Chapter Six

## The Lost Garden

*28th October 2016*

ALICE CRIED OUT when the first of the children seized hold of her, sharp tiny claws piercing the skin. Others lunged and caught at her too – they leapt, like cats, clutching at her arms when she raised them to shield her eyes.

The first thing she realised was that they were light – lighter than any child ought to be. They were like shells, or dolls of straw or papier-mâché; they hadn't the weight, and maybe that meant they hadn't the strength.

But they were still dangerous. She felt one coil around her feet, and kicked out, shrieking. Another leapt up, sank claws into her back; another still gouged at her buttocks. She ran at the wall, crushing the ones holding onto her arms between her body and the plaster; the weak, asthmatic hissing of their squeals, little more than high-pitched breaths, again had a feline quality.

She turned round and flung herself backwards against the wall. More squeals. But when she opened her eyes, the other children were gathered in the centre of the room and creeping towards her. If she could stay on her feet, see what she was doing, she could deal with them. But if they tripped her up, or if those claws got at her eyes, it would be another story; they'd press home their advantage, and they wouldn't stop.

Shaking and kicking the last of them away, she was surprised how calm she felt. She thought of clouds of gas swirling round the heart of a dead star: the outermost thoughts were of pain and panic, and dazed fright as to what these things were, what they wanted with her and why, but the hard, chill core of her was steady and calculating. Kat had told her, she remembered, that everyone had inner resources like that, survival mechanisms that kicked in when there was a crisis. You'd often surprise yourself with how well you coped.

*Get to the door, pull it shut, lock it if you can – keep the little bastards penned up in the room.* But even as she reached the door, she saw the children had considered the same possibility. One flung himself at the bedroom door to pin it back against the far wall; others darted through the entrance. Christ, they were swarming everywhere; it was pointless to try and stem the tide. She ran out onto the landing.

Two leapt over the banister rails and landed on the staircase, waiting for her. Others stood or crouched along the landing itself, between her and the top of the stairs. *Christ*, she thought, but she went forward anyway; there were others behind her. She tried not to think of one landing again on her back.

There was a noise above her. She looked up to see one of the children clinging to the ceiling. Its head swivelled a full hundred and eighty degrees to face backwards, grinning down at her.

There were four or five of the children on the stairs now, creeping forward, crouching ready to jump. The nearest was three feet away. She risked a glance upwards: the one on the ceiling had been joined by another. The children on the stairs grinned up at her, their white eyes avid.

White eyes, yes; they all had white eyes, the iris and pupil curdled over, milky in colour. They looked blind at first glance, but they weren't. They followed you, focused on you: they saw.

Couldn't go forward, couldn't go back, and the ones above were vying for her attention. They were herding her, trying to keep her distracted. Then a sudden attack, and with the banister to her right, it would be easy to send her over. A fatal fall on the stairs. *History of mental health problems. Loss of her daughter. Very sad.* Mum and Dad devastated by her loss as she was by Emily's, and blaming themselves, for the rest of their lives, without cause.

Alice charged forward, arms up in front of her, kicking out at half-visible shapes. They hissed and scattered. Another fell on her back, tangling in her hair; she reached the top of the stairs and drove her shoulders back against the wall, crushing it and shaking it free. It clawed at her ankles, hissing. She kicked it away.

*Straight down the stairs, no looking back. Kick out at the ones in front of you.* They flew away, bouncing weightlessly. She didn't look up, just grabbed hold of the banister and staggered down, eyes fixed on the front door. *Get out and then what? Go into Manchester, stay at a hotel? Never mind that now; what mattered was escaping these monsters.*

She reached the bottom of the stairs, ran down the hall. At the door she risked one backward glance; the children were sitting in rows upon the stairs, backs straight, feet together, hands clasped neatly in their laps. Their smiles might have been angelic if not for the blind white stare of their eyes.

They weren't following her. Perhaps their only purpose was to drive her out of the house, to keep it for themselves. In that case they could have it, and gladly. She jammed her key into the lock, turned it, heard the tumblers click. Then it was open and she was outside.

But something was wrong. Where were the streetlights? Where were the cars parked along the roadside? Where was the *road*? She couldn't see any other lights anywhere, and from this hill she should have been able to see the streetlights marching down Collarmill Road, the shops below, the cars going up and down and back and forth. Christ, the city of Manchester was right below her; it should be there, a million tiny lights, but there was only the dark. A power cut? But her lights hadn't gone out, and nor would those of the cars.

She could feel the ground under her feet; it should have been flat and hard, the concrete slabs of the garden path, but it was soft, undulating, grassy. The night was cloudy, but the moon and stars gave some light, and with the front door open, the light from the hall spilled out ahead of her. There was no front garden, no garden wall or gate, no pavement or road. Just a slope of grass and earth and rock.

There were noises from up ahead, from the dark: grunts and snarls that resembled speech, sounds of soft movement. And then from behind her came another sound – the giggling of children – and the spill of light in front of her narrowed.

They were closing the front door. Alice leapt, managed to thrust her arm through the gap so the door slammed on her shoulder. She yelped in pain and another chorus of giggles met her. Christ, she'd choke the little bastards to death, one by one, assuming that was possible. They slammed themselves against the door, but even combined, their weight wasn't that much, and despite the pain, Alice threw the door wide, scattering the children.

As she leapt back inside, fresh cries came from the dark and she looked back. Half-seen shapes flickered in the dim light, and then one ran into it, bellowing.

He was a man, but of what age she couldn't be sure. He was bearded, wore a tunic, together with a bronze helm and a breastplate, and when he saw her he shouted and cocked an arm back, with a spear ready to throw.

"Shit!" Alice slammed the door and ducked sideways from it, keeping low as the voice bellowed outside. For a brief moment it seemed the man might have changed his mind, but a moment later one of the glass panels in the door exploded, splintered glass showering Alice and the hallway as the spear sailed through, falling to bounce and clatter on the floor as it slid into the kitchen.

Alice leapt up. The dark beyond the front door was empty again, but when she turned the children were all grinning down at her from the stairs. The living-room door opened wide to her left; another child stood in it. Alice stumbled up the hallway – it was the only way left to go – looking up at the stairs, in case the children tried leaping on her. The door to the ground floor bedroom opened; two children giggled at her.

Alice ran into the kitchen. A backward glance showed the hallway filling up with advancing children. She kicked the door shut, propped a chair under the handle.

There was only one way now – the back door. But where would that lead? Into her familiar backyard, or elsewhere?

A crash, and the kitchen door jumped in its frame. Then again. The impact sounded impossibly heavy, even for all the children attacking en masse. It didn't seem possible they could muster such force, but if it wasn't them, then what was it? She hadn't heard the front door break open, but what if it was the lunatic with the spear? Or something worse, something she still hadn't encountered?

Alice ran to the back door, pulled the handle, but nothing happened. Well, of course not; she'd locked it. She fumbled out her keys. The kitchen door thudded again; she was sure she heard plaster dust trickle from the ceiling and patter on the lino.

The key turned; the lock clicked. She wrenched the door open and staggered out into the night beyond.

Again, the light inside the house lit up something of what lay outside, and once again it bore no resemblance to anything she'd expected to see. Her backyard consisted of a long stretch of yellowish grass and overgrown shrubbery, with battered plastic chairs and a table, concrete paving with plastic wheelie-bins tucked in one corner; plain wooden fencing between concrete posts, a wooden gate. None of that was visible here, and there was no streetlight, nor any sound of traffic.

On the other hand, it wasn't the empty wilderness of the hillside, either. The light shone on grass, yes, and on thick high growths of vegetation, but she stood on some kind of light-coloured pathway that crunched underfoot. She kicked at it, then crouched and touched it: gravel. It poured through her fingers. She could feel it. It was real.

Giggling sounded behind her, but even as she started to turn, the light from the open door was narrowing. White-eyed faces grinned at her through the gap as the door swung closed. She stood up, took an irresolute step towards the house, then stopped. The door swung shut. A moment later there was a click of a turning lock, and the kitchen light went out.

There was an implosion of darkness, rushing in to fill the space where the light had been. Alice blinked, squinted, rubbed her eyes. When she looked again she could better make out what was there, and also what wasn't.

There were trees and clumps of other plants, exotic ones grown wild and high. There were winding gravel paths, and here and there a statue. But no buildings. Her house was gone.

# Chapter Seven

## The Ogre

*28th October 2016*

Oddly enough, some of Alice's fear went away at this point. Yes, the house had disappeared, but so had the children. Nor was there any sign of the madman who had flung the spear. Wherever she was now, it seemed – so far – quiet and without any threat to her.

In the long run, of course, she needed the world she knew – the world she came from, of brick walls and streetlights, cars and streets half-cobbled and half-tarmacked. And, yes, the world of her dead daughter, too; that was reality, and she could do nothing but engage with it and face it on its own terms. How tempting the prospect of some other realm that her desires could readily shape; how tempting, and how illusory.

She must use her reason, must be logical. Rational. She was a scientist, or had been. She might be again. She must review her experiences. Monstrous children had appeared from nowhere and attacked her, trying to force her into a fatal accident. One reality outside the front door; another, completely different, out back. And neither resembled the one that should exist.

Logic offered only two possible conclusions: either her perceptions were accurate, and the normal laws of space and time had ceased to function in her specific case, or her perception was faulty. She was seeing things that weren't there. And hearing them.

Not to mention feeling them. The gravel crunched underfoot; she reached down and touched it again, felt it between her fingers.

The most likely explanation was that in reality she was wandering around inside the house or in her backyard, while the wild garden was in her heard. But there wasn't any gravel in the backyard, so where was she? Had she gone further afield without realising it? How awry had her perceptions gone?

These were questions without an answer, at least until she had more information. If this was a psychotic episode, it would end eventually. She'd find herself back at 378 Collarmill Road, Higher Crawbeck, and she could talk to her doctor about adjusting her dosage.

She liked the sound of that, even if she wasn't sure she believed it. In the meantime, the problem was deciding what to do. For the moment, she'd have to cope with the episode, and the best way of doing that was to find a safe place to wait until it passed. If she wasn't in an ornamental garden, she must be somewhere else, which could be anywhere from her bedroom to Browton Vale or the middle of Radcliffe New Road.

The safest thing to do, she knew, would be to stay still and wait it out, make sure she didn't step out in front of a car or off the top of a staircase thinking she was on a straight path. But somehow she kept moving. There was a sense of threat, of urgency, that kept her going.

It could be dangerous to listen to her instincts at a time like this; it could be just as dangerous to ignore them. She kept going. The path wound into a tunnel of trees and bushes, where overhanging branches interwove and meshed. Alice clenched her fists as she walked; it was dark all around her, except for the archway full of moonlight up ahead.

When she stepped out into it she breathed out in relief, then breathed in. The air was cool and clean, scented by unfamiliar plants, no hint of petrol fumes. The moon shone in the sky, turning rags of cloud into silhouettes beyond which lay the cobalt-blue night and the scattered dust of the stars. Normally you'd never see this many in a built-up area; light pollution rendered all but the brightest invisible. But here there were stars beyond counting, ranged by distance in layer upon layer. Alice couldn't remember the last time she'd seen a night sky like this; the holiday she'd taken with John in the Lake District, after they'd graduated, maybe. They'd gone out in some woods near Coniston one night, sipped beer and smoked a joint, but she hadn't really needed the spliff. Just the sight of that sky – and her realisation of its sheer vastness – had been intoxicating enough.

And it had also been about twenty years ago. Alice shook her head. All the same – she stole another glance at that unspoilt sky – as hallucinations went, it was extraordinarily detailed.

She looked down again, took stock of her surroundings. She was in a clearing of some kind – but not a natural one, she realised. No, this was a paved, circular space carved out of the garden, and in its centre there stood a statue; a noble, knightly figure with a broken sword, chin upraised, its posture defiant. Carved into the base was an inscription. Alice bent to make it out:

*Their name liveth forevermore*

She straightened up and looked at one of the paths that led away from the clearing. It angled steeply downward – this place, too, was on a hillside – stretching out across overgrown lawns before vanished into thick black foliage far below. Something in Alice shied away from there; it was too like a path in a fairytale wood, the kind the big bad wolf would be waiting down.

But then, she didn't have to go anywhere. She'd been looking for a place to wait out the episode, and the clearing seemed as good as any. There was even a seat, she realised, set into the low walls that marked out the clearing's boundaries. Alice sank into it with a deep sense of gratitude. Her feet were starting to ache, and so was the rest of her, as the adrenaline drained away. She was shaking a little.

She curled up on the stone seat as best she could, trying to warm herself. She looked up at the stars, and listened. It was quiet: none of the usual urban night-time sounds, no traffic or revving bike motors, no voices, no chatter of rotor blades as a police helicopter passed overhead. Only the gentle trickle of a nearby stream. Between that and the view, Alice thought she could put up with the hallucination a while yet.

When she heard the rumbling noise, Alice's first thought was of a roll of thunder, but then she remembered that the sky was clear. When the rumble became a rattling growl, she realised it wasn't coming from above her, but below. When it sounded again, she turned slowly until she was looking down the hillside at the path that vanished into the thick woods below.

The second growl was followed by another sound, one she knew from somewhere; a sort of medley of crashing and rustling and snapping. Undergrowth, leaves and twigs, she realised, as something big stormed through them. When she felt the stone seat vibrate under her, she recognised it; she'd felt it the other day – back in reality, or the reality she knew – out on Browton Vale. Something had been coming for her then, but had been stopped. Tonight, though, there was nothing to oppose it.

The woods below began to ripple and heave as whatever moved through it reached the perimeter. The moonlight gleamed on vast, feral eyes that saw and pinned her. And then there was another growl, and the thing burst free of the woods, rising and expanding as it lumbered towards her.

Its outline was vague at first, but grew clearer as it advanced. It was roughly – very roughly – man-shaped, but much larger than a man; hunched, and bristling with hair. Something of a man, something of a beast. And it was coming for her. Its eyes' unwavering glare told her that.

She had to run. She must get up, run down one of the other paths – but it was like one of those dreams where you feel someone sit on the bed but can't move, can't turn to face them. Sleep paralysis; she'd had that once or twice, especially after Emily's death. It came with certain dreams. So maybe this was a dream after all, in which case it didn't matter if she ran or not. She'd wake up at any moment.

Except what if she didn't? What *did* happen to you if you died in your dreams? She had no doubt that she would if the thing laid hands upon her. Another part of her cried out that this was no dream, couldn't be, was too real to be, but she ignored it. That part was surely impossible.

Whatever the truth, when the moonlight fell on the thing from the woods, her paralysis abruptly broke. It was nearly twenty feet tall and naked, with piebald skin. Its scalp and back were covered by black, bristly hair that stuck up in sharp spines like porcupine quills. The same hair sprouted across its chest, in a thick thatch around its groin and in random tufts dotted across its body. It gave the creature a dirty, matted beard that covered the lower part of its face. Its forehead was low, almost nonexistent, with a brutal ledge of a brow. Its eyes, in contrast, were a pale, almost delicate blue, with a cat's slitted pupils stretched wide by the dark. They looked out of place on that body, that face: they were poised above a wet, pig-like snout of a nose and a mouth that looked swollen and misshaped.

In fact the whole lower half of the face – what she could see of it beneath the beard – had a lumpy, malformed look, but when its mouth finally yawned open she understood. The lumpiness came from jawbones that had grown thicker and heavier than any normal human's should, and the knotted clumps of muscles that had thickened and swelled in order to work them. And the mouth was crammed with teeth too large even for itself: an array of canines and incisors like knives and chisels, and molars like the heads of club-hammers.

The sight was accompanied by the stench of its breath, which almost made her retch. The part of her that had screamed this was *too* detailed, *too* real, to be an hallucination no longer seemed so irrational. Whatever the case, her paralysis broke; she swung her legs from the seat and stood.

The thing had almost reached the clearing; saliva trickled from the gaping mouth, hung in wet, yellowish ropes from the beard. It reached out and parted the vegetation at the clearing's entrance. Its hands were dirty, its thick nails sharpened to points and clogged with filth and dried blood.

*Fee, fi, fo, fum...*

As it stepped towards her, Alice turned and ran. The path shuddered underfoot as the ogre gave chase. She came to turning after turning, path after path, taking each on instinct. Where she was going didn't matter, only that she kept moving, ahead of her pursuer.

A small, calm part of her – the part, perhaps, that had simply accepted what was around her as reality – told her she couldn't hope to escape the ogre. It was too close behind her; it was bigger and faster, and had her scent. As if to underline the point, the ogre roared, and she felt her innards shake from the thunder of it.

Something made her glance round. She screamed, or would have if she'd had breath: the ogre was almost on top of her, lunging at her with one enormous hand.

Alice dived forward, rolling on the ground, and the ogre's grip closed on empty air. But before she could rise, a huge foot slammed down ahead of her on the path, and another behind. The ogre loomed above her. The stench of it threatened to make her vomit: old blood and spoiled meat, stale piss, excrement and semen. Its hands reached for her and its jaws stretched wide as it bent forward.

And then there was a sound, and the ogre was still, a dazed look on its dull face.

She knew she'd heard the sound before, even as it slithered away from her. Her memory wouldn't hold onto it – but then, that was why. It had done the same on Browton Vale just after she'd arrived, leaving only a confused, jumbled impression of song, chant, horn, gong. But whatever it was, it stopped the ogre – just as, on Browton Vale, it had stilled the approach of another huge shape through the trees.

Feet crunched in gravel. She turned and saw them: they were long and white and bare beneath the hem of a red robe. She looked up; the robe flapped around a thin, spare body. The walker pointed with a pale hand. A tight red cowl clung to his head, framing a long, lean, masklike face. His lips moved and the sound came again.

The ogre moaned; she looked at it in time to see it flinch and recoil from the sound – whatever the sound exactly was. It stumbled away from her – or rather, from the figure in red – before turning to rush headlong down the path back towards the woods.

Bare feet crunched in gravel again. Alice looked up to see the Red Man standing over her, gazing after the fleeing ogre. He stayed like that until its grunting, and the crash and rustle and snapping sounds of its passage, had died away. Only then did he turn his head and look down on her.

# Chapter Eight

## Relics

*29th October 2016*

Alice woke up shivering with cold and stabbed with pain, curling up smaller in an attempt to warm herself. She fumbled for the bedsheets, to pull them closer round her, but they weren't there. Other details dawned on her; she lay with her cheek pressed against cold leather and she was fully clothed – right down to her shoes. She opened her eyes.

She was lying on the living-room sofa, with bright sunlight streaming through the front room windows. The time, what was the time? Her mobile phone was in her pocket; she fumbled it out and stared at it. Nearly half-past nine.

She sat up, shivering. She remembered the dream – it had to be a dream. The children had attacked her, driven her out into a hostile and unfamiliar night. The warrior, or whatever he'd been, throwing spears at her, and – the ogre.

Alice breathed out and smiled, amused and relieved in equal measure. When had she fallen asleep? Clearly, she'd never made it as far as her own room. Well, coffee would make it all clearer. She got up, wincing. Christ, she was stiff; well, that would teach her to fall asleep on the sofa. Her right shoulder was particularly sore. She flexed it, but that just seemed to make the pain worse. She yawned and went into the kitchen.

As the kettle boiled, Alice stretched and flexed a few muscles, trying to get the stiffness out. On the whole it was working, except on her shoulder. The soreness wasn't going. She prodded the area gingerly and winced, then pulled down the shoulder of her sweater.

"Bloody hell."

A belt of livid bruising ran across her shoulder. An image from the dream came back to her: the front door being pulled closed as she stood outside, her thrusting an arm through the gap so it closed on her shoulder instead. But it hadn't happened, couldn't have. It had been a dream.

She needed a better look at the bruise, to see how it could have been formed. She went out into the hall; she'd use the full-length mirror in her room. But she hadn't even reached the stairs when something crunched and gritted underfoot.

Gravel? Was the dream invading the reality already? She looked down and saw that perhaps it was, although not in the way she'd imagined. The hallway was strewn with glittering crumbs and shards of broken glass. In the same moment she became aware of a cold draught, and looked up. One of the glass panes was missing from the front door.

Alice steadied herself against the wall; all of a sudden, her legs felt weak.

Where had the dream stopped and reality started? It must have been local kids, throwing stones, perhaps a firework – they were only days from Bonfire Night, after all. The glass had shattered and she'd half-heard it, worked it somehow into her dream, just like the bruise on her shoulder.

She got to the bottom of the stairs, glanced up the hall once more before starting up.

And saw something else; something that made her walk

unsteadily towards it, on legs that felt less and less substantial by the step.

The object lay a few inches from the kitchen door. From it trailed a faint dark smear of what proved to be some sort of powder. It smudged her fingers faintly; when she sniffed them they smelt of damp wood. The smear was perhaps two or three feet long. Two or three feet that had rotted away. No. That was ridiculous; it could not be.

But the object couldn't be either, and it was. She touched it and her fingers found something cold and hard, pitted and worn, the edges nibbled ragged by time. She lifted it carefully, almost with reverence; it felt as delicate as a dried, fallen leaf. No leaf, though; no, this was a long, tapered spearhead of bronze.

THE JOINER CAME round within the hour, in a white van marked A.F. GRANT AND SONS LTD. He was younger than Alice had expected; twenty-two or -three, she guessed, in a smart-casual uniform of plain jeans, workboots, a lumberjack shirt and a baseball cap, offering his hand. "Miss Collier?"

She could have said *Ms*, but didn't have the energy to press the point. "Hi. Mr Grant?"

"Darren." He smiled. Nice white teeth, blue eyes – yes, and about half her age, too.

Alice glimpsed something to her right, at the edge of her vision – something white, something that grinned. She gasped, wheeled – but it was only another of those bloody plastic skulls, in the window of the house next door. "Christ," she said.

Darren followed her gaze and laughed. "Halloween, eh?"

The look on his face said *poor scared little woman*; on another day she'd have let him know in no uncertain terms that he was wrong, but she didn't have the energy today, so she forced a smile and said, "Yeah."

"So what's happened here?"

She indicated the broken pane.

"I see." He crouched to study the damage. He was very tanned, and it wasn't the kind you got from a sunbed either. Someone could afford to take foreign holidays, at a guess. Which was a good sign. Unless of course the money was really someone else's – she doubted he was the A.F. GRANT whose name was on the side of the van. His dad's, maybe. "How'd that happen, then?"

"Kids," she said. "I mean, I think it was. There was a stone, I found it in the hall. One of them must have thrown it."

"Little fuckers. 'Scuse me French. Want bloody hanging. Well, this shouldn't take five minutes, Miss Collier. Get a new pane put in in no time."

"No," she said. "I want a new door."

"A new –"

"A new door." She gestured weakly. "I mean, it's just got me thinking how vulnerable it all is. All that glass – anyone could just smash through it and get in."

Darren opened his mouth to argue the point, then realised there was a lot more money in a replacement door. "Yeah, course – see where you're coming from. Well, we've got wood and uPVC in stock –"

"UPVC's more secure, isn't it?"

"Yeah, that's right." He coughed and cleared his throat. "More expensive too, though."

"That's fine by me. I'd rather pay a bit more and feel safer."

"Right. Right. Okay, Yeah, of course, understand completely." Darren obviously knew enough not to look a gift horse in the mouth. "I'll just go get the catalogues and you can pick."

Darren crouched to measure the doorway. Muscles stood out under the jeans and shirt: pecs, biceps, abs. She studied the catalogue, occasionally casting glances at him. "This one, I think."

"Which?" he peered. "Okay, yep, that's fine. Right then, and I should be back about early afternoon – one-ish, two-ish?"

"That's great. As long as it's put in today." She'd waved a cash bonus under his nose to make sure it would be. "I'll feel a lot safer."

She hated how she sounded; jittery, anxious, needy. Of course, that was how she felt. Everything that had happened had left her scared, and she doubted this pretty-boy workman would have fared much better if he'd had an experience like last night's, but she didn't have to show how shaken she was. Even now, she had the nous and the self-possession to hide it. Perhaps she didn't want to: perhaps the new her, the broken, post-Emily her, had less pride and was more willing to play the scared, vulnerable little-girl-lost. Well, if it worked...

And yet of course it wouldn't. Because the spear had come through the door, the bruises on her shoulder were a lividly discoloured bar on either side of her body, as if she'd been slammed between two hard surfaces. Because it hadn't been any kind of dream at all.

"No problem then, love. See you later."

"Bye, Darren." Well, at least it was nice to know she hadn't lost whatever charm she'd had entirely; she'd caught him eyeing her several times. Probably thought she was going to play Anne Bancroft to his Dustin Hoffman. Good luck with that, young Darren. Then she shook her head; it was hard enough persuading herself she still had a right to even the simplest kind of happiness any more, without bringing sex into the equation.

Casual encounters had never been her thing anyway: for her, sex was the natural product of the right kind of emotional intimacy, the kind that became a lasting relationship. It had been like that with John – she'd been so sure they'd marry – and then with Andrew. Before John there'd been Tom Passmore at school – she'd given her virginity to him because she'd really believed it was love. Within a week she was dumped and he was practising his smooth talk on another girl. And after

John there'd been a brief fling with David, a work colleague's friend – God, she couldn't even remember his surname now. Everything had seemed pointless after the split; she'd had some idea that relationships driven by some great passionate love were doomed to burn out. Perhaps it was best to just find someone you could get along with and settle for that: share the mortgage payments and the bills, have someone to provide TLC and cuddles when you were ill or miserable (with the occasional shag thrown in, of course.) That had been David, and it had lasted all of three weeks. That had been the closest to a casual relationship she'd ever had. And, after that, there'd been Andrew.

Sex, moving in, marriage, babies. Was that still her personal equation? If not, what was? Celibacy? Or stolen afternoons of rutting with handsome young builders? She wasn't sure if she found the picture ludicrous or depressing.

She made coffee and shuttled, restless, between the kitchen and the front room. She couldn't quite bring herself to go upstairs. Christ, what next? Already she was letting her hallucinations confine her to one small part of her house. She needed to see Dr Whiteley again, and quickly, before she had a complete breakdown.

Except that it hadn't been an hallucination, no matter how much she wished otherwise. Or was she hallucinating the physical evidence too? The broken pane, the bruises, the spearhead – the spearhead most of all, because the other items were more easily rationalised. If she showed the spearhead to someone else, what would they see? A rusty old kitchen knife, perhaps.

She went outside, nursing the coffee cup, and sat on one of the lawn chairs. It felt a little safer than the house, although not much – last night, this had been the garden, after all. And there'd been the ogre – but she refused to think of that. Instead, when she'd finished the coffee, she nerved herself to go back and get the few gardening tools she'd brought – clippers, hoe, fork and trowel, gardening gloves and secateurs.

For the next hour or so, waiting for Darren to come back, she uprooted weeds and hacked at the brambles that overgrew the flowerbeds. She might leave a patch of them – after all, that would mean her own personal blackberry crop come the summer, which could hardly be bad. She filled a pair of bin-sacks, although rents soon gaped in them where the bramble-thorns had slit the plastic.

The clipper's blades clanked on something hard. Alice frowned, knelt, parted the brambles. Hidden beneath the hard, cable-like creepers was a hard grey block of stone, canted at an angle in the ground – buried, perhaps, but pushed slowly to the surface. Something about it made her want to look more closely; she took the secateurs and began snipping the brambles away.

Yes; she could see it better now. It was very regular in shape, or had been. On three sides it was neatly squared, the corners filed off, but the fourth side was jagged and uneven, as if cracked. Yes, that was it; this must be part of a larger whole. She clipped away at the brambles, until she was left with the thick knot of the central mass. She set to work with the trowel and fork. After that, a little more hauling with her gloved hands was all it took before the plant tore free of the earth, trailing roots like so much dead hair. Earth rained onto the grass, and over the stone; worms writhed in the hole where the bramble bush had been.

Alice reached out and brushed earth away from the stone. There was something about it; something familiar, she was sure, but she couldn't say what. Then she did see it; it was partial and worn and faded, but it was definitely there. Something had been carved on the stone.

She cleaned away more earth, peered closer, and saw it. Just one word, and a fragment of another, but it was enough: *...eth forevermore.*

# Chapter Nine

## A Question of Judgement

*The Confession of Mary Carson*

FOLLOWING THE INCIDENT in the music room, I passed the remainder of the day on tenterhooks. Mr Thorne had not seemed displeased, and yet... I was not wholly ignorant in the ways of men – or, indeed, women.

My father once warned me that most people have an image of themselves, of who they are or wish to be, but that this image is oft-times at war with their true desires and nature. Some care first and foremost for presenting an outward image to the world, and practise sin in secret – many are those who preach chastity in public, but in secret slink off to dens of vice.

But they, my father said, were as nothing to those who deceive themselves. Lustful men who believe themselves chaste; cowards who believe themselves brave; cruel men who believe themselves kind.

Or, sometimes, perhaps, might a man pride himself on his hard-heartedness, but at depth harbour softer emotions he dare not acknowledge, for fear they might rob him of the qualities that had earned him his wealth?

In either case, I remembered too well what else my father had said. "Such men are to be feared, for they will seek to silence the truth they do not wish to hear. And in doing so, they will strike out at any who behold them as they truly are."

From the first, Mr Thorne had shown me a face of unrepentant hardness, but now I had seen beneath it. What might he do to punish me for that?

It was no help to recall that if our next meeting ended in my discharge, I could blame but myself. If I had only stayed out of that wretched music room! But I had not, and must now accept the consequences.

You can, I am certain, imagine the trepidation with which I approached Mr Thorne's office the following day, Mrs Rhodes. My one hope, I thought, was that he might choose to behave as though the episode had never occurred; if I did the same, all might be forgotten and life resume as before.

Nothing had changed. The fire crackled in the grate – even in spring, the house was often cold – the portrait of a younger Mr Thorne stared down from the wall, and Mr Thorne himself sat waiting behind his desk, jotting down some note or other, barely glancing at me as I entered.

I waited for him to speak. At last he finished the note, but only glanced up and said, "Ah, Miss Carson. Take a letter, please."

He began dictating; I took it down, and so the rest of the day passed. By the time it was done any memory of what had happened in the music room felt like a dream. I breathed easily again: clearly he had decided the matter best forgotten.

So I was allowed to think, at least, for several days. We resumed our old routine and roles: the stern, flinty employer and the efficient, emotionless secretary. Soon I had almost entirely forgotten the music room, and then...

It was Mr Thorne's custom that we take luncheon in the

study at noon each day, for a period of precisely half an hour – no more, no less. There was a small dining-table and chairs by a window overlooking the garden; when the clocks chimed twelve Mr Thorne stopped speaking, sometimes in mid-sentence, and made his way there.

At that same moment, each day, the study door opened and Kellett entered, bearing a cold collation on a platter in one hand, and a pot of tea, with milk, sugar, cups and saucers, on a salver in the other. Mr Thorne and I would dine in silence until the clocks chimed the half-hour, at which he would return to his desk, sit and, as the chimes ended, begin where he had left off. And woe betide his secretary should she fail to be ready at her station when he did!

On this particular day, I happened to glance at the clock as I ate; I recall, quite vividly, that the hands stood at nine minutes past the hour, for it was at that exact moment that Mr Thorne, breaking our accustomed practice, spoke.

"Miss Carson?"

"Mr Thorne." I was startled.

"I would like to speak candidly to you, if I may."

"I would like to think you have always been able to, Mr Thorne," I said, but my stomach was tense and I felt my heartbeat quicken.

"It concerns what transpired in the music room," he said, dabbing the corners of his mouth with a napkin.

I put down my knife and fork. I could not have eaten another morsel; indeed, it was with difficulty that I swallowed the food in my mouth. Mr Thorne put down his napkin. After a moment, he began to speak again.

"I said at the outset that I come from humble beginnings. Allow me to clarify that statement. I was born not far from here at all, in Browton. My father was a farm labourer who drank most of his pay and beat my mother when unable to perform the sexual act. Do I shock you, Miss Carson? No matter. It is necessary that you fully understand.

"I was one of twelve children. A thirteenth was stillborn. Of all that brood, I am the last alive. Five never reached adulthood. Life, it seemed, was to be squalid, fearful and desperate – that, and short.

"When my father died, I and two of my brothers set off for Manchester and found work in a local mill. For lodging, we shared one room in a rat-infested tenement with six others, on a street no wider than I am tall, down the middle of which a constant stream of liquid effluent ran. Within two weeks of our employment, my elder brother caught an arm in the machinery and it was torn off. He died two days later.

"I contrasted the conditions of our lives with those of the mill owner, and concluded, as any man with a scintilla of intelligence would, that the second was infinitely preferable to the first. Therefore I sought knowledge – knowledge that would permit me to rise in society. For I had also observed that many mill owners had risen from lowlier stations in life. I knew what I desired was not impossible.

"On the one hand, I ingratiated myself with my employer. On the other, I set out to improve my own prospects. I could not read or write, but another employee at the mill could. When he received rough treatment at the hands of his more loutish colleagues, I persuaded them to let him alone." Mr Thorne's tone persuaded me not to enquire how this had been achieved. "In return, he taught me. Out of the money I should have sent home to my mother and younger siblings, I purchased books with which to educate myself. In the longer run, after all, my family would benefit."

The clocks struck the quarter hour. Mr Thorne paused to sip his tea; when the chimes had finished, he began again.

"I gained promotion at work, and with it came better and better understanding of business. I saved money, and was able to convince others to loan me theirs. Until, at the age of five-and-twenty, Miss Carson, the illiterate farm labourer's son could buy his own plot of land and build a mill thereon. A small operation to begin with – I was careful to select those employees who would work hardest for the least pay. My brother I employed as a foreman, but he proved incapable. I was forced to dismiss him – I ensured he found work at another mill, as an ordinary labourer. It would have been humiliation to reduce him in status and force him to work alongside... those others, in my employ. I shock you, Miss Carson?"

"No," I lied. "Not at all, sir. A business is a business, after all."

"And has no space for sentiment. You grasp, Miss Carson. There is, I fear, only one morality in commerce, one commandment: *thou shalt make profit.*" He actually smiled; it was a startling sight on that sombre face. "Forgive me. I forget myself – or rather, I forget that you are a good Christian woman."

I wondered if he was mocking me, but his tone gave no hint of derision.

"Nonetheless, it is true. Whatever awaits us in the next life, in this one we must live – and, for preference, do more than simply scrabble for scraps to survive, and perish leaving the world no different for our brief presence there. And no, Miss Carson, I have not forgotten that you too have known hardship. I mean no disrespect, but you were not born to it as I was; you did not have so high and steep a climb. To learn things you were taught in your cradle required great work and sacrifice on my part. I dared not fail – there were no guarantees of success, and it is easier, by far, to fall than to rise.

"And so I prospered, intending always to install my mother and siblings in comfort and luxury. Unfortunately, the intervening years were not kind: hunger, cold and sickness took its toll on them all. Only two of my younger siblings still lived; my brother took them in, but they were too weak from their privations to live long. As for my mother – she was by now a wreck, a shell. I ensured she was well-cared-for, for her few remaining days.

"And then I met Antonia. A fine woman. I found her,

picked her out of many others. She had been born to better circumstances than mine, but, like me, she sought to rise. I saw her hunger, her determination, and something else besides: that to be a rich man's ornament would not content her. She became my ally, my helpmeet. We married – for years she was my secretary, as you are now, Miss Carson. In business, in life, she was my constant and unfailing companion. In only one regard did she fall short: I have, as you see, no heir. She conceived more than once, but none ever carried to term."

I struggle to describe his tone of voice. It was calm, sober, without emotion, yet that only made its impact on me stronger. Arodias Thorne, I understood, was a man of iron self-control, of *will* above all else, and he laid out the facts of his life before me in plain. Had he made shows of remorse or grief, I would have thought them feigned; as it was, I believed he suffered, but concealed it well.

If nothing else, I felt I understood him better. He had, truly, had little option but to be single-minded, even ruthless, to succeed. And succeed he had. Considering the odds he had faced, it was impossible not to respect his achievement, or the personal qualities that had brought it about. Too, I now understood his disinclination towards sentiment or reflection; the cost of his prosperity had been such, he dared not look back.

At least, not until now.

"My wife's passing was unexpected," he said. "She was still a young woman – younger than I. It was a wasting illness. One day, without warning, she experienced pain and weakness; four months later she was a skeleton clothed in skin, in constant pain, barely capable of motion. And with her death, I am alone. I am no longer young, Miss Carson. When one finds oneself alone at my time in life, it's only natural to take stock. I am financially secure, as far as anyone can be – but sooner or later, I shall die. Without friends, heirs, family – what legacy, what memorial shall I leave? This house, my business, my properties, will pass to others or pass away. And it will be as though I never was. And then, of course," Mr Thorne took another sip of tea, "one's thoughts turn to the life to come."

He paused for a moment, seeking, it seemed, for words.

"All my life," he went on at last, "I have had little use for fear. It breeds hesitation, irresolution. Things I cannot afford. Time and again, I have steeled myself to press on regardless. But now, Miss Carson, there is a fear I cannot simply leap over or push aside."

Mr Thorne studied me carefully. Then he looked down, and began sawing at the remnants of his chicken with knife and fork.

"Judgement, Miss Carson," he said. "I fear judgement. What will they say of me when I am gone? How shall I be remembered?" He snorted. "I have hardly to guess, have I? I'm no fool: I know what's said of me behind my back. Old skinflint, greedy swine... do you know, Miss Carson, they say that I have never done a kind deed in my life?"

He pushed a piece of chicken into his mouth, chewed and swallowed. After a moment, he sighed, placed his knife and fork together on his plate, and looked back up at me.

"Perhaps," he said, "they're right. Of course, once I'm dead, words are nothing. 'Sticks and stones may break my bones', as the saying goes. But..." the grey eyes were intent upon me now "... but it is not the judgement of men I fear."

At last I found breath to speak. "Do you mean God, Mr Thorne?"

"Well, His is the judgement all men must fear – is it not, Miss Carson? It cannot be hidden from or ignored. And no amount of wealth will buy Him off."

"No," I agreed. I was no theologian, but I – everyone, I would have thought – understood *that* much about God.

"Therefore," he said, "as I still have some years left, I ask myself if it's possible to atone for my past actions."

I have no idea how I must have looked in that moment; I think I stared at him in uttermost astonishment. In fact, I know I did, because Mr Thorne chuckled. Chuckled! Perhaps you can guess how startling a sight that was. The smile had been out of place, but this was as though a lion had padded up to me and begun singing a comic song. "I'm sorry, Miss Carson," he said, "but your face was an absolute picture. In any case, what do you think?"

"Think, Mr Thorne?"

"What should I do? How might I devote myself to expiating my sins?"

Now my astonishment was complete. "Mr Thorne – you are asking my opinion?"

"Why, of course I am, Miss Carson. Who better?"

"Sir, I am no priest –"

"Your father was."

"But – surely there are clergymen you could ask –"

"Fools and hypocrites, for the most part," said Mr Thorne. "They spend the bulk of their lives flattering men like me, soothing them that their wealth will be no barrier to God's grace, no matter what measures they obtained it by. And always, always, their eye is on acquiring some donation for themselves. No, Miss Carson; I would be naïve to trust such men. You, on the other hand..."

"I?"

"I will not insult you by calling you a simple woman, Miss Carson – I have no doubt of your intelligence. However, you are not a trained religious. Your skills lie in administration and organisation: thus you helped your father's cause. You haven't been trained in clever sophistries. You have your father's example and, I believe, faith that is not simple but *straightforward*. Direct. Do you think that a fair accounting?"

"I – yes. Perhaps, yes."

"Good. *That* is what I have need of, Miss Carson. Now, tell me truly – without fear or favour. Am I, do you think, beyond all hope of redemption?"

"My father always taught me," I said, "that no human soul is beyond redemption. If there is repentance, true repentance, there can be salvation."

"Good," said Mr Thorne. "Good. It is what I hoped. I suspect your father would have said that actions speak louder than words, however – yes?"

"Of course. If you had been a trader in slaves, he would have expected you to give that business up."

"Naturally. So, a man must repent both in word and deed."

I am not sure even now if he expected any reply from me, but at that moment the clocks rang out the half-hour, and he stood. "In any case," he said. "To work! But thank you, Miss Carson. I will give your counsel a great deal of thought."

And with that he returned to his desk and readied himself to take up where he had left off. I hurried to my place and carried out my duties, transcribing his letters and memoranda. And so the rest of the working day passed.

Up, at least, until the final half hour, when Mr Thorne ceased dictating.

"Miss Carson?" he said, and there was a note in his voice I had not heard before. It was almost shy.

"Yes, Mr Thorne?"

"I was wondering if I might make a request of you."

"Of course, sir. You are my employer."

"Nonetheless, this is a request of a more personal nature."

I froze. What was he about to suggest?

"The music room," he said. "I wondered if we might retire there – and, if so, if I might prevail upon you to play again."

I hesitated. This was unfamiliar ground to me, in more ways than one. In terms of my relationship to my employer it was a new departure. In another, simpler sense... well, as I have said, there had been two suitors for my hand in my youth, but, other than my father, it had been a long time since I had had any conversation with a man beyond the purely professional. I had a sense of treading *terra incognita*, some hitherto uncharted domain of whose codes of conduct I was ignorant, where the penalty for a wrong step might be fearful.

If I said yes, what else might I be held to have implicitly

agreed to? But my very ignorance of these rules made me loath to refuse; perhaps the offer was, in fact, a sign of forgiveness for my earlier trespass in the music room – if trespass it had been – and to spurn it would be an insult. And besides, there was that piano, beautiful even beneath its dust, even out of tune. "It would be a pleasure," I said at last.

"Good." He smiled at me again. "Shall we go?"

It had been, beyond doubt, a day of surprises, and I soon learned that they were not yet over. When we reached the music room doors, Mr Thorne flung them wide, and I was astonished to see the transformation that had been wrought. The music room – and most of all, the piano – had been cleaned to spotlessness, and soft lights burned in their sconces on the wall.

"Miss Carson." Mr Thorne indicated the piano stool. "Please."

I sat there – much more self-consciously and with far less assurance than I had the other day. The piano looked brand-new, and expensive to boot. The deep brown wood gleamed.

Mr Thorne, meanwhile, walked past me and sat in the front row of the chairs, arms folded on his belly, watching me. I felt my cheeks burn with embarrassment; I felt awkward beyond words, and that, of course, was the problem. I was, most decidedly, uncomfortable, but I had no words in which to express my discomfort. Certainly, I saw no alternative but to continue with the game – if game it was.

I folded back the lid and cleared my throat. "What shall I play?" I asked him.

"I think," he said, "the piece you played the other day. You played quite beautifully, you know, Miss Carson."

Again I dared not look at him. I flexed my fingers, reached out and touched the keys. The sonata's first movement: *adagio sostenuto*. I played the first notes, then stopped. Not only had Mr Thorne had the music room cleaned, he had re-tuned the piano, and now the notes sounded as the composer had intended, full and rich and clear, gently wafting through the room.

Mr Thorne's presence continued to make me uncomfortable: I had no idea how to react to it, and so ignored it insofar as was possible. I did not look at him; I focused solely on the piano, the keys and the music.

Only once did my self-imposed resolve fail me, and I gave into the temptation of stealing a glance at him. He leaned back in his chair, his eyes closed, a slight smile hovering on his lips. I looked away, feeling as though I was intruding on some intimate moment.

And so on I played. First the *adagio sostenuto*; then, with barely a pause, the *allegretto*, and then at last the *presto agitato*.

At last I was done. I was angry, in a way; I'd found something private, something secret, some warmth and comfort in a comfortless place. Mr Thorne had robbed me of that, made it a command performance for his benefit. Was that how it would be now? The piano-playing as just another extension of my duties?

Fingers trembling, I folded down the piano lid as the last notes faded. As I did, I realised Mr Thorne was applauding.

"Very good indeed, Miss Carson," he said, getting up quickly. His voice was a little hoarse, and he did not let me see his face. "Very good indeed. Thank you." And then the music-room door swung shut behind him, his footsteps fading down the corridor's panelled floor.

# Chapter Ten

## Dating

*29th October 2016*

THE STONE IN the garden was fixed in place; Alice couldn't budge it. Instead she fetched her digital camera and took several pictures, close up. After that she busied herself on the rest of the garden, until she heard Darren's van pull up outside.

She brought him endless cups of tea and pretended not to feel his eyes on her when she turned away. Again that odd, guilty thrill of satisfaction: she still had it, whatever 'it' might be.

At last, he was done; a brand new uPVC door was in place, with a five lever mortice lock and additional locks at the top and bottom.

"Thanks, Darren," she said, counting out the promised notes.

He grinned back. "No problem, love." A pause. "Well..."

"Thanks again," she said, smiling at him. "Byeee."

She thought she saw the smile fade before the door clicked shut; he thought he'd been in there, no doubt. She'd been briefly tempted, all the same – a little warmth, a little companionship would go a long way just now – but it would cause more trouble than it was worth. It always did. She was quite damaged and complicated enough without any added ingredients, thanks very much.

She went to the window, watched the van drive away, then put the kettle on and studied the door. It made her feel a little better, but not much. There was danger inside, as well. She wouldn't fasten the top and bottom locks; she might need to get out. But considered again, that thought wasn't comforting either.

Indeed, she couldn't be sure if the children hadn't tried to drive her out of the house. Out front there'd been the warrior with his spear, and out back – she tried not to think of the ogre, told herself it couldn't have been real.

But still… there was the spearhead. She hadn't imagined that. She should have kept a sample of the dust that had lain beside it as further proof.

The phone rang; Alice jumped. Her hand went to her chest, felt the thunder of her heart. She was gasping for air; she made herself breathe slowly, in and out, as Kat had taught her to. The phone kept ringing. Alice sighed, went through into the front room and picked it up. "Hello?"

"Is that you, our Alice?"

She sighed again. "No, Mum," she said. "You're talking to a figment of your imagination."

A gasp. "Oh God, Alice –"

"Mum. *Mum*. I'm joking."

"Well, it's not a very nice thing to do," said her mother. "Your Dad and I have been worried sick about you since you moved there."

"Mum, I'm fine." Christ, that was a laugh.

"No you're not, Alice. No, you're not."

"Oh," she said, "yes, I'm sorry, Mum. Of course. I couldn't possibly have any awareness of my own mental state, could I?"

"I'm just trying to help, Alice. It can't be good for you, being on your own there."

Alice managed to stop herself bursting into laughter just in time. God knew what her mother would have thought of that, but she had to see the funny side if she wanted to retain whatever sanity she possessed, assuming she still possessed any. "Mum," she said, "really, I'm okay. I don't want to talk about –"

"Alice, you've *got* to talk about it. You're going through one of the worst things a woman can go through –"

"Mum, really, just leave it, okay?"

"No, Alice – you can't just hide in your room all the time."

"Look, Mum, for God's sake what do you *want*?"

There was a breath's worth of silence on the other end of the phone, enough to tell her that what she'd said had hurt. Which now meant, of course, that Mum would come back twice as strong as before.

"What do I want? I just want to be a mother to my daughter, that's all. What do you think I want? You're alone, you're grieving, you push everyone away, and I'm supposed to just leave you on your own?"

"I want to be left alone, Mum. Right now, that's what I need. I need some time to myself."

"You do *not* need time to yourself! That's the *worst* thing you could possibly have!"

"How do you know?" Alice could feel her control slipping. She knew what she was saying would make things worse: it was like watching someone fall from a height – it was terrible, but the outcome was beyond your power to change. "What makes you so bloody sure you know what I need?"

"I'm your mother! Do you think I don't know you better than you know yourself? It's the strongest bond there is, between mother and child –"

Mum stopped. This time the pause was of both their making. *Hell is truth learned too late*; Alice had heard that somewhere, and her mother had been just a second too tardy in realising what she was saying.

"Between mother and child?" she said. She felt her grip on the telephone handset tighten, felt the plastic casing squeak and crack. "Between mother and child? Who the hell are you to – *how dare you* lecture me about that? Who the hell are you to be so superior?"

"Alice, I'm sorry –"

"What did you do to protect your precious bloody daughter when Dad was gambling and drinking and pissing all the money up the wall? What did you do when the leg-breakers came kicking down the bloody door?" That was unfair and cruel and she knew it, but she couldn't stop. "What did you do to become the patron saint of Mums everywhere?"

She stopped herself – but again, it was too late. At the other end of the phone, she heard hitching breaths, then sobs. *Well done, Alice. You made your Mum cry.*

Alice put a hand to her mouth. *Say something. Just* say *something*. She didn't know if she meant her mother or herself. But Mum just cried and Alice couldn't think of anything to say. She couldn't carry on with this. She put the phone down and slumped back into a chair, then wiped her eyes furiously; she was beginning to shake. She felt sick. She got up and ran to the bathroom.

As she rinsed her mouth with cold water and splashed more on her face, she heard the phone ring again. She towelled her face dry and put her glasses back on. No, she wouldn't answer. She couldn't face Mum now.

When the phone had stopped ringing, she went into the kitchen, gently took the spearhead from its carrier-bag sheath and studied it again, then wrapped it once more. Walking down the hall she heard whispers, glanced up to see pairs of white, blind-looking eyes peer down at her from the stairs. She slipped the spearhead into her shoulder-bag and went out, locking the new front door behind her, walking toward the bus stop.

She got off on Chapel Street and walked until she reached the old Salford Royal Infirmary – now a block of flats – and the junction with Oldfield Road. Here was where the University campus appeared; on her right, down Silk Street, lay the Adelphi Building, which had been the hub for all the Performing Arts students.

She crossed over Silk Street and passed Adelphi House, a newer building that in her day had been filled with plasma screens and the like for better viewing. It stood above the Old Pint Pot, a pub perched on the bank of the Irwell. Now the A6 had changed, from Chapel Street to Salford Crescent, and on her right there was only a railing with a sheer drop to the swollen brown river below. Across the lanes of traffic was the Black Horse; she'd got drunk in there more often than she could count, but the windows and the doorway were covered now by sheets of tin, which in turn were plastered over with flyers for long-forgotten gigs and events.

Up ahead, where the river curved round, there was the main university campus, but Joule House was on her left, across the lanes of traffic. She walked up further, found a pedestrian crossing and used it. Then she went up the steps to the main doors, let herself through and approached the pretty young woman at reception.

"Hi."

"Hi. I've got an appointment to see Professor Fry."

"What name is it, please?"

"Alice Collier."

"Okay, just take a seat." Was it Alice's imagination, or did the woman behind the desk eye her with disdain? Alice could barely wait until she was sitting down before taking out her powder compact and checking herself in the mirror. She *had* showered that morning, hadn't she? *Had* remembered to put on make-up and brush her hair? The mirror reassured her that she had. She studied her clothes: jeans, trainers and a sweater. Nothing spectacular, but all clean on today and all good-quality brands. Unless – and she made herself laugh at the frightening traitor thought – unless all her perceptions were completely haywire and she was actually a nightmarish figure of dirty clothes, matted hair and old streaked make-up.

A door opened. "Alice?"

"Hi, Chris," she said, getting up.

Chris Fry smiled back at her and held out both arms, which went some way to dispelling her fears. His hug was tight, warm and above all, friendly – no attempt to be anything more than it was. "How are you, chuck? It's been ages."

"I'm" – Fine? Great? – "I'm okay."

"Oh good. Good." Chris shuffled from one foot to the other; a big, broad-shouldered man in his late thirties, he looked like a particularly large and amiable teddy bear blinking awake from hibernation. Like Darren, he wore a combination of jeans and lumberjack shirt, but in his case they strained noticeably in an effort to contain a physique whose lines, made generous by Mother Nature, had been made even more so by an excessive fondness for curry. Although the casual observer might have thought it was due to excess hair: Chris Fry was one of the most hirsute people Alice had ever known. His hairline was only just starting to recede, and his thick, reddish-brown mane, barely touched with grey, hung down his back. He'd made an attempt to tie it back in a ponytail, but about two-thirds of it had refused to be disciplined and spilled across his shoulders. Add that to a thick, bushy beard and the only parts of Chris' face still visible were his forehead, eyes and cheeks – which, she saw, were starting to redden as the awkward silence stretched out. "Come on up," he said. "This way."

"You want some coffee? I've got some of the proper stuff here. None of that instant crap."

"Oh, go on, then, thanks."

Chris's office, like the man himself, was in a state of amiable disarray, with papers heaped on his desk, on the spare desk up against the walls, and in the sorting trays. It was also a little home from home, with a tiny kitchenette tucked away in one corner, complete with a sink and fridge.

The bear's lair, Alice thought. He'd been no different when they were students together. A friend of a friend, who'd lived not far from her digs, Chris had plainly been smitten with Alice, but thankfully he'd also been far too shy and sweet-natured to be any kind of trouble. By the look of it, he still seemed fond of her. That wouldn't hurt.

Chris ambled over to the coffee machine, filled two mugs and cleared a couple of spaces on the desk for them before fishing a pint bottle of milk from the fridge. "Semi-skimmed do you?"

"Absolutely fine."

"Sugar?"

"No thanks. Sweet enough."

Chris chuckled. "Me neither, these days. Orders from She Who Must Be Obeyed."

Alice looked at the photos perched atop his computer. There was a photograph of Chris with a woman who might have been a magazine centrefold, and a picture of two adorable-looking young boys, one fair-haired, one dark. "You got married?"

"Don't sound so surprised. Yeah, her name's Marzena."

"Polish?"

"Yeah. She spoils me soft. Couldn't be happier. It'll be – Christ, just realised. Fifteen years next month." Chris grabbed a pen and a scrap of paper and scribbled a note. "Just reminding myself before I forget. Best book a table at Shere Khan's or she'll have me guts for garters." He nodded at the picture. "Those are my boys. *Our* boys, sorry. She's very strict with me on that. 'How much work did you do, Christopher? I was eighteen hours in labour just pushing out the first one!'"

Alice laughed. Chris grinned.

"The blonde one's Tomek – that's after her dad. Other one's Danny. Takes after me, God help him. So how old's yours now?"

The laughter died in her; she felt her stomach clench, as if a hand had crushed it like a paper cup. "I'm sorry?"

"Yours. Your little girl. Emily, right? How old's she? You had any more, or..." Chris trailed off. "Jesus, Alice, what's wrong?"

"You, um..." Oh, God. "You didn't hear?"

"Hear what? Oh Christ."

Haltingly, her voice shaking, she told him.

"Oh my God." Chris half-rose, sat down again. "Oh my God, Alice, I am so sorry. I hadn't a clue. The last I heard you were married – not to John. To Andrew, wasn't he called?"

"Andrew, yes." She forced a smile. Damn, she was crying again. Chris shambled over with a box of tissues.

"I hadn't heard anything of you for a few years," he said. "So I – oh, God."

"It's all right, really." The crying had stopped at last; she dabbed her eyes dry, fumbled for her make-up case, started rectifying the damage as best she could. It wasn't all right, of course; it never would be.

Chris sat in mortified silence. "Forget it," Alice said. "You didn't know. Shit happens." Her voice wobbled on the last word; she took a deep breath.

"What about Andrew?"

"Still in Sussex. I heard he's seeing someone else."

"The bastard." Chris had met Andrew at a couple of reunions. Alice had always felt he hadn't liked Andrew much. Maybe he'd still been carrying a torch. Didn't really matter.

Chris coughed, slurped what sounded like half his coffee and swirled the remainder in its mug. "Anyway. You didn't come here to... I mean it's good to see you, but..."

"But I said there was something I wanted your opinion on." Alice opened her shoulder-bag. "What do you make of this?"

Chris frowned at the object in its Asda carrier bag, looked up at her dubiously, then unwrapped it. He became still as he got his first clear look. "Good grief." He fumbled a pair of gloves out of a drawer, donned them and eased the spearhead out of the bag. "Where did you find this?"

"Grounds of the house I've moved into," she said. That was close enough to the truth for now.

"Amazing," he said at last. "Really quite extraordinary. It's in very good condition for its age."

"How old..."

"Well, I'll have to do more detailed tests to be sure. But if I'm right – and I think I am – we're looking at two, three thousand years, at least."

"Jesus. Really?"

"Well, it's made of bronze. That makes it a lot easier to guess at the age range. After the end of the Neolithic, before the Iron Age got going..."

"Of course."

"Do you mind if I hang onto this?"

"No. No, of course not. Just... if we can keep it quiet for now? I've only just moved in there and I'm finally getting settled in."

"Sure. I mean, I'll let you know if I think this is going to be the find of the century or something, but, you know, we're not just gonna storm onto your property and start digging things up. Illegal, for a start." He grinned, and after a moment Alice smiled back. "Look... if I think a dig would be a good idea, I'll get in touch and let you know, but it's up to you if or when anything happens on your property."

"Okay. Thanks, Chris. I appreciate it."

"That's... you're welcome. Are you gonna be all right?"

"I've no idea. I mean, not in the long run. Do you think you can ever get over something like this?"

It wasn't a rebuke but a genuine question, and to her relief Chris took it as such. She saw him glance at the picture of his two sons. "I don't know," he said. "I hope so, but..." he trailed off, caught between honesty and wanting to comfort her.

"Yeah," she said. "In the short term, though – yeah, I'll be okay. Relatively speaking."

"Here's my card. If there's anything we can do – even if it's just a friend to talk to... or if you ever want to come over, have dinner... I know Marzena would love to meet you."

That torch he'd carried, it had never completely gone out. "Thanks, Chris. I'll see you later."

When he hugged her, she patted his back and pecked his cheek and quickly slipped away before she could start crying again.

ALICE WALKED BACK down the Crescent and Chapel Street, then caught a bus into Manchester. She got off at Piccadilly, and once more flinched from the noise and heaving of it, the babbling, thundering, rushing crowd.

It felt as if you couldn't stand still for a moment, as if you constantly had to be alert and dodging other pedestrians, but she knew it wasn't so bad. Compared to London, say, Manchester was almost sedate. The fact was that she was too used to living far from anywhere these days, staying indoors and going for a ramble on Browton Vale. She'd have to start making more trips into town. Toughen herself up a little. Otherwise she'd end up a complete shut-in.

Somehow, she managed to get across the Metrolink tracks to Piccadilly Gardens. They'd changed significantly. When she'd last lived in Manchester, they'd been a big, largely untouched sprawl of grass, usually the haunt of the homeless and mix of subcultures – punks, goths, indie kids and crusties. Now the grass was trimmed and sculpted; there were benches and fountains, bijou restaurants and cafés. As she entered the Gardens, she found a Caffè Nero to her left; she wove through the outside tables and went inside. She found an empty table that was clean, unmarked except for a flyer advertising a double bill of *Dracula* and *The Wicker Man* at the Dancehouse for Halloween.

She grimaced and brushed it aside. She'd always found films like that hilarious; it had always infuriated John, who'd luxuriated in their atmosphere. Her taste had run to old black and white Hollywood movies – comedies especially – and subtitled European films, while Andrew had preferred thrillers. She was almost tempted to go to the screening, though. Given what she'd seen at Collarmill Road, Christopher Lee's plastic fangs would be just the kind of light relief she needed.

She ordered a skinny latte, donned her iPod earbuds and sat in a soft leather chair by the window, watching the faces swarm past. Except that now another dread kept building in her, then ebbing away again. It took her a minute to realise what it was.

The crowd moved like a tide at the shoreline, surging through seaweed and rockpools, then retreating. The bodies in it would cluster together or flow in unison along a route – and then part. It was when the crowd parted that she felt uneasy, she realised; every time it happened she was afraid of what it might reveal, what might grin or glare back at her.

But nothing did. Not this time, anyway. She breathed out. She wasn't a shut-in yet. Then again, that was hardly a surprise, considering what she'd be shutting herself in with. In fact, she might have to look for a hotel room in Manchester. Another night in that house – another one like last night – would finish her. She'd have to lay the ghosts – everything in her revolted at the term, but what else could she call them? – learn to live with them, or run away.

The last option was the only one she'd flat-out refuse to countenance. She'd meant what she'd said to Chris: she had no idea what kind of life you could have when you'd lost a child. Or, more specifically, what kind of life *she* could. Some people did rebuild – a new marriage, new children – but could she? She honestly didn't know. But to rebuild, you needed a foundation; you had to stop somewhere. You had to face the ghosts.

She looked away from the crowd and switched on her smart phone. The café had wifi access, thank God. She called up Facebook and scrolled through memes and cat pictures to distract herself.

With little success, though. The stone in the garden, the spearhead: they weren't products of her imagination, they were physical artefacts. The fear had plagued her, on the way to see Chris, that the spearhead might prove to be some innocuous piece of metal, like a rusty kitchen knife, that some kinked portion of her mind insisted on warping into something else. But Chris had confirmed it. Unless she'd hallucinated that too – but at some point you had to trust some of your perceptions, or you'd be paralysed.

There was a line, then: a line between what was real and what couldn't possibly be. But it was blurred. So, she had to establish what was delusion and what was actually real. A doctor could help her with that – unless he dismissed evidence that didn't fit his preconceptions, of course.

So on the other front, someone needed to examine the house –

She stopped. Then, after a moment, she began scrolling up her Facebook screen until the icons at the top were visible: notifications, messages and friend requests. She clicked on the last of these and a list unrolled.

A short list: there was only one unanswered request there. In miniature, Jon Revell's face smiled out at her.

Alice's finger hovered over the 'Confirm' button. Here was a whole can of worms and no mistake, Dad would have said. She hesitated, her coffee cooling beside her. Finally she clicked 'Confirm'. *You and John Revell are now friends.*

There was a lot more detail now. *Single*, his relationship status read. *Lives in Manchester*. She bit her lip. Maybe –

The phone beeped. *You have one new Facebook message.* Alice hesitated for a moment, then tapped.

It was from John.

*Hi there, Alice. Thanks for the add! John x*

After a moment, she typed a reply.

*Hi there handsome.*

She hesitated, then deleted the last word. It had come to her so readily – even though when she and John had first been dating, neither of them had so much as sent an email. But it was the kind of thing she would have said, or written, back then. Christ, it was so easy – almost frighteningly so – to fall back into old patterns. She'd better be careful about that.

*Hi there. How are you? Alice.* After a moment, she decided adding an 'x' would be okay.

She clicked 'send'. John replied within the minute. *I'm okay. Back in Manchester.*

*Me too*, she typed. *Didn't know you were away?*

*Here and there. Bristol for a bit. Then Reading. Glad to be oop North again, to be honest.*

*Yeah. It's cheaper, apart from anything else.*

*You're back in Manchester now?*

*Yeah. Moved back about a week ago.* She hesitated, then typed, *I'm in town, if you fancy meeting up.*

She waited, biting her lip, until the reply came through a couple of minutes later. He'd had to think about that one, she thought. How close had he come to refusal?

*That sounds nice*, he wrote. *When and where?*

*How about dinner at the Koreana? We used to like going there.*

*Are they still there?*

*Yup!* She'd idly checked online earlier today – or perhaps it hadn't been so idle. *About seven?*

After a small eternity, he replied.

*Okay.*

# Chapter Eleven

## One is One and All Alone

*May 2000*

It started over Colchester, of all places. But then it wasn't really true to say that was where it started; it had begun almost two years earlier, when Dorothea Revell had collapsed and died on her own landing, out of the blue. That had been the first cut, severing so many of the fibres that had bound John to her, but like many mortal wounds it hadn't looked that serious – at least not enough to be fatal.

But when both sides of a cut are pulled different ways – however gently, at least at first – the rent can only widen, until something vital is torn away.

"Babe?" called John.

"Mm?"

It was a two-bed flat in Prestwich, a neighbourhood that ranged from the posh to the grotty. Their street was neither the best nor the worst. It wasn't bad; it was acceptable for a young couple with their sights set on the kind of jobs requiring a B.Sc. (Hons) in Physics. Except that Alice wasn't sure if they both still wanted that now.

She was in the living room, curled up on the sofa, reading through a sheaf of papers for the job interview, jotting down notes as she went. John was in the kitchen, waiting for the kettle to boil.

Alice was twenty-five years old.

"I was thinking, tomorrow night – what do you say to a curry and a film?"

"Can't."

"You sure?" John came through, a steaming mug in each hand. "That *Gladiator*'s on. Thought you had a thing for Russell Crowe."

Alice stuck her tongue out at him, gratefully accepted one of the coffees. "Maybe the weekend? I'm not gonna be home until about nine."

"Say what?"

"I told you, didn't I?"

"Told me what?"

"I got an interview, for that job?"

"What job?"

"You know."

"Um..." John swept a hand over the top of his head, to illustrate the topic's trajectory in relation to him.

Alice frowned. "I didn't tell you?"

"Not unless I hit my head and forgot about it."

"Always possible."

"So, what job?"

"Researcher. At NuTech Labs. It's a plum job."

"NuTech? The hell are they at?"

"I told you –"

"– you didn't tell me –"

"– they're in Colchester."

"Where?"

"Col –"

"Fucking *Colchester*?"

"Hey! Will you not yell at me, please?"

John snorted through his nose. "Colchester? I mean, you know where the place is, right? Like, two, three hundred miles away?"

"It's just an interview, John."

"Yeah, but it's kind of a big thing, innit? Can't exactly commute from Manchester. We'd have to relocate."

Even then, had she been thinking *not necessarily*, thinking *you don't want to go, stay here*? Perhaps she hadn't quite articulated such thoughts to herself, but they were there, moving under the surface, silent in the deep and waiting their time to rise. "Look, jobs like this aren't exactly thick on the ground. We talked about this. You've got to go where the work is."

"And what about *my* work?"

Because, of course, his work was so much more important than hers. "Which work's that, John? Teaching A-Level stuff at an FE college?"

"It pays the bills."

"And it can just as easily pay them in bloody Colchester. You're in a rut. You're comfortable there and you don't want to move. Fine. But I do. I want to do some proper work, real work. Stuff that pays properly, not the kind where I'm always struggling to keep on top. But anyway, that's not the real work you're on about, is it?"

John glared, silent.

"No, what you really want is to keep spending your nights trying to record ghosts talking or looking at crappy blurred night-time photos and trying to convince yourself you can see a face. What the hell's that supposed to be?"

John turned away. "You've got your work, I've got mine."

"*Work?* It's not even *science*, John, it's just a load of airy-fairy wish-fulfilment bollocks –"

"Hey!"

"– and a few bloody chancers have come up with some sciencey-sounding names for the same old bullshit."

"You don't know what happens when you die, Alice. That's the whole point, no-one does."

"Yeah, right. Whatever. You die and you rot, that's it. All religion's about is controlling people and teaching them to hate anybody who's not them. And, and, talking a load of crap about an afterlife, that's for bloody losers, John, it's for weak people, stupid people who can't deal with reality."

She managed to stop then, but of course it was too late. She'd tried to tell herself in later years that she'd lost her temper and that her tongue 'outran her head' as she'd once heard it phrased, but she couldn't lie to herself now, not seeing it all, hearing it all, thinking it all again. She'd been angry at him – not just the parapsychology but the lack of ambition, the energy being poured away into something else instead of into advancing himself, the willingness to *settle*. Because John was softer than her, had known an easier – or at least more stable – upbringing, not the poverty and risk Alice had.

Maybe she'd wanted to snap him out of his apathy, or maybe, really, she'd just wanted him gone, and to do that she'd needed to hurt him. So she'd aimed for the tenderest spot, and hit home.

The two of them were glaring at each other: John angry and hurt, because all he'd asked was that she didn't openly mock his half-belief, his prayer, his hope that death might not be the end, that she at least left him that illusion, if illusion it was, and she'd rejected that. And her, proud in her own belief, holding it a weakness to spare religion or any such superstition.

He could have said something; so could she. Something to heal the rift. But neither did, and that was it.

She hadn't even got the job, either, in the end. As it was, it took another five months for the relationship to die; if she had got the job they'd probably have been put out of their misery the sooner. But she'd been miserable and preoccupied after the argument, by the thought of her and John drifting apart. And so she'd been off her game, no longer so sure if she even wanted the job, and she'd known even before she'd left that she'd blown it. And that, in its turn, had ensured that by the time she got back to Manchester, she'd been angrier still.

And five months later...

*October 2000*

Five months later she was stamping down the flat's stairs out to Dad's waiting van, a cardboard box of belongings in her arms. John stood at the top, watching; once he tried to pick up one of the boxes but she yanked it from his grip and walked off in silence.

Neither said anything; there was nothing left to say. John and Dad eyed each other uncomfortably, a mix of hostility and embarrassment and even maybe a kind of uneasy kinship. *We've both let her down*, Dad's eyes seemed to say; John seemed to nod fractionally in response.

Or perhaps she'd just been tired and she'd imagined it all.

She slammed the van doors on the last of the boxes and marched round to the passenger seat. She looked at John; he looked back at her, then turned and went inside, slamming the door shut behind him.

"Well," Dad sighed, "that went well."

Alice, trying not to cry.

It was autumn and leaves were starting to fall.

*February 2001*

It was late February and winter was almost done. When Alice went jogging in the park near her parents' home she saw crocuses bursting up out through the earth, daffodils on a green near the pond. The air was still cold, but no longer so cold it billowed from your mouth like smoke, as if the icy scorch of it had set your lungs on fire. The sunlight was softer now, no longer hard and glassy. The earth would wake. There would be renewal, rebirth; the seasons' ancient cycles would enter their next phase for the millionth, the billionth time, a time beyond counting.

Alice halted by the pond, bouncing lightly on the balls of her feet. What kind of New Agey bollocks was that? It was the kind of thing John would have come out with. The thought of him made her break into a run again.

She'd been doing that a lot since the break-up. Partly that was down to the weight she'd gained in those last horrible months with John, as she'd watched herself say and do things she hadn't wanted to but had been unable to stop herself from doing. Had it been the same for him? Whatever. She'd put on nearly three stone courtesy of chocolate, pizza and Chinese takeaways: the running helped burn it off. And it let her think she could outrace the pain of the loss. She couldn't, of course, but lately it had started to feel as though she was starting to widen the gap between her and the grief. It was weakening. One day it would be gone.

And on a day like this, when you could feel Spring coming, smell its freshness in the air – how could you not feel hope?

She jogged back home, ran upstairs and showered.

Her mood dimmed a little as she dressed in her bedroom. There were still posters of the indie bands she'd liked before heading off to college: James, the Stone Roses, Happy Mondays, Carter USM. That all seemed long ago and far away now. Another world and a different girl, a child who'd known nothing. She wasn't that girl any more, but her parents didn't know how to deal with her as anyone else.

She went downstairs. Mum was washing up. "Morning, love."

"Morning, Mum." They didn't say anything else. Her parents had tried to close the gap she'd left when she'd moved out as best they could. Their chick had flown the nest and they'd assumed she wouldn't return. Now that gap was too pinched and narrowed to fit her. Meanwhile, she worked in a shop in Manchester – she'd been teaching at a FE college, same as John, but they hadn't renewed her contract – paid some rent and saved the rest, building up a nest egg in between shuttling hither and yon in search of work.

The letter box clacked and rattled; she heard objects falling on the doormat. From the front room came the thwack of Dad flinging the Saturday paper down and bounding to the hall; he was still like a big kid when it came to the post, always hoping there'd be something exciting for him.

"Post!" he called, and walked into the breakfast room. "Morning, love." He bent and kissed Alice's hair, then put an arm round Mum's waist, squeezing. Alice winced; her parents had got a lot more touchy-feely with one another since she'd left home, and on more than one night she'd heard the squeak of bedsprings and other sounds from their room.

"Couple for you here." Dad dropped two envelopes beside her. The first had John's handwriting; the other was unfamiliar, but had a Hastings postmark. She didn't know why that seemed familiar, not then.

"Thanks, Dad." She finished her toast in silence, glancing occasionally at the letters. She wasn't reading them here; she never did. She had no idea if Mum or Dad recognised John's handwriting too, but the less they knew, the better. As for the other – could it have been David, he of that brief, on-the-rebound, affair? After they'd broken up, he'd moved away. Had that been down south? She really couldn't remember now. Either way, she'd feel more comfortable opening the letter in private.

She finished her toast and went upstairs. In her room she shut the door, sat crosslegged on the bed and held the first envelope by the corners each clasped between finger and thumb. For a moment she toyed with the flap of the envelope, but in the end she left it unopened, pulled the biscuit tin out from under the bed, took off the lid and put the letter inside to join the rest.

Four months on and the letters still came, even though she'd never replied – after all, it wouldn't be easy doing so if she never even read one. Each time one arrived she wondered if this would be the one she'd bring herself to open – and, after it, the others – but she never did. And the more the letters piled up the harder it got.

At first it had simply been a case of thinking: *No*. John would want her to come back, of course he would, because this *hurt*, for her as well as him. But he was who he was and wanted what he wanted, and she was herself and wanted her own wants. *And ne'er the twain shall meet*. Besides, too much had been said, too many angry words. *In ira veritas*, was that the Latin for it? *In anger, the truth*?

You couldn't go back. But had there been a little injured pride, too, a little too much concern over how it might look to her parents if she undid the grand gesture and went slinking back? If she was honest, yes, that might have played a part too. Not the only one or even the biggest – even without it her decision might have been the same – but it had been there.

So the first letter, the second – they'd been easy enough to ignore when they came. Even the third. Even if she hadn't been quite able to destroy them then, even if she'd set them aside, meant to read the story's ending when it was old enough to be without pain. But then had come the fourth letter, and the fifth, and she'd started to brood on what might be in them. Perhaps he wasn't giving up – or perhaps now he had. Maybe those first letters had held open the door for her return, admitted he'd been in the wrong or at least offered some sort of compromise, only for these later letters to slam that door in her face. *Fine then, Alice. It's over. I get the message*. Or: *I've met someone else. I hope you'll be happy*.

Other possibilities tormented her: what if one were a suicide note, or gave word of him going off to join some mad New

Age cult or religious sect, something she might have prevented? When that happened she had to harden her heart and tell herself that John would have done whatever he'd done whether she'd been there or not. He still had his father, his sister. If he was so weak as to be unable to face life now, or to need the crutch of faith – especially that kind – she couldn't possibly have saved him from it.

The need to know, in the end, was meaningless when weighed beside the fear of what she might learn. And with each letter, the weight on that side of the scales grew and grew.

Before she put the lid on the box, though, she still eyed the postmark on the letter. London, it said. So, he'd moved – or perhaps he'd been in London for the day, for a job interview or to visit friends or just for the hell of it. The questions each letter raised were a torment, surpassed only by the thought of what the answers might be.

Alice clamped the lid on tight, then shoved the box back under the bed.

That left the other letter. Hastings; what was it about Hastings? She slit the envelope and eased out the letter.

She saw the letterhead through the paper before she unfolded it. Amberson Electronics, Hastings. She remembered now: she'd gone down there for an interview – Christ, it must have been a couple of months back now. She'd hadn't heard anything since and had assumed she hadn't got it. That hadn't been a surprise; Amberson's stock-in-trade was research and development and while they didn't have the largest of workforces, a lot of money went into the place – into the equipment, the work they did and into the people they did hire. It was a pretty select workforce, and even applying for it, Alice hadn't expected to get the job. She'd been thrilled just to get an interview; although she'd prepared for it as assiduously as any other she'd gone for, the best she'd thought to hope for was to get noticed, her name remembered for future reference.

She unfolded the letter.

*Dear Miss Collier,*

*Thank you for attending the job interview on Friday 8th December 2000.*

*I am happy to inform you…*

Alice blinked. That wasn't right, surely? It should be *I regret*. That had to be a mistake; maybe she should apply to work there as a secretary. One way to get a foot in the door.

But:

*I am happy to inform you that we would like to offer you the position of Research and Development Assistant…*

The room spun; Alice rocked back on the bed. It couldn't be right. But she read the letter again, and it still said the same thing. The starting date, the starting salary: they hadn't changed either.

She put her hand to her mouth to stifle a laugh, and in the same moment felt her eyes prickle with tears. It was a job, it was a new start miles away from all she'd known; it was the kind of money that would let her live well enough without scrimping, and to save up too, to make sure she never risked the poverty and uncertainty of her childhood. This one letter, it changed everything.

In a moment she'd shout for Mum and Dad; in a moment she'd tell them the news. They'd be happy and sad, she guessed, but they'd cope. For now, though, she just sat on a bed that seemed to spin and spin and spin through space.

THE NEXT MONTH blurred by. Amberson's wanted Alice to start work at the beginning of April; in that time she had to find herself a home in or near Hastings. Amberson's paid a substantial relocation bonus, which was the cherry on the top as far as Alice was concerned.

She found a small flat in the town, put down a deposit, then returned to Manchester and began the task of packing.

It was hard to get her parents out of the house in those last weeks – she was flying the nest, and not just to the other side of the city as before – but she managed to at last, a few days before the move. They went out, for dinner and a film. Alice padded round the house, taking stock of the silent rooms: the framed pictures on the front-room mantelpiece, the old kitchen where Dad had fed her shepherd's pie after she broke up with Tom Passmore, the little domain Mum had ruled with a rod of iron and absolute calm certainty on Christmas Day in order to produce turkey with all the trimmings. She'd even gone into her parents' bedroom and walked round the bed, wondering why. She knew really, of course: it was a farewell.

After she'd done all that, she'd gone to her bedroom, taken the biscuit tin out from under the bed and gone downstairs, then unlocked the patio doors and gone outside.

It had been cold on the patio, but fresh; that February morning had made good on its promise of spring. But the barbecue Dad had built there stood cold and unused: it wasn't warm enough for that just yet.

Alice lifted the lid of the metal pan, opened the biscuit tin and took out John's letters; all of them, handful by handful. How many were there? She was tempted to count them, but didn't. She laid them on the barbecue.

There were two other items in the biscuit tin: a bottle of lighter fluid and a box of kitchen matches. She opened out the nozzle, squirted about half the contents onto the unopened envelopes and waited to let them soak until the reek of petrol made her head ache. Then she struck a match, let it flare, flicked it towards the barbecue and stepped back.

A muffled *whoomf* and the flames shot upwards. The smell of fuel gave way to that of burning paper. There was a poker on a stand behind the barbecue; Alice picked it up, poked and thumped at the burning items. The flames roared anew, finding fresh paper to attack.

She squirted on more lighter fluid – a spurt here, a gout there – until only char and scraps remained, on the bottom of the barbecue pan, having fallen through the grill. She poured the last of the fluid through so the remnants floated in a puddle of it, then dropped another lit match through the grill.

At last, only ashes remained. She shut the barbecue pan, buried the empty bottle in the dustbin, took the biscuit tin inside and shut the doors.

*April 2001*

"JUST IN THERE, please."

"Right-o, love." The removals man nodded to his assistant and together they picked up the sofa, huffing and puffing as they carried it through.

"All done, I think, love," the man said. He was in his forties – that seemed an eternity older than her, that day – with a rumpled face and salt-and-pepper hair.

"Yup," she nodded. "You want a brew before you go?"

"That'd be great, wouldn't it Sid?" The other removal man, a beefy lad around Alice's age, nodded and grinned. She put the kettle on.

"Nice place," Sid said.

"Thanks." The flat *was* nice, too. She hadn't been in so much of a hurry that she hadn't thought to check that everything worked, that the neighbours weren't deranged addicts or the neighbourhood itself the kind of place she wouldn't dare venture out of at night. It was bright and clean and roomy, and it was on the third floor of a building on the outskirts of Hastings, with a bus-stop close by. When she could afford it, she'd save up for a car, but for now it would make her journeys home of an evening that little bit safer.

"So how many of you are there gonna be?" asked Sid.

"Just me," Alice said. She could afford it: her starting salary was generous enough, and if she worked hard, applied herself, it could go a lot higher. There was opportunity here, and she was going to take advantage of it. She'd already set a budget to live on, covering the cost of living with something for the odd night out at the pictures, the theatre. The rest would be divided between two savings accounts; one to serve as an emergency fund, the other a high-interest one for her future needs.

"You got friends down this way, then?" said the older man.

"Nah."

"Boyfriend?" said Sid.

"Sid! That's not your business. Sorry, love."

"It's okay. No. No boyfriend, Sid." She made her smile bright and hard, stared him down as she added, "No girlfriend either, in case you were wondering."

Sid looked down, red-faced. The older man had reddened a little too, and not long after that they left, their cups of tea half-finished.

Well, it served them right, Sid especially. Even if he *had* been her type, he'd have been out of luck. There'd be no boyfriends for her, and no, no girlfriends either, not for a while: no nothing, just work. In five years' time she'd be thirty, and with any luck by then she'd have a good career and a decent nest-egg, and still be more than young enough to start a family. It wasn't that she didn't want one, after all; it was just that it could wait. There were priorities here.

CREATION SWUM AROUND her in glimmering blue and white. She reached out a hand that wasn't a hand, wasn't anything but atoms and energy moved by her will; she'd been dissolved into the cosmos, like fine sugar in warm water, and only her mind was left.

It could extricate her, that mind of hers: could put her back together, but only if it could keep itself in one piece, stop the demons and the memories and urges born of fury, grief and suffering from tearing it apart. If that happened, she'd vanish: just one more ghost story about 378 Collarmill Road.

Thinking of the house threatened to pull her towards it, towards John, threatened to make her true purpose fade, and that mustn't happen. Distraction was another enemy out here; you could so easily find yourself lost, your energy depleted, too far from home to ever find your way back.

Already the way she had to go was falling away from her, but here was a thread to lead her back. The way forward. That was how she'd been thinking, back then. What mattered was her career and her bank account, to winch her clear of the poverty she'd grown up in, the fear of the thugs kicking down her door. Nothing else counted; nothing else would be allowed to get in the way.

The foaming blue-white void about her hissed and seethed and shaped itself into a face that pushed towards her: the Beast's, Old Harry's, slobbering in its greed.

No, that wasn't her; it wasn't, it wasn't. But perhaps, at some forked point in the past, had she gone left instead of right, it might have been.

But it hadn't. She clung to that as she clung to the thread, and reeled herself back in towards her past.

*February 2002*

It was Valentine's Day that things changed, almost a year after she'd started at Amberson's.

The card was lying on Sally's keyboard when Alice came in that morning. Every machine in a lab, she'd rapidly learned, had its own name. The Amberson lab had Molly the Multimeter, Ozzy the Oscilloscope and a stereomicroscope called Ethel. In addition, it had three computer terminals – one attached to Ron, the main analyser, to input commands and check results, and two others in the data entry area of the lab, used by Andrew and her – dubbed, respectively, Tom, Dick and Sally.

A plain red envelope with *Alice* spelt out in slightly jagged block caps. Probably written left-handed to conceal the sender's identity. Silly custom. Alice sighed, shook her head, and almost consigned the card to the bin unopened, but on a whim she slit the envelope and took out the card.

*Be mine love...?* read the message inside in the same jaggedy left-hand sprawl. Unsigned, of course. Alice tossed the card back into her in-tray and mulled.

The lab was deserted, which wasn't unusual: Alice was often in before everyone else, head down and working. She planned on getting ahead, and didn't care who saw it. So the card must have been planted last night, after she'd gone home.

That immediately narrowed the suspects down to a shortlist of one: there were only three of them in the lab, and Teddy Ratner, Amberson's chief researcher, had already gone home before she'd left. Teddy was the motor that drove the lab work, while the two assistants – or 'minions', as he liked to call them – did the donkeywork.

In any case, Teddy was not only gay – 'camp as a row of tents', her mother would have said – and old enough to be her father, but had been happily boyfriended for nearly twenty years. Unless a piece of lab equipment had suffered a particularly bizarre malfunction and zapped him with a ray that had turned him straight, the card was unlikely to be from him.

Which left Andrew Villiers, a young assistant who'd joined a few months earlier: a tall, athletic-looking man about her age, maybe a year or two younger, with long brown hair tied back in a pony-tail. He liked to look the part of a rocker, although she was pretty sure he was quite posh. But ever since he'd started, he'd been trying to catch her eye, and smiling at her whenever he managed to.

He was quite the charmer, doubtless with a string of girlfriends or at least conquests to his name: after all, that smile of his was sufficiently bewitching that once or twice Alice had actually caught herself smiling back, which was something she *never* did. Villiers was far from the first man to flirt with her by a long chalk, and not even the first at Amberson's – single or otherwise – to do so, but he was the first to get a response.

Alice had kept to her self-imposed vows since coming to Hastings, but even if she *had* been looking, her work colleagues would be off-limits. Her fling with David, who'd only been friends with a work colleague, had caused enough embarrassment, and before that there'd been John – although admittedly that had worked out okay while they'd still been at college. So she kept the boundaries clearly marked and firmly policed. Even if doing so had won her the nickname of 'the Ice Maiden' at Amberson's. That Andrew Villiers had made her thaw, even slightly, said something about him. Even if Alice wasn't sure if what it said was actually flattering.

Andrew arrived about half an hour later, and Alice was tempted to get up and have it out with him then and there. But then she hesitated, wondering if that wasn't what he wanted; within a minute of that Teddy had arrived, and the opportunity was gone.

The next couple of hours went by in silence; they each had a near Bible's worth of data to enter onto Dick and Sally, so the only sound in the lab for a time was the clicking of computer keys and the faint strains of the Verdi opera Teddy was listening to on his Discman as he scribbled preliminary notes at his end of the office. Alice tried not to look at Andrew, but whenever she did he always managed to be looking her way. In the end, she coughed and called him over.

"Andrew?"

"Mm?"

"Do you want to come and have a look at this?"

"At what?" he was grinning, eyes wide and innocent. Alice ground her teeth, then forced a smile in return – the Ice Maiden, thawing again. "If you just come over here, I'll show you."

The smile stayed for a few seconds, the glint of pure mischief glimmered in his eyes, and it looked at first as though he was going to keep playing dumb. But Andrew wasn't the cruel sort, despite the heavy metal bad-boy looks. One reason why Alice found it hard not to return his smiles – under other circumstances, she might even consider him boyfriend material. He nodded and strolled over.

Doc Marten boots, ripped jeans, a studded belt, a Manowar T-shirt and a hint of deodorant. Muscled arms and long brown hair. Not entirely unpleasant, she had to admit. She picked up the card and whispered "I think this belongs to you."

"Me?" Andrew blinked. "I don't know why you'd think that. Maybe you were just *hoping* –"

"In your dreams, Mr Villiers." Alice found she was having to make a real effort to keep her face straight; he had that mischievous schoolboy's trick of being as funny as he was annoying. Made it hell to scold him. "I'm not interested, okay?"

That came out sounding blunter than she'd meant it. Andrew's smile vanished. "Shit – look, Alice – Miss Collier – I'm sorry. I didn't mean to –"

"You haven't offended me, Andrew. It's – well, it *would* be flattering. Nothing personal, I'm just not looking for a relationship right now."

"Whew." Andrew laughed. "Well, that's taken the wind out of my sails."

"Sorry." Though she shouldn't be apologising, really. *Embarrassment comes with the territory if you're trying to chat up girls, Mr Villiers.*

"No, it's okay. You don't try, you never know, do you?"

"If you try often enough, you'll succeed eventually." She grinned. "Law of averages."

"Yeah, but you know all that classical stuff goes out of the window when you get into quantum physics."

"True."

"And anyway – just so you know, I'm not in the habit of flirting with every girl I meet." He winked. "Just the ones I think are worth it."

A pick-up artist's line, or a truth hidden by a joke? It could be either. "Thanks," she said, in what she hoped was a tone that would suit both. "Anyway, I've got work to do."

"Okay." She bent back over her work; Andrew turned, but didn't walk away. She could feel him hovering there, hesitating. Finally she looked up. He turned back to her. "Look..."

"I'm looking."

"You don't want a relationship, that's cool. But – look, I think you're a nice lady. I like you. I like talking to you. I've... I haven't long moved down here, and I don't really *know* anyone in Hastings. So if you don't want to go out, that is fine. I will respect that, I won't flirt or anything like that. But – if we could be friends, maybe, that would be – I mean, go out some time for dinner or a film or – or whatever – I mean just as friends, nothing else, just that..."

She had to smile. He was the one blushing now. And there was something rather sweet about him. But did he mean it, or was it just another line? It might actually have been the first, given how his habitual cool had deserted him. She let him stew for a few seconds – at first she'd meant to turn him down, but then she found herself nodding, to her own surprise even more than his. "Okay," she said. "Tell you what. Dinner and a pub. Or a pub, then dinner. And we'll see how that goes. But –" she pointed. "*Just* as friends."

"Yeah. Yeah. Course. That's what I said."

"Just making sure you don't forget. You try anything and that's it. Home James and don't spare the horses."

"Promise," he said.

"Okay then."

"When do you want to..."

"We'll give it a try tomorrow night," she said. "You won't get a table anywhere this evening." And besides, she *certainly* wasn't going out with him on Valentine's Day. Even if it didn't give Andrew the wrong idea, it would give it to others.

"Okay."

"Back to work, children," Teddy called. "I appreciate today is one for romance, young Andrew, but you may wish to seek it in a more likely place than our Alice. Mother Teresa springs to mind, if you don't mind digging her up."

Now blushing a livid red, Andrew stumbled back to his desk in what looked like something of a daze. Alice bit her lips to avoid laughing and looked back down at her work.

It would be nice to have a friend, she thought. It was the one thing missing; someone to share the day's little triumphs and disasters with – best of all, someone who'd understand them too. She really hoped Andrew Villiers didn't try anything silly tonight; as long as he could accept that friendship was all there was, another aspect of her life in Hastings would click neatly into place.

# Chapter Twelve

## Memory Lane

*29th October 2016*

It was four o'clock; that gave Alice two or three hours to prepare. After some hesitation she went to a hotel just off Deansgate and booked a room for the night.

No, she had no intention of rekindling any romance with John Revell (*Single*); not ever, but certainly not now. She could only deal with one person at the moment, and that was herself. And, if she was honest, she wasn't always certain about that. But she wasn't going back to Collarmill Road, not tonight. She couldn't bear the idea of going back home – home! – not with what might be waiting for her there.

But hadn't she vowed to herself not to run away? Yes – but this wasn't running, or even a retreat; it was a tactical withdrawal. Falling back and regrouping in order to counterattack – and this time, with help.

She let herself into her room, looked out of the window. The hotel stood on the Manchester bank of the Irwell, so she could see up the river, which glinted dully in the autumn sunlight. Stone and metal bridges crossed it here and there. It was a different angle, another point of view, almost another city, and she gazed at it a while, entranced, for some minutes, before tearing herself away.

Alice studied herself in the mirror. She didn't look too bad; still the girl next door, although if she looked more closely she could see the shadows round her eyes. Speaking of her eyes, they were bloodshot. And she looked a little pale. A slightly more detailed make-up job would take care of that; for her eyes, maybe a wet flannel or some cucumber slices...

That pulled her up short. Was she planning a makeover? Well, perhaps it wouldn't do any harm. She checked her watch. Quarter to five. There was time, if she moved quickly. Kendal's department store was just up the road.

It was a short walk, but she had a taxi waiting – she needed every minute she could. She browsed in Kendal's long enough to settle on a plain, simple-looking black dress that ended just above the knee. It hid any bumps she wouldn't want to call attention to, and accentuated any she did. Add to that an ounce or two of very expensive perfume, a brighter-red lipstick than she normally carried, a pair of diamante silver stud earrings, a silver crystal pendant and a pair of black pumps, and her bank account was wondering what had hit it.

She rang a taxi to pick her up again and was back at the hotel at – she checked her watch – ten to six. She laid her new clothes out on the bed, and looked again at the bill. "Jesus," she muttered. She wasn't normally one for excessive spending on clothes; her idea of retail therapy normally involved the DVD and Blu-Ray departments on Amazon.

But – she may as well be honest – she wanted to look good for John Revell. No, that wasn't right: she didn't want to please him. She wanted him to see her after all this time and have his breath taken away. She didn't want pity from him: she wanted awe. If *he* still carried a torch for her, let it burn.

Apart from anything else, she had a favour to ask him, and after all that had happened between them it was a large one.

Alice ran the shower and stepped into it. Steam filled the narrow glass cubicle, turned the bathroom outside into a blur. Once, she thought she saw someone standing outside – a small, dark, figure – and she started, but when she rubbed the condensation away, nothing was there.

SHE WAS TEN minutes late, mostly because she'd forgotten how long it took her to properly get ready. The taxi dropped her on King Street West, outside the restaurant. She paid the driver and went inside.

The Koreana was in a basement; a flight of steps led down from the street entrance. The décor was simple enough, plain light colours, with traditional Korean costumes, musical instruments and the like on the walls. There was a huge plasma screen on the back wall, playing what appeared to be a cookery programme. And at one small table for two, she could see John Revell. As she came down the stairs, he saw her too, and stood.

A waiter met her. "Can I help you?"

She pointed in John's direction. "I'm with him."

She could tell as she approached that her 'makeover' had had the desired effect. Berry-red lipstick and nail polish; light pink blusher to put colour in her face and bring out her cheekbones; turquoise eye-shadow to bring out the blue of her eyes. Then there was silver jewellery sparkling in her ears and in the black dress' décolletage – and, of course, the black dress itself. For a moment, he looked lost for words. "Alice," he said at last.

"Hi, John." Thinking, once again, *I've still got it*. Whatever comfort that was supposed to be.

He hesitated in front of her; she hesitated, too. How did you greet an ex-lover after twenty years? In the end she stepped forward, kissed his cheek and hugged him briefly. It felt strange to do so; they'd gone from total intimacy to a complete withdrawal from it all those years before, and hadn't seen each other since.

"Shall we?" She motioned to the table.

"Good idea," he smiled. They sat. "You look great," he said. "You haven't changed at all."

"Neither have you."

"Black –"

"– don't crack," she laughed. "I remember."

It was true, as well. There were some crow's feet around his eyes and if she looked closely there were tiny flecks of grey in the close-cropped hair and goatee beard, but that was it. The biggest difference was how he dressed now: a red shirt under a wool sweater, tan corduroy slacks that matched the colour of the suede jacket hanging on the back of his chair. Back in the 'nineties, he'd been strictly a jeans and T-shirts man.

A waitress appeared. "You want to order drinks now?"

"Wine?" John suggested.

"I don't drink at the moment," Alice said. She hoped he couldn't guess the reason; alcohol didn't react well with antidepressants. "Just a Diet Coke, please."

"Bottle of Hite for me, then."

"Very good," said the waitress, and went away.

"So," John said, "look at you."

"I know. Back here again."

"Whereabouts?"

"Higher Crawbeck, near the Fall. Remember that place?"

"Remember it?" He laughed. "I remember going off the path and clambering up some slope with you because you wanted to check something out, slipping and going feet-first down it into the Irwell."

"You didn't end up in the river, John."

"Too bad. That slope was pure mud. I looked like I'd been dipped in cowsh –"

"I did my best to make it up to you."

He smiled. "I remember that too."

The waitress came back with drinks on a tray. "Diet Coke," she said, putting a glass in front of Alice, "and a bottle of Hite." She poured the pale beer into John's glass until it was two-thirds full, then stood the bottle beside it before taking a long-barrelled stove lighter from the tray. On each table, along with the cutlery and condiments, was a glass bowl containing a single tea-light. The waitress lit it. "Are you ready to order?"

"You?" Alice asked John.

"I know what I'm having."

She glanced through it. "I'll have the braised mussels for starters, please, and the *dak gang jung* for the main."

"Boiled rice or fried?"

"Boiled, please."

"Very good."

"I'll have the ribs," said John, "and the *ojingo bokum.*"

"Very good."

The waitress left. Alice grimaced. "Squid?" she said. "Don't know how you can eat that stuff."

"Don't knock it –"

"– until I've tried it. Yeah, yeah – change the record, Revell."

She grinned at him and he grinned back; then both of them looked away. They slipped back into the old banter so easily, as if the last twenty years hadn't happened. But they had.

John studied her. Candlelight glimmered in his eyes. He wasn't smiling now. "So how are you?"

She shrugged. "I'm okay."

"I mean, I heard about what happened."

"Yeah."

"Sorry – ah, shit. Alice, I'm sorry, I didn't mean to –"

"John, it's okay. I live with it every day, and it's like the bloody elephant in the room, you know? For me as well. Anything I talk about, whatever plans I make, it's all – touched by this. Shaped by it."

"I was sorry to hear, anyway. Sorry's not much of a word for it, I know."

"No, it isn't." Her eyes prickled.

"Hey." He touched her hand – light, hesitant – then withdrew. "You want to talk about what happened, I'm here and I'll listen. You don't? Fine, we'll talk about something else. Whatever you like."

"Thanks, John. What about you, anyway? How's your family? Is your dad –?" She stopped there, afraid she'd put her foot in it.

"Oh, he's fine. Church every Sunday, dressed to kill. I think there've been a few women."

"You think? You've not fallen out, have you?"

"Hell, no. But he's my dad. There are some things I *really* don't want to know about."

Alice laughed.

"No, he's still his old self," said John. "You should hear him. You know I went to Africa, a few years back?"

"No."

"Yeah. The Gambia. The whole 'Roots' thing. You know what dad said?" John slipped into his father's Jamaican accent. "He said, 'What you want to go over there for? Them still eating people over there!' You know what the old school are like."

"The old school." Alice smiled at him. "I'd forgotten, you always call them that."

"Yeah." The smile dimmed a little. "I do envy him, you know."

"What do you mean?"

"He's still got his faith. No doubts, no ifs, buts or maybes. Mum's in Heaven and when he dies he'll be with her again. That's how he copes. Everything else is just killing time."

Maybe now was the time to bring it up? It was an opportunity – but no, it was too early. Later, she'd ask him. And besides, the starters had arrived.

THE REST OF the meal passed in small talk. The old days at university, the mad things they and their friends had got up to, the old 'where are they now?' routine.

As they pored over the dessert menu, the topic shifted back to their families. Alice talked about Mum and Dad – still together, still maddening, still loved – and John about his sister, Carol, who'd just had her fourth child.

"Four now? Jesus. And hang on, I thought she was your *big* sister."

"Yup. Forty-four and a mother again. Back at work already."

"What about you?"

"Nah." He shrugged. "Never found the right woman, did I?" He didn't meet her eyes when he said it. "Few girlfriends, over the years."

"But no kids?"

"Nah." He studied the dessert menu with an air of deep concentration. "Think I'll have the rice cake. You?"

"Oh... chocolate ice cream, I think."

John beckoned, and the waitress came over. He'd always had that knack, she recalled. Alice had to practically stand on chairs waving semaphore flags in order to attract attention, and not always successfully then.

It was nice to be in his company again. Nothing more than nice – she was *not* here, she reminded herself again, to rekindle old flames – but it was that. His presence was warm, comforting. After the stresses of the past few days, it was a soothing balm. The sense of humour, the affection – God, the *warmth* of him. She'd forgotten that quality he had. He'd missed his vocation, she thought: he'd have made a great counsellor. But for all that, she mustn't forget why she was here.

After the dessert, they ordered coffee. Now, she decided, was the time.

"John?"

"Mm?"

"There's something..."

"What is it, love?"

*Love.* Oh God, she should have said this sooner. Heaven knew what he was imagining here, what hopes had taken shape in his mind.

"I need... John, I need your help."

"Sure. I mean, anything I can do to... what is it you need?"

"The house I've moved into. There's something – wrong with it."

"Wrong? What like? Rising damp? Subsidence?"

"No." A deep breath, and she looked him in the eyes. "The kind of thing you deal with."

"What?" He stared. "Seriously? Are you saying...?"

"Haunted, okay?" Shit, that had been too loud. She looked around, lowered her voice. "My house. I think it's haunted."

He stared at her, then snorted with laughter. "Very fucking funny."

"John –"

"No, it's hilarious. Really. I can't believe you wanted have a dig at me about that –"

"John, *I'm not having a dig.*" She leant forward across the table, spoke through gritted teeth. So much for the charm offensive. "There's something going on in my house, and it's not – it's not bloody normal, I know that. I've never seen anything like it."

"Really?"

"Yes. Really. I don't know what it is. I thought I was going mad – and you know something? I bloody wish I *was*, because at least then I'd know where I am. I'd need more therapy, more medication, more... whatever. But there's stuff that can't just be explained by me being mental. And that scares the shit out of me. I don't know where the line is between the real stuff and what's just in my head. I need someone who understands this kind of thing, John, and you –"

"And I just happened to be cluttering up your Facebook feed with a friend request."

"John –"

John kissed his teeth; his eyes darted round the restaurant. He was angry, but he didn't want a scene. "Should have known, but I thought no, give her the benefit of the doubt. I send you a friend request, and it sits around there with nothing happening for days. I mean, I could see that you'd friended some other people from uni."

"Oh, so you were stalking me?"

"Don't be stupid. We've got mutual friends on Facebook. I could see you were friending them – everyone else, all the others, but not me. I won't lie to you, that hurt. But then, boom. You friended me, and you wanted to meet, and I'm thinking wait a sec, this is going from cold to hot *way* too fast. I *knew* there had to be some sort of reason." He kissed his teeth again and shook his head, settling back in the chair, the anger subsiding or at least under control. "Just didn't want to believe it."

"It wasn't like that, John."

"Really? How was it, then?"

"When I first got the friend request, I couldn't decide. You think you're the only one with bad memories? But then, yes, *this* happened, and I knew there wasn't anyone else I could ask."

"You know what gets me?" he said. "This shit is what you dumped me for. Remember? *You're supposed to be a scientist, John* – that's what you said to me. *You spent three years getting a degree and now you're pissing it all away*. Any of that ring a bell?"

"John –"

"You finished it because of that," he said. "And now you come back and you say *John, help me, I've got a haunted house*. All of a sudden you believe in ghosts. What the hell happened?"

And then he realised, as soon as he'd said it, and his mouth snapped shut. Too late, though. He'd said it. Alice looked down. Her eyes were prickling. No, she mustn't cry. The make-up would run, and she'd spent time and money putting this mask in place.

"Shit. Alice..." He reached out, touched her hand.

"Leave it!" She snatched her hands clear of the tablecloth. Her voice had been louder than she'd intended. Heads turned.

Neither she nor John spoke for a while. Then she put a

hand to her face, cupped to hide her expression from others' prying eyes, and said, "Don't start thinking it's that. This is *not* about Emily. I didn't believe before she died, and I didn't start believing after. I've got a brain – I've got reason and logic and intelligence, and I use what I've got and I'm proud of it. Okay? I work off logic and evidence, not wishful thinking, not emotion."

"Yeah," he said at last. "That's true. You always did."

They were silent for a while, not looking at one another.

"Do you want to go and get a drink?" he asked at last.

"Okay," she said.

"All right," said John, and raised a hand. "Can we have the bill, please?"

AFTERWARDS, THEY WALKED onto New Bailey Street and dawdled across the Prince's Bridge.

"It's pretty." Alice leant against the bridge-work and studied the light glimmering on the darkened Irwell. Along the banks, brightly-lit buildings reared, and shone, reflected in the waters.

"Yeah, it is. I keep forgetting you haven't seen it in a while."

"Too long. I was happy here."

"So was I. We both were."

She didn't answer at first; at last she acknowledged that much – *were* – with a nod.

A long sigh, and John leaned on the bridge beside her. "So come on, then. Tell me. What happened?"

She started, and once she had she couldn't stop. Once or twice Alice heard her voice hitch and felt John stir beside her, reaching out, and had to wave him away. She wasn't after comfort, and couldn't let him get the idea there could be anything between them again.

At last she was done. "I really want to think I dreamt, or hallucinated it," she said. "I'm not scared of saying mental illness, because I've been there and it's not so bad. Just different. But the thing is there are these bruises and I don't know how I got them. There's this stone in my garden and it was in a – dream, hallucination, whatever it was – that I had *before* I found it. And most of all there's this bloody Bronze Age spearhead lying in my hallway one morning that Chris Fry's going bonkers over. Now, I couldn't have imagined that. And it didn't just get posted through my letterbox, did it?"

John sighed, watching the river flow.

"Look, John – you want me to eat humble pie? I'll eat humble pie. Yes, this is the kind of thing I always laughed at when we were together. If you'd told me a story like this, yes, I would have said it was bullshit, or that whoever it happened to was mad. But I can't do that, I'm living it, and I can't write it all off or rationalise it no matter what I do. So, yes – you are the only person I know, that I've ever known, who might understand this, believe it, have dealt with something like it. I need help, John, but I don't know what kind or how much, okay? That's why I'm asking you."

John Revell bowed his head, hands clasped as though in prayer. Finally he nodded, sighed and straightened up. "Come with me," he said.

JUST OVER THE bridge was the entrance to the Mark Addy; from it, a staircase wound down to the pub itself, a converted former landing stage on the banks of the Irwell, a relic of the days when the river was used for shipping. There was a river terrace, but at this time of night, and this time of year, the doors to it were locked.

The floor was carpeted; John went over to the bar while Alice found a table by one of the floor-length windows, with a comfy-looking armchair and a chaise-longue, which she perched on.

John came back with three glasses. "Two double brandies and a Diet Coke," he said. "Thought you might want a stiff one."

She raised her eyebrows. "In your dreams, Revell."

He laughed. "I only meant a drink. I swear to God. Anyway, then I remembered you were on the wagon, so I got you the Diet Coke."

He sipped his brandy; she studied the two glasses and thought *fuck it*. "I'll risk it for a biscuit," she sighed, and took a sip.

"Okay," said John. He was looking down again, the brandy glass cradled in his hands. "Look, Alice..."

"I'm not going to like this, am I?"

"I don't know what to tell you." He sighed. "See, the thing is – Christ, I should have updated that Facebook page months ago. The paranormal stuff? I don't do that any more."

"Oh."

"And more than that – see, you know how it started. You were there."

"Yes, I was. And, you know, I still kick myself sometimes."

"About dumping me?"

"Get over yourself. No, I mean... I don't know if we'd have lasted anyway – we were both pretty young, weren't we? Still had a lot of growing up to do. But bloody hell, I could have shown you a bit more understanding. You'd just lost your mum."

It had been a Sunday afternoon. She'd cooked a roast – leg of lamb with all the trimmings, (including Yorkshire pudding, which she was pretty sure wasn't supposed to go with lamb but John was addicted to.) They'd just finished that and she'd come back from the kitchen with the apple crumble – she really *had* been working on being the perfect little housewife – when the phone had rung.

*I'll get it*, John had said. *Sit yourself down*.

He'd gone into the kitchen. She'd served up portions of the dessert. They were never eaten.

*Hi, Dad*, John had said. *You okay?*

After that there'd been a silence. Then John had whispered, *What?*

Another very long silence, followed by the odd mumble from

John. Finally he'd said, *Okay, Dad. We'll be right over. Yeah. Right away. Yeah*. The click of the phone returned to its cradle had been so soft she'd barely heard it; wouldn't have if she hadn't been listening.

*John?* she'd called, but there'd been no answer. Then a single sob; the first of a torrent.

She'd found him sitting on the kitchen floor, face buried in his hands. He'd clung to her, finally managed to stop. He'd wiped his face with kitchen towels while he told her what had happened.

Dorothea and Elijah had gone to church, as they did every Sunday. She'd been dressed in her best, as she always was; sang louder than anyone else, as she always did. They'd gone home, eaten Sunday dinner, and, afterward, lazed in their chairs. Everything was as it was meant to be. Then Dorothea had got up to go to the toilet. Elijah, dozing in the summer afternoon's warmth, only realised something was wrong when he looked at the clock on the mantelpiece and saw that half an hour had gone by.

When she didn't answer, Elijah went upstairs. He found one of his wife's shoes halfway down the staircase. Dorothea herself was lying on the landing a few feet from the bathroom door. She'd wet herself on collapsing; that detail had haunted Elijah Revell for months afterward. *She would have hated that*, he'd kept saying. *She always liked to keep everything so clean.*

A blood vessel had burst; it was as simple and as brutal as that. A massive haemorrhage. There was no need for Elijah to torment himself with guilt at not noticing in time – although of course he did for months and years afterwards, probably continued to do so on some level even today – because there'd been no time. Dorothea Revell, *née* Stoneham, daughter of Nathaniel and Victoria, wife to Elijah, mother to Carol and John, had been unconscious in less than a minute and dead within five. The best medical attention in the world would have made no difference.

Elijah had called the ambulance and sat, stunned and weeping, on the stairs with his wife until they arrived. His world had fallen apart and refused to make sense; even his children had been forgotten. Only when they had taken Dorothea away did he stumble to the telephone and call first John, then Carol.

Alice had driven John over. Carol Revell had already been there, and was already handling her grief by organising furiously: notifying friends and neighbours, speaking to undertakers and the pastor of their church, finally getting into a furious argument with the hospital her mother's body had been taken to before the whirlwind of fury driving her had ebbed and she'd allowed herself to cry.

John breathed out, long and heavy. "Well, if we're blaming ourselves," he said, "you were right, in a way. I'd spent three years getting a Physics degree, after all. I *was* wasting it – I mean, I *did*. I let the grief just... take over completely, and for years as well." He took a large swallow of brandy.

"I could have been a bit more patient, though, couldn't I?" said Alice. "I mean, I look back on how I was and I flipping well *cringe*."

John chuckled. "I think that's pretty standard at our age."

Alice smiled back. "Yeah, maybe. Even so, though. You were grieving."

"You grieve for months, years maybe. Well, I don't think it ever goes away –"

"No, neither do I. Not now."

It had been a terrible time – for Alice too, who'd come to love Elijah and Dorothea. But the Revell family had dealt with the loss and gone on with their lives as before. All except John.

Everyone grieves in their own way. Elijah and Carol both had their faith to sustain them; Elijah had been raised with it and he and Dorothea had raised both children the same way. None of the Revells had ever questioned that faith; to them – to Dorothea most of all – the existence of God, Heaven and Hell, the divinity of Christ and His love for humankind, in general and in each particular case were facts of life, as self-evident and inarguable as the sun rising in the east and setting in the west.

None of the Revells, except for John. He'd spent too long watching science crowd God out of the spaces He'd existed in before, and he couldn't simply *believe* any longer. But nor could he give himself wholly over to cold logic and rationality. And out of that had come his fascination with the paranormal. Parapsychology: quite literally chasing phantoms – ghosts, rumours, tall stories – and trying to pin a scientific label on them. Trying to broker some sort of deal between his childhood faith and mature learning, to find some scientific principle that would let him say his mother wasn't gone – not wholly, not irrevocably.

He'd been trying to square one of the oldest circles there was: all logic said that the death of the body was the end. No persistence, no survival of consciousness, no soul. No future reunion with lost loved ones, no afterlife, only oblivion. But however certain it seemed in the face of logic, it was intolerable in the face of the death of your loved ones.

But Alice, back then, had been a militant atheist before the term was even coined. There was only science and reason. Religious belief could never be anything other than stupidity or madness, born from weakness of mind. At first, she'd tolerated John's burgeoning interest, albeit grudgingly, but her patience had run out. There'd been rows – and finally, the split.

It seemed so stupid now. Isaac Newton had believed in magic, hadn't he? There were other scientists, great scientists, who also professed a belief in a deity. None of that diminished their greatness, their stature. To have thought John's beliefs, born out of loss, to be an issue, now seemed so stupid. And besides, she'd suffered no loss by then: her parents were still alive and unharmed, despite the ups and downs her father's ways had brought in the past. Now, with Emily gone, she could imagine what John had gone through, and looked back at herself with incomprehension and shame.

"It's like a bad physical wound," John said. "It heals up, but it leaves a scar. You end up being able to carry on as before, but there's always a mark, or a numb spot, or a weak point. Shit, Alice, you know that."

"Just a little."

"Thing is, I've been doing it for how long? Fifteen years? That's way too long. And I don't know how much of that was me not wanting to admit I was wasting my time. You know how it is – the more something's cost you, the less willing you are to give it up."

"Yeah, I know what that's like. So when did you give up?"

"Oh, I finally decided to make the break at the start of the year. New Year's Resolution, yeah? It'd all been bubbling under for a while before I finally let myself admit it."

"Admit what?"

"Admit that... well, when I started out I was determined I was gonna be the one, you know? Catch lightning in a bottle, get a ghost, a real ghost, on film. Prove it, once and for all. I was gonna be the one to do that. They all believed Troy was a myth until Schliemann dug it up, or that the Earth was six thousand years old until Darwin came along. You get the idea. I mean – you know, *prove* there was a life after death?" He smiled, swirled brandy in his glass. "Just for a second, imagine how it would be if I did that – if *anyone* did that."

"It would be something," Alice admitted. Sod it, she thought, and took a sip of her own brandy. She remembered the old arguments. You couldn't prove a negative; you couldn't prove there was no God, no afterlife, no such thing as a ghost. Just as you couldn't prove the non-existence of invisible pink unicorns or a small teapot orbiting the planet; you couldn't disprove them, but logic and probability made them pretty unlikely. *Extraordinary claims require extraordinary proof; what is claimed without proof can be dismissed without evidence.* But to some people, that just meant the proof hadn't yet been found.

"Damn right it would. Whole *world* would change, somebody could prove that. Mum would've said that's *why* you can't prove it; we're not ready to be changed like that. I don't know about that. All I know is that when I started looking, it was still as a scientist. I was after evidence, real evidence – and if this case turned out to be a fake, or that one turned out to have a natural explanation – well, then, there were always others. The real deal was something rare, you know? Elusive. I'd find it and I'd show the world." He lowered his eyes. "And, yeah – after you left, that was just one more reason to keep on. I wanted to show you too."

"But you never found anything?"

Lips pursed, John shook his head. "Nothing. Not in all those years. Not one damned thing that couldn't be explained away. And then a couple of years ago I started using some of the gadgets the other 'ghost hunters' used – EVP recorders, that kind of shit. You know – the stuff that sounds scientific, but isn't?"

Alice chuckled. "Yeah. I seem to remember bending your ear a few times about what bollocks that was."

John laughed. "That you did."

Alice sipped more brandy. It made her feel warm, comfortable, for the first time in a while. Or was that John's presence? Maybe it was both. She slipped off her shoes and stretched out on the chaise-longue.

"Anyway – I was just trying to get a result. Something, anything. I started to think that maybe I'd been wrong. Maybe you couldn't find what you were looking for with the scientific method. I was trying to work out some sort of equation to show maybe you did need faith… and then, well – you know how alcoholics talk about having a moment of clarity?"

"Yeah."

"I had mine. Saw myself. Christmas was coming up and it looked like I'd be spending it same way I usually did, with the family. Dad, Carol, and her husband and kids – and me, on my own. I've been teaching at a sixth form college the last eight years. Oh, I've applied for other jobs once or twice, but my heart wasn't in it, and I'm pretty sure my little hobby didn't help. Forty-plus, no wife, no kids, not much of a job, not much money – and, you know, what for?"

"And that was it?"

"Not quite. I suddenly saw my house as well. Total fucking mess, the state I'd let it get into – pots in the sink, carpets hadn't been hoovered in months, all of that. And the spare room – that was my study. Walls covered in notes, pictures, this and that – I looked at it and it was like the diary of a fucking madman. And there was nothing scientific about it any more, nothing that wouldn't be laughed out of court in five seconds. I wasn't going to show anybody, not with what I had. I carried on a little longer, but I already knew, deep down. So, come New Year's, I took my website down. Oh yeah, I had one of those. John Revell, Ghost Hunter. Took the link off my Facebook page. The only reason it still says *paranormal researcher* is because I'd been dusting off my CV and started looking for something new. Wanted to put something better than what I had for a day job. Right now?" He shrugged. "I'm still there, but I'm saving up to go back to college. Get my Ph.D, then try and start again."

"I'm glad."

"Yeah?"

"Yeah. Why do you think I was so pissed off at you? Well, one of the reasons, anyway. You had all that potential, and..."

"I know. Shit, I've forgotten half the stuff we learned at uni. Quantum physics, shit like that? I had enough trouble getting my head around it back then."

"Tell me about it. It's worth the effort, though."

"So I heard. You did pretty well, didn't you?"

"I did okay, yeah. Financially, anyway."

"Right." John opened his mouth to speak again. He was going to ask about Emily, about Andrew; about the death, about the divorce. Alice didn't want that, not now, not with the brandy soothing the rough edges away.

"John?"

"Yeah?"

"How long do you think it'll be before you can do that Ph.D?"

"Couple of years, probably. If I'm lucky."

"What if you could go this year?"

"Say what?"

"Well, next year. The new academic year. What if you did one more paranormal investigation? A paid one? So well paid you could go back on the next course that's open, and not have to worry about student debt?"

"You any idea how much money that would cost?"

"Yeah. I can afford it, John. I was very well-paid. And I got half the proceeds of the sale on my old house. Homes in Sussex are a lot more pricey than they are in Manchester. Believe me."

"I do. Well, about the house prices. But this? You're talking five figures, Alice."

"I know. But I want to know what's happening, John. I *want* a rational explanation, I want something where I can go *well, that was a load of old bollocks*. And I think I can trust you to do that."

John chewed his bottom lip, frowning.

"Well? You going to help me, John?"

He looked at her long and hard, then finally nodded. "Okay," he said at last.

# Chapter Thirteen

## Thanksgiving

*The Confession of Mary Carson*

LIFE AT SPRINGCROSS House was ordered, and ordered by Mr Thorne at all times. Its equilibrium changed only rarely, and any disruption was brief. Order meant a great deal to my employer; any new element was either rejected, or incorporated into the whole.

So it was with my piano recitals. They became a part of my work day. When the daily round was concluded, I made my way to the music room with Mr Thorne, and played for an hour. My repertoire was somewhat out of date, but he seemed not to mind. Alongside other works by Beethoven, I played Pleyel's sonatinas, sonatas by Sterkel and, for variety's sake, Scottish and Irish airs – and, should I feel daring, the occasional piece by Mr Dibdin. You would not remember him, Mrs Rhodes, and even Mr Muddock's memory is unlikely to stretch so far, but in his day he was considered somewhat humorous, and even risqué. Throughout the whole performance, Mr Thorne would sit in the front row of the music room – now cleaned daily, and the piano regularly tuned – and would listen, eyes closed, showing every sign of deep content.

My pay, already generous, was further increased. I had no complaints on that score; indeed, I was pleased. I had little to occupy my time away from my labours, and the fatter my bank account grew, the happier I would be.

Our luncheons, however, were once more conducted in silence. Nor, after that initial display of confidence and intimacy, did Mr Thorne speak again of his wife, or of any topic of a personal nature. I accepted that I was, still, a mere servant, piano playing or no. He had learned I had an additional skill, one that he could make use of, and he had done so, nothing more.

I was fortunate, in many ways. He could, after all, dismiss me whenever he chose, and might well be tempted to, for now I might know him better than he was comfortable with. I assumed my competence and discretion, along with my musical skills, had impressed him to a sufficient degree that he preferred to retain me.

The piano sessions having been incorporated in my routine, I assumed there would be no further alterations. I was wrong, of course. With hindsight, it's hard to see how I could not have been.

Weeks became months; spring became summer. The air was warm, the days long. After the piano sessions, I would wander in the grounds with a novel and parasol. The gardens of Springcross House were in full bloom, the air rich with heady scents. The leafage was so thick it was easy to forget, at times, that I was in the grounds of a great house, near a populous city; I could almost believe I wandered in untouched woodlands, like those I played in as a child.

Looking back on my time at Springcross House, I recall this period fondly. It was the closest I came to real happiness there. But that time of innocence was destined to be short.

In literature and on the stage, Mrs Rhodes and Mr Muddock, life is full of omens. Reality, however – at least in my experience

– is a far more deceitful business, either devoid of omens or filled with those that falsely promise joy, rather than sorrow. If I am gay and happy today, with my husband and my children, it is because I have learned to treasure what I have while it is still mine, knowing that tomorrow, or sooner, it may all be dashed from me in suffering and shame.

The next phase of my time at Springcross House began – once more – on one of my days off. Mr Thorne was out, and I sat beneath a parasol outside the music room, reading. The music room overlooked a particular part of the gardens of which I was very fond, where a statue of a knight with a broken sword stood, a quotation from Ecclesiasticus on its plinth. Outside the French windows, a veranda stood above the statue, on a high embankment which made it impossible to see into the room from the garden itself.

Most of the staff were also out, but one or two chose to keep to the house – among them, on this occasion, Kellett. I did not hear the doors open, and was only aware of his presence when his shadow fell upon me.

I started; Kellett saw this, and made no effort to conceal his amusement. Though we remained publicly civil, our initial mutual dislike had only increased with time. I had found no friend or confidante among the other servants, but I had seen – and heard – what I had seen. Kellett was much given to casting lascivious glances at the prettier maidservants, and at night in Springcross House, sounds carried.

More than once I was much inclined to speak to Mr Thorne of Kellett's behaviour, but am ashamed to state that I always shrank from the task. Kellett had been in my employer's service for many years and was trusted implicitly; it was hard to believe Mr Thorne was unaware of his nature. More likely my employer valued Kellett's services to the extent that he overlooked his peccadilloes. As I have said, few of the staff showed what one might call a high moral character; Mr Thorne, it seemed, chose to wink at such practices under his roof.

Even so, I was troubled, for more than once I heard pain and protest in the cries from Kellett's room. I told myself, over and again, that the servants he consorted with were willing parties to his acts – you may be shocked to learn, Mrs Rhodes, there are said to be those who take pleasure both from receiving and inflicting pain. From snatches of overheard gossip, I gathered his days off involved more depraved activities still, although at that time I struggled to conceive what these might be.

Despite my loathing, I did my utmost to maintain a polite demeanour towards the man, which was far more than he did. Even now, as he stood over me, his gaze roved over my body. "Miss Carson," he said.

"Mr Kellett," I replied. Though fully clothed, I felt a strong urge to cover myself, but resisted it; he would only take pleasure in having discomfited me. "What can I do for you?"

Kellett ran the tip of his tongue along his upper lip, and I genuinely felt a moment's unease. Surely he would not dare take liberties with me? But if I was so sure, why should I feel such disquiet? In the event, he only gave his usual oleaginous smirk and said, "There's a gentleman asking to see you. A Mister Hardman."

"I know no-one of that name."

"Nonetheless, he's most insistent."

I sighed. "Very well. I will receive him in the drawing-room."

"Very good, Miss Carson." As I went back into the music room Kellett called after me. "What *would* Mr Thorne say about your receiving gentleman callers in his absence?"

I refused to be drawn. "The drawing-room, Mr Kellett," I said.

When I saw Mr Hardman, my first thought was that I should have received him elsewhere. He was small, with a podgy belly and thin, rattish face, dark with grime, and sported a weak moustache over a mouth filled with brown and yellow teeth, while his clothes – cap, kerchief, shirt, trousers and wooden clogs – were indescribably filthy. On seeing me, he swiped off the cap. "Miss Carson?"

"That is my name, sir," I said, sitting down and motioning him to another chair (over which Kellett or another servant had thoughtfully spread a protective sheet.) "But I confess I do not know you."

"No, of course not, Miss," he said, perching gingerly on the indicated chair. "I know who you are, though. We all do at the Thorne Mill."

That pulled me up rather short. "The Thorne Mill?" I said.

"Yes, Miss."

"You are employed by Mr Thorne?"

"Indeed we are, Miss, and, well, er – Mr Thorne himself gave leave for one of us to visit you here and convey our thanks."

"Your – your thanks, Mr Hardman? But whatever for?"

He blinked. "But didn't you know, Miss? Mr Thorne's made a number of changes at the mill, all on your account."

"Changes? And on my account?" I realised I was in danger of sounding like a parrot.

"Our pay has been increased, Miss Carson. There are to be repairs to the factory, and I understand that in winter it will be a good deal warmer..."

I was quite astonished, as you may imagine, to hear this account of quite unprecedented reform at the Thorne Mill. If Mr Thorne maintained this course, his reputation would be quite as reformed as that of Ebeneezer Scrooge in Mr Dickens' Christmas tale! Had I not been sitting down I would have been compelled to, else I might have fallen.

"Forgive me, Mr Hardman," I said at last, "but this all comes as something of a surprise – you say that Mr Thorne holds me responsible for these changes?"

"Yes, Miss Carson." Hardman screwed his face up. "He said you were a most – most excellent lady of the finest Christian virtue, and that your charity and goodness of heart were an example that had prevailed upon him to consider the lot of the poorest and meanest of his employees, alongside his own." Mr Hardman, having recited the entire speech by rote, here paused for breath. "As though he were ruler of a prosperous nation or head of an illustrious family."

My astonishment was redoubled; I could not speak. After a moment, Mr Hardman cleared his throat. "In any case, Miss Carson, we were all most grateful, and Mr Thorne at last agreed that one of us might come to call upon you in person to convey our thanks." He puffed out his chest in pride. "I had the honour of being so chosen."

I cannot recall what I said after that, so overcome was I. I stuttered out some few poor words of thanks, to my visitor and those he represented. After that, quite distracted, I retired to my room.

I was still in something of a daze several hours later, when Mr Thorne returned. Hearing wheels rattle over gravel, I peered from my bedroom window to see his coach come up the drive. Seeing him climb the front steps, I ventured from my room onto the landing.

Mr Thorne climbed the stairs and passed my room, almost without a glance at me – *almost*. But how great a difference such an *almost* makes, Mrs Rhodes! For Mr Thorne glanced at me and smiled – briefly, but with such warmth!

Any words I had meant to utter went quite out of my head; I replied only with a smile of my own – doubtless larger and sillier by far than his. Mr Thorne inclined his head, and moved on.

I returned to my room, my head all in a whirl once more. To think that I, alone, could have moved my flinty-seeming employer to such an extent!

It was only afterwards that it occurred to me how eagerly I had awaited Mr Thorne's return, how my heart had leapt at it – like a young maiden's, I thought, in the presence of her lover.

# Chapter Fourteen

## A Tatter of Red

*29th – 30th October 2016*

When they came out of the Mark Addy, John steered Alice down past Salford Central Station and under the big viaduct towards Chapel Street. "Don't know if you remember," he said, "but Deansgate can get kind of rowdy of an evening."

"So we go up here instead?"

"It's a shorter walk, too."

"Okay, I'm sold."

He offered her his arm. After a moment's hesitation, she took it and they began to walk.

"Okay," said John after a short while. "Ground rules."

"Ground rules?"

"If I'm gonna do this –"

"You already said you would –"

"All right! But there are conditions."

"If this is some attempt to get sexual favours, Revell –"

"Jesus, girl, have some respect for me. I hadn't even thought of anything like that." He grinned at her and winked. "But, now you mention it – ow!"

He hopped a few paces before starting to walk normally again. "You were saying?" Alice said, with the sweetest and most innocent smile she could muster.

"I was saying, there are conditions. *Not* that kind. But if I'm doing this, it's for one reason and one alone."

"Aw, thanks."

"Get over yourself. No, it's because you're claiming this is the real deal – that there's stuff going on that doesn't have a regular explanation."

"Hey, come on, John – I *want* there to be a regular explanation. Really and truly, okay?"

"Okay. Okay, I'll bite, but that means I come at this scientifically. I have to be a sceptic about all of it. Including what you've told me."

"What's that supposed to mean?"

"The spearhead thing, for a start?"

"What about it? I didn't make the spearhead up. Go see Chris Fry, he'll tell you –"

"But he won't have seen where it came from. The only evidence of where it came from is what you've told me. Same with the stone in your garden you told me about. I've only got your word you didn't see it until after the... episode, whatever it was."

"Do you believe me?" Alice's voice sounded very small, even to herself.

John sighed. "Alice, it's not about whether *I* believe you. I've got to think in terms of being able to produce compelling evidence –"

Alice pulled away and glared up at him. Small as she was, she felt ridiculous; at least she'd managed not to stamp her foot. "I know, I know, I *know* – for Christ's sake, John, I'm a scientist too – but do *you* believe me?"

She glowered up at him and he looked down at her, all kindness and understanding. It made her want to kick his shins again. "Yes," he said. "Okay? I believe you."

She breathed out, and let him take her arm once more. "Okay," she said. "Thanks."

"Look, I'm sorry," he said. "But it's not just for me. If this goes anywhere, you'll be exposed too."

"Exposed?"

"To ridicule. You know, from the Richard Dawkins brigade. The ones who sneer at people for being *weak* or *stupid* or *crazy* enough to believe in ghosts." John sighed. "It's not exactly a helping hand to your career, you know? I can speak from experience on that one."

"Okay. I understand, John. I get where you're coming from now."

"Good. I got to be careful with this. I'll be playing fast and loose with my ethical code as it is."

"Your what?"

"Ethical code."

"I didn't know there was one."

"*I* have one and so do some others. One of the big problems with the community is there isn't a standard code of ethics. Christ, I don't need to tell you about some of the chancers and nutcases who end up in this field."

"No. That's true."

John sighed. "Normally I wouldn't *touch* anything involving a recent bereavement, or stuff in someone's actual home. Ethically speaking, it's a minefield. In a case like this, though..."

"I appreciate it, believe me, John."

"I'll give you a written copy, but the basics are this – no spiritual or religious stuff during the investigation, and no pseudoscience. The objective is to find out what's causing this through rational enquiry."

"I told you, John, that's what I want."

"Now all of this will be done in strict confidence. I won't be approaching the media on any of it. I'm assuming you won't be either."

"Hell no."

He smiled. "Good. Re the confidentiality – I can't guarantee that if I discover evidence that a crime's been committed or that someone's at risk –"

"Like if I start trying to self-harm, right?"

He nodded. "I normally aim to produce a written report. If I do, you've got the option to have any identifying details censored. That's in written material, photos, audio stuff – the lot. Okay?"

"That everything?"

"It'll cover the main points, at least for now. By the way, did you get a surveyor in when you bought the place?"

"No. I thought I'd just buy a house and wait for it to fall down around my ears. Of course I got a survey done, John."

John grinned. "Great. I could do with seeing their report, see if anything jumps out."

"Yeah. I'll dig it out. It's around somewhere."

"And here we are at Blackfriars Bridge. This way, madam."

The hotel loomed up. His arm was warm and solid where it looped through hers; so was the rest of him, his body inches from her own. Maybe they hadn't grown so far apart after all. Maybe there were still enough loose threads on either side to pick up and knit back together. It would be very easy to invite him into the hotel bar for a drink, or back up to her room. If she stopped and turned her face up to his, closed her eyes and parted her lips, would he be able to resist?

Jesus, that double brandy had gone straight to her head and was having a merry dance-a-thon with her medication.

It was tempting, very tempting, but it was also a bad idea. She had a lot to deal with, a lot to get past and overcome, before she could even think of a new relationship, let alone rekindling an old one. So, no. Outside the main entrance she slipped her arm out of John's, stepped away from him and pressed a hand against his chest. "Okay, big boy. Thanks for walking me back."

He nodded up at the building. "Afraid of the ghosties and ghoulies, then?"

"What do you think?"

He opened his mouth and she knew he was going to try some line on her; something about it being easier to deal with when you had a little company. She put a finger to his lips. "Sh," she said. "Give me a call tomorrow."

"Yes ma'am," he said, sighing. "How about we swap mobile numbers, then?"

"Okay. Strictly for professional purposes only, Mr Revell."

He chuckled. "Yes, Miss Collier."

She gave him her number; he rang her mobile, and now she had his too. A long way from the 'nineties, having to ring people from payphones and jot numbers down on scraps of paper. "There," she said, and stood on tip-toes to kiss his cheek. "Good night, John."

"Night," he said. She went inside, turned back once to look. He was still standing there, watching her. She waved to him and walked to the lifts.

In her room, she splashed cold water on her face and refilled the bottle of Volvic she'd picked up along the way. She undressed, folding the new clothes neatly, eyed herself in the mirror again to make sure her body hadn't undergone catastrophic weight gain or breast droop in the past few hours, then pulled on the T-shirt she'd worn earlier and crawled into bed.

"Still got it," she murmured contentedly to herself. Guilt at the thought stirred again, but it was deep down and out of sight and she dismissed it. Grief couldn't occupy your every waking thought past a certain point; the old banalities crept back in. Sometimes that was almost comforting. She yawned, stretched, curled up, and then she was asleep.

Whispers woke her. Alice blinked and stirred in her cocoon of sheets.

*Can't let her…*

*She'll help him…*

*Not fair if…*

Children's voices. Dread stirred in her belly. She wanted to stay where she was, to pull the covers over her head and stay there, but she instead threw back the sheets and got out of bed, then padded across the bedroom to the door.

When she got there, she looked out onto the landing and saw the children standing there, gazing at her with white, hating eyes.

Alice braced herself for their attack, hoping she could slam the door and hold it shut, but they didn't move. Instead, they glared at her with intense concentration, their fists clenched. What were they trying to do? Attack her with the sheer force of their loathing?

Alice felt a wind rising, cold and hard, blowing down the landing towards her. There was a rattling sound; she could see the posts and railings of the banister begin to shake and threaten to come loose. Wood cracked. Something flew past her head.

Perhaps her guess hadn't been so wrong. But why did they loathe her so much? What cause could she have given them?

That didn't matter now. She grabbed the door knob and forced the door slowly shut, fighting the wind. Outside, the children screeched with rage as she slammed it. She pushed the bolt across, then stumbled back towards the bed. There was a key that would lock the bedroom door, but where was it?

Then she realised; she was in the house on Collarmill Road. But her last memory was of going to bed in the hotel off Deansgate. Had she lost time in between? No, she was sure she hadn't. This had to be a dream, then, or a nightmare. But it didn't feel like one. She was dressed as she had been in the hotel: a pair of knickers and the same T-shirt. The worn carpet felt rough and gritty under her bare feet.

There was a creaking, splitting sound; she turned and saw the bedroom door beginning to bulge inward. The key, she needed the key. Objects rattled on her dressing table: coins, lipstick, a mobile phone. The coins flew first, at her face – she ducked with a cry and heard them thudding into the wall behind her.

The wind rose; one of the door panels split lengthways.

Alice lunged for the window, wondering if she could climb out and down. She had little hope of that in any case, and the first glance outside confirmed her fears. Below her there was no street, no cars, only the slope of a bare hillside under a sky a-glitter with stars, unpolluted by the lights of a city. And at the foot of the slope there was movement. Something dark. A huge clump of shadow that stirred and heaved itself forward into the light. Even as the moon glimmered on its piebald, bristle-furred hide, the ogre lifted its head and gazed up at her with vast, lamp-like eyes.

Alice stared down at the ogre, and the ogre stared into her. A moment later it roared and charged up the hill. Would it smash in through the front of the house and batter its way up the stairs, or launch itself at the upper storey, smashing through walls and windows? Both seemed likely, but as Alice stepped back from the window, the bedroom door finally gave way and exploded inwards, in a storm of splinters and wood chunks.

Alice threw up her hands and flung herself to the floor. She heard the fragments thudding into the wall behind her. She didn't hear or feel any of them fall to the ground, so she realised they must have embedded themselves in the wall itself. She didn't want to imagine what they would have done to her if she'd still been standing; she pressed her face to the floor. The wind kept blowing, but nothing else flew through the air but puffs of dust snatched up from the carpet.

Alice started to get up. As she did, the first of the children filed in. They spread out to either side of the door, blocking her exit, then began to advance.

The wind rose, buffeting her; Alice tried to fight it, but it was too strong and forced her back. She collided with the wall. Splinters and jagged wood stabbed into her back and she cried out.

The children heard her cry, and grinned. They stopped, their brows furrowed, and the wind rose higher. The wood fragments dug further into her; warm wetness trickled down her back where they broke the skin.

And then the Red Man stepped into view, just at the edge of her vision, and shouted, or sang, or chanted – whatever that sound was, it stopped the wind and seemed to blow the children away. She couldn't be sure exactly what happened, because it took a fraction of a second, but it seemed the children were flung back through the door as if they were suddenly as light as paper, and caught in another wind much fiercer than the one they'd raised.

The room fell silent, and Alice stumbled away from the wall. The Red Man turned, lowering his upflung hand, and she stared into his face.

Except that the Red Man, as far as she could see, had no face. What appeared to be his face was in fact a mask, of some white substance like alabaster. Long and thin, ascetic in appearance, hairless and – of course – white, it was lifelike, but not alive. There were holes for eyes, neatly contained by the elegantly sculpted lids, and between the parted lips, but nothing beyond them, nothing but the dark.

Although it surely couldn't be possible, the impression she had was that the Red Man's cowl was entirely hollow, a rigid empty shell fronted with the white mask. On the other hand, Alice's entire sense of what was possible and what wasn't had been shaken pretty hard over the past few days.

And, as if to underline that point, the lips of the mask moved.

"They are becoming stronger," said the Red Man. His voice was strange. It sounded like four voices speaking together in perfect unison: the high soprano of a child, a feminine alto, a male tenor and another, deeper male tone – bass, perhaps. High and fluting, down to deep and rumbling. "And I must keep *him* at bay. I can no longer protect you from them."

Alice realised her legs were shaking. She felt dizzy. No, she couldn't, mustn't faint, not now. There were things she had to know – and now, they all came pouring out. "Who are you? What are they? Why are they trying to kill me? What do I do?"

The Red Man ignored all but the final question. "The time is getting closer," he said. "You must arm yourself with knowledge."

"What knowledge?" But now her legs gave way. No, no, no! Not this! Not now! She had to stay conscious.

His hands caught her. Her own fingers clutched at the worn red robe.

"First protect yourself," said the mask's lips. "A charm in rowan wood. *Listen to me.*" Alice blinked, focused on the white face. "Rowan wood is a charm. If danger threatens you on Browton Vale, hide among the rowan trees. Make a cross of rowan wood – bind twigs with your hair, or better yet, carve one. Do you hear?"

"Rowan wood. A cross." Alice was suddenly more tired than she'd ever been. Standing, even assisted, was impossibly wearisome, and her eyes were closing. Her legs collapsed under her, but hands clutched her tight, lifting her, lowering her to the bed.

"Good," said the Red Man's multi-toned voice. "Remember that."

ALICE WOKE WITH a muffled cry, thrashing in tangled bedclothes heavy with sweat. She threw them off, sat up.

The hotel room was empty; at least it seemed to be, in the dim light drizzling in through the window. There were still too many shadows, though, even when Alice switched the bedside light on. She stumbled out of bed and flicked the main light switch, then threw the en-suite bathroom's door open and turned that on too.

Light, beautiful light, chasing all the ghosts and devils away. Alice tiptoed to the window, parted the curtains. Yes, there was the river, and the city, just where they'd been. But the house, the house was waiting for her.

A cross of rowan wood. Alice snorted; Christ, even days before she'd have mocked the idea, but now... Which were the rowan trees, again? She'd have to power up the smart phone, Google it.

She pottered back towards the bed, then stopped, looking at something on the coverlet.

She padded closer and reached out to pick it up.

It was a piece of red cloth, a little bigger than the palm of her hand, frayed and tattered at the edges. When she looked at her hand, she saw wisps of the same-coloured material still sticking to her fingers. But the bedding was blue and white, and nothing she'd worn yesterday had been red.

# Chapter Fifteen
## Setting Up

*30th – 31st October 2016*

ALICE CHANGED BACK into her casual clothes, neatly folding up the black dress and boxing away the jewellery. She checked out early without bothering with breakfast – she had no appetite anyway – and caught a bus heading up to Crawbeck.

She got off a stop before her usual one, and popped into a charity shop. She emerged later with a worn old backpack and a Swiss Army knife. She put the second item in her jeans pocket and her clothes and shoulder bag in the first.

*Spending your money like water*, Mum would have said. True, but the plain fact was she didn't know what might be waiting for her at home.

Walking up Collarmill Road, Alice nearly laughed at the melodrama of it – but she didn't, because melodrama or not, it was also true. She didn't just have the Swiss Army knife in her pocket; the swatch of red cloth was there to keep it company. And before leaving the hotel, she'd peeled off her T-shirt and inspected her white back in the mirror. It had been studded with black and purple bruises, as if she'd been struck hard with a few dozen small objects. Or, alternatively, rammed back into a wall full of them.

Dead leaves dripped from the roadside trees. She passed flats and semi-detacheds, the little cobbled sidestreets that led across to the Brow. Finally Collarmill Road itself gave way to the cobbles and the iron rails of the old tramlines. Across the road, she glimpsed the plastic skull in the neighbours' window. HAPPY HALLOWEEN read a gaudy green-and-orange sign above it.

She eased the Swiss Army knife out of her pocket, gripped it tight as she reached the Fall and took the steps down. Two things would mark the rowan trees out for her, she'd determined: first there were the leaves, like rows of long thin blades pointing outwards, and second – assuming there were any left – there were the berries, orange or red in colour.

Alice breathed in the deep rich scent of the autumn air, felt fallen leaves crunch underfoot. The sky was grey and the damp cool air held a hint of mist. She'd always found autumn beautiful, but it was only now that it occurred to her that it was at least partly because of, not despite, its transient nature. All the beauty of autumn was of transition: the leaves falling, dying, summer cooling away into winter. It couldn't last. It was liminal, a borderland between one world and another.

She walked through the woods at a fast clip, glancing behind her. There was never anything there, but that didn't help. She hadn't realised before how full of sounds a wood in autumn was: the tick and snap of leaves breaking from their stems and falling to the ground, the flutter of birds and the scuttle of animals in the undergrowth. After the past few days' events, and last night's dream – if it truly had been a dream – the woods felt like an echo chamber of menacing noise, and the menace only gathered strength from the sense of its being poised, unseen.

Just for a moment she saw how Halloween could be – might once have been – something deeper, older, more primal than the gimcrackery of the shops and the neighbour's window, of the plastic skulls and jack o'lanterns and witches' masks. The Fall had the feel of a held breath, of a place between; between seasons, between worlds. Between the world she knew and another, whose occupants watched and waited in the deepening shadows beyond the light of fire and window, as the shortening days grew dark.

At last she saw the berries. They hung in bright red clusters from the branches of a stand of slender, light-coloured trees that stood beside the footpath. The leaves were still there, too, both on the branches and the ground.

Alice approached. Brittle twigs lay among the leaf debris – but what if they weren't all from rowans? What if some of them had snapped off other trees?

She reached for a low branch on the nearest tree. It branched in its turn, and several of its twigs were both close enough and thin enough to cut through with the knife's saw blade, while being long and thick enough to make a decent cross. She snipped through half a dozen of them – mumbling, as she did, a brief apology and thanks to the tree, much to her own surprise.

So much for the scientific mind, it seemed. A few nights of weird phenomena and she was calling in ghost-hunters and talking to trees? What next, Alice? Crystals? Homeopathy? Fairies? Dancing naked in the woods? She had to giggle at that; at least that would give the locals something to look at before she was carted off to the psychiatric ward.

Bushes rustled somewhere behind her. A moment later, a dozen or so twigs and branches snapped in a brittle, ragged volley, loud in the chill damp air.

Alice spun, but saw nothing. The woods were empty, and yet something had changed.

Stillness, she realised. All the wood's other little sounds had vanished. No bird sang or flew; no beast of any size moved among the bushes or the brambles. She couldn't even hear the sound of leaves falling from their branches. She breathed out, her breath billowing white and fading in the air.

More snapping sounds: louder, closer. *If danger threatens you on Browton Vale, hide among the rowan trees.* She stepped between the two nearest rowan trunks, huddled in the middle of the thicket.

More branches snapped. She pressed against the tree and shut her eyes.

The ground shivered; something huge and ponderous walked on it, plodding closer to her. A rank smell blew into the clearing, a stench of decay and uncleanliness that made her retch. She felt the febrile warmth of the huge shape nearby, and the dirty wind of its breath. She could *hear* its breath: a wet, clogged snorting and hissing. It roared and she almost screamed, clinging to the trunk as a thin, reeking slime spattered her, but she didn't; nor would she open her eyes. After a moment, there was an angry snarl, and then the breath and the furnace heat faded, the ground shivering again as it trudged away.

Alice opened her eyes. Her legs felt very weak. She held onto the trunk. She saw something in the corner of her eye. Roughly human-shaped, misty, pale, vaguely luminescent. She thought that it was female, but couldn't define what had given her that impression. The figure wavered, thinned; a moment later there was only a smudge of pale haze on the air, then even that was gone.

Footsteps sounded on the path, but then she glimpsed a blue anorak and relaxed, stepping quickly out of the trees and smiling at the other walker as he passed.

In one hand, she still held the Swiss Army knife; in the other, the rowan twigs.

SHE TOOK A deep breath outside her front door. She didn't know if she'd be safe doing this in the house, but then, she didn't know if she'd be safe anywhere.

She put the knife in her pocket, kept hold of the twigs with her left hand, dug her keys out with her right. She unlocked the door and pushed it wide, shaking and braced to run, but the hallway was empty.

Inside, she shut the door behind her, went through to the kitchen and spread newspapers out over the table.

Her hands shook. She listened. So far the house was quiet, but – Christ, they'd reached her in her dreams, at the hotel. She didn't dare go up and look at the room. But by the same token, here was as good as anywhere, and where else could she go to get the time and privacy needed for this?

*Make a cross of rowan wood; bind it with your hair.* Of course, the Red Man had made it sound so easy. For a start, she had to find a piece of hair long enough, which wasn't so straightforward when you kept it short. Luckily, as it went, she hadn't had hers cut in a while – was several weeks overdue, in fact – and there were a couple of big swatches at the back, starting to creep down her neck. She cut them off as close to the scalp as she could, weighed them down on the table with an old paperback, then set about trimming the rowan twigs, until she had half a dozen lengths of solid wood, a few inches long.

Now for the hair. She puzzled over that for a moment, then took a candle, a lighter and a saucer and set them to hand. Next she pinched a small bunch of hairs between finger and thumb, drew them off from the rest and carefully twisted them together. After that, she lit the candle, dripped some hot wax into the saucer and dipped the ends of the hairs in and out before it could harden. She did the same with the other end, then crossed two of the twigs and set to work, wrapping the hair round and round. Tying it off was a fiddly business, but she managed. Then she made a second 'rope' and bound the twigs in the other direction, so the two braids crossed and formed a X.

The result seemed reasonably sturdy, so Alice set to work using up the rest of her supplies to produce two more crosses, setting each aside as it was done.

Whispers sounded from the hall, growing closer. Alice

snatched up a cross, held it out before her. The whispers became gasps, then faded. The house was silent again.

SHE WENT UPSTAIRS to her room, steeling herself as she did. But, for a start, the door was whole and unharmed; when she pushed it wide, the room was undisturbed, or at least in no worse a state than it had been when she'd left yesterday.

Once again, Alice breathed out in relief. But not too much; the bruises on her back had still been real enough. At home or elsewhere, she decided, she was keeping the rowan crosses close.

She changed the T-shirt for a lumberjack shirt – and no, not for any pleasant associations with John Revell that it might carry. It was warm, comfortable, and more importantly it had a breast pocket. A good place to keep the crosses without risking damage to them. At some point she'd have to try carving one.

Those preliminary safety precautions taken, she went downstairs to the ground floor bedroom that still served as something of a storage space. She unpacked her old camp-bed and sleeping bag, having consigned them there when the new bed had been delivered, dragged them up to one of the spare bedrooms on the first floor, then added a couple of spare pillows. That should do. She should get a bedside table, though, to go with it, maybe a table lamp – she broke off, shook her head. Hopefully, John wasn't even going to have to stay long. Maybe a night or two. Please God, no longer than that.

It was done now. She went downstairs, wadded up the newspaper on the kitchen table and binned it, then made a cup of coffee, went into the front room and stuck an old Laurel and Hardy film on the DVD player. She sat there, stroking the crosses through the thin pocket of the shirt, and no-one bothered her.

* * *

JOHN ARRIVED A little after one in an old Volvo estate. Alice guessed it had been maroon-coloured when it had rolled off the production line in Sweden – which had probably been roughly around the same time she and John had been wending their drunken way through Freshers' Week at Salford – but it was hard to tell now. The long-suffering vehicle had been battered, scraped, spattered with mud and subjected, by the look of it, to pretty much every indignity under the sun that wouldn't have actually proven immediately fatal, but it was still in one piece and still apparently able to get from A to B.

*I know how you feel, pal*, Alice thought as John climbed out.

"Okay," he said, opening the boot. "Can you lend a hand?"

"Sure." She scampered back into the front room, pulled her trainers on and went outside. John came up the uneven path with a cardboard box full of gear. "Where can I put this for now?"

Alice pointed him to the downstairs bedroom and made her own way outside. God knew what the curtain-twitchers of Collarmill Road would be making of this display.

When John was done, he shut the boot, locked it and followed her back into the house. "So," she said, "where do we start?"

He shut the door behind him and grinned. "A brew would be great."

"Freeloader," she said, sticking out her tongue, but put the kettle on just the same. "Still black with two?"

"I was last time I checked, and it's been over forty years, so I don't see it changing now."

"Anyone ever tell you how funny you are, John?"

"Lots of people," he grinned.

"They were lying. Trust me. I'll try again: do you still like your coffee black, with two sugars?"

"Yes, Miss."

"So," she said, turning away, "what's your plan?"

"Well, first of all, I'm giving your place the once-over. I'll be looking for where to set up my equipment, and for anything that might provide a natural explanation for what you've been seeing."

"Fair enough."

John bit his lip. "You might wanna get another check up, too."

"What for?"

"Anything that might cause you to hallucinate."

She swallowed. "You mean like a brain tumour?"

He looked. "Or maybe hallucinogens."

Alice snorted. "John, I haven't touched anything like that in years."

"As far as you know."

"I've not been out clubbing it or anything. Shopping trips are pretty much my social highlight these days. No-one's had a chance to spike me, not unless they've been putting LSD in the water supply here. I should be so lucky."

"Part of the whole ethical thing," he said. "I need to know about any medical conditions that could have an effect." He grinned. "Maybe you've got magic mushrooms growing in the water heater. Stranger things have happened."

"Only in your dreams, Revell," said Alice as the kettle boiled.

John took an A4 pad and wandered round the house; Alice stayed in the front room and waited. He came downstairs with several pages' worth of floor-plans.

"Okay," he said. "What rooms do you normally use?"

She shrugged. "I kind of potter about, but the main ones – my bedroom and the bathroom – obviously – plus the front room and the kitchen."

"Right. And now one spare room for me." John reached into the cardboard box and took out a roll of clear tape. "So while this is happening, those rooms are the only ones in use. All the others are locked off for the duration. You okay with that?"

"If it that's what it takes, I can cope."

"I haven't got a theory that covers everything that's been going on, but these kids? You said you were physically attacked, right?"

"My back's covered in bruises," said Alice.

"I'd forgotten that. Can I see them?"

She turned away from him and took off the lumberjack shirt, fingers trembling on the buttons. What if she was unmarked? It was easy to imagine those little bastard kids delighting in such games, making her doubt her own sanity. Not to mention John doubting it. He was the only ally she had, except maybe Chris Fry.

But she heard him hiss through his teeth. "*Jesus*. Okay, hold still. I want to take some pictures."

"I did close the curtains, didn't I?"

He laughed. "Yes, you did."

"Just checking. Someone peeps in and sees me topless with a guy taking pictures, that's how rumours get started."

"You're not topless. You've still got your bra on."

She glanced back over her shoulder at him. "And that's how it's bloody staying."

"Damn. Another cunning plan foiled."

John took a series of pictures at different angles and ranges.

"Surprised you bothered," she said. "I mean, there's no proving I didn't do this to myself somehow."

"True," said John. "But this way we've documented the injuries you *have* got. And all the pictures are time-coded. If we get any others –"

"Let's hope not!"

"*If*, I said – we can date them. As of now, we're recording and documenting everything." John cleared his throat. "You can put the shirt back on now."

"Thanks." She rebuttoned it; her fingers brushed the breast pocket, felt the contours of the cross.

"Those aren't anyone's imagination," John said at last. "And if they *aren't* self-inflicted, the most likely explanation is that someone's got into the house and attacked you. So, I'll be booby-trapping all the unused rooms."

"You'll be *what*?"

He grinned. "Half the fun." John toed the cardboard box. "Got a whole bag of tricks in here – all sorts of cool ways to find out if anyone goes in or out when they ain't supposed to."

"In case I'm trying to fake something, you mean?"

"Or in case someone's trying to fuck with you." He turned serious. "Most of what I use is usually marketed for something else. Shit, I even use kids' toys."

"Seriously?"

"Yeah. Some of it's sold as 'spy gear.' Pretty funny, huh?"

"Jesus. I feel so much better."

"But a lot of the other stuff's used for home security. I've got alarm beams, for instance. Great way to make sure no-one's getting somewhere that's locked off. Anyone breaks the beam, we'll hear about it. So we set those up. Some simple clear tape across doorways, black cotton thread strung up in rooms – booby trap the hell out of the place."

"I'm starting to see the appeal of this."

"It does have its fun moments. I'll be setting up cameras too, so everything gets recorded. All clear?"

Alice nodded.

"Okay, then. Time for a few quick questions."

Alice sat on the sofa. John sank back into an armchair and crossed one long leg over the other. "Have you noticed any unusual cold spots in the house?" he asked.

"Not particularly, no."

"Not particularly?"

"Nothing I've noticed. I mean, it can get a bit cold without the heating on, but I've never felt unusually cold when anything's happened, if you see what I mean."

"Okay." He made a note. "So let's go through where things have actually happened."

"I've heard whispers coming from the hall, or seeming to come from there."

"Right. And you were in the hall when the spear thing happened too, right?"

"Yeah – well, I took a step or so outside. And then I ran through into the kitchen, and then out back."

"And it'd turned into this garden? Right?"

Alice's face was hot. She felt ridiculous now, trying to tell this story in terms of bare fact. "Yeah."

"Okay, and where else?"

"My bedroom, the landing, the stairs."

"Right..."

He was as kind to her as the questioning allowed, she knew. When he was done, he nodded. "Okay. Next point: journal." He took an A5 spiral notebook from the box and handed it to her, along with a fistful of biros. "From now on, you have any more experiences, you write 'em down. Look inside the front cover, you'll see what you got to do."

Alice opened the journal. Taped inside the front cover was a small laminated card; on it were printed a series of questions:

*When? (Time and date).*
*What was the weather like?*
*What were you doing?*
*What happened?*
*Who were you with?*
*How did you feel?*

"You answer those questions for each and every occurrence," he said. "Next step, I'm gonna look at where's best to set the cameras and shit. After *that*... it's mostly watching and waiting. That and homework."

"Homework?"

"That surveyor's report, for a start, if you got it."

"Shit. Give me a second." She went into the front bedroom

and rooted in the first of the remaining crates, which contained miscellaneous documents. She was braced for a long hunt, but as it turned out, the surveyor's report was one of the first things she found. "Here you go."

"Thanks."

"What are you looking for?"

"Anything I can find. Watercourses under the house, for instance – they can cause cold spots and any number of weird sounds."

"Hey, I told you there hadn't been any cold spots –"

"Just an example."

"Okay. Fine." She wouldn't mention what had happened in the woods this morning, then. Much less last night's dream, or the tattered red cloth. She didn't need to be made any more foolish, especially not about the rowan crosses in her shirt pocket. They made her feel a little safer, at least for now.

"So, what now?"

"For me, homework," he said, tapping the surveyor's report. "Seeing what I can find out about this site. After that? Sitting and listening."

"Listening?"

"To the house," he said. "Seriously. One of the best things you can do. You get to hear all the normal shit going on – the house settling, the neighbours, the wind." He shrugged. "Gives you a feel for what is and isn't normal here."

"Good luck working *that* out," Alice said. "I'm fucked if I know."

UNABLE TO SETTLE, Alice pottered around the house, going from room to room. The flat black lenses and gleaming red-light eyes of John's video cameras confronted her wherever she went. After a few minutes, she came downstairs, put on her coat and went into the front room. "What do you want for dinner?"

"Me?" John blinked. "I was gonna get a Chinese, or some chips."

"Yeah, I've been eating takeaways damn near non-stop since I moved in. Time I did something about it. Consider a decent home-cooked meal part of your fee."

John laughed. "Okay. Thanks."

"I was thinking maybe shepherd's pie, or spag bol."

"Either's fine by me, if you still cook 'em like you used to."

"I've had no complaints," she said, then quickly turned away. Any complaints would have come from Andrew or Emily. "Back in a mo."

"Okay. You all right?"

"Fine."

She went out into the gathering dark.

In the end she settled on the spaghetti bolognese, as her recipe – hardly changed since their university days – was the simplest: everything but the meat (tomatoes, onions, garlic, herbs, wine, Worcestershire sauce, etc) went in the blender. The meat was dry-fried and the fat drained off; stir in the blender's contents, throw in three or four bay leaves, cover, simmer and that was it.

She fished out the scrap of red cloth and studied it. From the front room she heard John humming. She remembered that habit from when they'd lived together. And here she was, playing the little woman for him again.

A sudden, horrible thought hit her. That saying people always bandied about when something dreadful occurred: *everything happens for a reason*. She'd come close to decking some New Age crap-spouting idiot who'd told her that after Emily died.

But what if it was *true*? What had followed from Emily's death? Her marriage had collapsed and she'd moved back up north. Moved here, where this had all begun... leading her to contact John again.

No. Alice actually felt dizzy for a second and had to grip onto the kitchen counter for support. But for a moment it was almost plausible. *There's a plan for everyone, and if you stray from it, the universe pushes you back towards it.* Was that it? She'd been meant to be with John, but had a family with Andrew instead. So, one little nudge from the universe and that family was gone, sending her flying back towards the man she'd been meant for.

No. No. No. Ugly, poisonous tripe. And people wondered how she bore the idea of a universe without purpose, without a guiding intelligence? It was actually far less terrifying than the alternatives: being the playthings of a god or gods with the attributes of sadistic children, or pawns in the crossfire of a never-ending war between God and the Devil.

Unless, perhaps, there was no intelligence, only purpose and pattern – laws of a science unknown as yet, maybe indecipherable to human minds. A big machine whose parts came in all sizes – subatomic particles, complex organisms, planets, galaxies – cycling through some unfathomable process of which Emily's death and all that had followed were just minor components.

Alice pushed herself away from the counter. She carefully placed the tattered red cloth on a sheet of paper, which she folded into a neat little packet and tossed into a drawer. Enough of that. Simple tasks like cookery could be a godsend at times like this. She stirred the sauce, and put a pan of water on to boil.

AFTER THEY'D EATEN, she washed up and John dried. She showed him where to put the dishes away. Again the slip towards the easy companionship of earlier days, half-welcome and half-not.

John's good mood didn't last long after dinner, though; he tried to research the area near the Fall online, only for the house's internet access to fail. Alice dug out the unused dongles, but neither of them were working either. They sat in moody silence, Alice reading while John worked his methodical way through a wordsearch book, glowering occasionally at the computer screen.

"Do you fancy watching a DVD?" Alice said after a while. He looked up at her and kissed his teeth. "What?"

"Ah, nothing. Just me in a bad mood. Have to go out tomorrow and try and dig up more info. I was hoping to get that side of things finished tonight. What movies have you got?"

In the end they settled on *Animal House*; it was an old favourite of theirs that Alice hadn't seen in years. She'd bought it on DVD but never got round to watching it; Andrew had seen it before and hated it for some reason.

The sofa was a big one; they sat at opposite ends. Alice kept a supply of comfort food in the kitchen; they passed a bag of popcorn back and forth. Neither got too close to the other, afraid to actually touch, but the warm companionship was there all the same.

The movie finished a little before midnight. Alice got up, stretched. "I'm going to get some sleep."

John nodded, frowning at the laptop screen. "You do that."

She padded upstairs, undressed and curled up in bed. She slept without dreams.

BIRDSONG WOKE HER; there were plenty of trees along the other side of Collarmill Road. Alice sat up, yawning, then pulled on jeans, sweater and slippers before going downstairs.

The guest bedroom's door was open, bed empty with the covers thrown back. "John?" she called. "You up?"

"Yup."

The voice came from the front room. Alice went into the kitchen, put the kettle on. "Want a brew?"

"Please."

Cooking him dinner, putting the kettle on for him – Jesus Christ, she really was playing the little woman with a vengeance.

"Fuck!" John barked.

"In your dreams, buster," she muttered; out loud she called, "What's up?"

"Gah." John stepped out into the hallway, barefooted in tracksuit pants and a sweatshirt. "Damned internet's still down."

"Seriously?" She made her way down the hall towards him, holding out a mug. "It's never been down that long before."

"Well, it is now." John took the proferred drink. "Thanks. Tried everything I could. Tested the connections, switched it on and off again, but there's nothing. I'm gonna have to head out."

"Where to?"

"Any coffee shop with wifi should do it. Unless this is screwed, of course." He tapped his laptop. "You'll be okay, right?"

"John, I've lasted forty-odd years, more than half of them without adult supervision. I'll be fine."

"Okay, then. I mean, you can come along if you want, but I'll be out and about for a while."

"I'll manage," she said. She had the rowan crosses, after all. She gestured around. "What about all this kit?"

"It'll run itself. Don't worry. If anything happens –"

"Journal."

"Right."

"Okay."

"I'll be back in a couple hours."

The front door closed. Alice went upstairs, climbed back into bed. Not a good habit to get into, but right now it was an attractive option. She dozed, read, finally got up again and went back down. In the kitchen, she refilled the kettle and put it on, spooning coffee into a mug.

And then she heard the whispering.

*No*, she thought. *No, no, no.* The cross, the rowan cross, warded them off. But she looked up and there they were, gathered in front of the back door, grinning at her, white-eyed.

*They are getting stronger*, the Red Man had said. She backed away; their heads swivelled as one to follow her progress towards the kitchen door. Their grins stayed fixed. Their bared teeth were sharp, the tips of their white fingers hard and pointed. She had to keep out of their reach.

But they weren't coming after her. A breeze blew through the kitchen. It picked up, began to push at her.

Then there was a rattling sound, and one by one the drawers to the kitchen units slid out. The rattling intensified; seconds later the blades of the kitchen knives rose into view, pointing ceilingwards, then swivelled slowly down to point at her.

The knives hovered, aimed directly at her.

And then they flew across the kitchen like arrows.

# Chapter Sixteen

## Moonlight Meeting

*The Confession of Mary Carson*

You may imagine, Mrs Rhodes, that it was a shock to realise my employer entertained feelings of a romantic, even carnal nature towards me. Perhaps, but not so much as you might think. Arodias Thorne, while not in the first flush of youth – he was in his fifties at this time – was still virile. Nor was he unhandsome.

Yes, not only was I flattered by Mr Thorne's attentions, but another, baser part of me – the one we women are expected to pretend does not exist, lest we be branded sluts, degenerates or wantons – was quick to imagine what yielding to Mr Thorne's desires (should he entertain any) might be like.

In fact, let me be truly honest here – this is a confession, after all, and I can hardly make it and maintain the fiction that I am the good, saintly woman folk take me for. As I said, women are not allowed to lust, are we? Men may lust after us, but we women – oh, we must guard our honour. Only the vilest of us admit to a lustful thought, and yet, we are considered to be the weaker sex.

So, let me confess it. It would be a more comforting tale were I the victim – the virtuous ingénue seduced by the wicked old roué – so long as I had no feelings of my own. But I did.

Despite his grey hairs, there was a strength to Arodias Thorne. Not like the strength my father had had; that had come from his faith, his unwavering belief in his cause and his selfless dedication to it, for which he would risk even his life, and, perhaps less admirably, the security of his loved ones.

Arodias Thorne was strong because what he wanted, he sought and took, with unstinting, single-minded devotion. Nothing barred his way: no law, no ethic, no difficulty of any kind.

My father's strength had been rooted in his compassion; Mr Thorne's was rooted in his ruthlessness. Yet were they total opposites? Each had pushed himself beyond normal limits, had striven and suffered to reach their goal. Mr Thorne had dragged himself from the very bottom level of society to a higher one, schooled himself, amassed wealth, by thrift, industry, and, above all, by *will*. His ruthlessness was unsettling, yet, at the same time, also deeply attractive.

I wondered briefly if his actions regarding the mill had been merely a gesture to win me, but almost immediately chided myself for such vanity. I could hardly imagine Mr Thorne playing for such petty stakes, or myself inspiring such extravagance. And whatever its cause, it had certainly improved the lot of the workers there. Something was working on Arodias Thorne – something, I dared hope, akin to grace. He was, quite clearly, not the monster some had thought him.

As the days passed, I watched for another sign of affection on his part, but in vain. Perhaps he felt he'd given sign enough, and now expected me to make some response? I considered the prospect and found it more than plausible. His actions must cost him dearly, eating deeply into his profits as they did. His dark grey eyes, surveying me at work in his study or over luncheon, remained inscrutable.

I was ignorant of how I might respond without embarrassing myself. Indeed, I feared that outcome so much I might have allowed the whole business to pass, except for the nagging fear that, should I do so, I might lose what chance of happiness I had in life. God helps those who help themselves, after all, and I'd prayed more than once for help in avoiding a destitute old age. How better to do so than by marrying a man of Mr Thorne's standing?

You must remember, Mr Muddock and Mrs Rhodes, that although a grown woman, I was largely a child in matters of the heart. We live and learn by trial and error. In these matters, as I'm sure Mrs Rhodes will attest, the sweethearts of childhood and youth are our instructors in truth and falsehood, but I had had none of these. Only, as I have told you, a brace of suitors for my hand, who had quickly abandoned their pursuit on seeing my devotion to my father's cause.

And so here I was, growing ever more certain that Mr Thorne desired me, but wholly ignorant as to how I should proceed. I concluded, at length, that the initiative now lay with me. It was like a game of chess; he had made his opening move, and now waited – patiently, I hoped – for mine.

But what should my move be? I could ask no help in the decision. I had, of course, no family to ask. All I could do was to make an overture of some kind, and hope I did not appear gauche or wanton.

I was afraid to, and afraid *not* to. As days went by I feared my chance might pass, and Mr Thorne find a younger and fitter subject for his affections, if he had not already. Or what if I had read the signs wrongly? I saw myself driven from the house in shame as a hussy, a harlot, a whore. All of which, I knew, would take place beneath Kellett's balefully gloating eye.

But there was nothing for it, I decided, but to make the attempt. I had to hope that even were I wrong, the worst consequences would be simple embarrassment. Surely, I had now been in Mr Thorne's service long enough to be valued.

And so I planned my move carefully; I made it one luncheon, at the little dining-table, watching Mr Thorne closely as he ate. You will see, of course, that over a cold repast such as the one Kellett served, it was easy for the diners' hands to touch by accident over bread or meat. I so contrived to 'accidentally' touch Mr Thorne's hand with my own, my fingers brushing over his... and then, in one of the most daring acts of my life, going on to rest upon the back of his hand and linger there.

I shall never, so long as I live, forget that moment. Time seemed to stop. Mr Thorne certainly did; he went utterly still. For how long? I could not say. No more than three or four seconds, certainly – but how long a time that seemed to me, Mrs Rhodes.

Then he looked up. Those dark, grey eyes fixed me with their stare... even now, the memory gives me a guilty shiver of mingled fear and delight. With his free hand, he dabbed his lips with a napkin, and then he smiled. For just a moment, he took my hand in his, then went back to his meal.

A moment later, I returned to mine, but was unsure what had happened. The smile, the holding of my hand: had that been only fatherly kindness? Was *that* the nature of his affection towards me? I had no idea.

I nibbled what little remained on my plate, then returned to work on the half-hour strike, until at last the working day was done and I returned to my room. I could hardly communicate my intentions more clearly than I had; the initiative now lay with my employer.

After the evening meal, which I partook of in solitude, I remained in my chamber, reading by lamplight beside the open balcony window, for it was a warm evening and the air was richly scented from the gardens below. It was perhaps ten o'clock when someone rapped lightly on the door.

"Who's there?" I called.

"Miss Carson?"

I started, at once enthralled and terrified. "Mr Thorne?"

The door handle turned – but, of course, I had locked the

door, as was my habit due to my mistrust of the other servants. "One moment," I called, and hurried to the door with the key. My father would have been scandalised – receiving a man in my rooms, clad only in my night attire? – and if I had allowed myself to think, I might have done differently. But I did *not* allow myself to think; I was resolved.

Fumbling the key into the lock, my fingers shaking, I knew very well what this night-time visit meant, and what he sought. But, I realised in that moment, it was no more than I wanted to give, and be hanged to the consequences. All my life I had shown care and moderation; much good it had done me. Let me be wild, then, wanton and abandoned. Let me be wicked!

Mr Thorne stepped into my room, bearing a candelabra and wearing a thick, brocaded gown. As he strode past me towards the bed, I glanced up and down the landing outside, but saw no-one.

"The servants are abed," said Mr Thorne. "Now, Miss Carson – or shall it be Mary?"

I smiled at him. "Mary – yes, Mary, if that pleases you."

"Mary, then. And I shall be Arodias to you, when we are private like this. Close the door, Mary, and come to me."

I did as he said. When I reached him, he sat upon the bed, and patted the place beside him. After a moment's hesitation, I sat, leaving a small gap between us – one I already regretted making, and wished to close, but at the same time feared to.

Mr Thorne – Arodias, as I must now think of him – had put the candelabra on a table, and the soft warm light lapped over his face. It was a kindly light indeed, for it seemed to smooth away not only the lines of age but the starker aspects of his countenance, making him appear not only younger but kinder. But the kindness had always been there; his actions at the mill showed that. It had only been hidden beneath the harsh demeanour he had been forced to cultivate.

"Mary," he whispered to me, and every dream of passion I had known was in that word.

"Arodias." It was the first time I had spoken his Christian name aloud. He reached out and stroked my cheek. How large his hands were, how broad and thick the fingers – yet how warm they were on my skin. I reached up to touch the hand. I gasped, as if stung, as the other unfastened my woollen dressing-gown and slipped inside. Again the warmth of his fingers, first caressing my ribs, then trailing up across my midriff towards my bosom...

Why, Mrs Rhodes, you are blushing! I have seen strawberries a lighter shade of red. And my dear Mr Muddock, are you shocked? Then be shocked. If you are, it is only a testament to your lack of self-knowledge. Desire is a part of us – not wicked, nor sinful in itself, but a natural thing. Had I not denied myself for so many years, I might have known a happier outcome than I did...

Still, I shall spare you both your blushes. Even in confessions, there are parts over which a discreet veil should be drawn. I will say only that he was a skilled lover. For my own part, I was surprised by how much came to me naturally, and for the rest, Arodias was quick to educate me. There was an instant's pain as my maidenhead gave way, but otherwise, that night was... joyous.

When at last he was content only to lie beside me in my disarrayed – and, as I discovered to my shock and embarrassment – bloodied sheets and take me in his arms, I felt... transfigured. In that respect, at least, I was fortunate, for I know now that neither all women nor even all men find their initiation into the acts of physical love a source of such delight.

But I did. I was outwardly the same woman who had retired to her chambers with her novel that evening, but now I was a world of experience richer and wiser, or so I thought. I was – I thought, I dared to hope – loved. And I was *in* love. I whispered it before I could stop myself. "I love you."

Before I fell asleep in his arms, I heard his reply, "And I you."

We did not sleep long. Waking just before dawn, I was pleased to find Arodias had no difficulty reprising his earlier performance. Nor did I – indeed, my passion energised me to the point where I felt I could have dispensed with sleep altogether. As we lay together panting, spent once more, I felt wide awake, oddly rested, and serene.

"We must, of course, maintain decorum," Arodias said at last.

I looked up at him. "What do you mean?"

"I mean that tomorrow, we can show no more familiarity than in the past." He smiled. "That can be saved for the evening – if, of course, you don't object to our repeating this encounter tomorrow night?"

Object? I would have near enough demanded it. Nonetheless, it raised a disturbing question. "Am I to be your kept woman, then, Arodias?" I tried to speak without bitterness – after all, I was now a woman of the world – and I knew that a mistress could, at least, hope to be reasonably well provided for. But I had hoped that I might become a bride; perhaps by giving away my virtue so easily, I had lost that hope. Men craved it, and I understood why. If Arodias had experienced half the pleasure I had received, the desire was easy to understand. That was not what angered me, but the hypocrisy men showed, where a woman who enjoyed the act or was willing to partake in it was considered unfit to marry.

But, to my relief and joy, he laughed. "No, Mary," he said, "nothing of the kind. In the fullness of time, should you consent to it, you will be my wife."

I was fortunate to be in bed already, because I doubt my legs would have held me up following that reply. "But," he said, "the time is not yet right. I neither expected nor planned for this. I sought only a secretary, not a wife, and Antonia is only a few months dead. There are those who would think nothing – indeed, who thought nothing at all – of the working conditions in my mill, but who would think much of my remarrying so soon after my wife's passing. It is a weak and foolish morality that does so, I think you will agree" – and I did, I did; indeed, I still do – "but unfortunately it is a prevalent one, and I should make enemies if I transgressed against it."

It was true; I could follow his reasoning all too well.

"And so," he said, "here is my proposal: that you remain here, as my secretary, until such time as a decent period of mourning may be said to have elapsed – shall we say a year? At that time, we shall announce our engagement, and be married as soon thereafter as may be convenient. As for… this," he said, and trailed his fingers up along my bare flank, over my hips, rump and back before finally settling on my breast, "well, we can, if you wish, have further night-time meetings such as these." He smiled; I remember how his teeth glittered in the dark. "Or if you would rather, we can defer them until we are married."

I laughed and reached up to kiss him. "I find your proposal more than acceptable, Mr Thorne. As for the question of another such rendezvous as this – I don't believe I could wait that long."

He chuckled. "No, I thought not." He leant forward and kissed my brow. "Shall we say tomorrow night, at the same time?"

"Let us say so," I laughed. I contemplated the sheets. "Although I dare say the state of these may inspire gossip amongst the servants."

He frowned. "I most sincerely hope not," he said. "I shall instruct Kellett to deal promptly with any servant uttering such rumours."

"Kellett has no love for me, I fear." I'd slipped back into the formal diction of a secretary; Arodias had abruptly become my stern employer again, and without even a conscious thought, I altered my own manner to match it.

"That is of no import," he said. "Kellett is obedient to me. And he will learn loyalty to you, and indeed to love you, for you will be his mistress."

I could not suppress a smile at that, for I doubted Kellett would receive that news gladly.

Sometime during the night, Arodias slipped away. I rose, feeling no ill effects beyond a slight soreness, and dressed for the day. As Arodias promised, he came to my room again that night, and so our days entered a new routine, where I played one role by day, and another by dark.

# Chapter Seventeen

## A Cross of Fire

*31st October 2016*

ALICE HAD TIME for a split-second of disbelief as the knives flew towards her; then her survival instincts kicked in and she flung herself through the kitchen door.

She felt the vibration as the blades hit home, thudding into walls and doorframe. Laughter sounded. She scrambled up and grabbed the door to pull it shut. As she did, a child's face appeared, almost touching her own, grinning its wide, shark-toothed grin.

Its white irises seemed to fluoresce for a second, as if trying to captivate her, but then she saw another gleam behind it: more knives, rising into the air. With a grunt, she shoved the door shut. A moment later, there was another flurry of thuds, and a dozen sharp knife-points drove through the thin wood of the door, several of them millimetres from her eyes.

Alice cried out and scrambled away down the hall on her bottom, then got to her feet. She felt a draught in her face. No, not a draught, she realised; a breeze, already strong enough to ruffle her hair. It was blowing from the door – through the gaps between door and frame, through the splits in the wood made by the knives. As she watched, the door began bulging inwards, towards her.

Just like the previous night's dream – but this time, when the door burst, it would be in a hail of knives. She turned and ran down the hallway, fumbled with the front door locks. She had to get out.

The locks turned; the door opened.

It was only as Alice went through the doorway that she remembered what lay outside the house at times like these. But by then she was already stumbling, because instead of the uneven pathway was a lumpen, rocky slope.

She swayed, took stock. Before, there'd only been darkness; now she was living her nightmare in broad daylight. In one way that made it even more frightening, but in another less so. There were no shadows or mysteries, only a landscape.

Parts of it she recognised. There was the Irwell, at least, some way below her – except that it shouldn't have been visible from where she stood. But perhaps it had been, once. After all, the road and the houses were gone now. The Fall was gone, too; instead a green slope reached down to the water.

She stood on a steep green hill above the river. Crops and spars of grey stone jutted from its flanks, and to one side was a wide grey apron of crackling scree. The hill itself was bare of woodland. The only trees in sight lay beyond the river; big deciduous trees, gold and russet with autumn. Alice suspected that if she'd been able to inspect them more closely she'd have found oak and hornbeam, the old, first-growth woodlands of prehistory.

The ground sloped markedly down where the house next door should have been. Of course; to build here, they'd have had to level off the ground, although it looked as though they'd added to the hill's height rather than reducing it

How long had she stood here, looking down? She'd lost

count of the seconds, caught only in the wonder of the moment. Because she'd quite forgotten to be afraid. This bare, empty land, lit only by a pale sun just visible through the grimy veils of cloud – this was what had been Crawbeck, Salford, Manchester, thousands of years before.

Giggles behind her, and the breath of the wind. Alice gasped and turned to see the front door swinging closed, the children grinning out at her from inside the house. She remembered what had happened the last time, when the back door had shut her out. She'd been trapped in the 'lost garden' and fallen foul of the ogre. Only the Red Man had saved her then.

And what had he told her? That he couldn't protect her from the children; that she had to protect herself. Protect herself with –

The rowan cross – she'd had the bloody rowan cross in her breast pocket all the time.

The front door was nearly shut when Alice flung herself forward and grabbed the handle. It jolted, briefly halting, but then was pushed shut – *almost* shut. She braced her feet against the ground, struggled to get a good purchase on the treacherous surface as she fought to hold it open. Thank God her trainers had a decent grip on them.

The house, she realised, was balanced impossibly on the narrow summit. It seemed wholly intact, but there was no sign of its neighbour; where 378 Collarmill Road should have merged into the next house, the brickwork simply stopped, as if sliced away with a knife.

A shout rang out from behind her. Alice looked round to see a gathering of ragged shapes at the bottom of the hill – men with long, wild beards and hair. More primitive than the spear-wielder she'd faced before, these wore animal skins and brandished what looked like stone-tipped spears. One was shouting and pointing up at her. He started forward; when the others hung back he turned towards them again and bellowed something, shaking the spear aloft. They shifted, stirred; then followed their leader in a bellowing horde up the hillside.

From behind the door came hissing and whispers and vicious giggling. The door was still open, but by no more than an inch. Alice pressed down with her feet as if walking forward, put her weight against the door to push it further open, then wedged her knee in the gap.

The door gave back under the pressure; the gap widened. The bellowing of the skin-clad men was getting louder. She could hear their feet pounding the turf. Something thumped into the ground. Alice looked back and saw a spear sticking out of it, no more than twenty feet away. The skin-clad men had halted a dozen or so yards away, their arms cocked back to throw.

Alice flung herself against the door again and again, slamming her body's full weight against it and pushing it wide. Inside, the hall was dim and grey. She saw the children snarling at her, their pale eyes almost luminous in the gloom. None of them were touching the door, but it still fiercely resisted her attempts to get it open. Moments later, their snarls turned to grins as the door began to force itself closed once more.

The cross. She fumbled inside her jumper for the shirt's breast pocket, felt the cross' outline through the material. Her fingers groped for the top of the pocket, slipped inside, found one of the rowan-twig arms. She pulled it free, fingers curled around it so it wouldn't catch or break on the lining of her jumper.

The children's faces gathered in the narrowing gap; they hissed and sniggered in triumph. A spear flew past, missing her by feet to splinter against the wall. Alice pulled the cross free and got hold of it by the upright. Now what? The Red Man had told her it would protect her, but how?

The skin-clad men charged, bellowing. She brandished the cross at them and the closest ones flinched back, but then came forward again when they realised it was no weapon. The children. She had to use it against them.

The door was inching closed. With a grunt, Alice thrust the cross through the gap. A frozen second passed, when she was sure it would be plucked from her fingers and snapped to pieces before her tormentors shut her out, leaving her to the skin-clad's spears. Then she realised a stillness had descended: the children's horrid sniggering had stopped. Before she could interpret their changed expressions, the cross smouldered for a second and then, like phosphorous exposed to air, it exploded into dazzling white flame.

There was no pain, nor even the least impulse to let go of the cross. There was a sound: a sort of hissing, sizzling, thundering noise that she later realised resembled nothing so much as the sound of a sea breaking on a shore, only amplified a million times.

As for the cross itself, for a second or two it was in her hand as a cruciform piece of brilliant light, then it lost all definition and turned the whole world white. The pressure on the door relented and it swung open. Alice had the briefest impression of a female figure, ablaze with light, standing in the hallway. The next moment she lurched forward, tripped over the front step and fell forward, arms out to break her fall.

THERE WAS A soft thump, and a click. Smooth, cool wooden tiling lay against her palms and her left cheek. When she opened her eyes, she saw the rowan cross lying a few inches from her right hand and, beyond that, her own familiar hallway.

Alice sat up quickly. The hallway was empty, and the thump and click she'd heard had apparently been the new uPVC door swinging shut behind her after she'd fallen through. Oh God, what had her neighbours seen?

She could worry about that later. She had to concern herself with the immediate danger. She got up and put her hand on the door handle. It took nearly a minute to nerve herself up to the simple task of opening it.

Outside was Collarmill Road, the same as always, the tarmac giving way to cobbles almost exactly outside her door, the trees across the road gently shedding their leaves. The sky above had greyed to near-blackness, and the first drops of rain splashed Alice's face. She breathed out, pulled the door shut and locked it.

An empty hallway; a kitchen door, hanging ajar, showed an empty kitchen too. No sign of the children. It looked as though the rowan cross had done its work.

She knelt by it, reaching to pick it up, and frowned. Its colour seemed different; the cross now looked entirely grey. And where was the hair that had bound the pieces?

In the moment before her fingers touched the cross she remembered what its appearance reminded her of; a cigarette of Dad's, back when he'd still smoked, that he'd left unattended. It had burned down to the filter to leave a grey tube so perfectly formed that she'd still been able to make out the cigarette paper's seam. But then she'd touched it, and seen it collapse into ashes.

Alice plodded back to the kitchen, found a dustpan and brush and swept up the ash. Then she went back to the kitchen door and stared at it, studying first one side, then the other. After that she checked the walls, but neither they nor the door were damaged in any way. Nor was there any cutlery lying around. When she opened the drawers, all the kitchen knives lay there, undisturbed. A tapping sound made her start – but it was just the rain, speckling the windows.

A faint noise stirred in Alice's throat. Then she remembered: the journal. She ran, found it, fumbled the cap off the pen and scribbled down her answers, fast as she could. She pushed the pad away, shaking.

She turned and studied the video camera John had mounted in the kitchen, saw that the baleful red eye of the recording light still glowed. When she went down the hall, the other cameras there were the same.

She went back into the kitchen and fumbled with the camcorder, stopping the recording and hitting *rewind*. The picture became a jagged blur; she pressed *play*. Yes, here she was, entering the kitchen, putting on the kettle.

She watched. Watched as she started, looking around, then

froze, staring towards the back door. Watched herself back away from something that she saw but the camera didn't, all the way to the door, and then dive headlong through it. Then the door swung shut.

Through all of this, Alice could see that the kitchen stayed empty and its drawers stayed shut. Not one knife stirred, and nothing else happened until she came back in some ten minutes later, staring around her to find the room unchanged.

It was a formality now, but Alice went through into the hall and played back the camera footage there. Much the same story. She watched herself dive to the floor and drag the door shut, then run down the hall to the front door, which swung wide open before swinging closed behind her – until she grabbed it, grappled with it, wrestled with thin air.

Alice cringed. Was that how she'd looked? Oh God, had any neighbours or passers-by seen? The madwoman fighting with her own front door, fighting with it and then –

And now the last part came. The camera, it seemed, was determined to offer her no comfort while sparing her no humiliation. She saw her forcing her own hand through the gap with its pathetic little cross, saw it thrust the useless talisman at thin air and then –

A flash, and the screen flickered; bands of static rippled across the picture as she watched herself trip and tumble into the hallway, sprawling. The cross spilled out of her hand. It was on fire. Brief fire, bright fire, that quickly flamed and danced to nothing, but fire, beyond doubt. And in the same moment, like a curtain closing on a play, the front door swung closed, as if drawn by a very firm hand.

Alice sat in silence. There was a hissing sound from outside as the rain fell; faster now, and harder. When she studied her fingers, she saw they were very faintly smudged with ash, but couldn't be sure if that had happened when the rowan cross had burned – heatlessly, painlessly – in her hand, or when she'd touched its crumbling remains afterward.

She watched the footage again, and got the same story. The footage of the kitchen actually gave her something new, the second time around. At the moment of the flash in the hallway, static buzzed across the screen in the kitchen as well. Alice suspected that to a greater or lesser extent, the same would be true of the other footage in the house.

She got up and went through to the kitchen. Her legs still felt unsteady. She wasn't sure if the cameras' evidence made her feel better or worse. Once again, there was no claiming it was *all* in her head.

Not by her, at any rate. But anyone else, even John? What was her evidence? A pair of twigs that burst into flame? She was still a scientist – enough of one to know how easy it would have been to fake that effect for the camera.

So, it seemed she was being spared the ultimate torment of doubting her own sanity – to an extent, at least. After all, she realised, that wouldn't have wholly been a torment; it would have been, at least, in part a relief. What she was being denied was the faith of others – it was almost like a punishment for all her years of stubborn doubt, for deriding John and those like him. *She* would know it wasn't all in her head – but she'd never be able to convince anyone else.

And, of course, she'd never be quite certain herself where exactly the dividing line was. Which was a far more insidious form of madness.

One thing she did know, though: the rowan cross had worked. But now it was gone.

Except that she'd made three. Alice fumbled in her breast pocket, looking for the others. Her hand came out clutching a jumble of snarled hair and splintered twigs.

When she'd fallen, they'd both been crushed. They were green wood, should have been much stronger, but they were in pieces. She searched the debris for the makings of a new cross, but there were none; she was defenceless.

And as she realised that, someone pounded on the door.

# Chapter Eighteen

## Diamonds and Rust

*31st October 2016*

ALICE CRIED OUT, and the smashed remains of the crosses slipped through her fingers to the floor. For a moment she was ready to drop to her knees and grub through the fragments for something she could use, but stopped herself. She'd already looked, and found nothing. Whatever had come for her now would at least find her standing, not grovelling on her knees.

She dusted her hands and stepped towards the kitchen door; as she reached for the handle whatever it was struck the front door again. She flinched back, then took a deep breath and opened the kitchen door.

What would the tape show? Would she fall dying from no visible wound – a heart attack, a stroke – or would she be remembered as 'killed by person or persons unknown'?

Two steps down the hall, then a third. The door loomed nearer.

"Alice?"

She stopped, gasped. "John?"

"Alice, you okay?"

"I'm fine."

"Can I come in? Please? It's pissing down."

"Sorry. I'm coming."

She'd forgotten; she hadn't given him a key. That would have been a little too much like old times for her preference.

Alice got to the door and opened it. John shoved through, shoulders hunched and collar pulled against the rain. "Christ's sake."

"I'm sorry. You made me jump." She stole a glance out of the door and breathed out in relief when she saw Collarmill Road was still there.

John was frowning. "Something happen while I was gone?"

She nodded.

He sighed. "Better tell me about it, then," he said, and walked through into the living room.

John switched on the digital recorder and Alice told him the latest, handing him the journal as she spoke. It already sounded silly and false even to her, and John's lips were compressed while he listened, his arms folded. Alice almost faltered and stopped, only managing to continue when she looked down and didn't meet his eyes.

"It's on the cameras," she said. "I played it back. Something is, anyway. The end. If you just watch –"

"I'll watch it," John said. Clipped, abrupt. Something had changed, and changed badly. He didn't sound like a former lover any more, or a friend; more like a policeman. "When did it happen?"

She told him. He went to the camera in the hall and played it back, nodding steadily. He kissed his teeth a couple of times, then looked up at her. "Nice trick," he said at last.

"Trick?" was all she could manage. She'd known how it would look, what any outside observer would say – but not John. She'd thought he'd try to believe her at least.

John sighed and leant back on the sofa. "What is it you want, Alice?" he said.

"What? John, you know what I want."

"I don't think I do. You come to me after all this time, pull the whole *Diamonds and Rust* act, then start talking haunted houses. But nothing actually happens when I'm there, only the first time I go out. And all there is on the tape is a little... conjuring trick, something any half-bright seventeen-year-old could pull off. You think I'm stupid?"

"I never thought that," she shouted at him. He flinched. She hadn't meant to raise her voice, but she was losing control. She was actually afraid of what she might end up saying. "Kind, yes. That you'd help me, yes. That you might actually believe me, yes. But I never thought you were stupid."

"That's not what you said when we broke up."

"For fuck sake, John, that was what, twenty years ago? I was young – Jesus, come on, we've both been over this. You know I wish I could take back some of the things I said. You know I do."

"Yeah. Yeah." But the anger and the suspicion were still there. "Is this some sort of crazy scheme to get me back?"

"What?" She couldn't keep the scorn out of her laughter and he looked away. "Get bloody over yourself, John Revell."

He breathed out. Finally he looked at her while he tapped his thumbs together. Alice managed not to smile – she didn't need him thinking she was mocking him now – but knew the mannerism of old; it meant he was thinking things over, planning tactics and methods. Finally he said, "Arodias Thorne."

"What? Who?"

"Arodias Thorne," he said again, watching her closely.

"What? Come on here, John, give me a clue. Am I supposed to know who that is?"

He didn't answer for several seconds; when he did, it was no answer. "Springcross House." He was watching her eyes and face, she realised, looking for the least flicker of recognition. When he found none, he tried again. "How about the Beast of Browton, Alice? Or Old Harry?" Then one last time. "What about the Red Man?"

"What about him?"

"You tell me."

"Oh for Christ's sakes." This was maddening. "John, I've *told* you about the Red Man."

He breathed out, still watching her. "Okay," he said at last. "One more name."

Alice sighed. "Go on."

"Galatea Sixsmythe."

"*Who?*"

"Galatea Sixsmythe."

"No idea. Never heard of her. Is it a her?"

John folded his arms. His face gave nothing away.

"Right, well, I give up. Who's she? One of Harry Potter's schoolfriends?"

John didn't chuckle – not quite. She could tell it was a bit of an effort on his part, though. But then his face hardened again. "One more question, then, Alice. Why did you *really* move here?"

"You *know* why, John."

He shook his head.

"Yes you do, John. I've told you."

"The real reason, Alice."

"I've *told* you the real bloody reason!" She took a deep breath, calmed herself, then managed to carry on. "I know this area. Used to live here. *We* did. And I used to love it. 'Specially the Vale. I wanted to be near Mum and Dad but not next door, and have something to do – that's why I bought this house. I *told* you, it's a fixer-upper, it's..." She shook her head. "Oh sod off, then. Believe whatever you like."

That, of course, was when the phone began to ring. Alice breathed out and pinched the bridge of her nose. She was tempted just to let it ring – but no, in the long run, that wouldn't do any good. "Hello?"

"How do, lass."

"Hi, Dad," she said, after a moment.

"So, how are you doing up there?"

"I'm okay."

"Yeah?"

"Yes. Yes, I am."

"Okay. Not meaning to pry. Just wanted to make sure. I know... look, I know you and your mother had a set-to yesterday."

"A bit," she said.

"Well, I'm not going to take sides, Alice. You know that I don't. Not saying you were right, to have a go like that or to bring up the past. You know how your mother feels about it. But, same time, I know how she can be. We're none of us perfect."

"I know, Dad."

"And I know that – God knows, I've no place preaching. I've tried to make it up to you since, but I was a bad father to you –"

"Dad –"

"I was. And a bad husband to your mother. Your mother feels guilty about that too – all the stuff you had to see as a kiddy, that you shouldn't have. But your mother's got no cause for guilt there, Alice. It was on me, all of that."

She could hear the strain in his voice. *Great work, Alice. Now you're about to make your father cry as well.* "Dad, I've never – oh God, Dad, please –"

"It's all right, love, I'm not having a go at anyone. Like I said, none of us can point the finger at anyone else like we've never got owt wrong. We all have, but that's not what matters. It's how you try and make things right again afterward." Dad snorted. "Bloody hell, listen to me. Sounds like some load of New Age crap from one of those bloody magazines your mother likes."

Alice laughed.

"Look, all I really wanted to do was call and say we both love you. I don't know how much good it'll do, but –"

"It's okay, Dad," she said. "Thank you. It does mean something. It does."

"Your mother would like to see you, Alice." She didn't answer. "Look, can we come up?"

"No. Not right now, Dad. That's nothing to do with you or Mum. I'm not angry with her – pretty bloody ashamed of myself, if you want the truth. Don't tell her that, though, I'll never hear the end of it."

Dad chuckled. "You've got a point there."

"I've just got something on right now. Got a friend over."

"Anyone I know?"

She looked at John. "I'll tell you about it when I next see you," she said. "Look, why don't you give me a call tomorrow, the day after – we'll arrange to get together, all of us. Is that okay?"

She heard Dad sucking his teeth on the other end of the phone. "All right," he said.

"Okay, then. Love you."

"And you."

"And tell Mum I love her as well."

"I will. Bye, love."

"Bye, Dad." She put the phone down, breathed out and turned back to John.

She couldn't keep meeting his gaze. Any minute now and he'd start pitying her, and that would be the last straw. She twisted round on the couch, staring at the smooth cushion, trying without success not to feel childish.

"Alice," John said. "Okay, Alice, I'm sorry."

"Sod off, John."

"No, I mean... look, I found stuff out today. A lot of stuff. And there's more, but I need to go and see someone to find out the rest."

"So?" Still she refused to look at him.

"So there's all this stuff I found out, just by going to the university library in Salford, and it fits what you told me. Fits it like a glove."

"You mean, too neatly?"

He touched her arm lightly. When she didn't flinch, he kept his hand there. "I found most of what I needed to know in about half an hour reading one old book on local folklore. Pretty obscure little tome, not the kind of thing anyone would come looking for – unless they were after something pretty specific."

"I see."

"But the librarian was adamant no-one else had come looking for that book in a long time. And it wouldn't be easy to find without their help."

Alice looked at him. John smiled at her. "But I had to make sure, you understand?"

She smiled at last, and turned back round to face him. "And now you think you have?"

John chuckled and stood up, stretching. "I've been doing this shit nearly twenty years. I'm like the human bullshit detector by now." He put his hands up. "I believe you, okay?"

"Well, that's a relief." Alice raised her eyebrows. "'The old *Diamonds and Rust* act'?"

John coughed. "Hey, you always liked that song."

"So did you."

"That's true." He smiled, looking into her eyes. She smiled back, but after a few moments had to look away; this was too close, too warm. "So," she said at last, "do I get to know what you found out today?"

John nodded. "You do. But I'll tell you en route."

"En route where?"

"St Thomas' Church, Pendleton. We've got to see a vicar – and if we get a move on, we might catch her before the evening service."

# Chapter Nineteen

## Two is Company

*July 2004*

ANDREW'S PARENTS LIVED in a small village near Eastbourne, and were members in good standing of the church congregation; they went there, regular as clockwork, every Sunday and more often than not they dragged Andrew, despite his avowed atheism, with them.

It was a beautiful little church, Alice had to admit as they walked out of it, perched on a small coastal road and facing out across the Channel. If you *had* to have a church wedding, she thought as the guests flung handfuls of confetti at them, you could do a lot worse than this.

Mum and Dad were there, dressed in their best and trying not to look too drab beside Andrew's family and the Amberson's staff. They were the only ones from Alice's side of things; Andrew's sister Mandy and her twin daughters had served as bridesmaids. Alice had thought of inviting John. Part of her had badly wanted to, but in the end she'd decided against it. She should have read those bloody letters of his, then she might have known how he felt, how he'd react to an invite. But it was too late now.

It was better this way, she told herself as they gathered in the church grounds and the cameras clicked. John was the past now. Christ, the last thing she needed on her wedding day was an ex with whom she'd left so much unresolved – *but whose fault was that*, a traitor voice demanded in her head? Who hadn't read the letters, who had refused to even try and remain friends? But even with everything between them laid to rest, would she have been able to resist putting John alongside Andrew, comparing the two men? But then what would it have said of her if she'd needed to do that?

No. Better that John stayed where he belonged, up north and in the land of yesterday.

Robert, Andrew's father, had a passion for restoring old cars: a beautiful old Humber sat waiting for them outside the church, grille and hubcaps gleaming. The JUST MARRIED sign and cans on strings trailing from the back fender looked brutally out of place, but that didn't matter. Nothing mattered except her and Andrew as they climbed into the back of the Humber, shut the door and kissed as Robert drove off.

THE RECEPTION WAS held just beyond the village, where an old manor house had been converted into a hotel.

Everyone, it felt like, got to make a speech, except Alice herself. Half of her bridled at that – here she was, done up like a giant bloody meringue for show and expected to be seen and not heard while everyone gawped at her – while the other half was relieved that she didn't, at least, have that to worry about.

Dad, thankfully, kept his speech short and to the point. "Alice has worked very, very hard to make her way in life. She's given up a lot, sacrificed a lot, and we're bloody proud of her." The 'bloody' provoked a few murmurs, and Mum poked him in the side. Dad coughed. "And we're even prouder of her today. She's found a very good man in Andrew, and we know they'll look after each other and we know he'll treat her right." He raised his glass. "The bride and groom."

He sat down, bright red with embarrassment. Alice reached past Teddy Ratner and squeezed his hand. "Thanks, Dad."

"No problem, love."

"Well said," said Teddy quietly.

"Thanks."

Teddy smiled. As the best man, he'd normally be sitting on the groom's side of the table, but given how few of Alice's friends or relations were there, they'd bent the tradition slightly, so he sat beside Alice, while Mandy was next to her brother. "You learn to appreciate it. You should have heard Robert's speech at Mandy's wedding. I swear three guests died of old age."

Dad laughed. Teddy had quickly charmed him and Mum, which was a relief. Alice had managed to make a new best friend at Amberson's after all.

The funny thing was that Andrew had been as good as his word on their nights out together, and never tried to take things any further. That had been Alice. After a few months of dinners, films, plays – and subsequently nights in at her flat or his with a pizza and a video – she'd finally realised (or admitted) her true feelings. So much for vows of celibacy. Even so, despite the distractions, her work didn't seem to have suffered.

Robert got to his feet, tapping a glass with a knife.

"Oh good Lord, deliver us," intoned Teddy under his breath. "Alice, I apologise in advance if I have to eat one of your parents to survive this speech."

"When Andrew was a little boy," boomed Robert, "he played a wonderful game of cricket. Used to say he'd play for England one day – well, maybe there's still time for that."

"Hope so," Teddy murmured. "The boy would look *ravishing* in whites."

Alice pressed her lips together in suppressed laughter.

"He's always been a good-looking lad," Robert went on, "and athletic."

"As I'm sure you can testify, sweetie," Teddy whispered, and Alice had to bite the inside of her mouth.

"When he was at school he was positively beating the girls off."

"I'll just bet," sighed Teddy, and Alice had to feign a coughing fit. She gulped wine and tried to glare at Teddy.

"But he's always been a good lad as well. Polite, respectful, hard-working. Gifted too. He was in the church choir when he was younger."

"And then somebody replaced him with this long-haired, head-banging monstrosity," murmured Teddy. "All right, I'll stop now."

"Please," said Alice. "If I wet myself this dress is a nightmare to get off."

"Of course, one of Andrew's greatest gifts is that of his intellect." From the corner of her eye Alice saw Teddy gaze at the ceiling with studied innocence. "Back in my youth I could hope to equal him on the pitch, but I can never hope to follow him intellectually. Very few of us in the family can, I have to say! But none of that changes our love for him, or our pride. I'm very glad that in Alice, Andrew's found a soul-mate who's a match for him in those stakes. But most of all – the biggest gift my son has is his heart. It's a damned big one. Maybe too big. His mother and I often worried that there are people out there who'd take advantage of that. But Alice isn't one of those." Robert harrumphed. He was a big man, portly in middle-age, with a drinker's jowls. "She's a lovely young woman. Kind, gentle, warm. I've never seen my son happier than he is with her, and – well, I know it's supposed to be the bride's parents who worry about whether their daughter will be in safe hands, but the groom's parents can do that too. Except that I don't – worry, that is. Because I don't believe that my son's happiness or heart could be in safer hands than it will be with Alice. I wish them many long years of health and happiness."

Robert sat down amid applause.

"That was rather sweet," said Teddy.

"Yes," smiled Alice. "Yes, it was."

THE RECEPTION GOT underway, and they sloped upstairs to relax.

The bridal suite was on the top floor, taking up the middle third of what had been the manor house's attic. A big semicircular window led onto a balcony. Below it spread the low green downs, and beyond them the sea glittered blue in the July sun.

Andrew shut the door. Alice sat on the end of the bed – king-size, four-poster – slipped off her shoes and massaged her feet. This was it: luxury. And the next thing she knew she was crying.

"Whoa, whoa." Andrew knelt in front of her, took her hands. "What's up, sweetheart? What is it?"

"This," she said. "Everything." She saw fear on his face. "No. I don't mean that. I don't mean it's *wrong*. I mean – I don't think you get it, how – this, all of this – it's so far from anything I ever thought I'd have. I mean... Andrew, do you even know we lucky we are?"

"Yeah." He smiled up at her. "I do."

"No. You don't. We've got money. We've got good jobs." *Your family's loaded* – no, she'd best not say that. "We've got some sort of security for the future. Just that, just having that – growing up, I didn't have that, and I wanted that so much. A nice house. Health. Bloody hell, we've got clean water and food on the table and a roof over our heads. Half the people on the fucking *planet* haven't got that. The room we're staying in tonight, that's got more than some people will ever see in their lives. Do you know what I mean?"

He didn't, she knew; God love him, he just didn't have a clue. But he said "Yes," and maybe he even thought he did, too. And then he was kissing her and she was kissing him back and his hands were pushing the great spilt froth of lace up over her pale thighs while her fingers fumbled at his shirt buttons and trouser belt. And then they were together on the four-poster bed – the first time, she thought, the first time as husband and wife – and all thoughts and fears and questions were gone for a time.

AND AFTERWARDS, THEY tidied themselves up and straightened their clothes, laughing, and Alice retouched her smudged and smeared make-up before they went back downstairs.

And they cleared the floor at the reception ready for the disco and the two of them took the first dance to *Carolyn's Fingers* by the Cocteau Twins, because that was the song that had been playing on the stereo in Alice's flat the night they'd first kissed, and everyone agreed that it was a funny sort of song for the bride and groom to dance to but that it sort of worked.

And then there was the disco and there was music of all kinds, and Teddy stole the show with his dancing while Alice and Andrew sagged on a couch, and Alice dozed off with her head on Andrew's shoulder.

And the next day they set off on their honeymoon to Portugal.

And through all of that, Alice never thought once of John Revell.

Not then.

*May 2006*

IT STARTED OUT as just another morning. They woke when the alarm raised them, went through the normal morning round of bathroom visits, coffee, and went out to the car.

The house was a cottage on the outskirts of Apsley, a village some miles inland of Seaford. No big stores yet, just a string of little shops. A kids' playground, nature trails, the River Cuckmere running through it, and the odd night out just a short drive away. It was perfect for them; perfect for a young couple, and perfect for a family. Which would follow in due course, just not yet. A couple more years, perhaps.

They drove to Amberson's. Afterwards Alice couldn't remember any details of the drive, although it often seemed to her that she should. But there wasn't much to remember; they'd lived together long enough by then that there weren't much in the way of highs or lows. They weren't feeling crazy in love all over again; they hadn't had a blazing row either. Nothing much was said; nothing of import, nothing she remembered. Perhaps because a faint sense of queasiness passed through her stomach, coming and going several times over the course of the car ride.

When they walked in through the reception area later, though, Andrew slipped an arm round her waist for an instant. She turned to face him and his lips brushed across hers, and then they were going their separate ways.

She went to the lab and waved hello to Teddy, who'd already been at his desk for half an hour, and the new lab assistant, Henry. The flat in Hastings, the first few months alone, setting off as dawn broke on winter mornings to be there first – all that was gone now, and so different a life. Another life, another woman.

"Oh, there you are. About bloody time. Some of us have work to do, you know."

"Morning, Teddy."

"How about a nice cup of coffee?"

"Great idea. You know where the kettle is." An old routine for them by now, worn smooth by countless repetitions.

"Dear God," said Teddy, getting up. "They are revolting, I tell you, Henry, revolting." Henry blinked. He'd joined two months earlier, after Andrew's transfer to HR, and still gave every sign of being an elective mute. Teddy made a quick mock-bow in Alice's direction. "Purely in the sense of rebellion, you understand, my dear – I intend no slur on your looks or personal hygiene. They're talking back to men, Henry. Do you hear? Answering back, driving motor cars, refusing to stay in the kitchen where they belong – by the Beard of the Prophet, they'll want the vote next."

Henry's lips twitched in a smile before he glanced at Alice and looked back down at his work. Teddy rolled his eyes and made for the kettle, adding "Milk and no sugar, I presume, milady?"

"Thank you, slave."

"And would madame perchance care for *un petit crème de Bourbon*?"

"Yer what?"

"A Bourbon cream, you peasant."

"Oh go on then, you old puff."

Henry kept his eyes down and on his work, except when temptation overwhelmed him and he dared to peek in her or Teddy's direction. Alice couldn't blame him, really. After five years, she and Teddy had built up the kind of banter that was impenetrable if not downright intimidating to a newcomer, especially one even fresher out of university than she'd been. She'd graduated, she supposed, from 'minion' to 'chief henchman.' Or henchperson. She powered up her desktop and yawned.

"*Une Nescafé avec le lait semi-skimmed et les biccies du chocolat*," said Teddy in a French accent that made Peter Sellers' Inspector Clouseau sound like the height of classical realism, setting mug and a china plate with three Bourbon creams on her worktop.

"Cheers. Who's doing the canteen run this morning?" Alice rarely bothered to eat breakfast at home. Amberson's had a good – not to mention subsidised – canteen, the bacon rolls of which were the stuff of legend. In the meantime, there were bourbon creams. Alice devoured the first in two bites, chased it with a gulp of coffee.

"Well, don't look at me, dear. I'm far too old for that sort of thing."

"You're too old for –" She never completed the sentence, and the sound that came out of her mouth defied spelling, even phonetically, accompanied as it was by the bourbon cream, the mouthful of coffee, the cup of coffee she'd had at home that morning, along with most of yesterday's evening meal and quite possibly, she later thought, lunch too.

"Fuck me," said Henry.

DESPITE ALICE'S PROTESTS that she felt fine, they sent her home. She called Andrew when she got back, assured him there was nothing to worry about, told him she'd see him later.

By the early afternoon, her stomach was growling. She cooked poached eggs on toast, which wasn't unusual for her – and nearly a full pack of bacon rashers into the bargain, which certainly was.

When she found she was still hungry afterwards and ended up eating anchovy fillets, which she normally hated, out of the can, alarm bells rang.

She went into the village and bought what she needed from the pharmacy – knowing as she did that word of her purchase would be all over the village by the time Andrew got home.

At home she unwrapped the pregnancy test kit and sat at the kitchen table looking at it for some time. Then she picked it up and climbed the stairs to the bathroom.

"YOU'RE *WHAT*?"

"Pregnant, Andrew."

He gawped at her. He'd only walked in from the office a couple of minutes ago, come into the living room to find her curled up on the couch, and then before he could even kiss her cheek she'd dropped the bombshell on him. Cruel, maybe, but she couldn't resist seeing the look on his face. "You – but – how?"

"How? Well, when a man and a woman love each other very much –"

"Oh bugger off." But he was smiling when he said it, which made things a little easier. He still looked a little dazed, though, and she could almost see the cogs turning in his brain, trying to crack the question of *how the hell are we ever going to afford this*? Because that was the funny thing about Andrew. Under all the heavy-metal bad-boy trappings, he was a good little son of the middle classes who took care of his money, budgeted and planned. Kids hadn't been on the agenda for a couple more years.

"We'll be okay," she said. "We've both got good jobs, we can afford childcare. You know, couples a damn sight worse off than us have children." Mum and Dad had had her, after all. If they'd waited until they were financially stable they'd probably never have had kids at all. "It's not the end of the world."

"I know, I know. It's just – whoa. Bit of a shock."

"Tell me about it. Look on the bright side. You're not the one who's going to be the size of a barrage balloon before this is over. Not to mention more bloody morning sickness."

"There's that. How you feeling now?"

"Fine, apart from craving flipping anchovies again. Well, I'll need my strength for pushing the bloody sprog out." She grinned. "At least I can pig out all I like with no-one pecking my head."

He grinned and climbed onto the sofa beside her. "I'm sure your Mum'll manage."

"Oi, cheeky." She poked him in the ribs. "Don't be dissing my Mum."

"Sorry."

"Besides, God knows what I'll have to put up with from your Mum. And Mandy."

"Guilty as charged."

He slipped his arms around her and she sank against him. Out of nowhere, she felt sad and afraid. Hormones, maybe? Or it might just be the sudden shock of realising everything would change now, had already started to – here was a new life, and it meant – it would have to mean – more than hers, than his, than both of them together. *This is a big job, so make sure you do it right.* "We'll be okay, won't we, babe?"

"'Course we will." His hand inched down, stroked her belly through the sweater, then slipped under it to caress the skin. "Me and you, sweetheart. And the Blob here."

"The Blob?" she snorted. "Last of the bloody romantics, you."

"What can I say? You bring out the best in me."

*November 2006*

Somewhere in the evening, fireworks popped and crackled. Alice peered through the kitchen window, saw the fields and woods beyond the village, their colours dimmed and faded by the coming of night.

She fished out the teabag, dropped it in the kitchen bin, splashed milk into the brew and then cradled it in cupped hands. Her fingers felt cold a lot these days; one of the quirks of this particular pregnancy. No two, they'd told her at the prenatal class, were exactly alike; each had its own little oddities.

Another firework popped. Pink lights glittered in the velvet dusk, dying as they fell through the sky.

Alice went back to the kitchen table, set the mug down, returned to her notes and her laptop. The chair was parked side-on to the table. Her belly was too big now for her to sit there comfortably, and she didn't like lying back in an armchair or lying on the couch these days. Her centre of gravity was all over the place and getting up again was a bloody nightmare. This posture was the best one for writing in, although it cricked her neck. And there was still a month of this to go. At least if the baby came on Christmas Eve, she told herself, they'd save money on presents.

Alice looked down at her notes again. A couple of months ago, a publisher had approached her about writing a popular science textbook for A-level students. Simple stuff compared to the work at Amberson's, but it would bring in some extra money and be another string to her bow.

With maternity leave coming up in her future, she'd agreed to it; she had no doubt she'd want something to keep her occupied. And so she'd spent her time feverishly jotting notes whenever inspiration struck – descriptions of experiments, explanations of principles and clever metaphors to demonstrate them, scribbled variously on A4 and A5 paper, the backs of envelopes from the bank, even, in one case, a receipt from Tesco's in Hastings.

They were spilled out in a heap on the table-top now. She'd spent the past couple of days making various stabs at a chapter-by-chapter plan to get the material into some semblance of order. After several attempts, she'd finished that last night – Halloween, after the bloody trick-or-treaters had stopped rattling the door every five minutes, after she and Andrew had watched a double bill of old Hammer horror movies and he'd gone off to bed. It was a tradition with them, and pretty much the only time they watched such films; as far as Alice was concerned, they were comedy gold. A few fireworks had gone off – five days early, she'd remembered thinking – while Andrew snored upstairs and bit by bit, the outline had finally come together.

Of course, the next step was actually starting to write the damned thing properly, which was proving to be a proper bind. She'd lost count of how much tea she'd drunk, mostly done in order to avoid work by brewing up, washing up or trotting back and forth to the loo. The new addition to the Villiers household – the Blob, probably a lot less blobby by now but whose gender remained indeterminate as they'd decided to wait and see – seemed to spend most of its time tap-dancing on her bladder, and the tea influx sent it into positive overdrive.

But here she was, back at the table, trying to get to grips with her nemesis, the heap of crumpled notes beside the laptop. First of all came the problem of deciphering what she'd scribbled down several weeks before, often under less-than-ideal conditions. Next she had to type them up. Then when she'd typed them up she realised that they were crap – they might have seemed clever and clear and perfect when she'd jotted them down, but when she read them back they seemed clumsy and stupid, so now she had to rephrase everything she'd written.

This was going to be a long job.

That was the last thought she had before the first contraction hit. She yelped, hunched forward in the chair and clutched her belly. *Christ.*

The first emotion was fear: the baby wasn't due for another month. Was something wrong, something she might have known about if she'd been a bit less bothered about waiting and seeing what sex the baby was? Then it passed. You could get the odd contraction in the weeks leading up to the birth. She turned her attention back to her notes.

The next contraction hit a few minutes later. Another followed, then another. Oh God, this wasn't right, something was wrong – and then there was a sudden hot gush of fluid down her thighs, and the maternity dress was suddenly sodden and plastered to her. There was a brief rush of shame – *oh God,* she thought, *I've wet myself* – and then the realisation of what had really happened.

*Stay calm.* She got up, picked up her mobile phone, rang the hospital. When they told her the ambulance was on its way, she got up and made her way to the front door, speed-dialling Andrew's number as she went.

SHE WAS IN labour for nearly ten hours; Andrew reached the hospital an hour after she'd called and stayed by the bed the whole time.

It hurt, obviously, and she didn't suffer in silence. Andrew joked afterwards that they'd probably heard her in Portsmouth, but she'd been too tired to reply. Beside, she'd gripped his hand so hard during some of those contractions she was pretty sure she'd damn near crushed his bones to powder, so Alice decided he'd been punished enough.

But just as all good things come to an end, so do the bad. At last, when the pain hit a crescendo she was certain couldn't be exceeded without killing her, it vanished, and its place was a baby's yowl.

"Oh my God," Andrew was saying. "Oh my God, oh my God, oh my God."

"What? Andrew, what?"

"It's a girl!" He was laughing and crying, all at once. "It's a girl."

The nurse wiped the child clean, wrapped her in a towel and put her on Alice's breast. She was tired and aching, her legs were slimed from blood and shit and amniotic fluid and her cheeks were sore and stinging because she'd cried so many tears of pain, but the second they put her child there all of that just went away. She reached up, stroked the tiny body through the towel, brushed her fingertips over the light down of the head, and her daughter looked back at her with big narrowed eyes in her tiny, ancient-looking face.

"Emily," she said. They'd talked about names and settled long before on what they'd be: Ethan for a boy, Emily for a girl.

"Emily," said Andrew. "Emily Villiers."

Emily Collier, too. Hell, it was Alice who'd done all the work. But it didn't really seem the right time to raise that point, somehow. And anyway, she was tired.

After that... after that there was haze. There were painkillers and there was cleaning-up, and her daughter was put in an incubator because she'd been early.

*So that's what love is*, she remembered thinking at some point. She'd thought she'd known before, but she hadn't, not until they laid Emily on her breast and it had come in a wave, blowing everything else away. Nothing else mattered: her career seemed an irrelevancy beside it, even her marriage if it came to that. Anything else, measured against her child, would lose every time.

And then she opened her eyes and looked to see Andrew slumped in his chair beside her bed, still in his office clothes and fast asleep, and she remembered what love was all over again. She reached out and touched his hand; he stirred awake, smiled blearily and held her fingers fast. Him and her and Emily, *just us*, she thought, *against the world*.

# Chapter Twenty

## History

*31st October 2016*

THE DAY WAS almost done; the sun was already sinking westward and the streetlights were coming on, rows of little red coals lighting the way to Manchester.

"So I spent a couple of hours in the University library," said John as she locked the front door, "and picked up a whole load of stuff. But here's the thing: when I try to find out more, I get nowhere. I get hold of Chris Fry – and my God, there's a man who's still carrying a torch for you –"

"Don't."

"Okay, okay. But it's true. He still thinks you're amazing."

And what did John think she was now? Alice was annoyed with herself for caring, but she did. "So you got hold of Chris," she said, "and...?"

"And there wasn't much he could tell me. There was some, but – here's the weird part – a lot of what we need to know is held by the church."

"St Thomas'?"

John got in the car, unlocked the passenger door. "Let's talk on the way."

"Okay," said Alice, and got in.

"When I say it's held by the Church," said John, starting the motor, "I mean Church with a capital C. Basically a whole load of documents ended up in the care of the Church of England – mainly, I think, because nobody else wanted to take responsibility for them. Hence our appointment with Galatea Sixsmythe."

"And who the hell *is* she, exactly? Can you tell me that now?"

"Yeah," said John, guiding the Volvo down Collarmill Road. "She's the current rector at St Thomas'. I spoke to her on the phone. She's expecting us." He glanced sideways at Alice. "And she confirmed that she had no idea who you were."

"But you still gave me the third degree?"

"Hey. *She* might not have known *you*, but that wouldn't stop you from knowing who she was. Anyway" – John made a right turn onto Blackburn Road – "you want to hear the story so far or what?"

"Fire away. Please."

"Okay. Well, Crawbeck as a settlement goes back the best part of a thousand years, maybe further. Started out at the bottom of the hill. It expands later, and that's when it becomes Lower and Higher Crawbeck. There used to be a church or chapel on the hilltop. But then in the early 1800s, along comes Arodias Thorne."

"Who was?"

"A mill owner. A filthy rich one. He bought the whole damned hill. The man was loaded. Get this – not only did he build himself a brand new home – all-singing, all-dancing – on top of the hill, he actually paid for the cost of building a brand new church further down."

"That wouldn't have been cheap."

"Certainly wouldn't. You'll have seen the church he built. Fact, there it is on the left."

Alice turned her head, just in time to glimpse the tall black silhouette of a buttressed, turretted square tower looming above the rooftops. "St. James' Church?" she asked.

"Just a few sidestreets down from you," said John.

"I remember the place. Went past there one night, back in the 'nineties, when I first lived up here. It was winter – about a couple of weeks before Christmas – and there was an evening service on. You could see the windows lit up. Beautiful stained glass."

John eyed her over the top of his glasses. "You just say something nice about religion?"

"I said the place *looked* nice. That's just an aesthetic judgement."

"Uh-huh."

"John, do *not* start trying to make out I've found Jesus."

"Okay, okay." John smiled, kept his eyes on the road. On the pavement, Alice caught a flicker of red. She started, looked, but it was just a child in a scarlet devil costume, accompanied by a witch, a werewolf and a sheeted ghost. *Trick or treat, trick or treat, give me something good to eat*. "St. James' is closed now. Back in 2002. Only congregation it's got these days are the local winos. *Anyway*, Thorne built this huge house that covered the whole top of the hill, including the part that eventually collapsed into Browton Vale –"

"And including the bit my house is now parked on?"

"Who's telling this story, me or you?"

"Sorry."

"And including the part now occupied by number 378, Collarmill Road."

"Thank you."

"It was called Springcross House, big stone mansion with a wall around it and ornamental gardens. Quite a place, apparently. The source of the Craw is up there somewhere, culverted."

"The Craw?"

"Craw, as in Crawbeck? It used to come out further down the hillside. Then the Fall happened and now it comes out somewhere in Browton Vale before feeding into the Irwell."

"What happened to the house?"

"Thorne didn't have any kids, and he wasn't a popular sort of guy. 'Never did a kind deed in his life,' was what someone said about him. Actually, that's a bit of an understatement."

"Nineteenth-century mill owners," Alice said. "They weren't exactly known for being softies."

"Even still," said John. "A lot of them liked to play the philanthropist. You know, build a public drinking fountain, give some land to the City Corporation as a park, that kind of shit."

"It was pretty much *de rigeur* in those days."

"Uh-huh. 'Specially when you start getting older and thinking about the next life." John chuckled. "One way of keeping yourself in the Big G's good books, anyway. Except our boy Arodias didn't seem to give a shit about that, because he never gave a penny."

"That *is* a little bit out of the ordinary."

"Here we are." They came up to the Pendleton roundabout, which the A6 ran across, changing from Broad Street into Bolton Road. St Thomas' loomed above them, lit up by floodlights. A St George's flag fluttered from the top of its tower.

"Same design as St James'," said Alice. "Or close."

"Waterloo churches," said John. "Commissioned after the Battle of Waterloo. Manchester, Salford – they were both growing cities back then."

He pulled into the small car park. "Church used to have a lot more land," he said, nodding to Brindle Heath Road, a small highway sloping down from the church towards the industrial estate below. "Those new houses there? That's where the old chapel of ease used to be. And just past them, there's the oldest Jewish cemetery in Manchester."

"Or Salford."

John laughed. "Or Salford. The Jews bought a plot of land next to the church for burials, used it up until they built the Great Synagogue out in Cheetham Hill."

"Mine of information, aren't you?"

"You look up *teacher's pet* in the dictionary, baby, you'll find a picture of me."

Alice snorted and shook her head.

"How you doing now?" No more third degree; when she looked, John's eyes were warm and kind.

"I'm better. Thanks."

"'Kay. Anyway, point being, you can only see a few graves and tombs round here. There'd have been more, back in the day – including one for Arodias Thorne."

"Is it gone now?"

"Probably. But not the man himself." John nodded towards St Thomas' floodlit façade. "He's in there."

"What? Is it haunted or something?"

"Not exactly." John got out, walked round, and opened her door. "Thorne's body was interred in the walls of St Thomas' after his tomb was repeatedly desecrated."

"Seriously?"

"No shit. This rassclaat was not popular."

Alice grinned: John had spent a lot of time in his youth with the 'old school', as he called his parents' generation; his command of patois was pretty damned impressive, and had a habit of popping up when you least expected. She'd forgotten that. She took his arm. "Thanks for bringing me along."

His answering smile was awkward. "I kind of had to."

"Eh?"

"Should have told you, really. Gave the Reverend a call before I came back to Collarmill Road – you know, I needed to know when I could see her. Anyway, I told her what I had on my hands here, what you'd told me, and..."

"And?"

"And she insisted I bring you with me."

Alice swallowed hard. "Right."

"It was all such a neat fit, like I say," John said. "That was like the last straw, got me thinking it had to be some kind of set-up. But since it's not, I think we'd best get in and see her. She's expecting us any minute now."

Alice's stomach had clenched, fist-tight. She turned and looked out for a moment. She'd forgotten how spectacular a view you got from here, stretching out across the whole Irwell Valley. So many trees and patches of woodland; you could easily think the whole landscape was forest, with only the occasional piece of concrete escaping the green stranglehold. It would be beautiful come the summer; Alice wondered if she'd be there to see it.

"Alice?" said John.

She turned to face him, nodded. "Okay, then," she said. "Let's go."

Together they walked towards the looming outline of the church.

# Chapter Twenty-One

## Conception

*The Confession of Mary Carson*

TIME PASSED, YET seemed to stand still. The memory of that summer remains almost precious to me; sorrow and delight are so bound up with my experiences at Springcross House I cannot recall one without the other.

Each night Arodias came to my bed, and each night I found fresh delight there. The difference in our ages seemed to disappear – in the dark, grey hairs were far less visible, and all that remained was his body's leanness and strength. His kisses were passionate and deep; his caresses, when our lovemaking was at an end, tender and consoling. I could not remember being so happy. I was loved, with the prospect of marriage, children and a secure future, and a husband I had redeemed from his earlier harshness.

It was like a dream, I admit – not least because, in daily life, we still played our accustomed roles of employer and secretary. Even our luncheon conversations rarely touched on any topic they would previously have avoided. From morning until night

I outwardly remained the upright spinster; smartly dressed, a pillar of rectitude. But after dark, when he came to my room... ah, then I lived in another world, Mrs Rhodes, one so glorious that when I woke some mornings I could no longer be certain what was a dream and what was not.

Below the hill on which Springcross House stood, the city churned out soot and murk, but the house's gardens were clean and bright. It was a glorious summer, at least to me; one, seemingly, without end. And yet, one morning I looked out of my window and saw the garden's brightly-coloured blooms dead or dying, the trees' leaves turning red and gold and brown, and falling to the paths. Autumn had come.

The days began to shorten. I, in my turn, took advantage of the evenings before they drew in too far, walking through the gardens after dinner to savour the rich scent of fallen leaves decaying into loam. There is a peace and stillness to autumn no other season quite possesses. It is a beautiful time, yet melancholy, for its beauty is born of dying and heralds the coming of winter. After walking, I would retire to my rooms to make ready for my lover.

And if, on those autumn walks, any doubt ever intruded as to my lover's promises, I dismissed them. I was happy, and wished to remain that way; and besides, to doubt my lover was to dishonour him.

Yes, that's how I thought. I was by then five-and-thirty years of age and thought myself wise enough, but in these matters I was as green and foolish as a young maid.

The end of my brief idyll – not that I so recognised it at the time – came one October morning, when I awoke feeling bloated and queasy. I waited as long as I dared for it to pass, but I could not delay rising indefinitely. When I did, I was forced to run to the water closet, where I was violently ill.

I assumed that I had eaten something that disagreed with me, although I had no idea what. The cook, Mrs Cowling, was as charmless and coarse-spirited a soul as any other servant at Springcross House, but her deficiencies did not extend to her kitchen skills: Arodias, after all, was scarcely likely to settle for a sub-standard bill of fare.

My nausea passed quickly. I made my toilet as per usual and went on to enjoy another day in that now-familiar pattern. But the following day, the sickness seized me again; and then, once more, the day after that.

Discreet enquiries among the other servants assured me that no other member of the household had suffered any digestive upset in recent days. I continued in my duties and daily routine, but I knew something was awry. To Arodias I said nothing; I did not want to voice my suspicions. Indeed, the two or three nights that followed were more abandoned than the rest as I sought to forget my worries – and to hope that the following morning would find me with settled stomach, the attacks of vomiting no more than a memory.

But, of course – as I am sure you, Mrs Rhodes, if not you, Mr Muddock, will have doubtless guessed already – that was not to be. The bouts of morning-sickness continued, and then, worse still, my monthly courses, normally regular as the tides themselves, did not come as usual that month. Nor, indeed, I realised with horror, had they arrived the month before.

Of course, it had been foolishness to believe I could sin without consequence. Had I but waited until Arodias and I were married, all would have been well, but as it was, what faced me but disgrace and the life of an outcast?

I could only hope Arodias was the man I hoped him to be, and would not prove some pious hypocrite. The thought had never occurred to me before, but I could not keep it away. I was no longer a woman of certain prospects, but one whose entire future hinged on whether one man chose to keep his word or not. He had been so concerned hitherto about his reputation, after all, not wishing to marry too early. How many times worse would this be? How much easier to cast me adrift and damn me for a whore, with child from some other servant? What would my word be against his?

I was surprised at the sudden sharpness of my fear and suspicion of the man I loved. Time and again I told myself that I was wrong to entertain any such doubt, but still almost a week went by before I dared tell him.

"Arodias, I am with child."

That is how I said it, Mrs Rhodes, in the middle of our customary half-hour luncheon. He went still, halting in the midst of chewing a mouthful of cold chicken, and looked at me for a long moment. Then he put down his chicken leg, swallowed a long draught of tea and set the cup down before saying, "You're certain?"

I nodded. I felt tiny, fragile, a withered leaf the first strong wind would blow away.

Arodias picked up a napkin and dabbed at his mouth. "We will talk further this evening," he said, "at the accustomed time." It was the first thing he'd ever said that made reference to how we spent our nights. He looked at my face, and doubtless read the fear and confusion there. For all my attempts at composure, I was, doubtless, an open book. Then he smiled, reached out and touched my hand. This, too was unprecedented, being the first display of affection he had made towards me anywhere outside the bedroom. "Don't worry, Mary," he said. "All shall be well."

Of course, his words only served to worry me more. I picked them apart and studied them as if under a magnifying glass throughout the hours that followed. What did he intend? There were those who could abort a child, once conceived: there were draughts you swallowed, or surgical instruments, intended to preserve life, bent to the opposing purpose. Was that his plan? And what then did he intend – to pay me off and dismiss me, or continue as before and marry me when the times were convenient? Could I countenance such a design? And if not, what else might he propose?

I passed the day in a daze, barely picking at the evening meal, wandering through the gardens in the twilight until it was very nearly dark. When I realised that the hour for our nightly assignation had almost come, for the first time I went reluctantly to the rendezvous.

I had no idea what Arodias expected. If he wanted to postpone all discussion until we had coupled, I was not sure I could oblige him. Thankfully, he spared me that. Entering the room as he usually did, in his brocaded robe and bearing a candelabra, he quickly set the latter down, sat beside me upon the bed, and took my hands in the tenderest fashion.

"My dearest," he said. "I am so sorry. This is all my fault. It should not have been a great hardship to wait, not for so little time as a year. I am to blame."

I had not expected this. I had expected blame and recrimination, so much so that I said, "So am I, darling. I should have thought to take precautions of some kind –"

But he was already shaking his head. "You're an innocent, my dear," he said. "Before you came to Springcross House, you were pure, unsullied. I am a man of the world. All my life I have had to consider the consequences of my actions, in order to ensure I attain my goals. It was always obvious that there was a risk of matters ending as they have."

"Ending?" The fear was back again, but he squeezed my hands gently.

"Developing, I should say. This is no ending. Rest assured of that, Mary. We will still be married. This changes nothing, do you understand me? Nothing. But... we must be wise."

"How do you mean, wise, Arodias?"

"As I told you, there are those who would care nothing about the conditions in my factory, however harsh, but would seek my ruin for a transgression such as this. It was politic to delay our engagement until a suitable time had passed. It is even more so that this matter be kept quiet."

My hands went, almost automatically, to my belly. "It will be a hard matter to keep quiet, surely."

"You rarely go far from the house. Work, and, if necessary, illness, can provide an adequate excuse for a low profile on your part until the child is born – and you may be certain that I shall ensure discretion on the servants' part," he added, "lest you have any concerns on that score. After the child is born, you can be seen in public again, and soon enough after that, our engagement can be announced."

"And the child?" I asked.

Arodias merely shrugged. "We will adopt him," he said. "He – or she – will live here, in secret, until in due course it can be announced that Mr and Mrs Thorne, unable to conceive children of their own, have chosen to adopt one whose lot would otherwise be bleak. And if we have more children" – he smiled – "we shall have confounded the doctors. It will hardly be the first time one of those quacks has been proven wrong."

I was speechless; the plan's audacity and thoroughness had taken me wholly by surprise. Arodias chuckled. "My wits and guile have been vital to my prosperity for more years now than I care to recall," he said. "I would be foolish if I had no idea how to overcome a crisis."

"But our child – to lie to him about the very circumstances of his birth –"

"Mary, my darling. Make no mistake – those who would use this to harm me would harm you and our child as well, without even a thought. Be guided by me on this, and we shall marry, with a child legitimate in the eyes of society and the law. He – and you – will be safe from calumny and ill-fame."

I could not fault his logic. Even should I decide honesty to be the better course and to take responsibility for my own weakness, how could I condemn an innocent child to suffer with me? "Very well," I said.

"We will find clothing that will conceal your condition as it progresses," he said. "When your time of confinement comes near, another story will do – illness of some kind, brought on by overwork. You'll leave the area for a spell – the Lake District, perhaps. When you return," my husband-to-be went on, "you will be fully recovered, and our child will be cared for in secret. Then, as I say, we announce our engagement at the required time, marry, and finally – *voila!* – present the child as our adopted offspring. And so the crisis is neatly averted and we are a family. No?"

I smiled. "It seems –" I wanted to say 'foolproof' but that would have felt too much like tempting fate. "It seems a sound plan."

He smiled back. "Indeed it is," he said. "All that is required is that you trust me. And now..."

With that, he began to kiss and caress me; I found I could not hold back.

We made love again, and soon Arodias drifted off to sleep – but rest, even though I was cradled in his arms, eluded me.

A life was growing inside me, that should have been cause for celebration and joy. But I could not shake the sense that any possible happiness was already tainted, because our marriage and our child's birth would be shrouded in deceit.

At some point, Arodias gently slipped out of bed. I pretended I was asleep too, and soon my bedroom door closed behind him.

Outside, a storm-wind blew, and the branches of the gardens' trees hissed and lashed the air, shedding falls of leaves. I lay sleepless and alone in my bed, coming – it shames me to say – to hate the child I bore for the shadow its scarce-formed life had already cast on mine.

# Chapter Twenty-Two

## Sixsmythe

*31st October 2016*

The inside of St Thomas' Church was warm with low and gentle light when John opened its heavy wooden doors. Alice followed him across the threshold and inhaled that oddly distinctive smell that churches have – must and wood polish, old books, candlewax, fresh and dying flowers.

She'd barely been in a church since she was a child, she realised. Her marriage had taken place in one and when Emily had been born, Alice had relented enough towards religion to have the child christened, if only to please Andrew's parents and her own. The low light gleamed on polished wood and brass holders, gleamed on tall slender windows.

Her footsteps clicked on the wooden floor as she walked up the aisle; even so, what caught her most of all about the church was its stillness. A Christian colleague had once spoken of going to church 'in search of spiritual peace'. She'd thought it, at the time, a trite and pretentious turn of phrase, but now thought she understood better. Where else, in a city, in the howl of daily life, would you find a building dedicated to silence and stillness? This was a place where you came for quiet contemplation, to take stock and think; to step away from your life's clutter and day-to-day concerns in search of meaning and understanding.

Well, it was now, maybe always had been for the privileged few. For the common herd, it had most likely been the kind of place where someone would scream at you from the pulpit about original sin, eternal damnation, and how the Labour Party was the Antichrist – at least, she vaguely remembered her grandmother, a Catholic, claiming the local monsignor had declared as much back in the 'fifties when they nationalised the railways.

She shook her head. She could quote chapter and verse – no pun intended – on the iniquities of organised religions, on the evidence of human hands in drawing up their rules and regulations to control the lower orders, of their deep loathing and fear of women – yes to all of that, you couldn't deny what logic showed. But at the same time there was no denying this place had some quality that called to her, that made her wish she'd come here on some other day, by herself, without mysteries to solve or ghosts to exorcise – or, at least, not that kind of ghost. It was like the feeling she experienced beside a sea, a river or a lake, or the heart of an autumn wood as it breathed. A sense of peace, of stillness, of connection to, or awareness of, something bigger. It was what she'd gone to Browton Vale for in the past, until the presence she'd sensed there – the ogre? – had corrupted it.

She'd picked a fine time to get religion, Alice thought; still, there was quiet and contemplation enough now. John seemed to feel it, too; Alice was grateful for that. She clicked her way down the aisle towards the altar. The pulpit stood to one side, a lectern to the other; a great cross of polished brass shone below the stained glass windows.

"The life of St Thomas," said a voice. Alice jumped, turned

to see a thin, grey-haired woman limping determinedly towards them with the aid of a stick.

"Sorry?" Alice said.

The woman smiled, pointed with her free hand. "The windows," she said. "They show scenes from the life of St Thomas. Only to be expected, of course, in a church named after him. Hm?"

The smile was mischievous, as was the twinkle in her bespectacled eyes; Alice smiled back. The woman limped closer, and Alice saw that under her thick jacket the older woman wore black, with a white dog-collar at her throat. "Reverend Sixsmythe?"

The smile brightened. "Ah – Miss Collier, I presume?" Sixsmythe switched her cane to her left hand, shook with her right. "Then this handsome fellow must be Mr Revell." Another handshake. "Very handsome fellow," she said. "If I were twenty years younger and didn't have a heart condition..." She laughed. "I'm sorry. Your faces are a picture. Yes, yes – guilty as charged. Galatea Penelope Sixsmythe, Reverend, C of E. Local historian, tea drinker and devourer of cakes. Spiritual guidance offered at an affordable rate. Come this way!"

Sixsmythe turned and limped around the front row of pews towards the left side of the church. Alice exchanged glances with John, and they followed.

Sixsmythe had stopped before a particular spot on the wall. As they approached, Alice saw there was a good-sized brass plaque set into it, glinting dully in the light.

"I think this is what you're here about," Sixsmythe said, tapping it with a bony knuckle.

*Of your charity, pray for the soul of*
*ARODIAS THORNE*
*1778 – 1851*
*'Judge not, lest ye be judged'*
*– Matthew 7:1*

"Arodias Thorne," said John.

"A man so well-loved that this was the only place they could give his bones a safe burial," said Galatea Sixsmythe, nodding at the wall. "But you know that already." She looked at Alice. Her eyes were dark grey, putting her in mind of Welsh slate in the rain, or cold iron. Hard, unyielding, but a strength to be relied on. "So, you're the new tenant at Collarmill Road?"

"Owner," said Alice, "I bought the place."

Sixsmythe smiled again. "I'm not sure anyone's ever really owned that spot," she said. "Not even *him*." She nodded again at the wall. "Let's sit."

Sixsmythe lowered herself into a pew. "Now," she said. "I've heard some little from Mr Revell, but if he doesn't mind keeping *shtum* for a minute or two, I'd rather hear it from the horse's mouth – not that I'm comparing you to a horse, my dear, in spite of one or two superficial resemblances."

"Eh?"

"Begin at the beginning, Miss Collier. I know Mr Revell well enough by reputation to guess that something's afoot in that house. So kindly tell me what you've experienced. Don't leave anything out."

"Did Mr Revell tell you –"

"That you're worried you might not be right in the head? It's a common enough concern, Miss Collier. But some things can't be suffered without leaving a mark. I think you know that very well."

"What –" she glanced at John. "What did you –"

"Mr Revell hasn't breathed a word regarding your personal life, my dear, you can rest assured on that. When we spoke on the telephone, he was in an agony of indecision about how much to tell and how much to keep to himself. But I'm not blind. Apart from the usual – births, marriages and deaths – people tend to come to their vicar with problems of one kind or another. So I can see when someone's been troubled. When there's been grief, or loss, or... well. You don't need me to tell you. In any case, the best thing I can suggest is that you tell me everything you've seen or think you've seen. If in doubt, spit it out. And I'll do my best to decide. All right?"

"Okay."

"All right, then." Sixsmythe beamed happily, clasped both hands atop her cane and propped her chin on top. "Whenever you're ready, my dear."

Alice reeled off the whole catalogue of events, spending most of her time studying the polished floor, occasionally glancing up at Sixsmythe, who smiled benignly back and nodded her eagerly on, or at John, who sat studying her with a hand resting on the back of the pew – not touching her, but resting only inches away, close enough to take without effort should she need it.

At last she was done. She omitted only the dream in her hotel room. She desperately wanted to believe that it *had* been only a dream, that the scraps of red cloth would prove to have a straightforward explanation.

She looked up at John, but he was looking past her, at Sixsmythe. When Alice turned towards the rector, her head was bowed, lips touching her clasped hands as if in prayer. Slowly the older woman looked up, and nodded.

"Well," she said, "you *have* got yourself in something of a pickle, my dear. I think you'd both better come with me."

She stood, wincing slightly as she straightened.

"Where to?" said Alice.

"Why, to the Rectory, of course. I can offer tea, coffee, something stronger if required, and – if we're very lucky – cake."

THE RECTORY WAS only a short drive away, in Irlams o'Th' Height. Sixsmythe went in a small, battered-looking Honda, while John and Alice followed.

"What do you think?" said Alice.

"I think we should listen to what she has to say," was all John said.

They rounded the Broad Street roundabout, went off the A6 onto Bolton Road, then turned down Park Road. Night had already settled over Lightoaks Park, and the line of bristling trees stood out against the light-polluted sky. It was still quiet when they pulled up outside the rambling Victorian townhouse that served the Reverend Sixsmythe as home.

Ivy clung to a trellis around the door, and a mock-Victorian lantern shone beside it. The lights were on inside, and a warm smell of spices and cooked dough washed out as the door opened. "Luck's in!" said Sixsmythe cheerily. "Dora's been baking, God bless her."

"That you, Rev?"

Sixsmythe motioned Alice and John inside and slammed the door. "No, Dora, it's the Yorkshire Ripper." To Alice's surprise, she was answered by a loud raspberry.

A young woman emerged from the end of the hall, wiping floury hands on an apron. She had short brown hair, no make-up, and wore jeans with turned-up cuffs, together with boots, braces and a lumberjack shirt. "Oh," she said. "Sorry, Rev – I mean, Reverend – didn't know we had guests." She had a soft Welsh accent.

"Yes, well, we do. Could you be a treasure, Dora? I'd kill for a cup of coffee."

"Coming up."

Sixsmythe turned to Alice and John. "You?"

"Er – coffee, please," John said. "Black with two."

"White coffee, no sugar," said Alice. "Please."

"We'll be in my study, Dora," said Sixsmythe.

"Right you are, Rev. Will you be wanting cake? Just made some coffee and walnut."

"Oh, go on then."

Dora vanished back into her fragrant domain. Sixsmythe shooed Alice up the stairs, John following. "Dora's my housekeeper. An absolute godsend. Cooks like an angel, too, as you'll see. Now – this way!"

Sixsmythe's study was in a front room, overlooking the road and the park. Streetlights glowed in cages of shedding leaves among the trees opposite. The Rector switched the lights on. "Take a seat, take a seat."

A wide, leather-bound desk was beside the window, with a well-padded swivel chair. A couple of leatherbound armchairs were braced against a far wall. The rest of the room was taken up by bookcases, bulging with elderly volumes of one kind or another.

"Unread, half of them," called Sixsmythe, flapping her hand as she crouched before the desk to address the door of a square black object tucked underneath it – a safe, Alice realised. "Now whatever *is* that bloody combination? I have a great appetite for broadening my knowledge of Scripture and theology and much else besides, but it does rather outstrip my reading time. Ah!"

She got the safe door open, and heaved out a large, heavy box-file.

"Now these," she said, "are just copies of the originals, which are in our safety-deposit box at the bank. As such, I can at my discretion let you borrow them. I suspect you'll find them useful, but I think you'll find it wiser and safer to peruse them elsewhere. Tuscany, maybe. I'm told that's nice this time of year."

"What are they?" asked John.

"Documents, Mr Revell," Sixsmythe said. "Documents pertaining to the site in question – 378 Collarmill Road, and its environs – and to Mr Arodias Thorne, formerly of this parish. Smoke?"

"Oh. No. Thank you."

"Miss Collier?"

"No, thanks. I gave up."

"Very wise." Sixsmythe slipped a packet of Sobranie Black Russians from a desk drawer, clasped a gold filter-tip between her thin lips and lit the black cigarette with a small silver lighter. She thumped a heavy cut-glass ashtray on the leather desktop before her and leant back. The smoke was richer-smelling than most tobaccos – in small quantities, even to a non-smoker, it wasn't entirely unpleasant. "Take it you've no objection if I do?"

"Your house," said John. "And you're helping us out here."

"True. But it's good manners to ask." Another twinkle in the eyes. "Just as it's good manners on your part to say yes. Anyway." She leant forward and blew smoke from the side of her mouth. "I take it Mr Revell has put you in the picture?"

"About –"

"About Arodias Thorne, Springcross House, St James' Church, the Red Man and the Beast of Browton, among other things?"

"Not the last two, not yet."

"Mm. Well, we'll come to them in due course. This is all connected in one way or another. But first, let me come back to the subject of Arodias Thorne. You know, of course, that he once owned the land your house stood on? That he built Springcross House on top of the hill now occupied by Higher Crawbeck?"

"Yes. Yes, John told me. And that he paid for –"

"The church, yes. St James'." Reverend Sixsmythe took a long, thoughtful drag on her cigarette. "That was quite a lot of money, as you can imagine. But you see, Miss Collier, Arodias Thorne wanted that piece of land. Very specifically, that piece and no other would do. So he was more than prepared to pay any price for it. The land – almost all of it – belonged to the Church. The old church on the hill – St Winifred's – had served as a chapel of ease for some years in any case, and the new one would in fact be far easier to reach for local residents. So the decision was made to sell. Personally, I believe that to have been *most* unwise. And others at the time felt the same way – it certainly *wasn't* what you'd call a unanimous decision among the relevant authorities. But they were greedy. A terrible sin.

Although comprehensible and forgivable, I think, where Dora's coffee and walnut cake is concerned."

The study door opened on cue and Dora slipped in, bearing a tray with three steaming mugs, a large cake, a knife and three sideplates. She deposited it on the table. "Dinner's in the oven, Rev," she said, "an Irish stew. Just pop it on for half an hour when you get back from the service."

"Spot on." Sixsmythe stubbed out her cigarette. "Thank you, Dora."

"Will that be everything?"

"Oh goodness, yes. Get yourself out of here." Sixsmythe smiled as Dora went out. "She has the loveliest little boy – her wife picks him up from school, but Dora always likes to be home in time for tea. Still, never mind that now. Where was I?"

"Greed, I think," said John, sipping his tea.

"Quite. Which reminds me – who's for some of this cake?"

Having cut them all a generous slice, Sixsmythe went on. "Yes, there were those who didn't feel the Church ought to part with that particular piece of real estate – and perhaps, too, those who felt that it certainly shouldn't fall into the possession of a man like Arodias Thorne."

"Why not?"

"We'll get to that, my dear. Just to clear up a pair of loose ends first: Old Harry and the Red Man. You weren't familiar with either of these?"

"No. But this Red Man –"

"In a moment." Sixsmythe, Alice decided, took a downright pleasure in spinning her tale. Her lips were puckered in that mischievous smile again. "Old Harry, first. Well, you've seen Browton Vale for yourself. Very pleasant spot now, of course, but in older times – and bearing in mind that Browton generally was pretty desolate – decidedly less so. The marshes there were considerably more extensive, the woods a lot wilder – at least until they were cut down to build houses. The marshes were drained at the same time, but up until then, they were considered very dangerous; a lot of children went wandering there and came to grief. And that, in part, is held to be the origin of Old Harry, otherwise known as the Beast of Browton. Have you ever heard of Jenny Greenteeth?"

Alice blinked. "No."

"Some sort of water-spirit?" said John. "Supposed to live in the Irwell?"

"Quite. A malign water-hag, a little like the Russian *rusalka*. There are different versions of her elsewhere in the country, and in many others. They haunt rivers, streams, pools, lakes – take your pick – and if anyone gets too close, *especially* unwary children, they're dragged into the water and drowned. But Jenny Greenteeth was specifically identified with the Irwell. She was said to have long, green hair, looking very like the growths of water-weed you'd see in the river any day. She was a monster who also made a very good cautionary tale to keep children out of danger."

"And Old Harry was something similar?"

"In part," said Sixsmythe, "but only in part." She was watching Alice closely. "You see, it's a very old legend. Goes back centuries. Anglo-Saxon times, at the very least. Perhaps earlier, but there's nothing about it in Roman accounts, although as I'm sure you know they settled the Manchester area. And they knew certain aspects of the local legends *very* well."

Before Alice could ask what that meant, Sixsmythe had breezed on. "But yes, the Beast of Browton. Put simply, Miss Collier, it was an ogre."

The room seem to grow still. "An ogre," Alice said.

"Quite." Sixsmythe plucked some papers from the box file, positioned her glasses further down the beak of her nose and read. "Let's see... 'About twenty foot in height, with a piebald hide covered in patches of fur... its general form is human, but for the greatest part it runs on all fours like some huge monkey or ape. A matted beard hangs about its dreadful maw. Its eyes, slit-pupilled as a cat's are, jar with its low and bestial aspect, for they are very large and a most delicate shade of blue...' Does any of that sound familiar, Miss Collier?"

Alice licked her lips. She took a gulp of coffee. "I think you know it does, Reverend."

"Yes." Sixsmythe put the papers back in the box-file, pushed her spectacles back up her nose. "Old Harry, the Beast of Browton, as described in a pamphlet on 'Folklore and Superstitions of Lancashire', circa 1850."

"Why 'Old Harry'?" said John.

"Not sure. Perhaps a corruption of 'Old Hairy'? Ah well, that's a puzzle for another day. The pamphlet says 'described variously as an ogre, hobgoblin or boggart,' but the first seemed the aptest of the three. Anyway, he – and it's most definitely a he, as a number of accounts of unfortunate women meeting a fate worse than death on Browton Vale testify, my dear, so you can think yourself lucky in one respect at least – he's been around there for quite some time. Sightings of Old Harry persisted well into the nineteenth century. In fact, I do believe the last recorded one..." Sixsmythe leafed through the box-file "... was in... yes... 1911! A courting couple in the woods below Browton Vale had their illicit session of nookie disturbed by 'a sound of twigs and undergrowth trampled underfoot' and reported seeing 'a huge black figure, covered in hair, with luminous blue eyes and pupils like a cat's.' Luckily for them, discretion proved the better part of valour and they lived to fornicate again. I don't think anyone put much stock in their story at the time, but in the light of your experiences, Miss Collier, I think you'll agree it's not to be dismissed out of hand."

"Yeah." Alice nodded, although she knew that a fortnight ago she would have done just that. It couldn't be true, she would have reasoned, and therefore belonged in this box or that – the ones marked *lies*, *hallucinations*, and *madness*. But now – Christ, what use were probability or reason as tools here, to determine what might or might not be true?

"Old Harry seems to have been most in evidence up to the seventeenth century, and the first half of the eighteenth. As the Industrial Revolution kicks into gear and the surrounding area becomes increasingly urbanised and so forth, his legend persists, but the old feller himself seems to become rather more bashful. Although, as you see, the last reported sighting was just over a century ago. But Old Harry's really just a sprog compared to the Red Man."

"Who is the Red Man? Please – I want to know what this is all about." Alice heard the strain in her voice. She couldn't stomach the thought of more of Sixsmythe's dancing around.

But the Rector just smiled and nodded. "And you have every right to, my dear. Now eat your cake and I'll tell you."

Alice exchanged a glance with John, who shrugged. His slice was already gone, with golden crumbs speckling his sweater while he stole what she suspected was only the latest of a succession of glances at the remaining cake. She took a bite, expecting little, but the cake was both sweet and richly flavoured, and she found herself chewing long and slowly to savour it the better.

Sixsmythe chuckled. "I've told Dora her cakes should be available on the NHS," she said. "So – the Red Man. He goes back a long way. A long, long way. He's a rather more persistent figure than the Beast; he was last sighted in 1972. He's also a rather more interesting character, too. More... ambiguous, anyway."

"Ambiguous?"

"In some accounts he's just a man in a red robe, like a rather unorthodox monk. But in others he's a warrior, a soldier – even a knight. And some stories present him as demonic, while others are more, shall we say, complimentary. It tends to depend who he was fighting against and who wrote the account, of course. One theme, however, remains constant throughout – that he is some sort of guardian."

"Guardian?" The last of her slice of coffee and walnut cake was already gone; Alice chased it with her remaining coffee and resisted the urge to look longingly at the rest of the cake. "Guardian of what?"

"Well, now – that's the big question, isn't it? The hill, Miss Collier, or at least, something on or in it. The Romans certainly appear to have had some sort of set-to with him."

"Really?"

"Oh yes. Did you never wonder where the name 'Collarmill' comes from? It used to refer to the upper part of the hill – the part that was by and large uninhabited until the late nineteenth century, when Crawbeck expanded so noticeably. The summit was known as Collarmill Height."

Alice shrugged. "I thought it just meant there'd been a mill there once."

"Oh no." Sixsmythe shook her head. "It's from the Latin. *Colle miles rubeus*, they called it. How's your Latin?"

"Very rusty, I'm afraid." They'd studied it at school, and it had been once of Alice's better subjects, but she'd forgotten most of what she'd learned long ago.

"*Colle* means hill, *rubeus* is red, and *miles* means soldier, warrior – even knight."

"The hill of the red knight?"

"Precisely. In fact, if you look at records going back before the Industrial Revolution – that is, back when Crawbeck was just a tiny village at the foot of the mount – you'll find it was simply known locally as Redman's Hill."

Alice realised she was still holding her empty cup and sideplate. After a moment, she propped them on the arm of her chair.

"So," Sixsmythe went on, "after tangling with the Romans, our friend the Red Man went on to knock heads with the Saxons, the Danes, the Normans – basically every fresh round of invaders who's thought to put their stamp on our green and pleasant land has had an encounter of one kind or another with him. Including the Church, when its fathers first attempted to build a place of worship there – back in the ninth century, as I recall."

"As old as that?" John said.

"Oh yes. I mean, the church itself was rebuilt several times for one reason or another, but... well, I take it you're aware that the Christian Church established itself in Britain less by destroying or banning pagan customs, festivals or holy sites but by – er – incorporating them, shall we say?"

John nodded. "Christmas replaced the pagan winter festivals like the Norse Yule and the Roman Saturnalia – that's where the tradition of giving gifts and making merry came from. And the Roman New Year supplied the traditions of lights, greenery and charity. Just like Easter w –"

"Yes, yes, thank you, Mr Revell." Sixsmythe scowled. "*I'm* the one displaying the breadth of her learning here. It's considered very ill-mannered, you know – for obvious anatomical reasons – to get into a pissing contest with a lady."

John opened and closed his mouth and might even have blushed. Alice bit her lips to avoid helpless laughter. Sixsmythe nodded, then shot Alice a wink. "Anyway, you understand the basic concept. Some aspects of paganism were demonised, and others... Christianised. As Mr Revell would no doubt have gone on to tell us, an awful lot of saints' days were pagan celebrations of one kind or another. I'm sure he hadn't forgotten that tonight is in fact one of the best-known, and was only saving it till last for maximum effect."

John harrumphed and looked down at the floor.

"I refer, of course, to Halloween. The greatest of all pagan festivals, and thus Christianised into All Saints – or All Souls – day. Or 'All Hallows.' As you were no doubt about to tell us, Mr Revell?"

John harrumphed again. Sixsmythe chuckled. "Quite. All Hallows Eve, or Even – Hallowe'en. Although the less said about the bloody trick-or-treaters, the better. By the same token," she went on, "pagan places of worship became Christian places of worship; pagan holy sites, Christian ones. St Winifred's Church, on Collarmill Height, was one such."

"So there was a pagan holy site on top of the hill," said Alice, "and the Red Man – guarded it?"

"Yes. Caused quite a lot of mischief to the early fathers, I believe, and there was much praying and exorcising and general gnashing of teeth. The official account has the Red Man's hash apparently settled once and for all, but luckily its author was long-dead and safely beyond embarrassment when the fellow popped up again a couple of centuries later to – er – remonstrate with the Normans. In every case, save one, the Red Man succeeded in his apparent aim: that is, safeguarding the source of the Craw."

"The Craw? You mean the stream?"

"Oh yes. The spring was in a cavern at the very summit of the hill, you see, and its waters collected in a small, circular pool outside the cave entrance. We're not sure if the pool was a natural formation or if early worshippers excavated it. Anyway, from the pool a small stream, or beck, emerged to run down the hillside. Hence Crawbeck. More cake?"

"Please," said John, trying not to sound too eager and failing.

"No – I mean, yes," said Alice, trying to consider her waistline and failing just as miserably.

Sixsmythe chuckled again and cut three more slices.

"So what was the actual sacred site?" said Alice. "The spring?"

"Holy springs are quite common," admitted Sixsmythe, "although it seems to have been as much the pool as anything else. There were various miraculous properties attributed to the spring waters, but only where they emerged fresh from the rock or collected in the pool outside the cavern entrance. The waters of the Craw itself were no more magical or blessed in nature than any others. Hence the belief in some quarters that the pool itself was man-made."

"Perfect place to let the waters collect," said John.

"Quite so."

"What kind of miraculous properties?" Alice asked. "I mean, you know, supposedly?"

"Almost any you can think of, Miss Collier," Sixsmythe said. "If you drank, or in some cases, bathed or were washed in the waters – well, it depended on what you were looking for. They were supposed to have healing properties, of course – there are a lot of claims of wounds healing magically, or even untreatable diseases such as leprosy being cured. But others talk of those who drank the waters seeing visions of the future, or of the past – where father buried the family treasure, that sort of thing – or of events occurring far away. What you got from the spring largely seems to have depended on what you needed. Some..." Sixsmythe paused, putting her cake down for a moment. "Some claimed to have seen the Virgin Mary, Jesus, even God Himself. The Virgin in particular, actually – there were quite a few sightings of her, or at least a female figure, all glowing and ethereal, that kind of thing. And not only be people who drank the water. Just added to the place's reputation. The Virgin of the Height, it was called locally. Of course..." Sixsmythe sighed.

"Of course what?" asked Alice.

"Well, much as I'd love to point to this figure as a miraculous proof of mine being the true faith – although my Catholic colleagues would probably point out that it rather vindicates theirs more – the fact is that the stories of the Virgin go back to pre-Christian times. She's been around for a while, this one. She was particularly associated with the groves of rowan trees that grew on the hill – it's a tree with various magical properties ascribed to it in folklore. People used to make little talismans out of the rowan twigs – dolls, and later crosses – to invoke her aid."

Alice swallowed.

"Another case of the Church incorporating a pagan symbol?" asked John, eyebrows raised.

Sixsmythe glared at him, and he looked away. "Cheeky, Mr Revell. But essentially, yes. The last sighting of her was in the mid-'nineties, if I recall. Interestingly, from the 1930s onward, she was also seen in the area called the Fall."

"The landslide," said John.

"Correct," said Sixsmythe. "Back in '29, a good-sized chunk of Collarmill Height ended up displaced into Browton Vale. And there are probably more rowan trees growing down there now than there are on the hill itself."

The glowing figure in the hallway when she'd used the cross; the hazy shape when she'd hidden in the rowan trees on the Fall. Alice clasped her hands together, tight.

"*Anyway*," said Sixsmythe, "all this is probably where the identification with the Grail came from, although some contend it was the Arthurian connection that came first..."

"Whoa, whoa, whoa." John held up a hand. "The Grail? Arthur? As in *King* Arthur?"

"*Yes*, dear." Sixsmythe frowned at the interruption. "A grail – or to use the Old English, *graal*, is, in the literal sense, more a bowl than a cup, and the pool was, according to contemporary accounts, a perfectly circular, bowl-shaped hollow in the ground – which was taken as more evidence for its being man-made. If you look back over the centuries, over the documents referring to the area, you'll see the name change. Crawbeck becomes *Crawlbeck*, then *Grawl-beck*, and, finally, *Graal-beck*."

"In other words, *Grail beck*," said Alice.

Sixsmythe smiled. "Quite so. The legends of the Holy Grail tend to ascribe miraculous properties – particularly of healing or longevity – to any water drunk from the cup. So the two were put together. There is a local legend that the Holy Grail was hidden for a time on Collarmill Height, guarded by a hermit or some such who used it to help deserving cases – and that afterwards, when the Grail was taken elsewhere, the miraculous spring first appeared. Another legend says that Sir Percival, while seeking the Grail, came to Collarmill and defended its heights against some horde of aggressors or other who wished to make evil use of the spring. It's only a fragmentary, local story – no connection to the big myth cycles – but it *is* interesting that it should be Sir Percival, specifically, of all Arthur's knights, who features in the story."

Here went Sixsmythe again, playing her little games and dangling her knowledge in front of them. The older woman's eyes were bright; she clearly couldn't wait for someone to ask her. Alice sighed. Might as well play the game. "Why's that?"

"There's more than one warrior known as the Red Knight in Arthurian legend," said Sixsmythe. "For example, there's a knight called Esclados who guarded a mystical fountain in the forest of Brocéliande. Interesting, no? Both Gawain and Galahad were known as the Red Knight in different myth-cycles – Perlesvaus and the Lancelot-Grail cycles respectively, if I recall. And yes, there's that Grail again. But Percival – out of all Arthur's knights, that's the one most strongly identified with the title. In Chrétien de Troyes' cycle, the original Red Knight is the Red Knight of Quinqeroi, who steals a cup from Arthur's court. Percival – who, in the beginning, is a boy of humble birth – vows to bring the cup back to Camelot: in fact, it becomes his quest, on the fulfilment of which his knighthood depends. And when Percival finds and kills the Red Knight in battle, he takes his foe's armour."

"So the Red Knight changes from being an evil character –" John began.

"To a noble one," finished Sixsmythe. "Quite so. And there's even a quest for a drinking-cup." She smiled. "And no, I'm not making any judgements as to the historical truth of the Arthurian legends here. What I do think is that the legend of the Red Man – and the Collarmill Spring – bore sufficient similarities that they were partly reworked into Arthurian myth."

"So is that why Thorne wanted that piece of land?" Alice said. "Because of the legend?"

Sixsmythe, pushing the last of her cake into her mouth, shrugged. "Who can say?" she said when she'd finally swallowed. "The original site of the spring itself was there somewhere – although the cave was blocked off and the pool filled in by the Roundheads during the English Civil War, as they considered it idolatrous. They burned down St Winifred's

Church as well; it was rebuilt during the Restoration, but the spring itself was forgotten. Obviously the source can't have been blocked entirely, as the Craw continues to flow. Perhaps Arodias Thorne hoped to find it and make some use of it. But it *is* hard to imagine what else Collarmill might have had to recommend it."

Sixsmythe settled back in her chair and lit up a fresh Sobranie. "Of course, I *could* be reading far too much into it. Perhaps Thorne was simply drawn to the otherwise unspoilt hilltop and its rather commanding view of the area? Perhaps. Perhaps. Perhaps he just liked being the monarch of all he surveyed."

"But you don't think so," said John.

Sixsmythe tapped the box-file. "You'll find a good deal more in here. He died childless, leaving Springcross House to a Mrs Wynne-Jones. She almost immediately sold it to the city corporation, on condition Springcross House be pulled down in its entirety and the site used for building new homes. As it was. Among them, Miss Collier, yours."

Alice wondered just how far her house was from the spring's source.

"Much of what I've told you," said Sixsmythe, "comes from the Church's own records. Some is from other sources, freely available elsewhere. But there were certain papers in Mrs Wynne-Jones' possession at her death. Her family wanted nothing to do with them, and so they eventually came to the Diocese of Salford, as the hill was under their jurisdiction – and thence into the safe-keeping of one of my illustrious predecessors."

Sixsmythe settled back in her chair, puffing contentedly on her cigarette. "So..." began John.

"So?" She eyed him benignly over the top of her spectacles.

"So what happens now?"

"Now?" Sixsmythe chuckled. "Now, I suggest you acquaint yourself with the material in this file. But as I've already said, I suggest you do it somewhere other than 378 Collarmill Road."

"You think it's dangerous?" said John.

Sixsmythe sighed. "What do *you* think?"

Alice looked at the box-file, then at Sixsmythe. "This isn't the first time, is it?" she said. "Something like this has happened before."

"Of course it has, woman!" Sixsmythe snapped. "Do you seriously think a place with *that* sort of history would just stay quiet until *you* came along?" She sighed, closed her eyes and breathed out. "I'm sorry." When she lifted her cigarette to her mouth again, Alice saw her hand shook a little. "There've been occasional reports from other houses on Collarmill Road. The Red Man is commonest, and the children."

"The children." Alice leant forward. "Who are they?"

"Alice," began John, but she waved him to silence.

"I think we need to know, John, don't you? Who are they supposed to be, Reverend? What do they want? Why are they trying to kill me?"

God, that sounded insane when she came out and said it, but Sixsmythe sighed again and nodded. "I can't give you an exact answer, I'm afraid, Miss Collier. But we can make educated guesses."

"Thorne," said Alice. "That's it, isn't it? He was some sort of child-killer."

Sixsmythe shook her head. "There was far more to Arodias Thorne than appeared at first glance. It's all here." She pushed the box-file towards Alice; it almost tipped off the edge of the desk and she had to catch it before it hit the floor. "What I *will* say is this: there were minor incidents and reports from other houses and locales around number 378, but nothing on the scale of what we've heard from *that* place over the years, Miss Collier."

"You mean – other people?" Alice saw John half-rising from the corner of her eye, heard her voice rise too, but couldn't seem to stop it. "Those things tried to kill someone else *and nobody said anything to me?*"

"*Sit down.*" There was a real whipcrack of authority in the Rector's voice and both Alice and John sank back in their chairs. All of a sudden, it wasn't remotely hard to imagine Galatea Sixsmythe preaching to her congregation about the torments of Hell. Her hands were clenched on the desk, brows bent in a frown, the grey eyes cold. "You came to me for help, Miss Collier. Don't forget that."

"I seem to remember John saying you were downright eager to see me."

Sixsmythe breathed out. "True. True." She lit a fresh cigarette. "Don't tell Dora," she said absently. "I'm only supposed to smoke five a day and this takes me over my limit."

"Dora's gone home, Reverend," Alice said.

"Oh, yes, of course she has." Sixsmythe puffed on her cigarette. "The answer to your question is yes and no, Miss Collier. There'd been reports of activity at 378 Collarmill Road for some time, but it's varied from occupant to occupant. People have heard children's voices at night when there weren't any children in the house. Some have even glimpsed them. From time to time there's been... well, I suppose the only term for it is poltergeist activity. Objects breaking suddenly, being flung through the air – bursts of loud, angry, inchoate energy that come and go, vanish as quickly as they appear."

She tapped ash from her cigarette. "The thing is that no two residents have had quite the same experience. Some have lived there and never seen – or at least, never reported – anything remotely out of the ordinary. Others get the sounds, or the sights, or the poltergeist activity, but all three at once, that's rare."

"And no-one's actually had the children try to kill them?"

"No. Or reported the experiences you've had outside the house – the cavemen and the chap with the spear. But there's usually something. Did the estate agent not tell you that 378 was unoccupied for a good five years before you moved in?"

"I think she may have mentioned something. But aren't they supposed to tell you if a house you're buying has that kind of reputation?"

"So I'm told," Sixsmythe said. "Sounds to me as if someone

at the estate agents was a bit naughty. I know – an estate agent, lying in order to clinch a sale? Surely not. It's like expecting a BMW driver to behave like an arrogant moron compensating for his erectile dysfunction." She coughed. "Anyway, it was rented out for a number of years, up until about '98, '99, I think. After that there's been a succession of owners. Some, as I said, complained of... incidents. Others didn't. But no-one actually stayed long. It might have been as little as a feeling that they weren't quite *welcome* there. But time and time again, it's gone back on the market."

"And no buyers in five years?"

"The last owner was a quite elderly lady, as I recall. Very independent soul. She fell ill – cancer of some kind – and died in the Christie hospice, in Manchester. She never reported any problems while there. Her family were scattered up and down the country. Some of her possessions they kept, the rest they sold, and the house was on the market ever since. And interestingly, while Higher Crawbeck isn't the back end of hell, it's hardly a crime-free paradise either. The premiums for buildings insurance on an uninhabited property are pretty damned high. In spite of which, the house wasn't broken into, or even vandalised, while it was on the market. And then you came."

"And woke the place up with a vengeance," Alice muttered.

"It certainly looks that way," Sixsmythe agreed. "If I'm honest, Miss Collier, I had a feeling I'd be hearing from whoever moved in there sooner rather than later, but the worst injury any civilian's suffered up until now has been a cut cheek from some broken glass. Whatever's there would seem to have a distinct interest in you, Miss Collier, which is why I suggest that if you are going to probe its mysteries, you do so at a safe distance."

"But... I mean, can't you do anything about it?"

"Such as?"

"What about an exorcism?" Alice felt a little dizzy saying the words; two weeks earlier she'd have said that only a superstitious fool would suggest it or think it could do any good.

"An exorcism?" Galatea Sixsmythe smiled at her, but it was a grim, mournful one. "My dear Miss Collier, whatever makes you think that hasn't been tried?"

"When..?"

"1989," said Sixsmythe. "A quarter of a century ago, while the Berlin Wall was falling down, two priests attempted to carry out an exorcism of 378 Collarmill Road. It didn't go very well."

"What happened?" asked John.

"One of the priests suffered a massive stroke. He never walked or spoke again for the remaining seven or eight years of his life."

"What about the other priest?"

"The other priest?" Sixsmythe winced as she stood. "The other priest," she said, picking up her cane, "still needs this to get around."

That revelation bought a moment's silence, which Alice finally broke. "I thought you said the worst injury anyone had suffered was a cut cheek?"

"No," said Sixsmythe. "I said that was the worst injury *to a civilian*. There's a marked difference between living under a wasps' nest and trying to smoke the wasps out, burn the nest or beat it flat with a shovel. Which is essentially what an exorcism boils down to. Take my advice – get out of there and read the file. Then take steps to sell the house, or rent it out – whichever you prefer. My advice, for whatever it's worth, is to sell it. Sever every possible connection to the place."

"That's it?" said Alice. She'd risen to her feet too, and was moving automatically towards the door.

"That's all the advice I can give. If what I've said hasn't convinced you, perhaps what's in here might." She'd picked up the box-file and held it out to Alice.

Alice took it. "Okay," she said. "Thanks, Reverend."

"Reverend," John said.

Sixsmythe shook hands with him. "Look after her, Mr Revell. God be with you both."

# Chapter Twenty-Three

## Smoke Without Fire

*31st October 2016*

OUTSIDE, THEY WALKED to John's car but didn't get in, not yet. The autumn air was cool and fresh after the smoky warmth of the Rector's study. Alice rested against the side of the car and breathed deep, looking at the streetlights in among the park's trees.

"You okay?" said John.

"Yeah," she said. "Just needed to clear my head."

"Not used to all that smoke, huh? Me neither. Even though I was *this* close to asking her for one."

Alice looked back at him and grinned. "Christ."

"Language!"

"Ha ha. I'd forgotten you used to smoke. You were on twenty a day when I knew you."

"Yep." John leant on his side of the car, chin resting on folded arms. "Got sent outside whenever I needed one when we lived together, even if it was pissing down or ninety below."

"It was never ninety below, John. We were living in Salford, not Helsinki."

"I'm exaggerating a little."

"A *lot*."

"Anyway, you could cope with living with a smoker better than you could a ghost hunter, right?"

"Ouch."

"Ain't digging. Just the truth."

She sighed. "I guess." She looked towards the park. "We used to live not far from here, didn't we?"

"Not far. Nice park, from what I remember."

"Really nice," she said. "Beautiful in autumn. I remember this one pathway, had huge trees on either side of it. Walking along that this time of year, with the leaves falling all around you..."

"I remember us doing that," he smiled. "Then inside for a bowl of soup."

"Or coffee."

John grinned. "Or something."

Alice laughed. "Don't get carried away, Revell."

Then she stopped laughing. There was a tree across the road, a fairly young one. The leaves... Alice crossed the road, reaching in her pocket.

"Alice?" said John.

She stopped beside the tree and looked. Yes, she'd been right – she could see the berries clustered under the blade-like leaves. She took out the Swiss Army knife, folded out a serrated blade and sawed at one of the twigs.

"Alice!" John crossed over. "What the hell are you doing?"

"It's a rowan tree," she said. "A cross of rowan wood, bound with hair."

"What?"

"I'll tell you later." She cut four twigs free in all and pocketed them. "Come on."

Alice opened the passenger door and got inside, resting the box-file on her knees. John climbed in beside her; they buckled up and he started the engine. Glancing upward, Alice saw a curtain fall back into place in a lit first-floor window in the Rectory.

"So WHAT'S THE plan?" she asked as they drove back along Bolton Road.

John drummed his fingers on the wheel. "I don't know yet. What you looking for?"

Alice rummaged through the glove box. "Sellotape?"

"Should be a roll in there."

"Yeah. Here it is."

"Okay," John said. "What do you think to this for an idea: we go back, grab what we need for an overnight stay, head back to a hotel and check out this stuff there?"

Alice pinched a few of her longer strands of hair, clipped them off and wrapped them around two crossed twigs. "What about all your ghost-hunting gear?"

"I can leave it overnight. Any weird shit happens, it'll catch it."

"That's one option," she said. She bit off a piece of tape and secured the twigs into a cross.

"You got another? You heard the Rev," said John. "Whatever the hell that is back there has a personal interest in you, baby."

"So you believe there's something there?"

John scowled. "Shit, I don't know. She talks about spirits and exorcism the way most people talk about a blocked sink. You know?"

"Yeah." Again, even a few weeks ago, Alice would have taken such talk as proof of religion's innate daftness. Now, though, the matter-of-factness and familiarity with which Sixsmythe had spoken invested her with the authority of someone talking about a subject they knew and understood very well.

"But if she's on the level, there's been all kinds of shit happening there."

"Except there's no proof any of this is supernatural, John. You know that as well as I do."

John turned onto the Broad Street roundabout at Pendleton; St Thomas' Church loomed up to the left, then fell away as they went down Broughton Road. "Yeah, okay. I know. That's why you're busy making *that*." He nodded at the cross.

Alice pushed it into her pocket. John sighed. "We got a load of old-time neighbourhood ghost stories and a bunch of weird shit that's *allegedly* happened to you." Alice had to smile at the way he emphasised *allegedly*. John was sounding more convinced than he had been a couple of hours before. "I know. Ain't nothing you couldn't have faked or hallucinated –"

"Except the spear."

"Except that. Which you could have got anywhere."

"Who are you trying to convince, John?"

"I don't know." John cleared his throat. "Okay – officially, I'm still sceptical. Unofficially? I think a night away from that place is looking like a better and better idea all the time. 'Specially if we can watch from a distance. But it's up to you."

"Better make my mind up, then." Alice tried a laugh while she said it, but it sounded brittle and false. They drove in silence for a little while; the Volvo crossed another roundabout onto Great Cheetham Street. Then he turned left and they were on Collarmill Road. Collarmill. *Colle miles rubeus*. The hill of the red knight.

"What about the house?" asked John.

Across the road, Alice could see a group of children in their Halloween costumes, plodding wearily along – homeward, she hoped – with laden carrier bags. She thought they were the group she'd seen before; one certainly wore the bright-red Devil costume that had caught her eye. "What about it?" she said.

"I mean, if it comes to what she said – selling up? Last time it went up for sale, it took five years."

"Yeah, I know." She sighed. "I've still got money in the bank," she said. "Enough to live on for a while. Maybe not enough to buy a new place outright, but I can put down a deposit. I need to find a new job, but –"

"With your qualifications, that shouldn't be too hard."

"No. Might need a place to stay in the meantime" – did his eyes flick over to her when she said that; did his lips part as if to speak? She hurried on quickly – "but I can sort that out. The bottom line is, I can handle it."

John nodded, cleared his throat again. "Okay," he said. "Here we are." He looked across at her. "You know what you want to do yet?

She took a deep breath, then chose. "Yeah. Let's get a hotel."

"Great." The Volvo pulled up in front of the house. "In and out," John said. "Grab whatever you need. *If* you need to go in. We can always pick up a change of clothes in town."

That reminded Alice of the clothes she'd bought before the meal at the Koreana – another overnight stay planned spontaneously. That, in turn, reminded her what had happened that night. "I'll pick up a couple of things," she said.

John sighed. "Okay."

She unlocked the door; he pushed past, darting into the front room. She went into the kitchen, opening the drawers until she found what she was looking for.

It was only then she realised she was still clutching the box-file. She put it on the kitchen table, pocketed what she'd taken from the drawer, then went upstairs and threw together a quick change of clothes and a make-up bag, stuffing them and her laptop into the backpack she'd bought from the charity shop.

Downstairs, she found him stuffing his laptop into his backpack. "John?" she said.

"Yo," he said, not turning around.

She took a deep breath. "There's something I should have told you. And Sixsmythe. I had another episode the other night. After the meal. That night or early in the morning. Not quite sure which."

John looked at her, frowning. "What happened?"

She told him.

"A dream," he said afterwards.

"A dream that told me about the rowan cross? I mean, that saved my arse when the children came after me again. You remember that little pyrotechnic show you caught on video? That cross caused it. There was no way I could have known."

"Subconsciously, maybe – something you read years ago and forgot about?"

"Then what about this?" She dug out the little package of folded paper, opened it out to show the tatters of red cloth. "I woke up clutching these."

John stared down, wiping a hand across his mouth.

"If it had just been a dream," she said, "then... well, it'd just be a dream. Wouldn't be any surprise if I had a nightmare or two after everything. But *this?*"

"And there was nothing else red in the room?"

"No. Just makes me wonder if moving out's going to do any good."

"Still got to be safer than here."

"But if it tries, you could be in danger too."

"Get your stuff. Alice?"

"What?"

John's manner had changed; he seemed almost shy. "Should we, uh, book two rooms or one?"

"One," she said. "Safety in numbers."

"Twin room?" he said. He didn't say *or double?* but the question was there, hovering between them.

Her answer right then would probably have been that they'd decide on the way, but she never got to speak as in that moment an alarm shrilled.

"The hell –" said John, clutching his ears.

"That one of yours?" she shouted.

He shook his head. Then she smelt it: smoke.

"Fire alarm!" John bolted out into the hallway, Alice a moment behind. The fire was in the kitchen, she could see the flames dancing. And there was someone there, silhouetted against them.

Alice ran down the hallway, John's voice raised in a shout behind her. She skidded to a halt at the kitchen door.

The fire was on the kitchen table. At its hot, brilliant heart, its outlines already beginning to shiver and crumble, was the box-file. The silhouetted figure seemed to be wearing a dress, or a long coat. It turned to face her, and Alice saw a white mask with black holes for eyes and mouth cupped in a red cowl.

"Who the fuck?" said John. "Who the *fuck*?"

The alarm screeched higher and the flames roared and swelled as the Red Man stepped towards them.

# Chapter Twenty-Four

## The Combat

*31st October 2016*

THE RED MAN advanced. Alice took a step back; John stood his ground.

"John," she hissed. He wavered but stayed where he was. For Christ's sake, no, not this, not now – the last thing she needed was John Revell trying to play the hero to impress her.

She looked from him to the Red Man. An ambiguous figure, Sixsmythe had told them: sometimes an ordinary man, sometimes a warrior, a knight; sometimes a hero, sometimes a demon. Closer too, the mask was clearly visible, and the glow of the flames, reflecting off the kitchen walls, glowed among its contours. He looked more the demon now – but at the same time, he'd saved her from the children. Had that been part of guarding the long-buried spring? But if so, was this now some part of it too?

The Red Man began to take another step towards them, then stopped, drew back his pale foot. He swivelled and stared at the table.

What was it he saw? There seemed to be something about the

box-file, or the blurred dark shape of it in the fire. But then a cold breeze was gusting down the hall, and Alice found herself turning towards it.

The children stood there. They were barefoot, the boys in ragged trousers, shirts, waistcoats and caps, the girls in torn, stained shifts. They weren't grinning this time; their faces were set and hard and their pale eyes glared. Alice fumbled in her pocket for the bony outline of the rowan cross and pulled it free, but they weren't glaring at her. No, they were looking past her and John, through the kitchen door at the Red Man.

"The fuck?" John said again. And then the wind began to rise.

'Began', in fact, was hardly the word. One moment Alice had an intimation that it was lifting above the soft strength of a breeze and the next it was driving past her with hurricane force. But it was tightly focused, a single narrow stream directed at the Red Man. The camera John had set up was flung down the hall, smashed into the wall and fell in pieces to the ground. Something slammed into Alice and threw her back against the wall. Across the hallway from her she saw John driven similarly against the plasterboard and wallpaper.

It was a hard, bruising impact that knocked the wind out of her, but it was mild compared to the wind's effect on the Red Man. He reeled, almost falling back into the fire he'd – presumably – started, then halted, steadied himself, and crouched as if to resist. But the wind's force was too much for him to stand against for more than a moment; a second later he flew backwards, shooting across the table and knocking the box-file aside before crashing headlong into the sink. He collapsed to the floor and lay still.

The fire had gone out. It seemed to Alice that it had been extinguished in the moment the Red Man struck the box-file. What really caught her eye, however, was the condition of the file itself. Smoke still rose in wisps from it and parts of it looked slightly singed, but other than that the raging fire seemed to have left it unmarked.

The pressure pinning her to the wall had stopped. She sagged, swaying and dizzy, and looked up the hallway. The children were still there, but thankfully she still wasn't the subject of their gaze. They continued to stare at the prone body of the Red Man – who, seconds later, stirred and rose to his feet, then turned to face them.

With a sweep of his arm, he knocked the table aside; Alice felt a wave of pressure pass through the open door; the children rocked and stumbled as it reached them.

The Red Man came forward, ready for battle. Little gusts of wind eddied back and forth in the hall. The children, silent, bared their teeth.

Alice heard no sound but the wind's movement and her own and John's ragged breath. Her scalp, the hair of her arms, prickled; the air was alive with static.

The swirls and gusts of air grew stronger. John clung onto the wall and Alice was almost dragged from it, her shoes slipping on the carpet. A whirlwind was building, where the opponents' strengths met. She was pulled this way, shoved that. But the trial of strength was just starting, she knew, and at its height she and John would be ripped to pieces.

That was when the roar came.

It shook the house; Alice felt the vibration of it through the wall, even as the wind and the air's static prickle died. Then it came again, and she realised it was from the street outside. Except that of course the street mightn't be a street at all, not any more.

The children and the Red Man stared at one another. Was the wind about to rise again? Did she and John have a chance to get clear before the battle recommenced, and if so, where to?

And then the children stepped aside, parting to leave a path clear. John stepped away from the wall to run through it, but Alice pushed him back. As he turned to glare at her, the Red Man stepped between them. He turned and stared at John, and Alice saw John shrink back. Then he turned and looked down at her.

"Do not trust the children," he said, in that strange, fluting voice that was four voices at once. "They want to destroy you."

And then he strode between the ranks of the children to the front door. He opened it, and outside was only a hillside lit by moonlight – that and a vast, vaguely man-like shape, bristling with fur, running towards the house.

The ogre – or, to give it its proper name, Old Harry, the Beast of Browton.

Its feet thundered on the ground and the house shook. The Red Man stepped over the threshold, hesitated for a moment, and then ran to meet the looming shape. In that moment, wind flurried down the hallway, the front door slammed shut, and the children vanished.

John stumbled away from the wall, swaying. "What?" he said. "*What?*"

"Welcome to my world," said Alice.

From outside came another roar. "What the hell do we do now?" he said.

"Before," said Alice. "The other time I ran into the Beast – the Red Man saved me. He drove it back, drove it away, or something. Said – after the last time he drove the children off, he said 'I have to keep *him* at bay.'"

"You think he meant... meant the Beast?" John stumbled over saying it, still struggling to process what he'd seen.

"I hope so. Otherwise it was something even worse." Alice went into the kitchen and prodded at the box-file, refusing to look out of the windows. It was warm to the touch, but that was all; when she opened it, the contents seemed intact.

"Fuck." John had made the mistake of looking out of the windows. Now he was staring. "Alice. *Fuck.*"

"John. John." She pulled on his arm. He blinked and looked away. "Come on."

"Where to?"

She tried to think. "Upstairs," she said at last. "My room." It probably wasn't safer than any other, but at least it would give the best view of events. Although she doubted that forewarned was forearmed in this case.

She ran up the stairs, taking the box-file; John panted behind her. At last they were at the top floor. Her bedroom door stood ajar a crack, inviting her to wonder what might be waiting inside.

Alice kicked it open. The room was empty. She breathed out, then slammed the door behind John. She doubted the actual lock on it still worked – even if she'd had a key for it – but there was a sliding catch you could push across, so she used that. It wouldn't hold the children back if they attacked with all the force they could summon, but little would – maybe not even the Red Man.

"Jesus Christ," she heard John say. "Alice. Alice. You've got to see this."

He was kneeling on the bed, staring out of the window. Alice went over to him, put down the box-file and looked.

The moon was full and bloated in a cloudless night sky, white and round, picking out their surroundings in stark detail. Below the window, below the house, the bare hillside reached down. The moonlight glittered on a ribbon of water winding down its flanks to join a curve of river that Alice assumed was the Irwell. Or had been. Or would be.

All that spread around them was heath and moor – that, and thick stretches of woodland. There were no houses that she could see, other than her own, precariously balanced somehow on Collarmill Height.

Except – wait. She saw lights gleaming on the plain below. Dim fire and candle-light, but now she saw it she could make out a huddle of low, rectangular buildings. And, gathered by them, a group of tiny stick figures.

"Look." John was pointing at the hillside. A body lay there – cloaked and hooded. As she watched, it stirred and knelt up, swaying slightly.

A deep, rattling growl sounded, shivering the window in its frame.

The Red Man shook himself, and rose to his feet.

The black woods stirred and shifted. Their perimeter swelled, gave birth to a dark shape that shook itself like a dog flinging water from its pelt and lumbered on all fours towards the hill.

"Jesus Christ," said John.

"Old Harry," said Alice.

The Beast approached the foot of the hill, slinking like a cat. It was an oddly graceful movement for something so crudely-shaped, especially when Alice remembered the stink of it and its caked, matted hide. The slitted blue eyes gleamed in the black silhouette of its body, gazing up, narrowed with hatred, at the Red Man.

Old Harry roared. The house shuddered; Alice was sure she heard things crack and shiver, heard loose dust fall and trickle. And then it bounded forward, charging up the hill towards them.

The Red Man crouched, ready to meet it. His hands rose – for what? Was he going to try and grapple with the thing? But whatever he'd planned, he had no chance to try it. The Beast snatched him up like a rag doll, whirled him round its head by one leg and smashed him into the ground once, twice, three times, before flinging him away and trudging the last yards up the hillside towards them.

*378 Collarmill Road*, Alice found herself thinking; *378 Collarmill Road.* Because that was such a normal name, because it conjured up – it *demanded* – a row of other houses like it, a street in place of bare ground, and all the twenty-first century trappings that went with that. Old Harry was heading towards 378 Collarmill Road, and that meant it couldn't be there, because it didn't belong in that world.

But they weren't in that world.

The Beast glared up at them, bared yellow fangs – knives and chisels, crammed to bursting in the stretch of its maw – and roared.

It made for the door – and behind it, the Red Man stood up.

Stood? It seemed to Alice that he didn't so much stand as *flow*

– flow back to his feet with ease and grace, brushing flecks of dirt from the undamaged red robes with his long white hands, as if there was no panic, no threat. As if he wasn't even bruised, never mind anything else – and by rights, after all, his bones should be shattered, skull crushed, ribs stoved in and driven through lungs and heart. But now he simply dusted his hands together and thrust them out after the Beast, as if lunging after it to grab its pelt, before closing them into tight fists.

Then there was a sound – that sound again that Alice had heard down on Browton Vale and in the lost garden, that sound that was between a chant and a song, a horn and a gong. It came as the Red Man pulled his hands violently towards his body, as if trying to haul something in. In the same moment he pivoted on one heel to face down the hillside, drove outwards with his fists and opened them again, releasing his hold on the air.

And the Beast, its own fists raised to pound on the house's door, flew backwards.

It hurtled past the Red Man, so fast it was a blur. The watching stick figures scattered with cries and vanished into their dwellings, and a moment later Old Harry smashed into the ground at the foot of the hill with an impact that shook the whole house. A thin hissing noise made Alice look up, and she saw plaster dust trickle from the ceiling, where the paint and paper had split.

"Jesus," she heard John say again.

She looked down and saw that where the Beast had landed there was only a hole in the ground. Perhaps it was dead? But no – something stirred in the dark and heavy, thick-fingered paws groped over the edges of the hole. Blue eyes blinked and flickered and shone in the dark and the low-browed shaggy head that bore them rose into the moonlight, teeth bared in a snarl.

The ogre – the Beast, Old Harry – pried itself from the ground and took a swaying step forward. The Red Man planted both feet square on the ground, facing it down the slope, and drew his hands back until they were level with his shoulders, palms spread.

Old Harry hesitated, lips flaring back from its teeth, and snarled. The two studied each other, waiting.

For a time it seemed as though the impasse might go on indefinitely, and Alice was about to suggest to John that they turn their attention to the box-file, but then Old Harry moved, leaping, and the Red Man thrust out both hands as far as they would go.

In the same moment, the *sound* came again, and the Beast was smacked out of the air and smashed into the ground once more. This time it didn't make a crater, but gouged a hell-deep furrow in the earth as it tore through the ground like a knife, hurtling towards the edge of the woods. When it hit, there was an almighty splintering crash Alice could hear even through the double-glazing. One tree crashed to the ground; two others lurched crazily askew and another flew through the air, uprooted wholly, before coming to earth in a thrashing and splintering of limbs.

The Red Man sagged and swayed for a moment before drawing himself erect, watching the woods. Alice watched too, with John beside her. Seconds, then minutes, ticked by, but the woods stayed still.

"Think it's dead?" John asked.

"Maybe. Wouldn't bet on it, though." Alice's voice sounded rough and croaky to her own ears, as though she'd left it disused for days. She nodded at the landscape outside. "*That's* still there."

"Then while we're waiting," said John, and scrambled off the bed to grab up the box-file, "we might as well take a look at this." He nodded at the window. "Looked like the Red Man was trying damn hard to stop us seeing it, didn't it?"

"Yeah, it did." Alice helped him get the file open. His hands were shaking, she saw, but that was hardly a surprise: so were hers. It was too dark to read, but there was a clockwork torch in her bedside drawer; she switched it on and shone it on the file.

"Where do we start, though?"

"W," she said, and sorted through the file's sections till she found that letter.

"Why W?"

"Wynne-Jones, remember?"

"Who?"

"The woman Arodias Thorne left the place to?" Alice looked up; John was frowning. "Remember? Springcross House? He left it to a Mrs Wynne-Jones. Sixsmythe said she couldn't get rid of the place fast enough. Shit."

"What?"

"Nothing there," said Alice.

"Try J, for Jones?"

Alice nodded. "Her family didn't want these papers, so they went to the Church instead. Sixsmythe made it sound as if they – fuck. Nothing here either."

John was frowning, looking down into the W section again. "Wait a minute."

"What?"

"Where was she from? This Wynne-Jones woman?"

"Why?"

"Was it Liverpool?"

"Could have been. Maybe. Yeah. I think. Why?"

John slipped a sheaf of documents free of the file. "Something from a solicitor's firm in Liverpool here. Got their letterhead on it. Look at this."

John handed over the document: a letter, typed on the stationery of J. Hughes, Garvey and Brandon, of James Street, Liverpool. "Addressed to the Dean of Manchester Diocese," he said.

*Dear Sir,*

*Regarding: Spring Cross House, Higher Crawbeck, in the City of Salford.*

*The enclosed document was dictated to my secretary by our late client, Mrs Wynne-Jones of New Brighton, in my presence, shortly before her death, with instructions that it be entrusted to the care of her family or to any relevant authority with whom the responsibility might rest.*

*Our late client's family has expressed in the strongest possible terms their unwillingness to be associated with this document in any manner, and indeed their desire to have it suppressed or destroyed on the grounds that it clearly demonstrates derangement on our client's part. Nonetheless, our client's wishes are the principal consideration here, and therefore we believe that the proper authority to undertake any study or action with respect to the enclosed rests with the Church.*

*On a private note, I would like to add that Mrs Wynne-Jones was a valued client of many years' standing. At no time during that period, nor at any time throughout the dictation of the enclosed, was I given any cause to doubt either the soundness of the lady's reason, nor her sincerity.*

*In the event of any query, or any further service that you may require, I remain,*

*Yr. obedient servant,*

*Elkanah Joseph Muddock*

Huddled together, leaning back against the bed, they began to read.

# Chapter Twenty-Five

## On Christmas Day, on Christmas Day

*The Confession of Mary Carson*

AUTUMN DEEPENED STEADILY into winter, and I settled into my new routine.

A few days into December, I was relieved of my secretarial duties. "You are now in a delicate condition," Arodias told me, "and should on no account strain or over-exert yourself." I protested – my mental faculties were quite undimmed, and my work required no physical exertion – but he brooked neither contradiction nor appeal.

I ventured out only rarely, especially when December came and snow fell lightly on the grounds. I was in a delicate condition now, carrying the master's child. I kept largely to my rooms, and the word was put about that I was unwell. I was uncertain how widely the truth was known throughout the household. Kellett knew, of a certainty, but whether or not he had told others I did not know. All depended on Arodias' commands.

Arodias, Arodias – always Arodias. By then he was supreme

master of my fate. My entire future was in his hands. Ruination awaited should I stray from the path he'd drawn for me.

I began at length to chafe at the degree of control my lover exercised over me. Even the most loving correction – for example, if he chid me for one of my now-rare walks in the garden, because of the cold – now seemed to have a ring of command, such that I was disinclined to remonstrate.

He never *did* command me, as such, or remind me of his power to cast me out – but, somehow, the threat always seemed to be there. It was no longer a conversation between lovers, or even between employer and employee: he was the master, and I must do his bidding.

And so, for the most part, I retreated to my rooms, where I could lie abed with a seemingly inexhaustible supply of novels, undisturbed save for the servants bringing me pots of tea, bowls of broth, or portions of steamed whiting.

A great fir tree was installed in the drawing-room, candles and baubles on its branches. Christmas was in the air; I wondered if it had always been thus, if Springcross House's chill atmosphere had ever thawed at this time of year, or if this change, too, I had brought about.

Nonetheless, I felt uncomfortable. Perhaps it was that I had never felt the unstinting love a mother should for the child I carried. Perhaps that hint of ruthless command behind Arodias' words and deeds, which made me ill at ease no matter how I berated myself for harbouring uncharitable thoughts towards my beloved. Even all these years later, I can't be sure.

I saw less of Arodias. He did not come to my room every night now, and on those I spent alone, I stewed in fear and uncertainty. On the nights he came, I found myself pathetically relieved to know I hadn't been forgotten. It was, he told me, the pressure of work. The new secretary he had take on while I was indisposed was not as capable, and it was harder, with pay increased and conditions improved, for Thorne Mill to produce as great a profit as in earlier days.

It was a bitter thing, Mrs Rhodes, to see the lines of care carved into my lover's face and know they were my ultimate responsibility. Therefore I contented myself with my lot. He had done much for me and pledged more still. To complain would have been demanding, selfish and ungrateful.

And then came Christmas Day…

What? My apologies, Mr Muddock, I was quite lost in recollection. Might I trouble you for a glass of the excellent brandy my husband spoke of so often? My thanks.

I was woken on the morning of Christmas Day by Arodias, bringing me gifts in bed. He brushed aside my apologies at having failed to buy any for him – how could I have, confined as I was? – and later, despite my protestations, I was brought downstairs in a bath chair for Christmas dinner. It was the bath chair I protested at, Mrs Rhodes, not the meal. Good Lord, I was chafing at the bit for a meal with some flavour and richness – one more plate of steamed whiting might have provoked me to murder! But I yielded to it. After all, he loved me, and I him.

Or so I told myself. I'd begun to wonder if my feelings for him were not at least equally rooted in desperation and necessity. One thing was for certain: I carried his child, and now depended on him.

We dined on roast goose, although 'dined' in my case might be an overstatement. I was permitted three thin slices of breast meat, a boiled potato and the merest dribble of gravy, followed by no more than a morsel of plum pudding, 'lest it prove too rich.' After much deliberation on Arodias' part, I was also permitted a sip of wine.

Arodias was kindness itself throughout the meal – indeed, those familiar with his reputation would have been astonished by the warmth of his manner. To me, though, who had come to know him far more intimately, there was a distance. We were seated at opposite ends of the table, with Kellett in constant attendance, and Arodias' table talk consisted only of conventional solicitudes.

It is more than possible, I can assure you both, to feel lonely beyond all words when every outward indication should point to the contrary.

"You look tired, Mary," said Arodias, wiping his lips with his napkin. "Kellett, please take Miss Carson back to her room so she may rest. I merely follow the doctor's advice, dearest," he added when I tried to object. "He understands your present needs far better than either of us."

He came to my end of the table, gently drew his fingertips down my cheek and kissed my hand. Then he leant in close and whispered, "I shall come to you later tonight, my dear."

AND SO I waited in my room, and I read because there was nothing else to do. Soon bored, I sat by the window and looked over the snow-covered gardens. For what seemed the first time, my gaze rose to take in the city beyond them, spread out like a black stain upon the land, a foul jumble of mire, brick and pain, its chimneys pouring black smoke to stain the pale sky. For an instant, I even thought I heard a thousand voices, crying out in anguish...

I tried to return my attention to the garden, but couldn't; that is, I could no longer simply blot out what lay outside Springcross House's walls. I felt as though I were on the brink of – dare I say – a revelation? Some great change in my understanding of things? But at that moment, the bedroom door opened and Arodias came in.

"Darling," I said, forcing a smile, but he neither answered, nor did his face show a smile in return. He locked the bedroom door, crossed the room and did the same to the windows before pulling the curtains shut.

At last he turned to face me, then crossed the room to sink into a chair. "Oh," he said inconsequentially, "something I had forgotten to mention."

"Yes, Arodias?"

"Yes. What was it – ah, that's right. There will be no wedding."

He took a cigar from his pocket and lit it with a match. "You've no objection, I take it?"

"What?" I said.

He held up the cigar. "To my smoking, I mean."

I shook my head. I confess I was utterly bewildered, Mr Muddock – that single casual phrase, if I had truly heard it, if it was sincere, had shattered everything. I could not believe I could have heard aright. "But... the wedding, Arodias?"

"I told you," he said, as if to a slow child, "there will be no wedding."

"But..." I sat on the bed, swaying, feeling weak. The room seemed to spin around me. "But... Arodias, why?"

"Christmas," he said. "Oh, I should probably mention that as well: it's quite meaningless to me from the religious point of view. All that fol-de-rol about fearing God's judgement and the life to come – all nonsense, I'm afraid, although it was rather useful, wasn't it, in gaining your affections?"

"Arodias, this joke is very poor taste – "

"Joke, Mary? Whyever should you think I am joking? As I was saying, Christmas is a meaningless event to me as far as religious feeling goes, but it is, by tradition, a time of celebration, of joy, of the giving of gifts. And so this is my gift to myself, Mary: honesty. You have no idea how wearying the pretence has become."

He drew deeply on his cigar and smiled in satisfaction. "I suppose I ought also to tell you that you are sadly in error regarding your influence over me. Your work as my secretary was purely a matter of convenience. And in the unlikely event that you haven't already realised, your influence over my actions or judgement is non-existent. I have done nothing, since engaging you, at variance with my own will."

As he said this, he smiled while watching me as a naturalist might study some new-caught animal.

"When first I heard of you, you were of little interest to me, until reports of your physical charms followed. When I met you in person, I knew you would be perfect for my purposes, which were twofold: satisfying my carnal appetites, and providing myself, through you, with a child." He smirked. "Neither was particularly difficult."

Does that shock you, Mr Muddock, Mrs Rhodes? It shocked me. I thought I had found love, and instead I'd found only the cruellest deception. The worst of it was the casual plainness with which he told me, as if to say, *Yes, I have done this. What can you do about it? Nothing. Nothing at all.*

"Conditions at the Thorne Mill remain exactly as they were before, and profits high as ever as a result. The gentleman you met, Mr Hardman? An actor, Mary, nothing more. I trust he gave a creditable performance? He was well paid for it."

Still he watched me, gloating over every sign of distress – and these were plentiful, for I could not hold them back. Arodias Thorne used words as a vivisectionist uses knives.

Forgive me, Mr Muddock, forgive me – I will need only a moment. To revisit such memories, even after so long, can be painful indeed.

"But why you, Mary, why you?" he went on. "That's the question you ask yourself now, isn't it? Out of all the women in the land, why you? Why not simply marry? Well, I did. I did. And she was entertaining in her way, for a time. But now she's gone, I've no desire to surrender myself once more to domesticity. I wanted a child. Nothing more, nothing less."

I gripped the bedsheets in handfuls. They were solid and tangible, and therefore real. I sought to cling onto some sense of reality. "Surely any common whore or slattern would have served your turn, for sufficient pay."

"True." He shrugged. "But even discounting the threat of disease, what good could come of breeding with such degenerate stock? No, my child must be *clean*, and the mother refined and educated and above all, if possible…" Oh God. I can't forget how he smiled then, or the look in his eyes when he said it. "...a virgin. You were all this, and pious, moral, upright. I will admit that I enjoyed the game. And there was some incidental pleasure gained from the whole business. In my experience, the more pious the woman, the more licentious she is at heart, if only she can be induced to admit it. But now I'm weary of the pretence."

I don't know if you will understand me if I say I felt the world was disappearing from me, falling apart and leaving me in a void. Everything – everything was being taken away, or had already been. My faith, my trust, any sense of my own worth or value. I could have died at that moment. I certainly wanted to.

"You were interesting, anyway, for a time," he went on. "Most people only pretend to be motivated by anything other than their own appetites. With them it's just a case of finding some acceptable cover. But you were one of those few who delude themselves. So I had to construct a more cunning and elaborate tale to snare you. Still, if nothing else, I think you'll agree in the end that I have made you a sadder but wiser woman."

I was torn between wanting to die and wanting to kill him. Had I only been able to lay hands on a weapon, any weapon, I would have flung myself on him. His life first, and then my own. But there was nothing to hand. My lover had been careful in these matters.

Very well, then. He had ruined and shamed and destroyed me and in the eyes of all decent society I would be at best a fool, at worst a whore, but I would not stay to see him gloat. Rather would I spend my night on the streets and sleep in honest filth, or drown myself in the Irwell, than give him another moment's satisfaction. Galvanised by the decision, I scrambled from the bed and hunted for my dress.

"Well," said Arodias, "what's this then? Wherever do you think you're going, Mary dear?"

"You have had your enjoyment from me, Mr Thorne," I told

him – I *did* tell him, I *did* – "but you'll have no more. I would rather starve than spend another night under your roof."

He roared with laughter, but when I started for the door, having gathered enough clothes to achieve some semblance of modesty, he called my name liltingly. I tried to pretend he was not there, but of course, the door wouldn't open, and I finally looked back to see Arodias dangling the key to the room. The smirk upon his lips was so vile and self-contented I could have killed him for that alone.

"The key, please, Mr Thorne," I said.

A snorted giggle escaped him and he shook his head. "Do you really think you could escape, in your condition?" he said. "Or that if you did, you would not be found?"

"Give me the key, Arodias."

He shook his head. "You're mine, Mary. Bought and paid for. And what I have, I hold. Nobody leaves me until I allow it."

I closed in on him. There might not be a knife or pair of scissors to hand, but I wasn't entirely without weapons. My fingernails were more than long and sharp enough to rend the flesh of his cheeks, to blind him if I could only get to his eyes. Do I shock you, Mr Muddock? Mrs Rhodes? Oh, but consider what he had done to me. Is it any surprise that in my desperation I felt capable of any act of violence against him? After all, I hardly had anything left to lose by now, and the man or woman pushed to that extremity of desperation is to be feared. For they may be capable of anything.

Perhaps that same thought occurred to him just then. More likely it had occurred to him long before, of course, because when I took another step towards him his smile vanished. He made as if to retreat – then lunged forward, taking me by surprise. He caught my hand and bent two fingers back, and instantly I cried out in agony. He forced me to my knees and stood over me, smiling grimly down.

"Understand me, Mary. You will, as you put it, remain under my roof, or you will find yourself in lodgings far less congenial.

I will have you declared insane, Mary, and committed to an asylum. You have no other kin, after all, and as your concerned employer I shall act *in loco parentis*. The child? A bastard conceived by some below-stairs dalliance, the father unknown or absconded. You will have gone mad from disappointment, and no-one will credit your fantasies about your upright and respected employer Mr Thorne. In any event you will carry my child to term: I shall see to that. And the child shall come to me, for my purposes. That will happen, no matter what. But once in the asylum, Mary, there you shall remain. Mad, Mary, mad. In filth and alone, and the plaything of the brutes that administer such places. For all the days of your life. Have I made myself clear?"

I had never been to an asylum for the insane, but had heard enough tales of what abuses might be practised on its helpless inmates. Such a fate would be the closest thing to a living Hell that I could imagine. With Arodias' wealth and influence, such a solution would be simplicity itself, far easier than murder: no inconvenient corpse to dispose of, and anything I said dismissed out of hand as a madwoman's ravings. Indeed, telling the truth would only confirm my lunacy. It gives one pause for thought – does it not, Mr Muddock, Mrs Rhodes – to think how many poor wretches in such places may in truth be innocent victims, of men like Arodias Thorne?

"Or..." he continued, "you can be sensible. Reasonable. Amenable to my will. If you do so, you will not only escape the asylum, but I shall see to it that you are well-provided for." A smile. "For services rendered, one might say."

I said nothing, for in truth what could I say? In a matter of minutes my whole world had fallen apart – my hopes and dreams for the future, every foundation I had built on for the remainder of my life. I was as lost as a drowning sailor, clinging to a spar in the stormy sea. And he knew that, and delighted in it.

He studied me. "I think I see a hint of defiance in your eye, Mary. A pity, but no matter. It will pass." He released my hand.

"We understand each other now. I think you can be trusted to behave in a reasonable manner."

I must now beg a moment's indulgence of you, Mrs Rhodes. And, perhaps, your forgiveness. There are things we do not speak of, not in so-called polite society. You may feel I have spoken more than enough of such matters already. But I must make my confession in full. You would have an old woman's eternal gratitude, Mrs Rhodes – for whatever that is worth – if you could steel yourself to record it.

Thank you. So, to resume my tale:

I bowed my head, my hands clenched into fists in my lap. "Is that all, Mr Thorne?" I said, with all the cold formality I could muster. I was determined to salvage what dignity I could. Of course, that was easier on my feet than on my knees, so I began to rise. But his hand descended on my shoulder, pushing me back down.

"Not quite, Miss Carson," he said. "Our nightly visits have been few and far between of late. I believe I have denied myself the pleasures of the bed too long in deference to your condition. But we shall remedy that now."

"Never!"

He sighed. "You disappoint me, Mary. I thought we had established that you would be *reasonable*."

I glared up at him. "What will you do, Arodias? Will you force me when I carry your precious child, and endanger its life?"

He laughed. "Why, when where is no need? The asylum, Mary, the madhouse. It is only to my advantage to keep you here if you are not troublesome. Now" – he reached for his belt – "for now, remain kneeling, if you please."

# Chapter Twenty-Six
## The Grail Spring

*The Confession of Mary Carson*

Be warned: there is more to come, much of which will be hard for either of you to believe. I was there, and struggle to credit it. At times I could almost believe what followed was a delusion or fever dream, but only almost. It was real. However, I do not require your belief. Only that you record what I have to say.

After Arodias had done with me, he left me in the room, weeping and bereft. But if I had thought my humiliation complete, in truth it had barely begun.

The following day, he resumed his accustomed routine with me as though nothing had happened. His nightly visits resumed in frequency, also. He was neither rough nor violent – there was the child to consider, after all – but he took me always without tenderness, revelling in freedom to use me however he wished, and his demands grew more... perverse. And it shames me to admit that I feared him too greatly to do anything but acquiesce.

The New Year came and went, and 1837 passed into history.

And then, on the last night of January, 1838, he came to my room as had become his wont, but what he did that night – I still consider it something of a minor miracle I did not miscarry from the horror of it. God alone knows what my fate would have been had I done so.

At the time the only explanation I could think of was that perhaps mere obedience had not been enough. Perhaps he had seen glimmers of hatred and defiance in my eye, and resented even that level of resistance. I thought so at the time, but... now, when I look back, I think the explanation is a simpler one.

Arodias had revealed himself to me in a way that he did to few others – most of them already corrupt and loathsome individuals such as Kellett. There was a special pleasure to be gained in it for him. All that mattered to Arodias Thorne was himself – his pride and vanity, his belief in himself as superior, magnificent, a man of genius, as one who had shaken off the bonds of convention. My horror and disgust was a source of pleasure to him – the fear of a sheep for a wolf.

And so, I believe, it went against the grain for him to conceal any part of his intentions, or any part of cruelty. That is the only explanation for what took place that night.

He had come to my room and made his accustomed use of me. Having satiated his desires, he left me on the bed and dressed, not speaking a word, before finally calling my name and beckoning me, without even turning round.

I rose from the bed and approached, still unclothed. Arodias turned to face me. He was smiling, and such was the gloating cruelty in it that I took a step back at once.

"Kellett!" he called.

The key turned in the lock behind me, and the butler slipped through. I cried out, trying to cover myself. What fresh perversion was this? Was I to couple with Kellett now, for Arodias' amusement? It shames me to say, Mr Muddock and Mrs Rhodes, that that might have been preferable to what was to follow.

Arodias motioned to me. "Restrain her, would you Kellett?"

"With pleasure, sir." The butler kicked the door shut and locked it, pocketing the key. Before I could move to evade him Kellett caught my arm, twisting it up behind my back. I howled. Surely someone must have heard – I remember thinking that very clearly. But then, I had never had any friends at Springcross House. Only Arodias, and I had been wrong even about that. I could scream all I wanted, and no help would come.

"Oh, and show a little care, Kellett." Arodias smirked again. "She's carrying my child."

"Of course, sir," said Kellett, pressing himself against me. He was aroused; I could feel it, and it make me sick.

Arodias came closer as Kellett pulled me to my feet. "I'm going to show you something, Mary," he said. His breath blew hot and rank in my face, like that of some panting beast, and it stank like carrion. "I'm going to show you what manner of man I truly am." His lips were wet; he wiped them on his sleeve. "The key," he told Kellett. The butler handed it over.

"Good," Arodias said, unlocking the door. "Bring her."

As Arodias stepped outside and Kellett dragged me to the door, I heard voices – male and female – and realised the landing outside my room was occupied.

I gasped and dug my heels into the carpet. Surely Arodias would not allow this, I thought. Surely he would at least cover my nakedness, or wait until all was clear before dragging me outside.

But then I heard laughter from the landing, and I realised the truth in the moment before Kellett forced me over the threshold.

The maids and manservants of Springcross House were gathered on the landing – Arodias' creatures, his spiritual brood – and as I was paraded before them they howled and jeered. What a fool I had been, to wonder why the servants had all seemed low, venal and unpleasant: such were the people Arodias Thorne surrounded himself with.

And now you look pale, Mrs Rhodes, for which I can hardly blame you. Nor you too, Mr Muddock. Perhaps you doubt my honesty – or my sanity. No matter. If you do not doubt it yet, be assured you shall have ample cause to do so before we are done.

I had one arm free, and struggled to protect what modesty I had left – but should I seek to cover my breasts, my womanly parts or the belly that proclaimed me a fornicator, bearer of Thorne's bastard? My arm went from one to the other, until Kellett decided the issue, shifting his grip on my twisted arm to hold it fast with one hand, then seizing my free arm at the wrist. That arm too was twisted painfully behind my back, leaving me totally exposed as I was manhandled down the stairs to the hall.

As God is my judge, Mrs Rhodes, I do not think I have ever came so close to genuine despair as then. I do not mean that I despaired of escaping or surviving – although if not, I came close to it. I mean despair at the world, at humankind itself. Had my father claimed the African as part of that family, the white man's equal? If so, he had ill-served them. If these around me were men, they were vile creatures indeed, baying like dogs and gloating at another's misery. I looked from face to face, seeking not help, but a glimmer of pity or compassion. There was none; only a revelling delight.

Kellett shoved me down a darkened corridor; Arodias led the way with a raised lantern. For all his talk of a child, I was half-certain they meant to kill me – but at least that baying crowd was gone. At least my death would be a private affair. Truth to tell, Mrs Rhodes, by that point I would have at least half-welcomed it.

Arodias flung open the doors to the music room. "Through here," he snapped, and marched inside, towards the French windows. Outside, the icy wind raged and white snow swirled against the glass. I shrank back, thinking perhaps he meant to cast me outside, naked as I was, into the gardens I'd once loved.

Kellett twisted my arms up tighter, sniggering through his teeth. Foul, foul, hateful man. I loathed him even more than my treacherous lover just then. Should I ever find the opportunity, I vowed, he would die a thousand deaths.

At the French windows, Arodias pulled the curtains shut, then knelt and pulled back the carpet. Underneath, set in the bare wooden boards, was a trapdoor. He flung it open, and cold air blew into the room from below. Arodias lifted the lantern; its light played over his face as he smiled that smile at me again. And then he'd climbed down through the trapdoor and disappeared from view.

Kellett dragged me to the trap and threw me down on the floor, then lit a lantern of his own. "Get down there," he said. "Right now. Or I'll take a whip to your pale arse and stripe it."

There was undisguised lust in his voice when he said it. I hurried to obey, just to escape him. Below the trap was a kind of chute of glazed red bricks, like the inside of a chimney. The light from Arodias' lantern gleamed off them, and on a series of metal rungs. Arodias was at the bottom, staring up. I didn't dare look at Kellett, who, just then, I feared even more than him. I began climbing down.

I must have climbed twenty or thirty feet, which I guessed placed me below even the level of Springcross House's cellars. I gasped in pain often as I went; my feet were bare and the rungs were not only searing cold, but narrow and almost jagged in places with rust. It was worse still when I reached the floor below, which was a mix of earth, water, gravel and loose rock.

We stood, I realised, inside a brick tunnel. The dank air was bitterly cold and I shivered, teeth chattering, stumbling away from the chute as Kellett climbed down. Arodias, almost gently, draped a blanket around my shoulders. I flinched but didn't move away; better even him than Kellett. Or so I thought until Arodias leant close to me and whispered in my ear.

"Have you finished your snivelling, Mary, or is there more

to come? It is most irritating, I must say. But not uncommon down here."

As I listened, I heard other voices, echoing down the tunnel. They seemed to come from either end and were little more than whispers and moans, but one resolved itself into a sobbed, despair-filled "Please..." such as I never wish to hear again.

"Shut up!" barked Kellett.

"Quiet," said Arodias. "Or there will be punishment. Yes, punishment." He turned to Kellett. "I'm going to show Miss Carson what all this has been for. But actions speak loudest, so I believe a demonstration is in order. Fetch a specimen."

"Yes, sir."

"For preference, whichever one just called out."

"Very good, sir," said Kellett, and moved away from us down the tunnel.

Arodias smiled at me and caressed my cheek. I wanted to recoil, but was too afraid to move. "Ha!" he said, then twisted a handful of my hair until I cried out. In the glow of the lamp I barely recognised him: neither as the tender yet virile lover – that pretence was destroyed beyond hope of restoration – nor the stern patriarch I'd met on my first day. His face was greasily slick with sweat and his breath came in hoarse panting sounds. His eyes never blinked and his mouth stayed twisted into that leering grin, save when he licked his lips.

"With me," he breathed at last, and leant close to lick sweat and drying tears from my face.

He pushed me along the tunnel, my hair in one hand and the lamp in the other. As we went I saw metal doors set into the tunnel's brick walls at regular intervals on either side, each with a barred window. From each came moans and cries, and a reek of filth and decay – and fumbling through bars came outstretched hands, almost black with filth but, under it, sickly-pale from lack of light.

"Back!" cried Arodias. "Back in your holes. I'll make use of you soon enough."

The tunnel bent around. He forced me along – my feet were soon cut and bleeding – until at last it opened into a semi-circular chamber in which the only sound was the dripping of water. The air was colder still – I could see my breath now – and the ground damper underfoot. Something else was different about this ground, I realised; it was uneven, and, although still gritty, softer than the tunnel floor.

Arodias turned to me.

"I shall," he said, "now endeavour to shed a little light on our situation." His smile was calm, composed, though no less cruel. "That means I must leave you where you are. You might be tempted to act foolishly. To run. You will understand, of course, why that would be silly. Even if you evaded Kellet and I and retraced the way you came, back into the house – what then? No servant of mine will help you, or look the other way. You would have to run into the winter's night, naked as the day you were born. And what then? Who will believe your wild stories about a respected local businessman? The asylum Mary – remember, the asylum. And be assured, Mary, that I will still have what I want." He motioned to my gravid belly. "If however, you're a good girl – if you do exactly as I tell you, exactly when I tell you – then you might not only leave Springcross House alive, but without a stain on your character and with every prospect of a secure and happy future. Well?"

"Do you expect me to believe that?" I sad at last. It was, I know, a poor response, Mrs Rhodes, but when one makes allowance for the circumstances I could have managed far worse. Arodias smiled.

"Probably not," he said, "although it is, in fact, true. I *do*, however, know you will believe I have both the means and the will to consign you to such a fate. Do you have any such doubt, my pretty little naked Mary?" His gaze roved over my body in the lantern-light.

"No," I said.

He smiled at me again, and the lantern's glow shone in his eyes like fire. "Then you'll see," he said, "that any slender hope of your escaping the madhouse rests on your continuing to please me. So I believe I can trust you to remain where you are."

Without another word he released my hair and vanished into the trickling shadows of that place. There was a scraping; a match flared. Light blossomed from a second lantern, hanging from the ceiling. A few moments later, he struck another match, and with it lit another. He repeated this procedure three more times; when he was done, the light filled the chamber and I could see where he had brought me.

The walls were stone and brick. The stone ceiling, about ten feet above the ground, was buttressed by heavy wooden beams. The floor was raw earth, dotted with mushrooms, in which worms and beetles crawled, and curved very slightly upwards, like a low hillock or knoll.

The room had only two features of note. The first was a sort of chair, although no chair in which I would want to sit – a single glance was enough to tell me that. It was bolted to a large steel plate, which in turn was bolted fast to the floor. There were leather straps to hold limbs and head into position, and clamps that I could only suppose were to prise the sitter's eyelids open so that they could not choose but look at what was before them. But these, Mrs Rhodes, were not the worst.

Mounted on the chair's frame on a variety of metal armatures was an array of probes, blades, hooks and wires, all connected to a sprawling, intricate clockwork mechanism fitted beneath the chair. Jutting up from this was a long brass lever with a carved handle of ivory, which, I assumed, set the whole monstrous engine in motion. Once the picture had formed in my mind of what the thing would do, I flinched from the very sight of it.

The room's other distinguishing feature was a sort of alcove, set into the centre of the semicircular room's straight wall; in it rose a broad thick hump of rock, about half again as tall as me. Dirt and chunks of moss clung to it, and there was an irregularly-shaped hole in it, large enough for a grown man to enter if he stooped – the entrance, I realised, to a cavern of some kind. I could not see how far back the cave went, but it echoed with a sound of trickling water, and from its mouth ran a bright, glittering rivulet that poured down the rocks to collect in a pool beneath.

Even in the dim lamplight, I could see the pool's water was crystal-clear. The bottom of it was smooth, almost polished-looking rock, with the thinnest layer of sand. I recall thinking that it could not be a natural formation, because in shape it was a perfect bowl. From it led a small, brick-lined channel that conducted a steady stream of water across the chamber to a grille at the chamber's outer edge.

"A spring," said Arodias. "Where we stand, Mary, was formerly Collarmill Height – the summit of what the locals, in my youth, called Redman's Hill. There was a church here, once; before that, a shrine of one kind or another. There was a crossroads too, of course. People once came from far and wide to visit this spring, as it was considered a holy well. Its waters healed the sick, gave sight to the blind, imparted knowledge of the past or future. Hence, Springcross House." He did not look at me as he spoke; instead he studied the streamlet and the pool.

"It took many years of patient work to restore this," he said. "Cromwell's barbarians filled it in during the Civil War. So much to be done, and all in secret. So I heaped fresh earth over the church's ruins, and built Springcross House atop them. And then under it all, I dug, and I searched, until I found what I had sought. And then reshaped the earth again to fit my design. It took much work, and great expense. But the shrine has been uncovered, the source allowed to flow free again."

"Source?" I demanded. "And why must it all be secret?" I was tired, angry and afraid, and had had my fill of his games. Of course, no sooner had I given vent to my brief flare of defiance than I flinched in terror of its consequences. Arodias, however, only chuckled.

"The source of the Craw," he said, "which flows yonder to join with the Irwell. Hence, Crawbeck. Craw – or, in earlier times, Crawl, from Graal, or Grail." He pointed at the spring. "The spring-waters once granted much to those who drank or bathed in them, Mary. But there is more – much more, as you shall see."

He turned and looked at me. "This, Mary, is far more than just a spring. As I say, it was a holy place for centuries. Thousands of years. Before Christ hung from his cross on Golgotha – if, indeed, he ever did. Perhaps even before Moses wandered in the desert or took down the Commandments on Mount Sinai. The spring itself is no more than a symbol, if you can imagine that. Perhaps you can – an intelligent woman like yourself, an educated one. You accept, do you not, that there are two worlds? Yes?"

"Two worlds?"

"Worlds, Mary! Worlds! The one we see and live in, day to day, and the one we *cannot* see. The invisible world. The realm of angels and demons, gods and monsters. Yes?"

"Yes," I said at last. It wasn't quite the language of my father's faith, but I understood its meaning clearly enough.

"The visible world is only a layer, a crust. Surely you understand that, Mary?"

"I believe that I have an immortal soul that will survive my body's destruction, if that is what you mean."

He shook his head. "No. No. That's not what I mean. Not quite. There *is* something that we might call a God, Mary. But He neither created us nor watches our every move. Heaven and Hell, Jesus, the Virgin Mary – these are no more than fairy tales we tell ourselves to make the vastness of Creation a less frightening place. The same with the Jews and their Torahs, the Mohammedans and their Koran. The truth is simpler, and very different. And, to the weak and frightened, terrifying. To Him, we are less than insects. Tiny motes. We exist, and then we don't. Nothing more. And yet – and yet – if we are wise, and seek for knowledge – seek it no matter what bars the path to it – we might know Him. Might claim the tiniest morsel of His power. Knowledge of the past, or the future. Healing. Even life eternal. *That* is the only immortality a human being can claim. When you die, Mary, you are but dust in the wind."

He cupped a hand under the flowing stream. The water shone and glimmered. He opened his fingers, and it fell like a rain of diamonds. "People came here to worship, Mary," he said, "and to sacrifice – yes, to sacrifice. Not to the spring itself, but to what it symbolised, what lay beyond it. They called it the Fire Beyond."

He crouched before the bowl-shaped pool. "There would always be a seer," he said. "A priest would work himself into an ecstatic trance through meditation. That, or a sacrifice would make the Fire manifest itself. Through my researches, I have concluded that a certain mental state is necessary to perceive the Fire Beyond. Either the priest's trance, or the sacrifice's suffering, reaching a pitch where he or she is beyond pain. Then they see the Fire Beyond, and in seeing it, they reveal it to others..."

He trailed off. By now, I was staring at him. He chuckled. "You think I'm mad, don't you?" He wagged a finger at me. "You think I'm insane."

As you will, I'm sure, be completely unsurprised to hear, Mr Muddock and Mrs Rhodes, that is exactly what I thought, but given my situation I considered discretion the better part of valour.

"That is no surprise," he said. "But no matter. No matter. I have a demonstration all arranged. Kellett!"

"Sir." The butler's voice came out of the darkness beyond the lantern-light, from the opposite side of the chamber.

"You have one?"

"Here, sir."

"Then bring him."

# Chapter Twenty-Seven

## The Moloch Device

*The Confession of Mary Carson*

KELLETT MARCHED INTO the light, his lantern in one hand; the other restrained a gaunt, pale thing, naked but for a few tatters of soiled cloth, that was, or had been, a boy.

He was very pale and thin – his eyes, I remember, seemed enormous in his poor starved face. I remember this, Mrs Rhodes: every maternal impulse that I had tried and failed to feel for the child I carried seemed now to wake, directing itself at this other victim of Arodias Thorne.

"Thank you, Kellett," Arodias said, taking the lantern from the butler's hand. "Now if you'll put him in place, please."

"No!" shrieked the boy. Thin and famished as he was, his voice rang clear, for all the good it did in that place. "Please, sir, not that. Please just kill me. Please! Just cut my throat, sir, please!" I cannot forget that, Mrs Rhodes: I cannot forget how I heard a child beg for death.

"Quiet." Kellett cuffed the boy on the side of the head. He slumped, dazed.

"Careful, Kellett," Arodias said. "Don't damage him."

"Sir."

Arodias nodded. Kellett dragged the boy to the chair.

"Arodias, no!" I caught at his arm, but he threw me off and I stumbled away, losing the blanket in the process.

"Never," he said through his gritted teeth, "*never* put your hands on me again. Not without my express permission. And *never* tell me what I can or cannot do. Remember where you are, Mary, and where you will go at a word from me." At a nod from him, Kellett, having stripped the boy of his few remaining rags, shoved him into the chair and secured his limbs with the cuffs and straps.

"You can't change his fate," Arodias told me. "Or that of the other wretches down here. They're like you, Mary. I bought them, I own them, they belong to me. *I* decide – I and no-one else. You can either learn from what I show you, or die as a madwoman. Is he ready, Kellett?"

"He is, sir."

Arodias waved the butler away. "As I've told you, Mary, the Fire Beyond could only be seen by the priest in his trance – or through the sacrifice, in his suffering. A human sacrifice, of course. In olden days, they had to create the necessary mental state manually: a messy business and a clumsy one, and not particularly efficient. With luck, through such methods, they might see the Fire Beyond for the blinking of an eye. But as with so much else, the right machine can do the job faster, more neatly, and far more effectively."

"Please!" The boy in the chair began screaming again. "Please, Mr Thorne, please – I'll do anything – I'll be good – I'll –"

Arodias reached down, and the boy's screams were stifled. When Arodias stepped aside I saw a rubber ball, secured on each side by a leather strap, had been forced into the boy's mouth. "There's a risk of the subject choking on its tongue," Arodias said, "but the noise is distracting. Now, come here."

He glanced at my nakedness and scowled. "And cover yourself up, for God's sake."

I wrapped the blanket around myself. I hated jumping so easily to his commands – but I was, after all, at his capricious mercy and bitterly cold to boot. The only reason I had not reached for the blanket before was fear of how he might react to my making another movement without his permission.

I approached. "Closer, please," he said. "*Closer* than that, Miss Carson. Now. See. Observe the intricacy of the mechanism. I designed it myself. I am far more than just another businessman, Miss Carson. Far, far more."

He stroked the chair; the boy whimpered through the gag. "I call this mechanism the Moloch Device. I'm sure you'll appreciate the relevance of the name. But now, watch – and learn."

He pushed the brass lever forward. The boy's cries and whimpers rose to a crescendo – then ceased as the lever moved, with a dull clunking sound, into position.

The first cogs stirred and shifted, grinding against their neighbours. Then these, too, began to turn, until the whole mass of cogs and gears, wheels and levers, was in motion, like a morass of brightly-shelled insects swarming over a corpse to pick it clean. Through all of this the boy in the chair stared out at me, with wide, pleading eyes.

And then the other parts of the machine began to move.

A hook sank into flesh, before rising upwards, lifting a tent of skin in its wake. A blade pierced, cut, then cut again. A little blue flame flicked into life, and the three-inch length of stiffened wire above it glowed first red, then white, before sliding home with horrid precision. The boy shrieked and bellowed against the gag, face scarlet, his screwed-shut eyes seeping tears.

"Watch!" barked Arodias as I turned away. I forced myself to obey. If I could do nothing else, I vowed, I would be a witness, I would testify and record. Although as you and Mrs Rhodes are no doubt thinking, Mr Muddock, I have been all too tardy in keeping my vow.

I could not say how long that dreadful process took, for there was no way to reckon time. It seemed to last for hours upon hours, and no doubt it seemed so to the boy. Arodias' machine was indeed ingenious, I will grant him that. Ingenious, and an abomination. Over that period of time, however long it was, I watched it cut, tear, flense and burn until the boy's ghost-white skin was a horror of red and black – fresh blood and dried, raw flesh and charred skin. And still the Moloch Device worked, until white bone gleamed through the carnage, and all the while the boy shrieked and shrieked against the gag –

"There. There!" Arodias seized my arm. "Look. Look there. Now!"

He was pointing, of course, towards the spring. I tore my gaze at last from the atrocity in the chair; looked, and saw.

The waters of the spring were burning. Not an ordinary fire; cold, blue, lambent flames that danced on the surface of the pool and the water streaming from the rock, and lit the glistening walls of the cave.

"That," said Arodias, "comes from the Fire Beyond, and gives those waters the power they possess. But it isn't the Fire Beyond itself. Keep looking, Mary – keep looking and you may see."

I obeyed; it freed me, at least, from witnessing the Moloch Device's bloody work. The only distractions were the muffled, fading screams of the boy in the chair. The blue flames danced brighter, brighter – and then the rock and water themselves disappeared, almost completely: they became shadows of themselves, ghosts. The bowl-shaped pool remained, but now it was empty of water; in its place was a column of pale blue fire that brushed the chamber roof.

I saw it only for a moment, but... I do not think I could ever fully describe the nature of the experience. If you ever looked into a fire as a child and saw shapes in it – faces, figures – it was a little like that, except there were so many shapes, so many things. If I looked long enough, I thought I might fully understand what I was looking at, and I thought I might see...

everything, Mrs Rhodes, Mr Muddock. What had been, what was to come. Perhaps even the face of God Himself. To do so, of course, might kill me or drive me mad, but it might be a price worth paying.

And then it was gone, and there was only the water trickling from the cave, no longer afire, and the chamber was silent but for the churning of the Moloch Device's gears and cogs.

"There," said Arodias. "There we are. You saw?"

"Yes," I said, and turned. I rather wish I had not done so, for then I saw what the machine had left of that poor boy. But, having seen, I forced myself to record every detail, as penance for having looked away at all.

Arodias pulled the lever back to its 'off' position; the Moloch Device wound down into silence, and those bloodied hooks and blades fell still. The boy lay still, his torment at least at an end, his dissected corpse steaming in the chamber's chill air.

"WHAT YOU SAW in that final moment, Mary, was the Fire Beyond."

Arodias Thorne said this to me on the morning of the 1st day of February, 1838. Up until that point I had almost convinced myself that the previous night's events had been a nightmare. Almost, but not quite – not enough to dare venture from my room and face any member of Arodias' staff, much less Kellett or Arodias himself.

After the Device had ceased its work, Arodias had summoned Kellett once more, and the two of them had taken me out of that chamber. I went without demur, for I was almost numb from what I had seen; the beauty and rapture of the Fire Beyond on the one hand, and on the other the obscenity that was the Moloch Device.

On returning to my rooms, two maids took charge of me. I heard Arodias instruct Kellett to 'dispose of the used specimen' and clean the Device before closing off the chamber once more. A bath was drawn. I was washed and dressed in a clean nightgown, then led back to my bed and tucked in like a child. I knew both maids for hard, coarse, slatternly women, but they were almost gentle with me then. Did they know what went on in that secret chamber? Or was my condition such that they pitied me, no matter how they'd despised me before? I shall never know.

One of them put a cup to my lips. There was a drink, warm and sweet – hot milk with honey, I think. And after that, nothing, until I woke the following morning, with bright clear light filtering through the curtains.

"You're awake." Another maid – not one of those that had tended me – stood beside the bed. "I'll let Master know." She was gone before I could speak. I lay there, trying to decide whether the previous night's events had been real, or a fevered dream. In my warm bed, in clean linen, they seemed impossible.

"Ah, Mary," Arodias said. "You're awake." He planted a chaste kiss on my forehead and sat beside the bed. "And how are you today?"

He was smiling, but his eyes were fixed and cold. It was the Arodias I'd seen for the first time last night. And so then I knew; had I not been lying down I would have fallen. As if from a distance, I heard Arodias chuckle.

"Yes," he said, "you remember, Mary, do you not? Good, very good. You saw the Fire Beyond – that is what matters most of all."

"I saw everything," I told him – my tone, I hoped, conveying the full extent of my loathing.

"I'm sure you did, but who can you tell? It would be the work of moments to have you committed. You can't have forgotten that part of our conversation."

"I have not," I said at last.

"Good. But the Fire Beyond is the important part. Why, you ask? I shall tell you."

Arodias linked his fingers together, and strangely, this was when, for the first time, I felt a glimmer of hope that I might escape the asylum after all. I was his audience, the witness to his genius. Better that I live, free but ever in his power, rather than the doomed and broken inmate of a madhouse.

"I spoke of the spring's properties," he said. "The waters could heal, grant knowledge of the past or the future. Whether they did or did not do so, by the way, had nothing to do with the any divine whim, or still less the deserts of any individual supplicant. It is far simpler. Have you ever seen a child use a burning glass – perhaps used one yourself?"

"Of course," I told him.

"Two things are needed to produce the required result," he said. "On the one hand, the light of the sun; on the other, a magnifying lens to focus them in a single point of intense heat. Yes? Well, then. Imagine that the spring is the lens. That remains present throughout. The source of the Fire Beyond, though – that comes and goes, as the sun rises and sets."

"You mean," I said, "that there are times when the spring is only a spring, and nothing more?"

"Precisely. Now, the Moloch Device works, if you will, as another lens – or a set of lenses – each focusing the sun's rays with greater and greater intensity. The spring waters, at the right time and place, can do much, but are only a shadow of the source itself, as the heat of a stone lying beside a fire is as nothing to that of the fire itself. What you saw last night, although only for a moment, was that source."

"The Fire Beyond," I said.

"Which," said Arodias, "can do *far* more than heal a few bodily ills. Hence those ancient ceremonies, to make it appear. When you saw the Fire Beyond, Mary, a doorway was open – just for a moment – through which a man might pass. You see, Mary, if a man can enter the Fire Beyond itself, all that power will be his. All knowledge of the past and the future – and life eternal."

Insanity, you might well think. And so might I, had I not seen what I had.

"But it wasn't open long *enough*," Arodias continued. "In addition, the connection between the Fire Beyond and this world of ours is too tenuous at this time. It is a matter of proximity, like the cycles of the planets and stars. Thirteen years from now, by my calculations, the Fire Beyond will be at its greatest strength. Like the *perihelion* – the longest day of the year, when the Earth draws closest to the Sun. Meanwhile I continually refine the Moloch Device's operation to prolong the effect, in order to open the doorway for a sufficient period when the time comes. All I need, Mary" – he looked at my belly then and smiled – "is the right subject."

At last, I understood, and my hands went to my womb. For the first time, I felt as a mother should feel towards my child.

"If you attempt to run," Arodias said, "you *will* be found, and I *will*, still, take your child. Understand that, Mary. You cannot prevent it, and you will end your days in the madhouse."

Unless I ended my own life, cheating him of his prize. But still he smiled, and I knew he knew my thought. It was as though I ran through a maze where each exit was blocked even as it came in sight. Arodias had planned this from the first, before I even set foot in Springcross House; he held all the cards. Within the house his power was absolute, and outside it I would be only an impoverished fornicator whose every utterance would condemn her – even before he made good on his threats.

"You are not the stuff that Christian martyrs are made of, Mary," he said. "But then, I would not have chosen you had I thought otherwise. No further unpleasantness is required between us, only a few months' submission on your part, after which – so long as you have pleased me – you will be free to go, and well provided for." He stood. "So long as you have pleased me."

He went, and I was left alone. And so my wait began.

# Chapter Twenty-Eight

## The Inheritance

*The Confession of Mary Carson*

YOU HAVE BEEN both patient and forbearing, Mr Muddock, Mrs Rhodes, and for that you have an old woman's gratitude. You'll be glad to hear my ramblings are almost at an end. There is little more to tell, and in most respects we are past the worst.

In most.

I had discovered my maternal condition, you will recall, in the autumn of 1837. It was later established that my pregnancy was by then some two months advanced, meaning that the child was due in May the following year. And so I spent the next four months – four lonely months of fearful speculation – quite literally confined to my rooms at Springcross House. The doors were locked, my meals brought by servants. Otherwise, I was almost entirely alone – except, of course, for the occasional visit by the child's father.

I had my books, which I read and reread to distraction, and could look from my window at the gardens, even open them to take the air. There was no-one to see or hear me shout for help. Besides, the one time I tried, Arodias had the windows shuttered for a week and denied me lamp or candlelight for the duration. He relented for the sake of the baby's health, but assured me that next time, the room would be shuttered permanently. Privately, I thought that if the child had survived the cruelties heaped on me over Christmas – and where had his concern for it been then? – a little darkness could do no harm, but I dared not say so.

And so I obeyed without question, as what choice did I have? Arodias became the god of my circumscribed world – capricious, inscrutable, rarely seen or heard. While I had no friends among the servants, I would have given anything for a minute's conversation, but they had been instructed to say nothing to me; even those who'd howled and cackled loudest at my degradation spared me neither word nor glance, kind or cruel.

Except for Arodias' rare visits, I was alone with my memories, and these turned vicious as time passed. I'd known only four people with any real intimacy. And that included Arodias Thorne, who, it seemed, I had truly known only in the Biblical sense. I had been wholly ignorant of his true thoughts until he had flung them in my face.

But now, I felt, I *did* know him – and there was little enough to know. Beneath his fine speeches, airs and pretensions, he was a child. We forget, I think, what children are, Mr Muddock – do you agree, Mrs Rhodes? The current fashion is for sentiment; sweet and simpering cherubs. Angels, we call them – and perhaps in that is an unwitting truth. It was God's angels that destroyed the Cities of the Plain; an angel of God who slew the Egyptian first-born. The innocence of children is not as we think. Children know no evil, true – because they don't know what evil *is*, any more than good, until we teach them. Nothing can be crueller than a child; they can be utterly selfish, and pitiless in that selfishness. Most have love, at least, to temper that. If Arodias Thorne had, he'd never understood it. In any case, he had looked on the world and coveted, and whatever he coveted, had taken by force or guile. He'd clawed his way up, made his money, but even that was not enough. He would never feel safe if his playthings could be taken away from him, whether he still wanted them or not.

So what hope had I of ever escaping his control? I was his; why should he relinquish me? Even if he let me go, with wealth and feigned respectability, he would always be able to take all of it away with a word, if he chose. Even when he died, he might conceal some final twist of the knife in his will.

Yet oddly, that gave me hope. With the knowledge that Arodias' punishment would always be a Sword of Damocles above my head came a kind of calm, born from resignation. Sooner or later the blow *would* fall, and accepting that drove the worst of the fear away. I could not prevent that, but by guile might delay the event for as long as I could, and find what joy I might. *That* would be my victory.

But first, I had had other torments to face. Do you know Milton, Mrs Rhodes? There is a line of his: *the mind is its own place, which can make a Heaven of Hell, or a Hell of Heaven.* And shut off from all human intercourse, as mine now was, it can turn upon itself, like a trapped fox gnawing off its foot to escape.

The other three souls I had known well in life were my father, and the two men whose offers of marriage I had refused: Tristan Moreland and Denys Landen. None of them, thank God, could see me as I was now, but my fancy now ran amuck, and my memory was able to furnish it amply with all it needed to raise them – from the dead, in my father's case, and from happy marriages and prolific families in those of Tristan and Denys – to sit in judgement on me.

In my mind's eye, my father turned from me, pity and loathing in his eyes; Tristan and Denys, cruel having been spurned, mocked my erstwhile piety and present misery, parading sow-like wives and hordes of children. Some nights I screamed aloud at them to leave me – then clapped my hands over my mouth, lest my cries rouse Arodias' fury. They never did, thankfully, but my imagination taunted me with pictures of Kellett and the other servants listening and sniggering amongst themselves to see the haughty Christian woman who had thought herself so pious and full of rectitude brought so low – brought, indeed, to the very threshold of madness itself.

Arodias' visits were the nearest I had to relief. He was my only flesh and blood companion, though whether they served as any respite depended entirely upon his mood. Sometimes he was kindly, bringing some small gift – sweetmeats of some kind, or a new book – although he would, often as not, taunt me with it until I'd abased myself sufficiently. At other times he was full of lust, despite my condition, and woe betide me if I did not give him his way quickly enough. Or, sometimes, even if he did.

At other times he would come only to torment me, holding up a mirror to my wretched state – crawling in that now-filthy room, in clothes little more than grimy rags. Occasionally he brought me new clothes to wear, and hot water to wash in, but that was for his pleasure, not mine.

The days, the weeks, the months passed by; I thought my ordeal might never end. That was how I strove to think of it, for an ordeal, at length, comes to an end. But at times it seemed as though all the years of my life would be spent this way. More than once I thought that Hell would be this room, but for a true eternity, without even the hope of release through death. At other times I wondered if, indeed, I *was* in Hell – if I had died in my sleep to pass unknowing into that realm of eternal misery.

I would not allow myself to believe it, because this much theology I knew: the worst sin of all is despair. To believe oneself to be beyond God's mercy is an act of supreme wickedness and arrogance. So I told myself, over and over, that I still lived, and therefore still had hope of redemption.

But I came close; dear God, I came close.

Even though Arodias had dismissed the very idea, I was

tempted, at least every other day, to end my own life and that of the child in my womb, to spare it the fate Arodias had devised for it. But I dared not. Suicide was a mortal sin; so was taking the life of an innocent. And more practically, should I make such an attempt and fail – or worse, end the child's life but not my own – Arodias' vengeance would be terrible.

I did not doubt the existence of God, but as to His will or nature I now felt utterly ignorant. At times I could almost believe Arodias, that God was no loving Father, personally concerned with the fate of my soul, but a cruel and capricious deity to whom we were all no more than insects. "As flies are to wanton boys..."

But if God was, indeed, the God of my father and *not* that of Arodias Thorne, perhaps temptation was being put in my way. Perhaps this was a test of my faith, an opportunity for redemption; bear whatever blows this life had to offer with Christian fortitude, and I might hope for salvation; self-murder or infanticide in an attempt to evade worldly suffering would assuredly condemn me to Hell.

I was tempted still – less for my own sake that that of the child to consider. But neither the will of God, nor the future, can be known. Who could say what future events might deliver my child from Arodias?

And so I prayed. I prayed morning and night, for guidance, for mercy, for forgiveness.

I clung to my reason by the slenderest of threads. All too easily it might have given way, and then it would have truly been the madhouse for me, from which Arodias would have ensured I never emerged again. I was on the brink, until one day – one dark night, indeed...

I cannot be sure, now, that it was not my fancy. I was, after all, near madness at the time. But at the time, I was certain: perhaps I felt I had no choice but to believe and hold fast to it.

A figure appeared in my room – a female one, its arms held open. I could not see her face in any detail; it was pale and indistinct, and it glowed, with a soft, gentle light. It was the Virgin Mary, Mr Muddock, Mrs Rhodes, of that I had no doubt.

You will ask, no doubt, why I should have seen so – well, so Romish an apparition, and I have no answer for you. It was that, indeed, that convinced me of what I had seen. It was one thing for my father, my suitors and other images from my past to haunt me, but this was... something other. God had revealed Himself to me in a form I could not mistake. Let Arodias sneer at my faith and call it a child's tale. I *knew* again, once more, that my God was real.

And there at last I came to my final hope; that, whatever my ending on this Earth, I might still find grace after death: reunion with my father, and the happiness that had eluded me here. In that darkness, Mrs Rhodes and Mr Muddock, I found my faith and my God anew, and prayed. Over and over, in the morning, at noon, at sundown and in the night, I prayed for His mercy, and dedicated myself to Him.

You might ask why, having seen the Blessed Virgin, I did not turn to the Catholic faith. Perhaps it was because, as Arodias knew so well, I am not the stuff of which Christian martyrs are made, I am too prone to doubt and question at leisure. The comfort of my father's faith was easier to embrace once more. More practically, as a Catholic I must make a full confession of my sins – and that I did not believe I could bear to do. And indeed I could not, until now.

Only a week after this, I felt the air outside change. There was, even through the distant reek of the city's smoke, the scent of something else. A freshening, a taste of something better to come.

In the garden, green shoots sprouted, and buds appeared on tree and bush. Leaves unfurled. As my belly grew, trees blossomed, like a carpet of brilliant foam. Winter became spring. I cannot tell either of you what that meant to me. There was the sense of change and renewal, of rebirth, redemption, that that whole season brings.

I found memories now that were a comfort: the services my father had held at Easter, the hand-painted eggs. But most of all, I knew now that, try as Arodias and the rest might to make me despair, *time was passing*. To all things there was an end. A day would come, and with it my child. Perhaps my death also; perhaps not. But in either case my current state would not, could not, continue in perpetuity. I would die in Springcross House, or live outside it. If the first – I could not be certain of God's grace, for I had sinned and there had been no minister to counsel me, but I had prayed and repented, and had, at least, the *hope* of salvation. If the second, I would build as decent a life for myself as I could. Nothing excessive, for had I not seen how poisoned a chalice wealth was? If I might still have a family of my own – a loving husband, children – that would be the highest bliss on Earth. And if not, my eyes were set on Heaven.

And then, at last, the birth came. I cried out for help when the pains began, and they went unanswered. But when at length my waters broke – ah, *then* I understood, and cried out that the child was coming. I cannot help but smile, despite everything, when I remember how great a difference *that* made – his whole damned household came running at that!

What a panic and a performance that was. A doctor was sent for, with a nurse. Were they Arodias' creatures, like the servants, or simply paid to perform a task and keep silence afterward? I do not know. They had kind faces, I recall, but I was well aware of how little *that* meant.

What else? I remember the pain of childbirth, of course – but I shall not describe that in great detail, Mrs Rhodes, as Mr Muddock is beginning to look distinctly bilious. Forgive my levity, sir, I know none of this can be pleasant to hear. I can only say it was still less pleasant to endure.

At last, the pain ceased and a small wailing red-faced thing was placed on my breast. I am hard put to describe what I felt then. I experienced a wave of love and tenderness so great as to set the rest of my ordeal at naught, though I knew it was valueless in the face of Arodias' earthly might. Even should I escape, he would spare no effort to hunt me down. So I told myself then, and tell myself now. I had no choice. Even had I killed him, Kellett and the rest would have avenged his death and disposed of the child. Yet had I done that, at least the child would not have been his to dispose of...

But I had only bare minutes with my child. Then they came and took him, and I was too weak to fight. I howled in my anguish, and so did he. But I never saw him again.

"A MISCARRIAGE, MISS Carson," said Arodias several weeks later. "Or stillbirth, perhaps. Such things are unfortunate, but they happen, and must be endured."

"Yes," I said, "perhaps that would help."

We sat in the garden, sipping tea. I wore a white dress and bonnet, he, as always, an immaculate suit. It was July, I think.

I was a little uncertain of time, since following the birth and abduction of my child I had been on the very edge of madness, if indeed I had not crossed over for a time. I'm not sure if, having returned from such a state, one can ever be entirely whole again, but I regained a degree of lucidity, at which point they told me my child was dead. I did not believe them, of course, but a part of me wished to.

Looking back, I have no doubt Arodias knew that. When I review my time with him, the skill he manipulated me with is almost impressive. First he had been the stern man of business with a hidden heart; next, the cruel and arbitrary master who drove me to the point of desperation and made me a cringing slave. And now, having almost destroyed me with his cruelty, he resumed his kindly mien. The fiction he maintained was that I had 'fallen' through a dalliance with some scoundrel who had subsequently absconded, to be rescued by Arodias' charity. I dared not say otherwise for fear of the madhouse, and in truth I almost wondered at times if perhaps I had only imagined what had gone before.

"Here is my proposition," he said. "You will leave Springcross House, and restrain yourself from making any utterances that might – shall we say – embarrass your former employer. In return, a discreet silence shall be maintained about your own – ah – fall from grace?"

He sat there, eyebrows raised; finally I nodded assent.

"Excellent," he went on, and laid some papers on the table by the tea things. "These documents detail your marriage to Captain Hartley, an officer in a Guards Regiment, now deceased." Captain Hartley himself, Arodias assured me, enjoyed the advantages of having been quite real, as well as undistinguished and entirely without close friends or family. Favours owed to Arodias by certain public officials on the one hand, and by a highly accomplished forger on the other, had done the rest.

"This Will and Testament," he went on, laying down a further sheaf of documents, "and these solicitor's letters, confirm you as sole beneficiary of his not inconsiderable estate." The real Captain Hartley's 'estate' had consisted of gambling debts and a good deal of indecent literature, but it served as a suitable fiction to explain the very generous sum Arodias had provided me with.

"No blot on your reputation," he said, "and you will live out your remaining years in comfort. I am a man of my word, Miss Carson – or should I say, Mrs Hartley?"

Yes, he was a man of his word – when it suited him. For motives best not thought on, it did so now.

"But remember," he added, leaning across the table, "that what I give, I can take away. Very, very easily, Mary. Never doubt that."

"I will not, Mr Thorne," I told him. I had neither stomach nor desire for argument; I only wanted to be as free of him as I could ever hope to be, and at once.

Birds sang in the trees; a host of blooms perfumed the air. Rarely have I known surroundings more beautiful or tranquil than the gardens of Springcross House. In them, the past few months seemed an impossibility. I could almost believe the version of events he related.

"Then I believe our business is concluded. Kellett will take you wherever you wish to go, when you are ready to leave. Goodbye."

He rose, gave a short bow, and walked away.

And that, Mrs Rhodes, was the last time I ever saw Arodias Thorne, save in my nightmares.

I wish I could have found the courage to defy him at the last, but I could not. How damnably well he knew me. He saw my weakness of character, and, perhaps, my capacity for self-deception. In the years that have passed since leaving Springcross, I played my part so well I came to believe in Captain Hartley, that I was his widow and the mother of his stillborn child. Part of me, of course, wished to, rather than admit the truth. At times I found the courage to admit the lie, if only to myself, but I refused to look beyond the deceit that lay below it, that Arodias Thorne had saved my honour and reputation when I fell pregnant through an illicit love affair. At most, I might have acknowledged that Arodias was the child's father, but not the worst truth of all – the truth of the Moloch Device and the Fire Beyond.

Until now, of course. Soon enough I shall discover at first-hand exactly how merciful – or otherwise – my God is.

What else was to be done? I went to my rooms. They were unrecognisable either as those I'd moved into that first day or as the filthy, stinking chambers I'd spent my confinement in. While I'd been lost and raving, the servants had stripped, cleaned, repainted and scrubbed, then burned all that could not be cleansed. They gleamed and shone as new and were utterly unwelcoming, alien to me.

My belongings were packed, and I had already arranged lodgings in Liverpool; Sodom and Gomorrah could not have been more loathsome to my sight than Manchester by then. I would have dearly loved to return to Burscough, but feared I would be unable to deceive the people among whom I had grown up. Instead I had rented a clean, roomy house where I would have quiet, for the prayer and repentance I had resolved to spend my life in.

I heard soft footsteps on the landing, spied a shadow at the periphery of my sight; Kellett, his usual smirk upon his lips. "Ready, Miss Carson?"

I walked by him without a word, loathing even the sensation of my skirts brushing him as I went past.

We are almost done, Mrs Rhodes, and indeed Mr Muddock knows my history since then. Within two years of moving to Liverpool I met a gentle Welshman, a childless widower called Geraint, whom I can honestly say was the one true love of my life. You knew him, of course, Mr Muddock, for he became my husband: within a year of that meeting I was a bride – truly one, for the first time – loved, and cherished. My life was transformed, and for the better, in every way.

And in very short time, I was a mother again. Despite my age, I bore Geraint three healthy children – a boy and two girls – all of whom have survived to adulthood and borne children of their own. I am, Mrs Rhodes, truly blessed. I could almost believe that God was recompensing me for past hardships... but then I think on my sins, and my greatest dread over the years has been that He will take my loved ones from me as a punishment.

But all through our first decade of marriage it was not God I feared, but Arodias. He had no reason to expose me, of course, but might, for all I knew, do so out of petty spite. And there were the other servants – Kellett, most of all. I knew it could only be justice if the axe fell, but the thought of the suffering such an event would cause my loved ones was too much to bear. Oh, it's true – Geraint, God rest him, was devoted to me, but could he have forgiven me, had he known? I wanted to believe so, but did not dare put that to the test. And so I suffered in silence and watched my children grow, my worldly joys all tainted with dread…

And then, in December 1851, a miracle: Arodias Thorne died.

I learned it from his solicitors. It seemed I was, almost, his sole beneficiary. The mills were mine, his tenements, his warehouses – all of his considerable estate. Including Springcross House and the lands appertaining.

Briefly I wondered if it might constitute some gesture of repentance on his part, but this I thought unlikely. More probably, it was Arodias Thorne's last, black joke. It certainly caused surprise – and, I think, suspicion, in my husband's case. I was able, I am glad to say, to convince that good man that Arodias Thorne had entertained nothing more than a paternal affection towards me, an emotion for which he had found no other outlet in his prosperous but lonely existence – hence this final and startlingly generous bequest.

Why did he really do it? I have often pondered the question. On the one hand, who else was there to leave his worldly goods to? Perhaps it was a means to leave one last mark on my life, by forcing me to remember. Perhaps he hoped to poison my marriage with suspicion; with a man other than my husband, he might have succeeded. Most of all, though, I believe it was so that I would know what he had done.

What *had* he done, you ask? Well, I have no proof, merely conjecture. To understand what that conjecture was, and how I arrived at it, requires an account of my final visit to Springcross House.

I wanted nothing of his. I made arrangements for the immediate sale of his properties and businesses – vetting, wherever I could, the prospective buyers in the hope Arodias' tenants and employees would enjoy kinder treatment and conditions than before. As for the house – that was why, early in the February of 1852, I returned to Manchester for the first time since leaving Springcross House as Mrs Hartley.

When I was made aware that Springcross House was now my property, my first worry was how to deal with the servants – would any there remember me, after all these years? However, I soon learned I need have no worries on that score.

You'll remember, Mr Muddock, my saying I was *almost* the sole beneficiary of Arodias' will; the other was Kellett, to whom Arodias had bequeathed one hundred thousand pounds – more than enough to keep him in whatever manner he desired to become accustomed for life, no matter how depraved that manner might be. Those monies had been made available even before the reading of the will; Arodias's solicitors had been instructed to that effect. At which point the butler had, taking the wages of his many sins, vanished.

With Arodias dead and Kellett gone, the servants – most of them, I have no doubt, with histories that might not bear close scrutiny by the authorities – had looted the place for anything they could carry away and fled. No record of their names could be found; any such record had gone with Kellett, we knew not where. Since then, the great house had stood derelict, open to the elements and any who sought its shelter.

My husband was against my going there alone, for who might now have made their abode in Springcross House? I might have answered that no-one could have been viler than its former master, but forebore. For my own part, I was adamant Geraint should not accompany me, lest he stumble over some incriminating matter left there out of carelessness, or – more likely – by intent, to inflict a final ruinous blow on me. If there were any ghosts from my past at Springcross House, I would face them by myself, and lay them to rest if I could.

By way of compromise, I agreed to take Thomas, whom I had hired when I first moved to Liverpool and had served me faithfully ever since – a former soldier, stolid, loyal and dependable. He had always been my, rather than my husband's man, so I felt secure regarding both my physical safety and any potential threats to my reputation. My husband was satisfied with this. Thomas, though in his forties by then, was strong and fit, while Geraint was my own age and – as I'm sure you'll agree, Mr Muddock, having known him – while a good and kind man, was no warrior born.

And so we took the train from Liverpool to Manchester, and then a carriage from the station. As I said before, I took little notice of the city, nor of Crawbeck as we passed through it, but doubtless it had changed as one might expect, with more low, mean tenements sprawling up the hill slopes. Even if it had been unchanged, I was not; spying my reflection in the glass, I saw a plump matron with greying hair, but was more than content to be so. It was hard to recognise the woman who had ridden this way in 1837, or believe I could once have stirred the passions of Arodias Thorne. That sense of distance enabled me to contemplate Springcross House with a smaller measure of fear.

The gates of Springcross House had been forced asunder; a length of broken chain lay on the gravel path, and the journey to the house itself was decidedly bumpy. When we reached the house itself...

I'm sorry, Mr Muddock. Might I trouble you for another small measure of your brandy? I vowed to avoid any such stimulant until this testament was completed, but it has been a most fatiguing day.

Many thanks. Yes, the house.

Arodias had not been dead two months when I visited Springcross House, yet the condition of the building and grounds suggested a far longer period of neglect. Windows were broken; great pieces of stucco had fallen from the walls, ivy writhed across the frontage and slates were missing from the roof. And the once-beautiful gardens, the one aspect of the place for which I cherished the least glimmer of warmth, were wild and overgrown, the trees, shrubs and plants stripped bare and withered by the winter winds.

It was as if Arodias had allowed the whole building to fall into disrepair once I had gone, yet my enquiries showed he had done no such thing. It was as though, like Jonah's gourd, it had grown up, then withered, in a day. It is only one more mystery amid the rest.

Inside, the impression of desuetude was much the same, but the explanation was more readily apparent. The servants had departed like a plague of locusts, leaving only when they had stripped the house bare. Even the carpets and light-fittings were gone. With no servants to clean them, the empty chambers were already accruing layer on layer of dust. There were pale gaps on the walls where paintings had been taken down; the kitchen's drawers and cupboards had been emptied. In places one could hear the drip of water and the scuttling of rats.

One painting remained in the house. I invite you both to guess which one. Yes, Mrs Rhodes: that damned portrait of Arodias in his study. I can well imagine how even those depraved souls might have feared to touch it. I had Thomas take it down, then slashed its face to ribbons with a knife. We lit the fire in the study, and the portrait, torn and broken, went into it.

At one point, I thought I heard a chuckle from behind me. Well, no; let me be precise. *His* chuckle. A middle-aged woman's fancy, no doubt. But still.

I wished to remain no longer than I must, but there was another purpose to my visit. You see, Mr Muddock, one small detail regarding the death of Arodias Thorne continued to worry me.

The circumstances of his passing were somewhat gruesome. If one believed in poetic justice one might have even called them apt. Arodias, it appeared, had been stricken with a violent apoplexy while reading late at night. Not even time to pray forgiveness for his sins; I confess to having taken a most uncharitable satisfaction from that, which made me feel guilty. After all, I hoped, and still hope, for forgiveness for my own.

But that is neither the poetic part, nor the detail that concerned me. Allegedly, the apoplexy had not killed him outright; he had risen from his chair, then fallen. To be precise once more, he had pitched headlong into the very fireplace in which I had burned his portrait. Where a fire had been burning.

Why, Mrs Rhodes, you have gone quite pale. Do you feel faint? Mr Muddock, I believe another small measure of your excellent brandy might be in order. Indeed, you look as if you yourself might benefit from a little...

To resume: I mention that rather unpleasant aspect of Mr Thorne's death not to revel in his suffering, but because his body had been identified – could *only* be identified – from its clothing. The head, face and hands had all been burned beyond recognition in the fire.

I can see from your expression, Mr Muddock, that you divine my fear correctly. Arodias Thorne was not dead – the body discovered was doubtless that of some poor unfortunate he had made away with, using the fire to disfigure the face and hands beyond recognition – although whether he was still *alive*, in any commonly accepted sense of the term, is harder to say.

But why should such a man so cavalierly dispose of the wealth he fought so hard to gain? Ah, but even his wealth was only a means to an end. He wanted *power*; he wanted *control*. Wealth gave him that in earthly terms, but sooner or later death must take it from him. What he truly sought – his ultimate goal, if you will – was what he called the Fire Beyond. Through it, remember, he believed he could attain immortality. Eternal life, and – and, I think, a kind of transcendence. Where he was going, money was unimportant.

For myself, I cannot say what the Fire Beyond truly was. I can testify only to what I saw, on that long-ago Christmas night I wish I could believe was only a horrible, fevered dream. It might have been a trick, or a delusion of Mr Thorne's that I briefly came to share. I do not know. Still less can I say if it would, indeed, fulfil him in the ways he dreamt of. I *do* know, however, that he believed it would do so. The Fire Beyond, immortality – they may have been pipe-dreams on his part, but believe me, Mr Muddock and Mrs Rhodes, the Moloch Device, and the children who perished in it, were all too real.

The child I had borne Arodias – the one he had told me had died at birth, but about whose fate I could no longer delude myself – would have been thirteen years old at the time of Arodias' 'death'. The age of reason, we are told, and the time he referred to as 'Perihelion' would have coincided with that development.

That underground chamber, I believed then and now, was where Arodias' story truly ended – or, perhaps, truly began. It was also where the body of my first-born child, along with those of countless other innocents murdered in the Moloch Device, lay. If nothing else, I hoped to ensure them a decent Christian burial. And if I could find some way to strike a blow against Arodias – although I supposed him to be far beyond the reach of any justice but God's by now – then I'd do that, too.

Yet, search as I might, neither Thomas nor I found any trace of the hidden entrance in the music room, still less the place it led to. It was as though they had never been.

At the last, I was forced to admit defeat. I had Springcross House pulled down, every trace of it erased – yes, Mr Muddock, even the gardens. The land was sold to the Corporation of Manchester. A hard choice, but one I felt I must, for my own sanity, make. I *did* also make arrangements with the Church authorities – in exchange for a sizeable donation – that the site be blessed and consecrated. If I could not find my child's remains, I could at least be sure that he, and the others, rested in holy ground.

KELLETT'S DISAPPEARANCE REMAINED a source of disquiet to me for another five years. He moved, it later emerged, to the district of Whitechapel in London, where any appetite, however base, was readily sated. He fell in with a crew of procurers who specialised in abducting women and young girls for the use of men like him; all he and his kind need do was select a victim.

However, he made the mistake of choosing the young – the *very* young – daughter of a soldier who had just returned from the Crimea, with others of his regiment. These young gentlemen, having alerted the police, took the law somewhat into their own hands thereafter, and fortunately so; they found the girl in good time to save her virtue, her sanity and her life.

Mr Kellett, it seems, reached under his jacket to draw out his wallet, being convinced that this would be sufficient to extricate him from any difficulties, but the girl's father, in addition to his quite natural outrage at the whole business, assumed him to be reaching for a weapon, and shot him several times with a revolver. I am pleased to report that the father and his confederates were subsequently exonerated of any wrongdoing, but more pleased yet to report that Kellett expired two days later, in what appears to have been extreme agony. I have tried in vain to repent my lack of Christian charity in this matter.

Through all the years I have feared to tell the tale, because there have always been those who might be hurt. My husband, my children... I often thought of coming to you in the past, Mr Muddock, as Geraint always trusted you implicitly, but knew that to confide these matters to you would place you in a most invidious position, as you and he were not only close in business, but friends. But now Geraint has passed away, and the problem no longer arises.

I fear judgement, Mr Muddock and Mrs Rhodes. It has been hard enough to speak of what I have done, and been, before yourselves. Before the eyes of the world I dare not speak more – such is the measure of my cowardice. But I fear that other judgement too – the one I cannot escape, and must face, sooner rather than later. And the dread that Providence would bring the Lord's wrath upon me in this life, through my family, has never left me. Not even now.

And that, I think, is all, save for the end.

My name is Mary Wynne-Jones, widow of Geraint Wynne-Jones, shipping merchant, of the City of Liverpool. I was born Mary Carson in a small Cheshire village called Burscough, in the Year of Our Lord eighteen hundred and two. This is my Confession. I believe it to be as full and comprehensive as needs be, and I leave its disposition in your hands. And now, Mr Muddock, I hope I might trouble you for another – and more copious – measure of your brandy.

# Chapter Twenty-Nine

## Perihelion

*31st October 2016*

ALICE REACHED THE end of Mary Carson's narrative in silence. She didn't dare glance at John. After a moment she heard him breathe out, then settle back on the bed. That was when she finally turned to him.

He looked back at her, eyes bloodshot. "You know," he said at last, "when Sixsmythe said Thorne was more than he seemed, I thought –"

"That he was better?"

"Yeah. He'd got a bad reputation, but under it, he was..."

"I get you. I thought the same way when I started reading that. But he was worse."

"Yeah."

"That poor woman." Alice turned away and peered out of the window; the slope outside was deserted.

"You feel sorry for her?" John asked.

"Hell, yes. You *don't*?"

"'Course. I just thought you might – I mean, giving up her

baby and all."

"Because of Emily, you mean?" Alice glared. John looked away. "That bastard went to work on her, John. He took her apart psychologically. In the end, she was in no shape to outwit him. The blame's on him. Not her."

"I knew that. But she blamed herself."

"Of course she did. There's no way you can't."

She realised they were both speaking in whispers. The house was silent. She looked back out of the window.

"Nothing doing?" whispered John, crawling onto the bed beside her to look out as well.

"Can't see anything. Not even the Red Man."

"That's a long time," John said. "Normally it's only a few minutes, and then it's back to our world."

"I know. Maybe this is the end-game."

"In which case," John pointed out, "it's our move."

"I know. But what are we supposed to do?"

He rubbed his face. "The children want something, right? We can see that. And the Red Man wants something else – enough that he's stuck his oar in with the kids."

"Yeah," said Alice, "and I'm caught in the middle. Question is, which side should we be rooting for?"

"The Red Man's protected you, and the children tried to kill you. But at the same time, the Red Man didn't want us reading that box-file, and the children stopped him burning it."

"Maybe we shouldn't be backing either side, then. At least..."

"At least what?"

"At least until we understand what the fight's about."

Alice got off the bed; suddenly she felt charged-up, full of energy. *I'm close to something*, she thought. *It's at my shoulder, behind my back, maybe even right in front of me, but it's like a ghost and I can't see it – can't see it, unless. Unless what, though? Unless what? Unless something happens to make the ghost visible. What would do that? Did the ghosts need to absorb more energy from their environment to register visually*

*– absorbing heat radiation to convert into a visual image? Wasn't that why ghost-chasers like John claimed haunted houses grew cold when ghosts appeared?*

"Alice?"

She shook her head, held up a hand to ward him off. He had the sense to fall silent: he'd seen her like this when they'd lived together, when some train of thought kicked off – except that it was more like lines of dominoes, each knocking over the next to show some odd pattern on the underside.

The ghost. Yes, the ghost. The ghost she couldn't see but had to. What made a ghost become visible? Did the ghost have to do something, or was it the viewer? Did she need something, some shift of perception – the kind the Moloch Device had created in its victims, or the ancient priests had achieved in their trances?

Perception, observation. The Fire Beyond. *Perihelion.*

"Perihelion," she said. She turned to John. "It's about proximity. In certain times, in certain places, the Fire Beyond can be reached more easily. A force – and/or a *location* – that lets you see the past or the future. Or heal the sick or the dying – whatever. Something that lets you make changes to something at a fundamental level.

"We've been assuming that all this is supernatural in nature. Paranormal. Magical. But what if it isn't?"

"I don't get you," said John.

"What if all this is natural, scientific phenomena? Just stuff that's been badly understood and poorly explained?"

"You've got a scientific explanation for this? I'd love to hear it."

Alice snorted. "Don't know if it's anything old Doc Peabody back at Salford would have had much time for. You remember her?"

"Don't I just," said John. "She was the one always telling us *not* to get quantum mechanics confused with magic or the paranormal."

"Just try this for an idea. What if this place – Redman's Hill, Collarmill Height – what if it was some sort of soft spot?"

"Soft spot?"

"Remember how they told us to picture space and time as a flat sheet?"

"Right," said John.

"Yeah. But there's this thin, quantum foam theory, which suggests that space-time isn't of a constant, uniform texture – there can be areas of instability."

"Right," said John. "And this –"

"The Fire Beyond. That's what it is. It's a point where everything's unstable, in flux. And if you can locate that, *connect* to it in some way, you can control it. You could, say, open a wormhole."

John clicked his fingers. "Wait a sec, I know the technical name – an Einstein-Rosen bridge, right? It's like you fold the sheet over and push something through, make a hole going from one side to the other."

"Yeah." Alice snatched up an old envelope and a biro, then drew two dots, one marked 'A' and one marked 'B', at different ends. "Points A and B are separated in space or time or both. But fold the envelope like so, and –" she unfolded one of the Swiss Army knife's spikier components and pushed it through, transfixing both dots. "Ta-da! You've got a hole that links them. You can put something into that hole..."

"And it'll come out on the other side," said John. "At a different point in space or time. *Instantly*."

"Instantly," Alice agreed. "Halfway across the galaxy, or a hundred years in the past. Or in the future."

"And if you created the right kind of bridge," said John, "you could, say receive light signals through it. From another time, or a remote location."

"Yeah," said Alice. "You could see into the past or future, or watch something happening far away. Or you could perceive matter on the quantum, sub-atomic level. And then manipulate it."

"Creating fundamental changes on the basic composition of matter." John was nodding now. They were slipping even further back into old intimacies. These were the kind of conversations the two of them had had at university, bouncing ideas off one another over bottles of red wine or rum at silly o'clock in the morning. "Like lead into gold, right? Or, say, miraculous healing. But control it? Control it how? And this is just a freak occurrence? It sounds a little too useful for a natural phenomenon."

"Maybe it isn't natural," said Alice, "maybe a thousand years in the future, someone built a machine to look through time or manipulate matter at the sub-atomic level, and this is just like a side-effect from it, or the result of an accident. Or maybe there's been some sort of trillions-to-one-against naturally-occurring freak event. Maybe there's something in the cave walls that amplifies the effect. Essentially it acts as some kind of tachyon detector or attractor. Either way, to see it, to connect with it, you have to be in a particular state of mind, like an ecstatic trance or the state one of the sacrifices went into."

"A sort of heightened level of awareness, so you could perceive things you normally wouldn't?"

"Right."

"But then wouldn't the sacrifice be the one who controlled the thing?"

Alice shook her head. "The sacrifice would barely be capable of any conscious thought – my guess is that once the Fire Beyond became visible, it would be first come, first served."

John scratched his beard. "And the children, the ghosts? Where do they fit into it?"

"If there's some kind of mental connection with the instability," said Alice – she knew she was winging it, but she knew, *knew*, she'd make some sort of breakthrough here – "then maybe some trace of their personality gets caught up in it, like old computer files on a network."

"Ghosts in the machine," said John. "Literally. Cheery thought, huh? But that might explain the hill's reputation, the time travel, even the children, but what about..." he nodded out of the window "... those two?"

"On that," sighed Alice, "you've got me."

"And this 'Perihelion'," said John, "that means it's close – or that it's stronger than at other times. That tracks with Halloween, because it's traditionally when all sorts of supernatural shit is supposed to go crazy. So, okay, the Moloch Device makes the initial connection, so the Fire Beyond becomes visible, and then what?"

"What Thorne said he wanted. To enter the Fire itself and use it. He could plug in directly, step outside time and space. In theory, at least, he could live for ever."

"Except he didn't," said John. "He died, remember?" He picked up the Confession and turned to its final pages. "See? She says here they found a body."

"And you saw what else she said."

"Come on, that can't have been –"

"Can't it? According to whom?"

John sank back onto the bed; Alice slipped the Confession out of his hands.

"What do any of this lot want?" he said at last. "The kids, the Red Man, the Beast, any of them? I mean, if we knew that..." He snorted. "Like it matters anyway. We should have just left this place behind and forgotten about it."

"*You* could have," Alice pointed out. "I don't think the place is done with me. The kids, the Red Man – they've all got plans that seem to involve me, somehow."

Whispers came back to her, from when she first moved in, *Does she know? Will she help? Help who? Him or us? She'll help him. It's why she's here. Can't have that. So we're going to have to –*

"*She'll help him*," she said.

"What?"

"When I first moved in, I heard whispers – the kids again, I guess. They were talking about me helping someone else.

'Him', that's all they called him. Whoever it was, they didn't want it happening. And not long after that –"

"They tried to kill you."

"Yeah." She plopped down on the bed beside John.

"So, who's this 'him'?"

Alice took the Swiss Army knife and the remaining rowan twigs from her pockets, fumbling at her scalp until she found a few more longish hairs. She snipped them off. "At a guess, the Red Man. Or Arodias Thorne, if there's anything left of him."

"Always assuming they aren't one and the same."

Alice stopped and blinked. For some reason that had never occurred to her. "I don't think they are, you know."

"Why's that?"

She bit off another piece of sellotape and wrapped it round the juncture of the twigs, over the hair that bound the cross. "Something about the Red Man himself. There's something almost... kind... about him, somehow. Maybe not *kind*, exactly. I can't put it into words. But he isn't cruel. Arodias Thorne was."

John puffed out his cheeks. "He might have been two hundred years ago. If he's still around now – if he managed to reach the Fire Beyond – he might have changed."

"Yeah." Alice passed him the second cross and got up. "He might be worse."

# Chapter Thirty

## Descent

*31st October 2016*

ALICE PULLED THE handle, and the bedroom door swung open. It only took a second, but the moment stretched out and out; with every inch of darkened landing it exposed she expected a leering white-eyed face to appear. But none did. The landing and stairs were deserted.

She stepped out, raising the cross before her. "Dark," she heard John mutter behind her, followed by the clicking of the light switch. The light didn't come on.

"I think we're some way from the mains supply right now," she said. She heard her voice shake and sucked in a deep breath. "Like a couple of million years."

John moved to her side and took her hand. "What do you reckon Collarmill Road looks like right now?" he murmured. "Is there a big hole where 378 used to be?"

"I don't know." Maybe it would only be gone for a split-second, too brief a time for anyone to notice. There and back. When it came back, its return would fit seamlessly into its departure. But before it did that, it could spend a near-eternity here. Or rather *now*.

She passed the spare room; the doorway gaped blackly at her, the tape across it a weak glimmer in the dark. There was a flicker of something pale and she recoiled with a gasp, but it was only an A4 notepad she'd left on the writing desk at the end of the room. Alice breathed out.

The spare room was empty, and so were the bathroom and the box room at the end of the landing. The staircase was empty too, and the landing below. But there was a light down there: it was pale, bluish in colour and it flickered down in the hallway.

She looked at John. He raised his eyebrows. "What you reckon?"

What, indeed? "We won't get anywhere by hiding out up here," she said. "We've got stuff to do."

"What stuff?"

Alice began tiptoeing down the staircase. She could feel her legs shaking, but she gripped onto the bannister and carried on.

"Alice!" John hissed. She glanced behind her, saw him hesitating at the top of the stairs. He was afraid too; as much as her – if not more, because however little she understood, he understood still less.

"Babe," she said and held out a hand. "Come on. It's okay. Trust me."

He let out a short, nearly silent laugh, then sucked in a deep breath. "Okay," he muttered. "In for a penny and all that shit."

They reached the floor below; all was silent and still. The doors hung ajar and the rooms beyond were dark. Anything could have been waiting there… but somehow, she didn't think so. "Let's go," she said.

"Okay," muttered John. "But, uh, *where* we going, exactly?"

Alice crept to the top of the last staircase and peered down into the hall. That faint bluish light still wavered and danced over the laminate flooring, but there was no other motion. Everything looked still and empty. Of course, that didn't mean it was. In fact, there would be one part of the house that most definitely wasn't. The question was whether she'd correctly identified which. She couldn't resist the impulse to glance over her shoulder at the empty first floor rooms. It would be so easy for one of the children to leap out of the dark and send her headfirst down the stairs to break her neck. But she didn't think they would.

"Remember the stone I found in the garden?" she whispered at last.

"Stone?" John frowned. "Wait – with the inscription?"

"Yeah. I saw it – the complete version – the first time this place... went back. It was still Springcross House that time, only... derelict. After Thorne died, I'm guessing. Thing is, I recognised it from what Mary Carson put in her confession. A quotation from Ecclesiasticus. I knew I was trying to place the inscription. 'Their bodies are buried in peace...'"

"'...but their name liveth forevermore,'" said John. "Ecclesiasticus 44:14."

"Chapter and verse."

He shrugged. "I was a star pupil at Sunday School. What's your excuse?"

"I read it in a book somewhere. Anyway, it was Mary Carson's favourite spot in the gardens, remember? Right outside the entrance..."

She saw the lights go on in John's eyes. "To the music room," he breathed.

"And right under the music room there was..."

"The chute, the shaft, whatever you wanna call it. Down to where he was sacrificing those kids."

"Yeah." Alice tried not to think about the Moloch Device or the torments Thorne's child victims must have suffered. "And more importantly, to the spring. That's why all this is happening – that's why it's *this* house that's the haunted one, not the bloody builder's yard or the place next door. We're directly on top of it – the shrine, the Fire Beyond, whatever you want to call it. If we can find our way down there, we might be able to pull the plug."

"Didn't she say she'd looked all over for it and couldn't find it?"

"Yeah," said Alice. "Well, let's just hope she was getting short-sighted in her old age. Come on."

"They built a whole *street* over where that house used to be, though," said John. "The shaft'll be gone. Filled in."

"Maybe not. There'd have been some record if they'd found anything when they pulled down Springcross House."

"Maybe there is, and we didn't get to it."

"Could be, but Mary Wynne-Jones would have probably got to hear about it if they had."

John nodded. "True."

Alice crept the rest of the way down to the hall. The front door was shut tight. The living room and spare room's doors again stood open, with only shadows inside.

The kitchen door, though, was almost shut. Almost; it was just open enough for the flickery blue light inside to spill down the hallway. Alice took a deep breath and strode forward.

"Alice –" John caught her arm, but she pulled free. Three more quick strides took her to the door; she flung it wide before she could let herself think about it.

"Fuck," said John. His hand came up, clutching his cross.

The children were gathered in the middle of the kitchen. The table that had stood in the centre of the room lay against the far wall, broken and shattered. The camera that had been set up in the room was a tangled heap of charred and molten plastic and crumpled metal tubes. The children were silent, hands clasped before them. At first, because they were lit from behind, she saw them only as silhouettes, save for their dead white eyes which stared out at her, almost luminescent. She raised her own crucifix, but they made no move towards her.

Behind the children, rising from the kitchen floor to lick the ceiling, was a column of blue fire. Pale and lambent, it put Alice in mind of the Bunsen burners in the school lab, but was the light blue of a summer sky. It didn't seem to have damaged the ceiling in the slightest. This flame, she knew, wouldn't burn her.

As her eyes accustomed themselves to the kitchen's dimness, the children's faces began to resolve themselves out of the dark. They were all screwed up in pain. Some looked close to weeping; a couple, she thought, were sobbing outright, but there was no sound.

She took a step towards them, but John caught her arm. "Careful," he said.

She nodded. Yes, this time he was right to urge caution. It was hard for any mother to see a child suffer, whatever that child had done, but these had tried to kill her, and more than once. And yet they'd helped her too, saving Sixsmythe's box-file from the Red Man's fire. Perhaps their goal had changed, whatever it might have been before.

"Jesus," she heard John say, snapping her out of her reverie. The children were *fading*, in and out of existence, first growing transparent, then becoming mere outlines before, at the last, the process reversed itself. But no sooner had they regained solidity, they began to fade.

A grinding crack; the floor shuddered. The sound came again, drawn out into something more prolonged and tortured; stone cracking, brick breaking, rock grinding against rock and powdering into dust. There was a cracking, a splitting, a rumbling below them. Alice thought of some huge machine, long-disused, cogs of brick and gears of stone all oiled with dust, stirring finally back into life. The floor shuddered again, then tilted sharply down. Off-balance, Alice stumbled forward, towards the children.

John shouted her name, but she swayed, steadied herself. The children faded almost to nothing, then began solidifying again, but the process was happening more slowly, and seemed less likely to complete. From what she could see of their faces, they were howling in anguish.

The ceiling cracked across and bowed; plaster dust billowed through the air. Alice coughed and spluttered. The blue flame turned the dust to a glowing mist. A shape loomed up beside her: John.

The floor tilted again and there was another splitting crack. As the billowing dust thinned, she saw a huge rent running up the kitchen wall.

"Fuck," said John. He pulled at her arm. "We've got to get out of here."

"And go where, John?" Alice shook him off. "There's nothing out there for us. Our only way back's in here."

She was amazed how calm she felt. But then again, she thought she understood. There was a purpose to this, and she was a part of it; that purpose wouldn't allow her to be hurt by chance. Or perhaps that was delusion on her part – perhaps no purpose governed events here, only chaos and randomness. Maybe every theory – hers, Arodias', Sixsmythe's – were all just hopeless attempts to find method in the madness. And after Emily, wasn't she desperate to find a meaning, a reason, behind all this? Hadn't even her atheism been shaken by her daughter's death?

The kitchen window shattered, and they both ducked, arms raised to guard their faces. The rumbling died away; the house wasn't shaking now and the dust was settling.

The blue glow dimmed. As the dust dispersed, Alice saw the flame had dwindled to a thread. The children had faded to shadows on the air; a moment later, they were gone.

The flame lingered like a thread of luminescent smoke, wavering and sputtering towards extinction as it rose from the floor – no, Alice realised, not from the floor, but from the gaping hole in it.

The kitchen floor had sagged in the middle. The lino had split and rucked to expose the stone beneath, which in turn had split into wedge-shaped segments, separated by narrow crevasses. The kitchen sink had pulled loose from the wall.

The floor had sagged down, and right in the middle of it, at the bottom of the shallow, cracked bowl it had become, there was a hole – a perfect circle by the look of it, the edges smooth. And from its exact centre issued that last surviving thread of a flame.

Alice pocketed her cross, braced herself and started down the incline.

"Alice," began John, then broke off. "Fuck it," she heard him mutter, and then he was following her down.

She had to place her feet carefully. The wedges of floor tapered to their narrowest points as they neared the centre, the gaps on either side of them widening. She didn't have *that* blind a faith that there was a purpose to this – and, after all, blind chance and accident stood ready to fuck up any purpose you had at the best of times, so it was hardly sensible to assume this would be any different.

Through the broken floor, she could see the pipes that had run below it. No smell of gas, at least – but then, the gas that supplied her home in 2016 was probably still brewing somewhere under the earth.

Below the stone floor were the brick foundations; below that, raw earth, and then –

And then, gaping at the centre of it all like a ravening throat, there was a brick-lined shaft, leading down.

"No fucking way," John said.

Alice leant forward, peering down into the dark. The blue flame was almost cotton-thin now; tiny flecks of it gleamed off the damp bricks and rusted iron rungs.

"Hang on a second," John said, and inched back the way they'd come, to where the gaps between floor sections diminished. Plaster dust hissed and pattered down from the ceiling above them.

"Where you going?"

John brushed at his dust-clogged goatee and spat. "Ain't gotta be Sherlock Holmes to know you want to go down there." Gingerly, he put some weight on the section of floor beside theirs. "Right?"

"Yeah? So? Jesus, John!"

He'd already leapt onto the neighbouring section. Now he inched across it towards the shattered sink unit. "So, I seem to remember seeing a couple more of those clockwork torches in that drawer." He tested his weight on the floor section where the unit belonged, then stepped across.

"John, be careful!"

"You said it yourself," John didn't look back at her, his eyes on the floor. "Our only way back's here." He nodded at the shaft. "Or rather, down there."

In the shaft, the last of the blue flame flickered, then went out.

The sink unit's floor section canted badly; John swayed fighting to steady himself. Alice felt her hands rise to her mouth. There was nothing she could do. If he fell, what then? The gaps between sections looked quite big enough to swallow him up, and what would be waiting for him? Even if there was a purpose for her, it didn't necessarily extend to John. He was expendable. But he managed to pull open the drawer and pick out first one, and then a second torch. Each had a rubber lanyard dangling from the butt; John looped both over his right wrist and picked his way back towards her. Twice he wobbled, nearly losing his balance, and she flinched; another time, one of the floor sections sank a few more inches with a harsh grating noise, but he barely wobbled and the floor section halted. A moment later he was beside her again, handing her a torch. "Here."

"Thanks."

"Glad to be of help."

With the torches switched on, they shone them down the shaft. The rungs were intact, all the way down to the clinker floor below.

"Right," said Alice, climbing down. This time John didn't protest.

The beginning was the worst; she had to hold on as best she could to the cracked and crumbling end of the floor section, testing first one, then another rung with her full weight before stepping down, until she was at last low enough to take hold of the topmost rung. After that it got easier. Above her, she heard John muttering as he moved into position to climb down after her.

The air got colder: chill, and dank. The shaft's brick walls gave way to an open tunnel. She hung from the last rung, her feet in empty space. When she looked down, the torch hanging from her wrist showed the floor below her – how far below? She couldn't tell. John was climbing down above. Alice took a deep breath and let go. The impact was jarring, she'd only dropped a couple of feet.

She stepped away from the shaft and shone the torch around. The tunnel – brick-lined, like the shaft – extended both in front of and behind her.

John landed beside her. "So," he said, "which way now?"

Had Mary Carson's account specified the direction? If it had, Alice didn't recall. "This way," she said at last, and started up the tunnel.

It curved round as they followed it, and soon enough an archway appeared on the right. It opened into a room. More archways lined the walls there on the left and right, but they were screened across with iron bars.

Alice stepped inside. This room felt colder than the tunnel had, and there was a smell. Decay, filth, or at least the memory of them. In one corner were a table and chair. A tin mug and plate sat on the table, beside a bunch of rusted iron keys.

"Ah Jesus," John said.

He was facing one of the walls, shining his torch back and forth through the arches. "Don't," he said as she approached. "You don't want to –"

No, she didn't, but perhaps she *had* to. She aimed her own torch through the nearest arch. The tiny room inside was perhaps six feet wide, only a little taller and no more than ten or twelve feet deep. There was a wooden pallet and the remains of a blanket, a few pieces of straw at one end that might be the remains of a rough pillow. A tin bucket at the back of the room; a plate, a mug, a knife and fork beside the bars. She inspected the rust-pitted bars more closely. On one side there were hinges, on the other a lock.

"Cells," she said. "He kept the children here."

"Yeah," said John. "Fucking bastard. Now come on, we need to –"

"John?" There was a thickness to his voice she didn't like, something that suggested he'd seen more than just an empty cell. "John, what is it?"

"Don't," he said, turning away from the arch that neighboured hers and spreading his arms, trying to ward her – no, she realised, *herd* her – back towards the tunnel. "You don't want to know."

But of course she did; she had to. Anything left down here was necessary. It was information, it was a clue; it was fuel for her anger, her resolve. She side-stepped, dodged past him, and John lowered his arms, head bowed, acknowledging defeat as if he'd always known this would happen. He probably had as well; after all, he'd known her long enough. But at least he'd cared enough to try.

Something stuck through the cell bars. Her first thought was that it was an old broom, the kind with a brush made out of bound twigs, but then realised it wasn't. The twigs were too few and too thick; both they and the broomstick were too light a colour.

"Oh," she said. She understood now. But still she shone her torch through the cell bars, and onto the pathetic huddle of rags and bones from which the outstretched arm protruded. The skull was angled back and propped against the wall; the jaw hung open, dangling by a hinge.

She went to the next cell, then the next, then stumbled across the room, ignoring John's voice calling her name, to check the other row. Each wall held ten cells; no more than a third, in total, had still been occupied, but that was enough. It was too many.

"They were... just left here," she said. "To starve."

John nodded. "Thorne."

"Not Thorne," she said. "Kellett. Whether Thorne was dead or... somewhere else, Kellett would've known they were down here. He just took his money and scarpered, and I bet you he never even thought of them again."

"Bastard," said John.

"Yeah." She took a deep breath and let it out, tried to stay calm. She'd need a clear head down here: to give way to rage, terror or grief would be fatal. "Come on. We've got stuff to do."

They went back into the tunnel. Another archway appeared on the right, but the room it opened into was empty and featureless. No cells in the brick walls, and nothing else, but Alice was sure there was something about the room she ought to notice.

The next room was the same, except that there was something propped against the wall. Alice went inside, shining her torch on it. "A shovel?"

Beside it was a pick-axe. John shone the torch around the room, frowning. Alice crossed the floor towards him, and that was when she realised what was different. The floor sloped up, then down again. A mound.

She let out a muffled cry and scrambled clear, flashing her torch over the chamber floor. Yes, it was a mound – a low one, but a mound none the less. She pushed past John, went back to the chamber before and studied the floor.

"Burial chambers," she said. John stared into the chamber with the shovel and pick, then looked back at Alice. She took more deep breaths, forced herself to stay calm, then walked on. "Those are mass graves, in both of those rooms."

Her legs were trembling again. She kept walking; it was easier than trying to stand still.

There was another archway to her right. She made herself peer through it. There was a door of iron bars here too, but set in the archway itself, although it was standing ajar. It squealed as she pushed it further open and stepped through.

There was a bed – a rusted iron frame and the rotten remains of blankets and a mattress – a desk and chair with a jug and ewer on them, a shelf with a few mouldering books, a cobwebbed chamber-pot. The books were swollen with fungus and damp, their pages beyond reading. Even the leather bindings were so badly cracked that she couldn't read the titles on the spines. Lanterns hung from hooks on the walls.

Compared to the cells it was almost palatial, but in a way that made it worse. It was still a prison, and Alice thought she could guess whose. She backed out of there quickly; the air itself there smelled, *felt*, horrible and wrong in a way she couldn't define. John put his hands on her shoulders. She started, gasping, then relaxed when she realised who it was.

"Easy," he said. He didn't sound any better than she felt.

She patted his hand, slipped free and walked on. The tunnel bent round. From up ahead she heard a sound of trickling water. Then the tunnel opened out into a chamber; into *the* chamber.

It had to be. It matched Mary Carson's description: a semi-circular room with stone and brick walls and a stone ceiling buttressed with stout wooden beams. Unlit lamps hung at intervals and a narrow brick-lined gutter crossed the floor to empty into a sodden, weed-clogged drain in the corner. And the straight wall was living rock, and in it was a hole – the cave entrance – from which water coursed to fill a bowl-shaped hollow that drained off through the gutter. The Collarmill Spring, the Grail-beck's source.

And, in front of the spring –

"Oh Christ," said Alice, and nearly dropped the torch. But she gripped it tight; she wouldn't look away.

"Fuck," said John.

It was a chair, or at least it resembled one at first. Until you got in close and saw the clamps and straps that held the occupant in place, the tangled mass of gears and cogs crouching underneath it, the long brass lever with the ivory handle that stuck upwards from its base and the blades and hooks and other implements it bristled with. They were barely tinged with rust; in fact, what had looked initially like rust looked more like something that had dried and crusted on them. Stainless steel? Unlikely, if this was of Thorne's making: his death had come long before its invention. Silver plating, perhaps; whatever it was, the machine's parts were barely touched by decay despite the damp air.

The same could be said for the Moloch Device's occupant. Comparatively speaking, anyway. The other children who'd died down here were rags and dust and bones, but this one was more than that. No rags, because there would have been no clothes: Arodias Thorne would have put him naked into the Device's embrace. But both the skin that hadn't peeled off him and the skin that had were still there, had dried hard like perished, buckled leather. Alice had no idea how it could have happened, because she'd always thought it took dry heat to make a mummy – or freeze-drying, maybe, in a handful of cases. She could feel the air's dampness here, and, while chill, it wasn't even close to either of the extremes of temperature that would have preserved the corpse.

And yet, and yet, here he sat. Yes, it was, had been a he – she couldn't keep her gaze from straying to the dead youth's groin, and what remained of the genitals, little though it was, was unambiguously male. Beneath the holes in the skin the Device had made – gaping bloodlessly now, stretched wide by the skin's drying – the muscles were gnarled, blackened cords, the viscera hardened and translucent. Shrinkage had turned the victim's last expression monstrous, pulling the jaws tight shut, while the lips writhed back in a simian grimace from teeth turned to blade and chisel-like fangs by the withering of the gums, and the nose had shrunk to a crumpled little snout. The eyelids retained their natural shape, but the eyes themselves were gone, unless their shrivelled and deflated remains still rested inside the emptied sockets; hair hung down to the shoulders, bleached and faded to white.

"Mary Carson's kid," said John. "Right?"

"I think so." Her throat felt constricted, choked; tears stung her eyes. Another dead child. How old would he have been? Arodias Thorne's death, if it had really been a death, had been in December 1851, six months before the boy's fourteenth birthday. Thirteen years; six more than Emily had ever got. But at least Emily had known the light, the sun, green grass and rain. What had Mary's child known except this dark? She thought of the cell with its shelves of books and iron-framed bed. Had he lived out his whole life there, like some pale grub in the dark? Christ, had Thorne even troubled himself to give the child a *name*?

"Babe?" John's hand settled on her arm. Alice realised that she was crying. She shook her head, squeezed his hand and stepped away from him. "I'm okay," she said at last, but she wasn't, and she doubted John was stupid enough to believe it either.

If he'd ever had a name, this boy of Mary Carson's, it had gone unrecorded. All so long ago now, long ago and far away – but it still felt close. He'd lived in the dark and died in it, this nameless boy – alone and companionless, without love or comfort, and his last minutes had been a crucifying agony as the machine had pulled him apart. Alice found herself kneeling by the chair, wrestling with unoiled clamps and stiffened, dusty straps, freeing the mummified limbs from their bondage. Wrists, ankles, chest and waist, then finally the head. The body didn't slump or sag; it lolled stiffly sideways, the whole of it in one unyielding part, like stone. Something crunched in its side, and dust shivered from its hair.

"Easy," muttered Alice. She rose and steeled herself, then reached out to touch the body.

John said nothing, thank God. This was hard enough even

with everything she had focused on the task. Her skin writhed at the prospect; when she'd been a child even the sight of a dead bird had made her recoil, and now this. She shut her eyes and bit her lips, clasped hold of the body, afraid it would break apart at the pressure of her touch.

It didn't, though. It held. Alice stepped back and lifted, and the mummy came with her. It was heavier than she'd expected; the thing in the chair had looked like an empty husk, desiccated to the point of weightlessness.

She looked down at the floor, so that she could see where she was going without looking at what she carried. The corpse's bare feet swung below her. Bony as they were, with the nails grown long and black until they resembled talons, they looked like the paws of an animal.

She knelt and lowered him to the floor. Finally she allowed herself to look at the boy. He'd suffered no further damage, but he'd never look peaceful in death. His father had seen to that.

Alice stood, then stumbled back, her revulsion at what she'd touched kicking back in; she scrubbed her hands frantically against her jeans until they were sore.

Her torchlight was waning. "Shit," she muttered, and began winding the handle. The darkness fell in upon her; it made her think far too much about being buried alive, about tons of black, silent soil flooding in to drown her. So dark. She looked around, but couldn't see the other torch. "John?" she said.

No answer. She turned, flashed her torch at where he'd been, but there was nothing. The torch dimmed again. She wound the handle frantically, shining it around, but found nothing and the beam continued to fade.

Then light bloomed on the walls.

The lanterns hanging around the chamber first glowed, then brightened, all in perfect unison. There was no-one near them; no hand she saw lit the wicks. The yellow light that spread to fill the chamber might have been comforting, Alice thought, in another place or time.

"John?"

"Alice," said a voice. Voices. None of them John's.

It was a voice that sounded like four speaking in eerie chorus. It came from behind her, and so she turned.

The Red Man stood behind the Moloch Device, his pale left hand pressed to John Revell's forehead, bending his head back. In his right was a knife. Its silver-shining blade, flashing where it caught the light, rested on John's throat.

# Chapter Thirty-One

## The Fire Beyond

*31st October 2016*

How long did the silence last? Alice couldn't tell. She couldn't look away from John or his captor. It would be the work of a second, the simplest movement of a hand, as long as the blade was sharp. And it would be, of course.

John was still, teeth clenched, lips peeled back. Angry, afraid, but not so much of either that he'd do something stupid. The Red Man was silent and still.

Alice studied him; she'd seen him before, of course, but fleetingly, and with the quality of a dream. There was nothing dreamlike about him now. She could see every detail.

Close to, it was hard to believe what she'd seen him do to the ogre. His scarlet robes were tattered and frayed: grimy, worn. The white mask was scratched and pitted – she thought she saw a hairline crack in it – and expressionless though it was, it somehow looked ineffably weary. Yes, this was an endgame of some kind. The Red Man was very close to done.

Another thought: the rowan cross. She fumbled it from her

pocket and thrust it towards him. The Red Man didn't move, but the lips of the mask stirred, and that strange choral voice came out.

"That will drive back the children," he said, "but not me." He inclined his head towards John. "I do not wish to hurt him, but I will cut his throat if you do not obey."

"All right." Alice pocketed the cross and raised her hands. "Just don't hurt him. Okay? Please?"

"This is what will happen." The Red Man inclined his head towards the Moloch Device. "I will bring your friend here. He will sit in the chair, and you will strap him into place."

"No. No, please."

The Red Man motioned slightly with the knife; John gasped, blood on his throat. Alice cried out.

"A scratch only," the Red Man said. "Listen to me, Alice Collier, and understand. I do not wish to kill. I have *never* wished to kill." Was there a note of bitterness in that voice? "But my will is not my own. I have no choice. But I pledge you my word that I will help you, both – if you obey me now."

"John?" Alice whispered.

"Do it," he said. "I'm not dead yet."

"He speaks truly," said the Red Man, and marched John round the front of the chair, then – keeping the knife at his throat – pressed him down into it. "Now secure him," he told Alice, not looking at her.

She ran forward, knelt and set to work. Her fingers felt thick and stiff and clumsy; the straps and clamps were stiff too, through age or rust or disuse. But she secured John's ankles first, then his wrists. Then a strap around his waist, another round his chest, another still round his forehead.

She was crying again. Oh, if she only didn't care. It would be so much easier if she didn't care. But she did. *All the times you made me laugh, John; all the ways you made me smile. The warmth of your arms. I tried to forget them, even tried to hate you, but none of it worked.*

"I'm sorry," she whispered. "I'm sorry, I'm sorry."

"It's okay," he said. "It's okay, babe."

His eyes were wise and kind.

"I," she began, then "I," again. No, that was wrong. "John," she said. "John –"

"I know, babe. Me too." He smiled and shook his head, as much as the strap allowed. "I never stopped."

"I thought I had." Her hand gripped his. "I didn't, though."

A tapping sound; she looked up, saw the Red Man's blade rapping lightly on the frame of the chair. The white mask stared down at her; John tried in vain to crane his head up and see it too.

The Red Man moved round to face both of them. "You must listen now," he said. "You will both need your courage, and your strength." He looked from John to her. "I cannot say which of you will need it more. It will be hard – it will be terrible – for you both."

"Jesus," said John, "go ahead and sell it to us, why don't you, mate?"

Alice blinked. For an instant she was sure she'd seen the mask's lips turn fractionally up at the corners in some approximation of a smile.

"You will both be in great danger," said the Red Man. "But if you can endure, I will help you all I can. Then, with luck, you may both survive this night."

"If," said Alice. "May."

The Red Man inclined his head. "I have told you – my will is not my own in this. None of this is, or has been, by my desire or choice."

"Only obeying orders," said John. "Heard that one before."

"You do not understand," said the Red Man. "But if you live, you will. Now listen, for time is short."

Alice looked at John, squeezed his hand again. "Okay," she said. "Go on."

"Perihelion approaches," said the Red Man. "You understand the term?"

"Halloween," said John.

"There are times and places," said the Red Man, "at which the Fire, in one form or another, is close to this world, so close it takes little effort to reach. This is one such time; that is why it was once an occasion for worship and sacrifice. The Veil between the Worlds is easily parted tonight, and the flame revealed." The mask turned towards Alice. "And when it is, you must step into it."

"What?"

"I will be with you," said the Red Man, "And I will be your guide."

"Oh, *shit*," said John. They both looked at him. "And I'm the poor bastard who's got to open the way, right?"

The Red Man inclined his head. "I am sorry."

"Wait a sec," said Alice, suddenly angry. "You can't do that – not with John. It's got to be – got to be my child or something."

The Red Man shook his head. "Arodias Thorne knew much, but not everything. For this he can hardly be blamed. The books he followed, after all, were only written by men, no matter what they had witnessed, no matter what inspired them. Ties of blood are unimportant. All that matters is the correct sacrifice at the correct time."

Remembering the Confession, Alice felt sick. "Then everything he did to Mary Carson..."

"Unnecessary," the Red Man said. "Although it doubtless gratified him in some way." Again, Alice was sure she heard something like bitterness in his voice. "Before you say it, yes: John must be embraced by the Moloch Device in order to part the Veil."

"No –"

"*Listen to me*. There is something that must be corrected, and that can only be done by entering the Fire Beyond. I cannot do it alone, else I would. When you have done what must be done, I will bring you back. As long as John is still alive, there will be hope for him." The Red Man pointed to the waters of the Collarmill Spring. "I will help you heal him, and then you are released."

"How can I trust you?"

"I cannot answer that. I could say that I have saved your life, but –"

"You did it for this," said John.

"Yes. I can only give you my word, and tell you that it has never been broken."

"And if we refuse, we die."

"Yes. I will be compelled to."

Alice swallowed hard, looked at John. Die for certain, or risk what might be worse? At last, she nodded; a moment later, he nodded back.

"Okay," she said, and stood. "What do I need to do?"

"For now, only wait." The white mask turned to contemplate John. "His task comes first."

John took a deep, shuddering breath. Almost gently, the Red Man touched his shoulder. "Are you ready?"

"No. Yes. Fuck. I'm as ready as I'm ever gonna be." John gritted his teeth; his bound hands balled into fists. "Do it."

The Red Man motioned to Alice. "You must."

"Oh God."

"Do it," John said again.

Her hands shook as they grasped the lever, then pulled. At first she thought it wouldn't move, that it was rusted into place and that the whole horrible contraption was dead, broken beyond repair, just an ugly relic of Arodias Thorne's cruelty and madness, but then it shifted, with a gritting, grinding sound. With a dull, solid *clunk,* it slotted into place.

Cogs and gears ground. Below the chair, the machinery of the Device stirred and moved.

"Don't look," said John. "I can handle it if you don't look."

"Look instead at the spring," said the Red Man. He came to Alice's side; his hand rested on her shoulder. "It will not take long."

"Depends on your point of view," she said. She could hear John breathing harshly through his teeth.

"You are thinking of the boy Mary Carson saw die in this chair," the Red Man told her. "Do not. That was a long way from perihelion, and Arodias Thorne had nearly fourteen years after that to perfect the efficiency of this device. It parted the Veil in minutes when he put her child in there." He bowed his head, as if in shame. "But there was no-one here to stop the Device once its work was begun."

She heard the sound of other parts moving now, as the Moloch Device's battery of implements were set in motion and went to work. John grunted and growled through his teeth.

"Watch," the Red Man said again. "Be ready – when the Veil parts, we go through. If you care for him, every moment is precious now."

The water bubbled and trickled.

John screamed. A sob burst from Alice's throat.

"*Watch!*"

She wiped her eyes, focused. John screamed again, and again, and the Moloch Device's cogs and gears ground on.

How long now? How long? What if it didn't work? Arodias' victims had only been children, but John was a grown man – wouldn't he be more resistant to the pain, less ideal a subject?

As if in answer to the thought, another scream ripped the air behind her.

"*Watch.*"

The gears and cogs ground and the screams rang, on and on and on. This was Hell, this was how Hell would be, an eternity of this – except of course that there were worse torments, there had been the loss of Emily, there would have been (she forced herself in desperation to think it, to make this bearable) the torment if Emily, had she lived, had been in the chair instead of John. She tried to hold the image in her head, but it was too vile to stay and no imagining, however bad, could compete with the reality taking place behind her, the one she could only hear but had to fight not to turn around and face. It would go on forever, or at least until John was dead.

And then the waters of the Collarmill Spring burst into bright blue flame.

It was that same pale lambent glow she'd seen in the kitchen. It lit the inside of the cave, and she could see all the way to the back of it. It was small, Alice realised, reaching back no more than ten or twenty feet. From the stone face at the back of it, she saw the water gushing out, burning bright and flowing along the cave floor, flickering off the damp stone walls. As John screamed again, the flames brightened and intensified further, streaming upwards, until the spring, the chamber – and yes, even the screams from behind her – seemed to dim and fade, to became shadows and the breath of the wind.

The only real thing was that column of blue fire, and this, she realised, was what Arodias Thorne had sought his whole life, had perfected the Moloch Device in order to see. The Fire Beyond, close enough to touch, real enough to enter and to pass through, to whatever lay beyond. It had taken years – years, and how many children's lives? Surely more than the ones Alice had seen. Maybe they were just the vanguard of a spectral, suffering army, united in their need for vengeance.

The Red Man stepped forward: at last, something almost as real as the fire. He held out a hand to her. "Quickly," he said. "Now!"

Alice reached out and took his cold white hand. The blue flames flared brighter. Her gaze was drawn to them, and they seemed to grow and encompass her; so much so that she barely noticed when the Red Man strode forward and, drawing her after him, walked into the Fire Beyond.

# Chapter Thirty-Two

## Behind the Mask

THE WORLD EXPLODED into blue fire, then white. Alice cried out and flailed in her blindness, but the hand that held hers only gripped tighter, so tight she cried out again from the pain. But the pain anchored her, focused her, reminded her the light was only something that she passed through.

She floated. A million voices screamed and sang, and there was no ground beneath her feet but she did not fall.

She floated; she flew. It was exhilarating and it was terrifying. A wrong turn here and there was nothing to stop her hurtling on into space, into eternity.

And then, a swooping descent; even though she couldn't see anything she could feel it rushing up to meet her. She pedalled with her feet – and then they hit solid, if uneven ground, and she staggered forward as the world crashed into her.

She stumbled, almost fell; the cool grip on her hand steadied her. Brightly coloured lights flashed in her eyes; she blinked hard to clear them, then looked about her. It was daylight. The sky above was overcast and grey. She stood on bare grass. They were on top of a hill, one bare of any sign of human habitation. Below them Alice saw a wide valley, a winding river nearby. The whole street, even her house, was gone, but the spring was still there, bubbling from the cave entrance, now set into a low grassy hump, emptying into the same bowl-shaped pool before draining into a small thin stream that zig-zagged down the hillside. The water that poured from the rock, that filled the pool, was still burning. Some flames still flickered weakly on the stream's waters as they emerged, but died away quickly as they ran downhill.

"We are here," said the Red Man.

She turned and faced him. Wind flurried his robes.

From below them came shouts. Beyond the hill were thick woodlands, and near them Alice saw the same low wooden buildings as before. Tiny figures emerged, gathering at the base of the hill. Men clad in crudely-stitched leather and animal furs, pinned together with needles of bone. Some held spears and axes; others, burning torches. One wore what looked like a wolf's pelt, its emptied head snarling above his black-bearded face. He was shouting and pointing up the hill towards her. The few words Alice could make out meant nothing to her, but their importance was clear enough. What had he called her, she wondered? A witch? A demon? Nothing, at any rate, that could be allowed to live and pollute the sacred spring. Whoever he was, he was marshalling the others to attack.

"You're afraid," said the Red Man, in his strange four-in-one voice. "Don't be, Alice. There is no need."

The man in the wolf-pelt screamed something, weapon held aloft. Then he was running up the hill, and with a howl, his tribe followed.

Alice tried to step backwards, but the Red Man held her fast. "Watch," he said.

The roar came, the bellow; not the many-throated roar of a mob, but a single one, from a vast lone throat. The forest hissed and crackled as dead wood fell from the trees and living wood split and cracked from the passage of something huge and remorseless. The wood rustled, heaved and broke open, and something huge and piebald ran from it on all fours towards Redman's Hill.

It rampaged through the village; its foot caught one wooden dwelling and tore half of it away in a hail of boards and splinters. A chorus of screams came from the village. The tribesmen, a third of the way up the hill, had already turned and frozen. Now they scattered, screaming, as Old Harry came charging towards them, fury on that shaggy, low-browed, slobbering face.

Only the pelt-clad man was not fast enough; the ogre snatched him up and flung him down like a toy. He hit the ground and rolled and did not move. By then, the remaining tribesmen had fallen back to the village and formed a defensive ring around their remaining homes.

Old Harry, the Beast of Browton, reared up, howled and beat its chest, then climbed further up the hill before turning to do so again. The tribesmen broke and ran back inside their homes. They'd be praying to whatever gods they held dear, Alice guessed; nothing else would shield them.

Old Harry roared again, then began to descend, lumbering towards the village.

Alice looked towards the Red Man. He let go of her hand and pushed her aside. "No more," he said, then shouted it after Old Harry. "No more!"

The ogre looked back over its shoulder and snarled, then turned away and continued downward.

She heard the Red Man take a long, rattling breath and raise his arms. A moment later, the *sound* come out of him – whether from his mouth or some essential core of his being, she couldn't tell, but she felt the ground shiver with its force. The Beast turned and snarled, struggled as if straining against a hundred ropes that bound it. For a moment she thought it would break away and tear down towards the village – but at last it sagged down onto all fours and crawled up the hill, glaring balefully at them both, every step of its ascent.

The Red Man groaned and fell to his knees. Old Harry raised its head and watched him through narrowed eyes, but the Red Man looked up at him, meeting that cold blue stare with whatever lay behind those blank eyeholes. Another snarl, and the Beast lowered its head and climbed on.

Alice knelt by the Red Man. "Are you okay?"

"I can hold out a little while yet."

"Long enough to get me back? And to save John?"

He didn't answer. She caught his arm, then snatched her hand away. Something about it hadn't felt right. The Red Man made to move away, but she caught hold of him again. Another time, she suspected, he would have been too fast for her and too strong, but controlling the Beast had weakened him, at least for now.

The arm underneath the wide red sleeve was thin – impossibly so, it felt. And hard. She made a fist, gripping the loose material, and pushed it up before the Red Man could move to resist.

The arm was bone. Not even the two thin bones of a human forearm, but one long thick bone. Along its side ran a long narrow panel of glass; inside it, Alice saw cogs, levers, gears – a whole intricate nest of clockwork – that turned and clicked and worked and moved.

The Red Man tore free of her grip. In doing so, the cowl slipped back. What lay beneath was what appeared to be a skull, except that its bones blended seamlessly into the mask of the Red Man's face. Again, there were glass panels set into it, and behind them more bone clockwork turned.

The Red Man stumbled away, twisted clear of her, struggling with his clothes. The Beast growled. The Red Man rose to his feet and turned to face her. His robes were once more back in place.

"I did not wish for you to see that," he said at last.

Oddly, Alice wasn't afraid. "What are you?"

"An automaton," he said. "A machine. A servant. A... perhaps the best word would be a *familiar*. What animates me is not mechanical; it merely amused my maker to shape me in this way." The Red Man ran his hand along the sleeve of his robe, as if worried the bone might still be visible. "I was created for a purpose which I am unable to fulfil alone. To do that, I need your help."

"What purpose? Who created you?"

"Can you not guess?" The Red Man turned and pointed to the creature just below them. "He did. Machines were his lifeblood, his wealth – but in private, he preferred to work with flesh and bone. In me, it suited his humour to combine the two."

"*Him?*"

"He was not always as you see him. With your help and mine, he will be as he was again." The Red Man turned back to Alice. "He will become the man he once was. He will become Arodias Thorne."

# Chapter Thirty-Three

## On Collarmill Height

OLD HARRY – THE Beast, the ogre – stirred and started at the mention of the name, growled softly; the Red Man waved a hand, and it subsided. Its eyes flicked towards Alice. She looked away, and moved back towards the Red Man.

"How can that be Arodias Thorne? There've been legends about Old Harry for centuries – he's been around for hundreds of years before the bastard was ever born. And you?" She waved her arms at the surroundings. "Collarmill Height – Collarmill, Sixsmythe told us what that meant. The Red Knight's Hill – in *Latin*. You were – how could – you were here when the *Romans* came, for Christ's sake. How can you have been made by him? He wasn't even *born* until –"

"Haven't you understood anything, Alice?" The Red Man went to the cave-mouth. "Where we are now – the spring, the Fire Beyond? From where we are now, we can see for miles. More than you'd think. Across the world. Further. The moons of Jupiter, if you want. Distant stars. And not only through space. Time, too. The past, the future. And more than look. We travel. It's only a matter of seeing things as they are – as they truly are."

The Beast growled; the Red Man eyed it for a moment, then turned back to her. "Old Harry," he said. "Old Arry."

"Arry," said Alice. "Of course. From Arodias."

The Red Man nodded. "He roamed through time at will, but nowhere near as far in space. Not after he became this. It was familiar to him. Browton, where he'd grown up; Crawbeck, where he'd lived. He'd roam far and wide, looking for whatever he craved – young women, mostly. He'd aim to satisfy one appetite or another with their flesh, be it his hunger or his lust. Sometimes both. And I... I would pursue him, find him. Sometimes in good time and sometimes not." Was that guilt she heard? It was hard to tell with that many-toned voice.

Alice looked at the ogre; she could smell the stink of it from where she stood. "That... *thing* is Arodias Thorne? How? I mean, what happened?"

"'Be careful what you wish for; you may get it.' That's the proverb, isn't it? Arodias Thorne got what he had desired so long. The Fire Beyond. He controlled it, and so he had – *has* – eternity, together with the ability to reshape physical reality in accordance with his desires. But that was the problem. Everything, in theory, became subject to Thorne's will." The Red Man sighed. "I think that what happened was... a trick? Perhaps too strong a word. I don't believe that the Fire Beyond has a mind of its own, as such. But I do believe that the kind of power Thorne sought is hard to attain for good reason."

"You mean," Alice had to smile, "that there are some things man was never meant to know?"

"Or woman?" Incredibly, the Red Man smiled. "Not exactly. I mean that the Fire Beyond, by its nature, *cannot* be controlled for long – not as he wanted to control it."

"I don't get you."

"As you use the Fire – as you change things with it – the Fire also changes you. It amplifies both flaws and virtues, shapes not just reality but one's own form and nature to fit them. And the Fire reshaped Arodias into what he had always truly been

– a creature of rapacious greed. His intellect, everything else he might have been, all of that was gone, subsumed into... *this*. But he had time to know what was coming, and to create me."

"To make him what he was."

"That's right. He couldn't stop what was happening to him, but he could create a being like me, who could watch for someone like you."

"What's so special about me?"

"You can reverse what has happened to him. Restore him, to the man he was. I cannot. I can only serve."

"How am I supposed to change him back?"

The Red Man pointed to the burning grail pool. "There is the Fire Beyond in its purest form. If you drink it, you will see."

"*What* will I see?"

The mask's dark eyeholes met hers in an empty stare. "Everything. All you have to do is survive the experience."

"You're a cheery fucker, aren't you? And you're taking a lot for granted."

"Only I can return you," the Red Man reminded her. "And if you would save John Revell, only I can help you do so."

"But... why me? Why me, out of everyone?"

"There are no wizards," said the Red Man, "or none that I could find. None who understand the mysteries and rites that Arodias drew on."

"Well, I certainly don't."

"Yes," the Red Man said, "and no. You are not schooled in those rituals. You do, however, understand the concepts and principles involved. You and John understood them at the last."

Alice remembered the conversation in her room. "You mean I was right about all that?"

"Close enough, shall we say."

"So you want me to turn Arodias back into a man," she said. "No wonder the kids wanted me dead. I suppose they thought it poetic justice of a kind, didn't they, seeing Arodias turned into a slobbering beast? As much of it as they'd get, anyway.

And then you come along to take even that away from them."

"*It is not through my choice.*" She stepped back from the real anger in the Red Man's voice. He sighed. "I am sorry. But you behave as though I had a will of my own in this. Arodias… built constraints into me. I *cannot* betray him, or disobey. Whatever my own feelings. If I had a choice, I might choose differently. He made me enough like you for that. But at the same time, he denied me free will. I have been his keeper, even his gaoler, for this long; given free will, I might have continued to be, throughout eternity. Or sought to put an end to him. But this was denied me. Perhaps he guessed that he made me too human to be entirely trusted. And so I have reined him in, sought one like you, and protected you from the dead. All you need do now is what I ask – and then you can go."

"And John?"

"And John, if we are quick enough to save him. I can promise that, and what promises I can make, I keep."

Alice studied the Beast and thought of the brute hunger with which it had pursued her, of Mary Carson and all she had undergone, of the Moloch Device and the children who had screamed in its embrace, of the withered husk she had prised from its grip. And she thought of John: John as she had known him, the kind, clever eyes, the anger and the warmth of him, and then of the screams that had echoed out behind her as the way had opened to this place. "All right," she said finally. "Show me what to do."

"Just drink the water," said the Red Man. "I told you: drink and you'll see. And then you'll be able to do what has to be done."

"If I survive."

He nodded.

The Beast growled. Somewhere, the Moloch Device had John. Alice walked to the spring and knelt. The children had tried to kill her to stop this. Now they'd failed, and she'd robbed them of their justice.

"I'm sorry," she muttered, then dipped cupped hands into the water. She'd steeled herself for pain – of course there'd been none when she'd passed through the flame, but that had been a gateway, not a fire for drinking. But there was no pain now, either. The fire licked around her wrists, and she felt nothing but a light tickling, tingling sensation. She scooped up the water; flames danced on its surface and on the skin of her hands.

*I'm about to drink fire. Do it quick, before you think yourself out of it.*

She put it to her lips and gulped. The water was cold and clear and she could taste the purity of it, feel it. A line of pale fire from her lips, down her throat and into her – and then spreading outwards, filling her.

Alice rose. Her hands were glittering with light. At first she thought it was the last of the spring water, but then she realised the light was coming from within.

The world spasmed and lurched. The earth was the sky; the water was the earth. The Red Man's placid mask watched her. The Beast cringed and howled. Chanted prayers rose from the village below. Everything was packed with shadows: the shadows were the past and future of each object, and not only one future but many, all possible ones.

A wave of dizziness sent Alice to her knees beside the grail pool. The grass swam in and out of focus, and then she could see the blades of grass and the crumbs of earth and the ants and mites that crawled amongst them. Now she saw smaller things, smaller and smaller. In the grail pool she saw a water boatman rowing on the surface, in such pin-sharp detail she felt as though she were hovering alongside a battleship, eyeing the grooved chitin of its back, the steady metronomic beat of its paddles. But there were smaller things too: rotifers and tardigrades, hydras and daphnia. She looked away, back at the grass, and now she saw the individual cells with their green cellulose walls. Bacteria teemed in the water, on each blade of grass, even her hands.

Already her sight was reaching further, further. One of the plant cells rushed towards her, expanding to the dimensions of an office block. The cell wall, the cellular membrane. Here was the nucleus, there the green spheres of the chloroplasts, suspended in the cytoplasm. Then she eyed the nucleus, and it rushed up to meet her. She thought of a golf ball with the outer shell peeled off, a globe made of strand on rubbery strand, wrapped and interwoven. She looked at a single strand and there it was, thick as a tree-trunk beside her. Here was a strand of DNA, that intricate double helix that was at once the recipe for any living creature you cared to name and the machine that would build it. She not only knew the individual molecules – this was cytosine, this guanine, that adenine, the other thymine – and the sequence they stood in, she understood the messages they spelled out, the grammar and syntax of genesis itself.

Now she started to understand the power of the spring water, how it worked as it had. If she wished it, she could rearrange the molecules of the DNA as easily as she might the tiles in a Scrabble set and reshape the organisms they composed into a dodo, a quagga, a passenger pigeon or a great auk. Any one of a hundred extinct species could live again at her whim: all she need do was to reach out and touch.

With what? She wasn't sure, at this level, what her thoughts would move to achieve the desired result, only that they would do so, beyond doubt. What she wanted would happen. And the water that had emerged from the spring in the old days, the one that had become a shrine, that had only been a shadow of this – enough to seize upon this man's desire for health or life, another's to know what was to come or what had been, and grant that wish before its touch, its union, its insight departed again.

And then beyond the DNA, she was falling in among the atoms and beyond them. Here was an atom of carbon: the protons were heavy spheres of red, the neutrons heavier purple ones, while around them, high above, zipped the tiny blue electrons.

And then she fell beyond: a proton loomed up, the size of a planet, and she tumbled into it. Two up quarks, one down quark, and flickering between them, the gluons that bound them together. *Oh, Andrew, Teddy, if you could see this now. To behold this sight with your own eyes* – if, indeed, it was her eyes with which she now perceived this.

And now at last she was at the simplest level, where matter was both a particle and a waveform. Where every choice, every action, spawned new realities. Where pasts and futures shimmered out behind and ahead. Go this way, and see the dinosaurs walk the earth; go that and watch the death of the sun. Reach out a hand and change reality.

I am it and it is I. I am he as you are he and we are me.

I am everything and nothing; the potter and the clay.

There was no she; no Red Man, no Arodias. No John and no Mary. No Andrew and no Emily. Emily. It was all one thing, one great swirling shifting mass of energy that formed here and there into patterns and eddies like shapes in the fire. Patterns of abstract energy in motion through space-time. Emily. There was no point now where she ended and the rest of existence began; in this moment she was everything and could do anything.

Emily.

She understood something of what had happened to Arodias now. Her thought potentially controlled everything now – but what controlled her thought? A subconscious whim could command all the force of a conscious desire. She saw her mind for a second as a flimsy structure of biases and ideas, ethics and philosophies imperfectly cobbled together in an effort to create a make-do framework – something to house and cage and channel the fast dark waters of her soul. And that current was now the torrent that swept all else before it, altering even its own shape and course like a river in flood as it wore away the weaknesses in its banks, or shaped islands out of silt and gravel.

Alice opened her mouth and tried to scream.

Was she the first one the Red Man had waited for? Had

there been others, who had drunk the water but been unable to withstand what lay behind the veil they'd lifted? Perhaps she was about to join their number.

The torrent buffetted her. Emily. Emily. Emily Emily Emily. She couldn't, mustn't think of it. But she couldn't *not* think of it. All she could do was surrender to the torrent and hope she could learn to ride it. Instead of drowning there.

The torrent grew faster and the waters rose. No air, no light, and no longer able to hang on.

Alice let go, and let the water take her.

# Chapter Thirty-Four

## A Nation of Three

*August 2014*

Alice leant back in her chair, rubbed her eyes and breathed out. From upstairs, she heard singing, and the sound of Emily bouncing around her room. How someone so small managed to sound so heavy was a puzzle even quantum physics couldn't solve; it sometimes sounded as if she was about to come through the ceiling.

Alice yawned, put her glasses back on and stared at the laptop screen. No, the rest of the book hadn't magically written itself while she'd taken a breather. More was the pity; the deadline was coming up and right now the writing was like pulling teeth.

It didn't help that the kitchen was hot, the air close and thick. It was like trying to breathe cotton wool. The summer had been fierce. A long hot spell had been broken by thunderstorms and torrential rains only a couple of days before – the river running by the village was still swollen and fast – but the blistering heat had quickly reasserted itself. Andrew had wanted to install ceiling fans when they'd redecorated last year, but Alice had vetoed it. She wished now she hadn't: it would have done a lot to make the kitchen more bearable.

A pain was gnawing behind her left eye. Always the worst place, meaning a world-class bastard of a headache was on the way if she didn't do something PDQ. Outside the sun was bright, the trees explosions of glossy dark green and the grass bright emerald. Clear blue sky without a cloud; the song of birds.

But all that was outside and she was inside, staring at the screen and its single winking cursor. *Finish the chapter and you can go out*, she told herself, but she'd been telling herself that all day and here she was now at two in the afternoon with barely a paragraph written. She'd manage a few words, a desultory and unsatisfying sentence or so, and then she'd abandon the work, leafing through a book or surfing the net instead. As if the part of her that did the writing was a sulky child who wanted to go out *now*.

Alice grunted, got to her feet and went to the sink, where she filled a half-pint glass from the tap. They kept their medicines in a cupboard above the sink; she popped two ibuprofen out of a blister pack and swallowed them with water.

"Mummy?"

Alice turned and smiled. "Hello there, chucky-egg."

Emily bounced into the kitchen. The blue eyes might have been Alice's, but where she'd got her ash-blonde hair from was anyone's guess. Or that tiny heart-shaped face, which they both agreed was going to break hearts one day. Andrew was already joking about investing in a shotgun to deter potential boyfriends. "Look. New picture."

Alice knew she was biased, but honestly thought Emily had real talent, although the subject matter was a bit worrying at times: here was another sword-fight, starring a young woman with blonde hair and blue eyes who appeared to be cheerfully dismembering her way through a mixed bag of disreputable-looking humans and other creatures of uncertain origin. "Wow. That's good."

"Can we go out and play now?"

"Emily, Mummy's working."

"*Pleeeease?*"

Working on her textbooks had been an easy enough job after Emily was born; she'd often set up a folding table in the nursery with the cot only a couple of feet away and beavered away on the laptop with breaks for feeds and nappy-changing. The first textbook had been a big enough success for her to have been offered more work, and that work had come often enough and paid well enough – not as well as the work at Amberson's, it was true – for her to work from home. It wasn't the big-bucks career she'd dreamt of a few years before, but she was content with it. Motherhood changed you. Andrew had the high-flying career now, and if Alice privately thought she was actually the brighter of the two of them, if she ever wondered if maybe she should be the one still at the lab while he stayed at home and wrote textbooks for school kids then, well, life was like that. There'd always be something you regretted or wondered about.

All the same, an infant in a cot was a lot easier to manage than a seven-year-old with fully-developed motor skills, boundless energy and demands of her own. "Oh come on, Mummy," Emily said. "We've been here all day."

"Well go and play in the garden, then."

"*Bo*-ring."

Alice took a deep breath, and then the phone rang. Probably for the best; she didn't want a row with Emily right now. "Hello?"

"Hi, sweetheart."

"Hey, babe."

"Hiya daddy!"

"Say hello to the little monster for me."

"Daddy says hello."

Emily waved, then climbed up onto one of the kitchen chairs. "What can I do you for?" Alice said.

"Well, thought you might like to know. It's about Teddy."

She felt cold. "What about him?"

"It's his last day today."

"*What?*"

"Yeah, he gave in his notice a while b –"

"And you didn't tell me?"

"You haven't seen him in ages."

Alice felt a pang of guilt. "I know, but… anyway, never mind that. Why's he going?"

"Early retirement. Seems he's put a lot of money away for his old age, and – well, he had some bad news. You know, health-wise."

"Oh God. Oh no."

"Alice, it's okay. It was the 'if you hang up your boots now you should be fine' kind rather than the 'six months to live' sort, if you know what I mean. But him and Stefan are moving abroad. Flying out to Spain in a week."

"Next *week*? God." She hardly saw Teddy these days, but the news still came as a blow. Even before Andrew, Teddy had been her friend – the first one she'd made when she'd moved down here, the first crack in the armour she'd built to keep out the world after John Revell. His humour and his kindness had meant a lot to her. If he hadn't befriended her and started to winkle her out of her shell, she wasn't sure if she'd have said yes to Andrew or not.

"Yeah, I know. I'm gonna bloody miss him. We both are. Anyway, listen – that's not what I'm calling about."

"What's up, then?"

"Well, we're going to need a new chief researcher. You know we've got a lot on at the moment – there's that big MOD contract for a start – so I really need to start looking for a replacement for him. It'll need someone with a solid background in physics, and experience in that kind of work, of course – but if I could also get someone who's worked at Amberson's before and knows all the drills and procedures, *that* would be really handy."

In the moment following that, Alice was sure she felt the kitchen perform a single slow, graceful rotation around her. She looked at Emily, who sat, arms folded, at the table, pouting. Sulking because mummy wouldn't come out and play.

"Alice?" said Andrew. "You still there?"

"Yeah. Yeah. Me? Is that it? You asking me to come back?"

"Have to go through the interview procedure, of course, but I think you'd walk it." He hesitated. "It'd mean some changes, of course."

"Yeah, it would, wouldn't it? No more working from home."

Emily looked up at her sharply.

"You need some time to think on it?" Andrew asked.

"Yeah. Maybe. Yeah."

"Okay, well, we'll talk about it some more this evening. I'd better go."

"Okay. Speak to you later."

"Bye."

"Bye."

Alice put the phone down. Across the kitchen table, Emily glowered at her – despite which, she still managed to look adorable. *Who could leave all this?* Alice sighed and managed a smile. "Let's go to the park," she said.

It was the right thing to do anyway; by the time they got there the headache was gone. Emily stayed quiet when Alice helped put her blue trainers on, quiet as they walked into the village, but there were children she knew at the playground and she ran off to join them.

Alice relaxed on an unoccupied bench. Not that she had anything against the other local mothers – well, apart from the fact that a distressing number of them were small-minded cows who thought that immigration was responsible for everything wrong with the country – but right now, like Garbo, she just wanted to be alone. There was a decision to be made, after all.

It was like a crystal that changed colour depending on how the light struck it: on the one hand, here was a chance to resurrect the glittering career she'd been mourning only seconds before Andrew's phone call. On the other, how much of Emily's growing would she now miss? How many little triumphs and tragedies, that in the normal run of things she'd witness, would now be seen instead by a childminder or a crêche supervisor? By some stranger, working for pay, because Alice couldn't be bothered to –

Oh, for Christ's sake. If the shoe was on the other foot – if it was Andrew contemplating a return to his old job after years juggling childcare and working from home – no-one would bat an eyelid. No-one would accuse him of neglect or of selfishly putting career before child. But if you were a woman, it was different.

That said, it still came down to whether Emily would spend most of her days with at least one of her parents or with somebody else. How would the girl feel? Just the hint of it before and her face had fallen. Would she feel abandoned, unloved?

*She'd get over it. Kids got over worse all the time. Alice had.*

But Emily wasn't 'other kids', anymore than she was Alice: she was herself, with her own personal strengths and vulnerabilities. She might cope, adapt and shrug it off, or the abandonment might fester in her, bear some horrible fruit of neurosis or depression in later years.

Or maybe Alice was worrying too much. It was a stone-cold fact that if you worried over every possible thing that could go wrong, every potential negative consequence, you'd never make a choice or a decision again, go through life paralysed by *what-ifs*.

*Well, if you're so concerned, ask her then. Ask her how she feels.*

But wouldn't Emily automatically want her mother to stay? Wouldn't she instinctively fight the change?

*Maybe not. But what if she did? You're still an adult, Alice – you still have a life, a mind, of your own.*

Yes, she did: one that came with responsibilities attached.

*So you have to consult your seven-year-old daughter before any life decision?*

Emily would be affected by any decision she made.

*Doesn't mean she's best equipped to judge for the best. Would Andrew ask her first if he had a choice like this?*

He might. Emily was his little girl, after all.

Emily screamed. Alice blinked out of her reverie, looked around. *What's happened? Where is she? Oh God – what will I tell Andrew – I looked away for a second and –*

But, no – there was the flash of the red T-shirt her daughter was wearing, a blur as the roundabout whirled round and round, and yes, there was Emily, shrieking and giggling with laughter as she clung to the ever-faster-spinning roundabout. Alice settled back.

*She's stronger than you know.*

Alice nodded as if in answer to the thought. Emily *was* stronger: now and again the *fact* of her daughter hit Alice anew and dizzied her with wonder. Here was this tiny person, so herself, showing a glimmer of Alice or Andrew here and there – a mannerism, a gesture – and yet neither of them; complete in herself. With the talent for drawing and the sweet tuneful singing voice: her daughter. *My daughter. My child.*

"Come on," she said at last.

Emily bounded over – but flush-faced, sweat-damp, grass-stains on the knees of her jeans and her brimming reserves of energy lessened just a little – grinning, with all bad humour gone. "Where now?" she said.

"How about the village?" said Alice. "I think I know a little girl who'd like some ice-cream."

"Yeah!"

They started walking, along the footpath on the river embankment. Emily grabbed safety rails as she passed, swung on them, leaned on the top rail to peer over at the rushing brown foamy water of the Cuckmere.

"Get down from there," Alice said. "You'll fall in."

"No I won't."

"Emily. Get down."

"O*kay*."

Alice chuckled and shook her head, fumbling in her handbag for her phone.

"Mummy, look, it's a lizard!"

"Oh, that's nice." There it was; she flicked it open, cued Andrew's number up and pressed CALL.

She looked out over the river for just a second as it rang. Just a second to take in the view of the river, the village, in the afternoon, of the stay-at-home mums whose ranks she was about to leave, before turning back towards Emily. She was halfway through the turn when Andrew's voice sounded in her ear – "Hello?" – and, in the same moment, the screaming started.

"What –?" she said, and "What?" said Andrew's voice, puzzled, but the screaming went on. It was from the other side of the river, from a woman with a pushchair, and the woman was pointing across the river at – at Alice? No, not at Alice, but just ahead of her, at –

"Emily!"

It was a scream torn out of her gut. It came because she completed the turn she'd been making to look at Emily, to where the screaming woman was pointing – and there was nothing there. Nothing but a gap in the railings, the prints of trainers in the soft earth beyond them – *look, Mummy, a lizard* – and then a sudden skid-mark gouged in the earth. That, and when she ran to the railing and looked frantically down, the telltale flash of a red T-shirt in the brown and foaming water, whirling faster and faster as it was swept away.

# Chapter Thirty-Five

## Things Fall Apart

*August 2014*

ALICE HAD NEVER learned to swim, and so all she'd been able to do was run along the embankment, screaming – *my baby, my little girl, Emily, Emily* – as she tried to keep that little red scrap in sight and pray, pray that Emily was fighting to keep her head above water. Mummy couldn't swim but Emily could: she'd had lessons at the baths in Hastings, she'd be all right, wouldn't she?

Unless she was stunned or winded by the fall. Hadn't Alice read somewhere that women floated face-down in water when unconscious – *when they didn't have any control over it* – and men face-up? Or was it the other way around?

"Emily!"

She kept running – but oh, God, it had been too long since she'd visited the gym and she was already out of breath, the rhythm of her run failing and breaking up, and Emily spun away from her, the little red scrap shrinking and shrinking, and then up ahead she saw it – the weir. And she screamed, but a scream could do nothing, a scream couldn't change the laws of physics, couldn't stop a body in motion, driven by water pressure.

And Emily hit the lip of the weir. And there was white foam in the water. And Emily was gone. And Alice finally registered Andrew's voice, shouting her name, over and over, from the phone. And she ended the call, switched him off, because she couldn't tell him, not yet, couldn't tell him because she knew that this was the end of them, of their life together, the life that had seemed so perfect two minutes ago, and she couldn't tell him what she had to tell him, not now. And she dialled the emergency services and put the phone to her ear and said police, said ambulance, said things she could never remember later in a ragged sobbing voice just an inch away from screaming. And then when it was done she dropped the phone to clatter on the ground and sank to her knees as people ran towards her, and she ignored it when it began to ring again because it was Andrew and she still couldn't tell him. And then at last she screamed again, screamed across the thundering water, screamed her child's name.

THE POLICE CAME, and they were kind; the paramedics came too, and so were they. There was a hot drink and a blanket round her shoulders. There were questions from them and monosyllabic answers from her that she had no conscious part in making. About her and about Emily, and about her husband: about how his name was Andrew Villiers and how he worked at Amberson's and how they could reach him on this number.

And there was the hospital, where doctors and nurses shone lights in her eyes and tested her reflexes. And at long last there was Andrew, and she couldn't look at him, and at the same time she couldn't refuse to look at him, because it hurt her to do so, but she deserved to hurt, deserved to feel pain, deserved to suffer. *You took your eyes off our daughter and she went in the river and now she's dead. Drowned. Lost. Gone. All your fault. All your fault.* He didn't say any of that, of course. Perhaps he didn't even think it, but she doubted that. How could he not, for Christ's sake? Emily was dead because of her.

"It's all right," he told her. "It's all right."

"It isn't," she said, "it isn't." And of course he couldn't answer that.

"It's my fault," she said.

"Don't say that," he told her. "Don't blame yourself. I don't blame you. I don't. It was an accident."

But *accidents don't happen, they are caused.* That was what Dad had always said. And what had caused this? Emily climbing through a gap in the railings to try and catch a lizard; slipping, falling. And why had she climbed through, why had she slipped and fallen? Because someone hadn't been looking, someone had been thinking about her career instead of her child and *look what had happened.*

"I don't blame you," Andrew said again, whispering, holding her, whispering in her hair.

But something in how he held her felt wrong. As if he didn't really want to hold her; as if, despite their physical closeness, he was withdrawing from her. Even in his arms, she felt alone.

THEY WENT HOME. At some point they had a pizza delivered. Didn't seem right to be hungry after what had happened; everything should have stopped with Emily going into the water. The growling of her stomach seemed to say *well, fuck it, life goes on* – and of course it did, went rattling blindly along, indifferent to the deaths of good men and bad, good women and bad, of children, of the old, the crippled and the whole, the black and the white and all other colours in between. But it shouldn't. Not with Emily gone.

Nonetheless, they were hungry and they ate. They went to bed but didn't sleep. Didn't speak either. She heard Andrew draw breath a couple of times, as if to say something, but then he'd breathe out again and whatever he'd meant to utter was forgotten. Perhaps he knew – how could he not know? – that virtually anything he might say was certain to trigger the end of everything between them.

And the bedside clock ticked and the night went by and still she couldn't sleep and nor could he and still they waited. And Alice wanted the phone to ring and wanted it never to ring, because if it rang then at least she'd know, one way or the other, but while it didn't ring, while she was still waiting, it meant there was at least a chance, at least some tiny sliver of hope of Emily washing up on a riverbank bedraggled and cold and crying and scared, hurt and hypothermic and ill, needing hospital time, yes, very sick for a while, yes, but alive. That sliver was all she had to cling to, that thousands to one chance; it was her marriage's only chance of survival, perhaps hers as well.

And then finally the phone rang. Not the mobile phone; the landline. It rang several times in the dead silence of the house with neither of them moving – Andrew must be hoping she'd get up and take the call, just as she was willing him to. Alice was lying on her side, her back to him, staring at the wall. The figures on the digital clock on her bedside table glowed blood-red in the darkness: 2.07 am. And she lay on her side, breathed in and out, nice and regular, as if she was sleeping through it.

"Alice," Andrew said. "Alice?"

She didn't answer. Did he know? He must know. The phone continued to ring. At last he muttered something under his breath and got up. She felt the bed creak and shift. His footsteps padded away.

Abruptly the phone stopped ringing. A beat of silence. Had the caller given up? But then she heard Andrew say, "Hello?"

More silence. Could she hear, if she listened closely, the faint sound of the voice on the other end of the phone?

"I see," said Andrew. More silence. "No, it's okay. I can meet you at the, I can meet you there." Meet you at the what?

What word had he just stopped himself using? But of course she knew. "Where is it? Right. Okay. We'll be there in half an hour."

*We?* No. No. She didn't want to see what had happened. But at the same time, having failed her daughter so profoundly, how could Alice refuse to look on her one last time?

"Thank you," said Andrew. Thank you for what? For calling with that news? She tried to tell herself that maybe it wasn't *that* news. It might be good. They might have found Emily alive. But if that was true, why was Andrew's voice so dull and flat, so empty and so drained?

After that, a silence. Then the click of a phone going down.

The house seemed to wait and breathe. A moment or an hour later, she couldn't tell which, she heard Andrew's footsteps, creaking on the floorboard, coming back to the bedroom door.

*No. No. Stay away. Don't come in.* But of course he did, and turned the bedroom light on. His face was grey – he looked drowned. He looked dead.

"No," she heard herself say. She didn't want to hear it. But he was going to say it; of course he was going to. She wanted to shout, scream, drown him out, shout him down, but nothing would come beyond that tired little whimper of sound.

"They've found her," he said.

*Please say more*, she silently begged. *Say she's in a bad way – hypothermia, broken bones, anything, but clinging on. Say it's touch and go and she might not make it because then at least there'll still be hope, still a chance it might not be –*

"They want us to go and identify her," he said.

And then her voice worked again, when it was too late to drown out the news, and she howled, and even as she did it Alice marvelled at the sound, the agony of it, as if made by something whose guts were being torn out of its body. But it was her who made it, just as she had on the riverbank before. And she fell to the bedroom carpet and curled up around the pain, howling again until she thought her throat was bleeding.

And Andrew dressed, then laid her clothes out and stood and waited until she was ready to go.

She'd already believed their marriage would be dead if Emily had died, but hadn't realised until that moment that she'd still nurtured some tiny embryo of hope that she might be wrong, that somehow they would get through it, survive, repair – maybe even, maybe, somewhere down the line, have another child. That hope died the first time she looked up to see Andrew waiting by her neatly-laid-out clothes, his hands behind his back, his face like stone. Waiting with an executioner's terrible patience for her wailing to stop and for her to come with him. Because no entreaty on her part would prevent his demanding her presence, witnessing the consequences of her inattention. He would make her. Not because he needed her support or because it would in the long run be best for her to see the body and be sure that it was their child, but because he would suffer and wanted her to suffer alongside him.

And it was only just, she decided, that she should.

She climbed off the floor and stood. Her joints felt stiff and achey, as if she'd grown very old lying on the floor. Andrew just stood and looked at her. Unable to meet his eyes, she took off her nightgown and began to dress.

*March 2015*

"WELL?"

Sat at one end of the table, hands clasped tight in a bony knot, Alice glared at Andrew.

If she'd expected any real reaction from him – shock, fear, anger, contrition – she was disappointed. He just looked down at the pair of black lace panties on the table, said "Well what?" then took his jacket off and hung it on the back of the kitchen door, turning his back on her as he did so. He cared that little. He was that indifferent to her now. Her heart cried out for the sweet, long-haired boy she'd married. But he was gone; long gone.

Andrew sat down at the other end of the table. He loosened his tie, took it off. "Go on, then. Say what you've got to say."

Alice pointed at the panties. "Those aren't mine."

"I know they're not."

"Who is she?"

"You don't know her."

"From Amberson's?"

"No."

"Where, then?"

"I don't think that's any of your business."

"Not my –" she fought for words, as if for breath. "Not my business, Andrew? Not my fucking *business*? I'm your fucking wife."

He just looked at her and breathed out.

"Is that all you can say?"

"I met someone. Yes. And yes, I care about her. I could actually sleep in the same bed as her given the chance, instead of the spare room. Is that what you want to hear?"

"Want? No. I don't *want* any of this. I suppose I was at least hoping it was just fucking, nothing else. Going off and getting your oats because you're not getting them here."

"You make it sound like it was you who cut them off. There's a reason it's me sleeping in the spare room, Alice. I was the one who chose to –"

"Then why are you still here?" Alice heard her voice shake. She knew the best thing to do right now was to stop talking. Throw the panties in the kitchen bin, end the conversation and pretend it had never started. Then they could carry on as they had, presenting at least the semblance of a marriage to the outside world. But she knew as well that she wouldn't, that neither of them would or could stop now. The machine was in motion and it wouldn't halt until the last of their marriage was in ashes.

Andrew sighed, then shrugged. "Habit," he said at last. "Less trouble this way, isn't it?"

True, of course; they both knew everything between them but the appearance of being a couple had died with Emily. She had thought, more than once, about leaving, about divorce. Why hadn't she? Because she didn't want to be the one who left, who abandoned her grieving husband? *What a heartless cow*, people would say. Because some part of her had still refused to give up hope that there was something to be salvaged? Because her pride rebelled against her sneaking home to Mum and Dad with her tail between her legs – because honestly, if it was comfort she wanted, if it was love, where else had she to go? Or, like Andrew, because it was just less effort to keep on going through the motions, maintaining appearances? It might have been any of these, or all of them at once.

It didn't matter now. She'd had one last illusion to cling to: that it would be her decision what happened, that she'd choose whether and when to stay or leave. Now even that was taken from her.

"You bastard," she said. It was his blank, tired indifference that hurt most of all, the way he'd confessed to the affair as if it was nothing much. She wanted to break that, to hit him with something that would hurt. "You rotten, adulterous bastard."

"I was going to let you know soon," he said, as if she hadn't spoken. "The next few days. She's asked me to move in with her."

"You bastard." This time it came out of her in a scream. Alone, abandoned, only Emily's ghost for company. "You fucking bastard. You're just leaving me?"

"Yes, I am. Come on, Alice, it's time, we both know –"

"I need –" She needed him? For what? "You can't leave me on my own," she said. It sounded weak and whiny and she hated the words and herself for saying them as soon as they were uttered. It made her sound like a victim, and she had never wanted to be a victim. More to the point, she refused to accept she had a right to call herself one. Her single, cataclysmic fuck-up lay at the root of all that had happened: this was just the latest consequence. For Alice to call herself a victim was an insult to the dead.

And by the look of it, Andrew felt the same way, because she saw anger and maybe even loathing on his face then, and he got up. "Can't I?" he shouted. "Why not? *You* left *her*!"

Alice opened her mouth both no words came. *Andrew, please, no. Don't say it. Don't.*

"My little girl's *dead* because of you," he said.

She screamed something, looked for things to throw, found nothing. Andrew had already thrown open the kitchen door and was striding down the hall. She screamed after him, telling him to fuck off and never come back, calling him every ugly name she could think of, but he didn't turn around, never even slowed down. Just opened the door, flung it shut behind him and by the time she got it open his Audi's engine was already roaring into life. He tore down the drive and off onto the main road as she stumbled through the exhaust fumes, coughing between obscenities.

The car's roar died away. Silence returned. A bird trilled somewhere. Nature: the Green Machine. Mindless, indifferent, chugging along through its endless, millennial cycles. Emily was dead and the Machine ground on. A huge mindless mechanism that worked and turned without a mind, and what did it matter in that great schema if one tiny mote, one little pattern of energy that had appeared to be matter and appeared to be alive and conscious, had changed its form and behaviour? It was grist to the mill. Emily's ashes had been scattered and would be assimilated into the ecosystem, would make new organisms grow. That was all. None of it had a point; none of it meant anything.

The bird trilled again. Across the road, a hedge rustled as some small creature moved in it.

Alice turned and went back inside the house. She shut the

door. She went up the stairs. She went into the bathroom and she opened the medicine cabinet. She took out the two packets of paracetamol she found there and sat on the edge of the bath looking at them for quite some time.

THE BLUE AND white void of energy and light heaved and writhed. Faces swam before her. Before it had been the ogre's, Old Harry's, Arodias Thorne's, but this time they were the children's, baying and snarling. Children taken too young, lives snuffed out like Emily's had been – but by design, not accident.

Arodias Thorne had plotted the children's deaths: not out of sadism or perverted lust, but merely as a means to an end, for him to attain the immortality he'd sought. Her crime? Her guilt?

She was guilty of imperfection. She was guilty of being flawed. She was guilty of a moment's distraction. How many parents were guilty of it? All might be: it was only ill-luck or blind chance or the casual cruelty of whatever power did preside over this world that had caused that brief distraction to coincide with a moment of life-threatening danger to her child.

It was so easy to say it – so much so that it sounded glib to her own ears – but it had been hard, the work of months of therapy, to say it with anything that even approached belief. It would be years before she truly believed that, assuming she ever did. But she had managed to say it, and would again; had begun the slow and tortured process of self-forgiveness.

She remembered that moment, and reached for it, held fast to it through the raging of the sea.

*MY DEAREST ALICE,*

*I hope this email finds you well – as well as the circumstances permit, at least. It seems an obscenity to hope somebody is 'well' in a situation like this. I'm sorry, but I'm at something of a loss for words. I'm used to being clever and witty, and none of that is really appropriate here.*

*I should have sent this email a long time ago, and I'm sorry for that as well. Stefan and I were busy settling in, and we've rather lost track of our friends in the UK. But even before that, I hesitated – we hadn't spoken for some time before this awful tragedy happened; I was afraid you might have come to think of me more as Andrew's friend than your own. As excuses go, that seems decidedly pathetic now – but of course, the longer I left things, the harder it was to write.*

*My darling, I cannot express how sorry we both are for your loss, and nor can I even begin to imagine the pain you must be suffering at this moment. I'm trying to find something to say, but I can't. I'm trying to think of something amusing, or wise, or kind, or healing, something that will make you feel better, but I know that there are no such words. I wish only that I could hold you in my arms and let you cry, but I can't even do that. Things being what they are financially, I have no idea when we'll next be able to come over to Blighty – I would love to tell you that I'll be on the next flight across, but unfortunately that's something only characters in a Hollywood movie are able to do – or perhaps, the kind of people who write, direct or star in Hollywood films, as they can afford to jet off anywhere at the drop of a bloody hat. I'm sorry; I'm trying to be clever again. I will be there in person as soon as I have the opportunity. In the meantime, please get in touch. Whatever has happened, whatever you feel yourself to be guilty of, you are still my friend.*

*Stefan also sends his fondest wishes.*

*With love,*

*Teddy*

* * *

*April 2016*

"Was it my fault? Yes. But on the other hand… I don't know, can anyone, ever, say there wasn't a second when they should have been looking and weren't?" She dabbed at her face. She was crying freely.

"Probably not." Kat, her therapist, looked back at her. There was no judgement in her face, only kindness and warmth and acceptance. That was how it worked: she wasn't there to judge, she'd told Alice at the beginning, or to guide or to advise, only to listen to Alice and help her see her way to a solution. Always assuming one existed, of course.

"That's what I thought," said Alice.

"How does it make you feel to consider that?"

*I don't know*, she wanted to say, but didn't. It was a sort of unwritten rule of their sessions, although Kat had never actually stated it. In fact, Alice had a feeling that the rule was of her own invention, because she knew she'd get nowhere unless she made herself answer. "It hurts," she said, "of course it does. If I could go back and change things… but I can't do that, can I?"

"No," said Kat, "it only goes one way."

Alice took a deep breath. "If I'd looked away at any other moment, it would have been a near miss, or nothing at all. I…" Deep breath. This was so hard to say. "I made a mistake anyone could have made. At the wrong time. Can I forgive myself? I…" *Don't know*. "I'll try. Maybe – I mean, after Andrew left, I took the pills, yes. But then I changed my mind. I rang the ambulance. I could have just given up and laid down and… you know, gone. So even then, part of me still wanted to live. Maybe even thought I'd deserved to."

Kat nodded, waited, but Alice couldn't think of anything else to say. After a minute or so, the therapist asked, "So how are you feeling right here and now?"

"Here and now?" Alice blew out a long breath. "I'm not sure how to describe it. I can't say I'm happy or at peace or any of that bollocks... any of that... stuff... you probably want to hear."

Kat smiled.

"I still miss Emily more than I thought it was possible to miss anything. Every day I see something that sets me off again. A toy, or a flower or an animal – she loved animals, you know, used to beg us to buy her a dog. Nature as well, wild animals, all of that. All of that, any of it, makes me think of how Emily would have loved it, and that can just send me over the edge. Or seeing parents with their kids – mums especially. Mums and little girls. Sometimes I end up watching them like a bloody hawk. Just in case the mum's concentration slips. Just to spare her what I went through."

Alice stopped, thought for a moment, then went on. "No," she said, "I've got to be honest here. Haven't I? It's not about them, it's about *me*. If they fuck up, if their kid's put in danger, then if I'm watching I could save the child. That child would owe me their life; to that mother, I'd be a heroine, a saviour. Be nice to see myself like that. Like a superhero with a special power."

Kat laughed. "Yeah, it would."

Alice snorted, her own smile fading. "Wouldn't make much of a film, though, would it? Not really. This mad woman who hangs around on footpaths or in supermarket carparks, almost wanting someone to make a mistake and endanger their child's life. When I saw myself that way – when I realised that *was* what I looked like, not some sort of heroine – you know, I realised I couldn't just... it was just another way of trying to make the pain go away with a magic wand."

"Do you still think you're mad?"

"No. No. Just in pain. I probably always will be now. I've accepted that. It's just letting it become... manageable. People live with chronic pain all the time, don't they? And they still manage to have lives. I'm not there yet, but... you know."

Kat nodded. "And what are your feelings now about Andrew?"

"Andrew?" She shook her head. "I just realised this morning, before I came here, I didn't really feel anything much. Nothing bad, anyway, for him. I felt sad for him, and I remembered a few things, like when we got married. It was sad, but I could still remember the good times, and that they were good. I didn't feel any more anger, or bitterness – I suppose I just realised that I'd forgiven Andrew ages ago. He was in pain and he was blaming me – we both were."

"What do you think will happen between the two of you now?"

"Nothing. It's too late for anything like that. I don't think we ever had a chance of staying together after..." *After Emily died.* "After what happened." She was stumbling through language like a newborn foal; words were a shifting, treacherous rubble. "Never mind getting back together again."

"Do you think you'll stay in touch? Maybe stay friends?"

"No. No, I don't think so. Things went too far. Things got said, done... no."

"So what *has* been achieved?"

"The hate's gone. Or it's going anyway. We're just ending things and walking away" She shrugged. "I think that's as good a result as we could have hoped for."

Kat nodded. "We're coming to the end of our time together," she said. "Both this session and the ones you've arranged up to now. How do you feel about where we've got to?"

"Somewhere important, I think. I'll try to forgive myself, if I can. God knows how that's going to happen, but I'll get there."

"Are you still planning to go back to Manchester?"

"Yeah. There's nothing left for me down here now."

"Do you want to arrange further sessions before you go up?"

"I don't think so, at least not for now. I think I need to – you know, just go off and try get on with things. Have a life. You know?"

"Yeah," said Kat. She scribbled something down on a piece

of card. "Well, if you ever feel you're struggling and you need to talk to someone, you can get in touch with me and we can arrange something. Or if you need something a bit more local, these are a friend of mine's contact details. Same line of work. She's based round Manchester and she's very good. If things get bad, you could contact her. Or me, if you want."

"Thank you."

"Right, then."

"Yeah." Alice stood.

"Good luck."

WHEN THE TIME came to go back up north Alice insisted on driving herself. Her parents begged her to let them come and pick her up, but she said no.

It was a small thing, but important to her, that she made the journey under her own power; drove herself back, out of choice, rather than be picked up and carried away like a broken, helpless, crying little girl. Perhaps somewhere there'd been a faint memory of leaving John, of Dad loading her things into the car. Daddy coming to sort things out, because she couldn't any more. *Take me home, Daddy. Wrap me up in blankets and cotton wool, and coddle me from the world.*

That wasn't her. She would not admit to being so weak, so broken. Nor would she accept such comfort when it was undeserved. She was not the child; the child was dead.

It was a long drive from Sussex all the way back up to Greater Manchester, that sprawling conurbation that had subsumed parts of both Cheshire and Lancashire into its mass. The lanes of the motorway unrolled beneath her, like an endless path. It felt as though she were hardly driving at all, as though the car just slid along of its own accord, along a predetermined path. More than once the idea crossed her mind that if she took her hands from the wheel, her feet from the pedals – even crawled into the back seat to sleep – it would still ferry her home. Once or twice, she actually felt her hands relax their grip as if to put the idea into practice, but caught herself in time and took hold once more. She would not tell her parents of that; she would not tell anyone. They must not know how close she'd come.

At last she turned off the motorway and down a succession of B-roads; at last she was turning down the little cul-de-sac in Sale, pulling into the driveway of a bungalow. She remembered their old house and the men who'd kicked down the door. The Pinstripe Man. Such a long way away now. Her parents had come far; they'd done well, for themselves and for her.

There was movement inside the house, behind the glass of the front door. It opened; Mum came out first, arms outstretched. Dad ambled out of the house behind her. Alice took a deep breath and got out of the car.

"Oh, Alice, love." Mum threw her arms around her, kissed her forehead and cheeks. "Oh, love, what do you look like? You look so pale. When did you last have anything to eat? You look half-starved –"

"Give her a bit of space, Ann," Dad said. He put a hand on Mum's shoulder, his other arm going round Alice's. "It's been a hard time for her. Hard time for us all."

Mum hugged her tightly. Dad's arms encircled them both; his lips brushed Alice's hair. A line of Robert Frost's came back to Alice, about home being the place where they had to take you in. But she remained stiff, unbending, wouldn't accept the comfort she had no right to, not when her own child was ashes. But something broke and she fell against them. The crying tore out of her as if she'd swallowed cogs of metal on a chain and now they were being wrenched free of her, tearing and gouging.

Her sobs became howls, but her parents didn't speak; they just held her. For all their faults and their mistakes, this was constant, this endured. She didn't think she had or could have loved them more than in this moment; beautiful in their fragility and humanity, flawed and burdened by failures, but striving still.

* * *

In the writhe of the sea, the shifting patterns of blue and white, that fragile self-forgiveness was a raft and she clung onto it, steadying herself before dragging herself aboard. And then she crouched, balancing against the storm.

As she did so, the wind died and the sea levelled out.

Alice stood. *I am the sea.* All creation rolled beneath her, ready to change at the lightest touch of her will.

All creation; past, present and future. Time flickered before her and she stood on Collarmill Height, looking down. Days and nights flurried past: years, centuries. Men in rags of fur knelt before her, with fire and weapons and stone; she saw men of bronze and men of iron. Men in chainmail and women in linen knelt at her trickling shrine. Cavaliers fell, and Roundheads shouted of idolatry, heaped stone and earth upon her spring and took fire to the church above it while she watched, her arms held out.

The ruined church rose again, then fell. And a great house rose about her, a wall and garden rising beyond the walls. The servants came, and then one came in particular – a woman in her thirties, brown-haired and blue-eyed, unworldly yet graceful. Mary. And the months flickered on.

And Alice knew what she must do next; she rose now, drifting upwards, rising through ceilings and walking through walls until she found Mary Carson's room, found it on the night the shattered, brutalised woman grovelled in her own filth on the brink of insanity. *I know that place*, Alice thought, *I know that place so well*. And it only took a moment to let Mary see her, to fill the room with light. And that was all it took to convince Mary of grace and pull her back from madness – to ensure she'd live and thrive.

And to ensure that one day she would inherit Springcross House and leave her testimony behind, to arm Alice with knowledge in the future.

The rowan wood called to her; she wavered, witnessed a hundred people in different times holding talismans and crosses of that wood aloft. Collarmill Height faded, and the woods of the Fall appeared. She saw herself now, hiding among the trees, heard Old Harry's growling approach. With a thought she drove him back. And then she was on the Height again, and standing in the house she'd bought, 378 Collarmill Road – she clung to that tiny, mundane detail, that little anchor to reality – to drive the children away from her. She saw herself falling through the door into the hallway as the children vanished, saw the armed men outside the door vanish back into the past.

The sea rolled and calmed. She was everywhere and nowhere, but falling back towards where she'd come from.

– *If I could go back and change things... but I can't do that, can I?*

– *No. It only goes one way.*

Except that it didn't, not here.

She could go back to that day, to the lizard, the path by the Cuckmere. She could be watching when she needed to be. Emily could live again. All she had to do was reach into this shifting ocean, change a single detail.

And what then? Would none of this have happened, be only the fading echo of a dream? Or would Arodias Thorne still be working to bring her to him; would he find another way for Emily to die?

Had Emily's death truly been accident, blind chance, or all a part of some terrible pattern? And whose pattern? Arodias', the Red Man's?

Or had some greater pattern brought her here, to do what had to be done, end this violation that Arodias had begun? Had Emily's death just been one step along the way to deliver the right object to the right point in space and time, the click of one gear in a machine vaster, more intricate and more cruel than the Moloch Device could ever be?

And then there were the other children to consider, all the ghosts of Collarmill Height.

*Emily.*

There might be time; there *would* be, she'd make sure of it. But first, this had to end.

She put all other thoughts aside and focused. The water became sparks of blue and white glittering light, and then at a thought from her, the focus shifted, moved out. Galaxies of quarks and quanta coalesced; another order of magnitude, and these shrank, flew together, and she contemplated the electrons whirling around atomic nuclei. Back again and the atoms joined together into molecules; zoom out a little further and now she could begin to see the structures those molecules fitted together to combine.

*Back, back, further back – let me see, for now, as I always did.*

And with that, the chains of molecules became cells – plant cells with their cellulose walls and bright chloroplasts – and those cells became a blade of grass, and the blade one blade among many on the ground before her, and the ground the top of Redman's Hill.

# Chapter Thirty-Six

## The Render of the Veils

*31st October 2016*

ALICE STOOD, SHAKING. Her legs trembled; her heart thundered. How could she describe what she had just witnessed, what she'd just undergone? She doubted she ever would, exactly, be able to describe how it felt. She felt a little as she might have felt if she'd just climbed off a rollercoaster ride, and a little as though she'd just narrowly escaped death by electric shock.

But something else trembled inside her: vibrated, hummed, groaned for release. The heightened perception that the spring's waters had given her still remained, but for now, at least, under some sort of tenuous control – and with it, the ability to influence what she saw. The power of the Fire Beyond itself.

Both were fleeting, of course: the power and the control. In mental or emotional terms, she'd merely reached a plateau, and couldn't remain there indefinitely. Her self-forgiveness for Emily's death was still an ongoing project, and one that might never be completed – *could* never be completed, perhaps, only developed to the point that life was bearable. There would be more guilt in her future, more anguish, more moments when she wished to die – except there need not be, if she was wise and quick, because she could wipe that whole reality away – but for the moment, she was balanced and at something close to peace, and controlled the Fire Beyond rather than being controlled by it.

How long did she have now? Minutes? After that the effects of the water she'd drunk would wear off and she'd just be ordinary, powerless Alice Collier again. But in that time, what couldn't she do?

Emily would be almost ten by now. Ten tomorrow, in fact.

"Alice," said a voice, a voice that was four voices in one; the Red Man's voice. "Alice, time is short."

She looked up. He stood facing her, by the pool. Behind him stood the children and down the slope of the hill, slinking half-willingly towards them, was Old Harry.

Alice stood up, nodded. First, the children. One glance at them showed her what they were: innocents who'd died in bewildered, tortured anguish, trapped here between worlds and wanting only the release they'd been so long denied – or, failing that, to keep the tormentor trapped in his bestial state, the only vengeance they could hope for.

They'd tried to kill her, yes, but she forgave. If she could forgive herself, how could she not forgive them?

There was power enough for what she needed to do. She waved a hand and undid what had been done, the things that bound the children and held them fast. The change was instant: the curdled whiteness left their eyes, their deathly pallor lessened, and she glimpsed their harrowed faces breaking into smiles – but only for an instant, as she turned away. The main task still lay ahead.

Old Harry, the ogre, the Beast, Arodias Thorne, crept towards her and grovelled at her feet. Alice looked down on him in silence.

"Time is passing," said the Red Man. "Not just for you, Alice. For John, as well."

*John.* Of course. A pang of guilt – in reliving her life with Andrew and Emily, she'd forgotten him. What might have been had she stayed with him, treated his pain with greater understanding? Might they have stayed together, raised a child or children of their own? And if they had, what might have happened to their child?

She knew now, looking down at Old Harry and letting her focus shift: she knew now what to do, what had to be done.

"Don't," said a voice. She turned, saw one of the children stretching out a hand as if to stay her. He was tallish, with shoulder-length fair hair, and the other children seemed to be gathered round him. Was it his body she'd pried from the Moloch Device's grasp?

"I'm sorry," she said. "I have to."

The children stared back at her in dismay. Where would they go now? To oblivion, or to some other place. Some things were beyond even her sight.

Alice turned back from them to the Beast. She reached out, but didn't touch that reeking, matted pelt. Just the thought of doing so seemed to soil her. It didn't matter, anyway; she didn't need to touch him. The gesture was enough.

*Adjust focus, and –*

Arodias, the Beast – his, its, body expanded before her, a constellation of molecules, atoms, finally energy itself. She could see all that he was and had been, and somewhere in the warped DNA, distorted physiology and attenuated psyche of the Beast, the man who'd raised himself from squalor – down in Browton Vale, only a turn of her head from where she now stood – to being one of the magnates of the new city, the untitled lord of Springcross House and the maker of the Moloch Device, who'd sought ownership of the Fire Beyond, was still there.

It was simply a case of finding him, and having found him, restoring him to what he was.

And so she reached back: because she didn't just see the Beast, she saw all he was and had been. A chain of Beasts and men, reaching back through the centuries as a single unbroken entity. Here, back here – somewhere around 1851 – something had changed. All she needed to do was reach back to that point and prevent those changes from occurring.

*There.*

And just one more thing...

Alice closed her hand into a fist, and pulled.

The blue and white constellation of the Beast's body whirled, convulsed, collapsed. Alice released her focus, returned to her normal angle of vision, and saw the looming hairy bulk of the Beast lurch and stagger, shrink and change colour. The fur pelt fell away, the coarse hairs vanishing before they struck the ground. The piebald, filthy skin grew white and unmarked; the few torn rags and scraps still clinging to the body grew and merged back into clothing, the immaculate suit of a nineteenth-century gentleman. The beard fell away; the vast knife-and-chisel teeth shrank, whitened, became straight and small, disappeared behind thin lips. The low slope of the forehead rose and became high and domed. The hair of the head, filthy and matted, grew clean and neatly brushed, iron grey with long sideburns. The snout became a fine, aquiline nose. And the eyes, aflame with the blue of the Fire Beyond – the eyes closed, then opened and were grey.

The figure – diminished but upright, tidy, human – swayed, then straightened, then advanced the final few steps up the hill to approach her, the Red Man, the bubbling spring.

Arodias Thorne met her eyes, adjusted the cuffs of his shirt for neatness, inclined his head and smiled.

The children wailed, as in a single voice. Thorne glanced towards them; Alice was glad to see the Red Man move between him and them. Whether it would do any good, against a master who could make you step aside at a command, remained to be seen.

*Emily.* All that remained was to make that final change. But it was fading; the blue ocean glimmered for a moment and she could almost see the thread she had to tweak and snip to change it all. But then it was gone, and she was only plain Alice Collier again.

The spring – she moved towards it. Arodias turned, wagged a finger, smiled and shook his head.

But the children were free. They had to go, and now. She didn't know if Arodias could snare them once more, but it would be madness surely to take the risk.

She opened her mouth to warn them, but Arodias turned back to her, put a finger to his lips and whispered, "Sh."

His eyes would not move from hers; a smile hovered around that cruel mouth.

She swallowed hard, then turned away from Arodias, towards the Red Man. Strange how a man made of bone and clockwork could be more human than one of flesh and blood. "We need to go back now," she said. "We need to help John. You promised."

"Did he?" said Arodias. His voice was a purr, like that of some great cruel cat, preening its contentment over a trapped mouse as it prepared to begin its work with claws and teeth. He turned and addressed the Red Man. "Have you been making *promises* to her?"

The Red Man seemed to waver before that stare. Alice tried to catch his eye, or at least the holes in the mask that served for them. "You said you'd take me back," she said, trying to keep her voice steady. "You promised. You'd take me back and get John out of the Moloch Device."

"Yes." The Red Man straightened. "I gave my word. Come –"

"Stay where you are." Arodias didn't even raise his voice: he sounded offhand, even bored.

"I kept my side of the bargain," said Alice.

"Bargain?" Arodias laughed. "Who on earth told you it was a bargain? You fulfilled your role. Nothing more, nothing less. And this – John? Who is John?"

"Her... friend," the Red Man answered. "She... cares for him. I had to use him to operate the Moloch Device. I gave my word that we would release him. There is still time."

"Why would I want to release him?" said Arodias. "Or her, for that matter?" He smiled at Alice with what seemed genuine warmth, and she understood how Mary Carson could have fallen so completely for this man. "I assure you it's nothing personal, madam, but I think some secrets should *remain* secret, don't you?"

"There's a bloody great hole in the kitchen floor leading to your underground hideaway," Alice said. "That won't keep your secrets very long."

But Arodias Thorne, smirking, was already shaking his head. "Merely a temporary measure," he said. "One that will have been rectified by the time the house returns to the year you came from – what year was it?"

"2016," the Red Man said. Alice could see his white hands coiling and uncoiling into fists.

"2016," repeated Arodias. "Did it really take that long? But then again, time means very little here, in any direction, does it? But, yes," he said, addressing Alice again, "there'll be no sign of any damage to the house when it returns to 2016. The hole in the floor will be mended. Your friend can remain in the Moloch Device, safely out of sight and mind. His suffering will only be a matter of minutes – albeit rather unpleasant ones, from his point of view."

"And me?" said Alice.

"And you," said Arodias. "Well, what about you?" He looked her up and down, and there was no mistaking the look with which he appraised her. "I'm sure we can think of something." He smiled. "Probably something that hurts."

"I gave my word," said the Red Man.

"I've never understood this tendency on your part," he told the Red Man. "*You gave your word*. These pretensions of yours to morality, to integrity –" he broke off. "Ah, of course.

Integrity." He approached the Red Man and studied the face, stroking his chin. "Some feeble attempt at rebellion on your part, to assert you have an identity of your own, independent of me." He shook his head. "We'll have to do something about that. You're a machine, nothing more. Can't have something that's nothing more than a tool getting ideas of its own." He smirked, turning away from the Red Man. "You don't even have a name."

"Oh, but he does," said Alice. "The Red Man. The Red Knight." The Red Man looked at her. "Even Percivale." The Red Man cocked his head. "The Grail Knight."

"If you're trying to turn him against me," said Arodias, "you're wasting your time. I built him, Miss..."

"Collier. Ms Collier."

"Mizz?" Arodias frowned and shook his head. "I built him. His limitations are hard, solid things, Miss Collier. He can no more refuse my commands or raise his hand against me than a spinning jenny can talk. So, there it is. You and your *friend*, John, both disappear – and even if they did find your friend's remains at some future date, they'll never find yours. Just another mystery; another of Collarmill Height's innumerable ghost stories." He took a step towards her. "All that remains is deciding your fate – and I think I've made that decision already. There are certain appetites I've had denied for far too long."

He took another step towards her. The Red Man stood against the rising, buffeting wind, and the children began to wail.

# Chapter Thirty-Seven
## All Souls

*31st October – 1st November 2016*

THE RED MAN let out a cry; he swayed, staggered, fell to one knee. A grinding sound issued from his head.

Arodias raised an eyebrow. "Ah," he said, and turned back to Alice with a shrug. "That's the only problem with tools, of course," he told her. "Sooner or later, they wear out or break. But when that happens, all one need do is discard them. And then, manufacture a replacement."

He walked over to the Red Man and kicked him once. The Red Man cried out and keeled over. The children moved; Arodias took a step towards them and they recoiled. "Still afraid of me," he said. "And they could do nothing to harm me in any case."

"Are you sure of that?" asked Alice.

Arodias studied her. "One thing I have noticed about women," he sighed. "They always think they understand everything, when they understand nothing. But please go on, Miss Collier. Amuse me. Tell me what it is you think you know that I don't."

"You're a man again," she said, "but that's all. You don't have any great powers." She nodded to the pool. "I had to restore you to how you were before. So I did. You're just a mortal man again, Mr Thorne. No immortality. No special powers. Just yourself."

"Just myself? That was more than enough to get me here," he reminded her. "And do you really think you can keep me from that spring? Even if those pathetic little wraiths took a hand in things, you couldn't prevent me. I have fought too long and too hard. I've earned this. I will drink from the spring, and I will claim it – claim the Fire Beyond as I did before. And this time – this time – there won't be any mistakes."

Mistakes? Still he didn't really understand. The spring amplified what was already there: it wasn't any weakness of his cast-iron will, but his selfishness and greed that had warped him into the Beast. It was only a matter of time before it happened again – and what happened then? The Red Man, repaired or replaced, would go in search of another like her. And until the Beast overwhelmed him again, Arodias would find new ways to prey upon the world, and when he'd devolved once more the Red Man would try to contain his excesses. More death, more suffering, added to the bill.

"No," she said, "there won't be any mistakes. Because you won't be there to make them."

Alice hadn't opened her fist since she'd closed it while restoring Arodias. Now she opened it, and something lay in the palm of her hand. *Just one more thing*, she'd thought, and here it was. She took it between finger and thumb and held it up: a tiny vial of glass, with a blue glass stopper. Filled with a fine white powder like caster sugar.

"Oh?" Arodias chuckled. "Now what's this? Poison, Miss Collier?"

"It isn't –"

"Let me guess, you plan to throw it in the spring?"

" –poison, Mr Thorne."

"One swallow of the water and I'd heal myself with a thought – not poison? Do tell, then? What is it? This is, I take it, the fearsome weapon with which you intend to destroy me?"

"It's time, Mr Thorne. That's all there is in here."

Arodias smirked, but there was a little less certainty in it than there had been before. "Time? What are you –"

She nodded toward the spring. "That isn't really water. It's something else, put into a form we can understand. Some things here are what they are, and other ones are something else. Yes?"

Arodias didn't answer. Alice shook the vial. "You're just a man again, Mr Thorne; an ordinary mortal man. An ordinary mortal man who would by now be... let's see..." Alice thought back to the dates on the plaque in St Thomas' Church "... about two hundred and thirty-eight years old. Men don't live that long, Mr Thorne."

Arodias' smile faded.

"So I had to stop you ageing. Oh, I took that effect away from you, but I did keep it. This is a rather nice little symbol, don't you think? The dust in here is time: all the time you should have aged since you 'died' back in 1851. It can't affect you, of course. Not as long as this vial's intact."

Arodias wasn't smiling at all now; Alice thought she saw a muscle twitch in his cheek, and his thin lips were compressed, growing white.

"But if this glass breaks," she said, "and it is *very* thin glass, then all that time will find its way to you. All those years will fall on you, and in seconds. In far less time than it will take you to reach that spring, Mr Thorne."

Arodias looked from her to the blue flames flickering on the surface of the pool. Here it was, all he desired, almost within arm's reach. Could it really be that this *woman* could deny him that?

"So," he said, "what do you propose? Safe passage? The Red Man to escort you back to where you came, free what's left of your... *friend*... from the Moloch Device? Very well."

"No," she said. Not because his proposal was insincere – although of course it was, he would break his word in a moment. Not even because he would feel safer, but purely because it would amuse him. She remembered what they'd found in the chambers below the house, what Mary Carson, the children, the apprentices in Thorne's mills, had suffered at his hands. Arodias Thorne was living proof that a human being could be beyond all hope of redemption.

"No?" said Arodias. He was very still, his posture close to crouching. A cat ready to spring.

"No," she said. "No deals, Mr Thorne. I just wanted you to know."

Arodias leapt at her with a roar.

Alice pressed thumb and finger together, and the shell-thin glass splintered and broke.

The white dust hissed out in a stream like smoke. Defying gravity, it didn't drift down or dissipate: it shot through the air like a vaporous arrow towards Arodias Thorne, and struck him.

He screamed and fell before reaching her, fell writhing to the ground. The Red Man stood; the children rushed forward, gathered to watch.

His hair greyed and whitened. His face seamed, thinned, stretched tight on the bone. Cataracts exploded in his eyes like pale dead stars. His hands became clawed, then knobbled with arthritis.

And then age was joined by decay, even while he lived and screamed. Green and black stains spread across his flesh, rotted into holes. Maggots teemed in his flesh, darkened into pupae, exploded into flies that swarmed upon him and fell dead even as their children boiled out of the rot they'd battened on. Flesh fell off, peeled away, liquefied. His scream split his decaying cheeks wide and they slid off to make his face a laughing skull from the nose down. His screams gurgled, then perished as his throat rotted. But still what had been Arodias Thorne moved, while the muscles and tendons were still there to twitch the bones, until they fell away and became a tar-black stain on the grass of Collarmill Height.

The stain faded, steamed and dried. The bones beneath twitched a few more times, though what could have moved them Alice didn't know. The jawbone worked as if Arodias was still trying to scream, and then was still. The bones bleached white, grew porous, cracked and collapsed. In seconds there was only dust: fine, white dust, like the powder in the vial.

The wind blew over Collarmill Height, and cleaned the dust away.

Alice brushed crumbs of glass from thumb and forefinger. She heard the children laugh, but when she looked up they were gone.

Done. Arodias was gone; the children were free. Now: *Emily*. She stepped towards the spring.

"Alice."

A hand seized her wrist.

She turned. "Let me go!"

The Red Man was swaying. As she watched, he fell to one knee, then forced himself to his feet again. "I am dying," he said. "When Arodias goes, so do I. That is how I was built." His other hand extended, to point at the spring. "But first I will keep my word."

"No," she shouted, "wait –"

The flames on the water surged up, brightened. *A pillar of fire*. So bright Alice could barely look upon it.

"I will keep my word," he said again. "Wait!"

But the Red Man walked into the fire, dragging her after him.

DARKNESS, BROKEN BY lantern-light and a chill blue glow; a smell of dirt and damp. Water running; a man's voice whimpering in agony.

Alice opened her eyes. In front of her was the Moloch Device, and John. Or what remained of him. "Oh God."

"Step aside," that four-toned voice called behind her. She obeyed: looking back, she saw the Red Man standing in the pool, in the column of fire. He raised a shaking hand and pointed; the Moloch Device grated and ground to a halt. Then its blades and hooks and heated wires peeled outwards, its clamps opened and its straps snapped, and finally the chair itself shattered, splintered in two from top to bottom. And John fell, torn and bleeding, barely recognisable, to the floor, moaning.

"The water," said the Red Man. There was effort in his voice and every line of him as he stood in the Fire Beyond. "Give him the water… heal."

The water was on fire. Blue fire. Alice ran to it, caught it in cupped hands, ran to John as he rolled onto his back, his mutilated lips gasped. She poured it between his lips; the blue fire lit the shattered cavern of his mouth. He coughed, choked, spluttered – but the water went down.

The chamber shook and rumbled; a thin stream of dust poured down from above. Alice looked up, but couldn't see if the ceiling had cracked or not.

"Alice?"

She looked down. John blinked up at her – unwounded, unhealed. "What the fuck?" he said at last.

The Fire Beyond still danced on the water. There was still time; a mouthful was all she'd need. Alice lunged for the water – but in the second she did, the flames flickered out. "No!"

She scrabbled at the water as if she could dig the fire back out, but there was nothing. She gulped a handful of it, but it was only water, cold and metallic-tasting. There was, maybe, just the faintest flicker of the power it had held seconds before, but it was a ghost; the ocean wouldn't come. "Emily," she said, in little more than a whisper.

"Go," gasped the Red Man. "Quickly."

John grabbed her arm; she pulled him to his feet and they ran for the tunnel. He went quickly: he had only the memory of pain to haunt him now. Rubble crashed behind them.

"Here!" John shouted. "Come on."

He pushed her to the rungs in the wall. She climbed up through the shaft, the rust gritting under her fingers.

Dim light at the top: she could barely see it for her tears. She reached it: yes, it was her kitchen floor, complete with gaping hole. The house shuddered and a stench of brick dust came billowing up the shaft. "John?"

"I'm here, I'm here." He scrambled to the top. She caught his hands and helped drag him out.

The house shook again. The floor tilted. Clouds of dust. Screams. She dragged John towards the door.

Then the dust was falling, and so were they.

And after that, nothing.

MORNING. BIRDSONG. LIGHT.

Alice opened her eyes, stared at laminated wood. Something soft and warm pressed against her back. It snored softly. Then grunted. "Alice?"

"John." She got to her knees, then stood, wincing. Then she went through into the kitchen.

The floor was level and unbroken. The sink unit was undamaged, and no fire had marked the table or the ceiling. The camera stood in its corner; it was intact, but its light was out.

Outside, there was a blue, open sky and the sunlit yard. Squinting at the glare, Alice thought she saw a group of figures outside the window: small ones, gathered round a taller one robed in red. But when she rubbed her eyes and focused again, the yard was bare.

On Collarmill Road, an engine growled and a car passed by. There were voices, the clatter of boots on cobbles; the laughter of children.

But one child's laughter was missing. *I could have restored it*, Alice thought. *I could have brought her back.*

But the chance had gone. Even if she brought workmen and drills, tore up the floor, she knew she wouldn't find the spring again.

She would tell herself it was better that way, or at least try. If she could believe, she might build some sort of life.

"We're back," said John.

She took his hand in hers. "Yes," she said. Her voice cracked; she fought to keep it level. "We are."